Rebecca Tinsley w[...]
to Britain in 1970. She studied law at the LSE and in
1983 was the youngest parliamentary candidate to stand
at the General Election. She worked on the BBC's
Newsnight programme, and was a Lobby Correspondent
at Westminster. Now she writes articles on travel and
architecture, and lives with her husband in Lincolnshire.

Her first novel, SETTLEMENT DAY, is also available
from Headline Feature:

'Complicated plot and characters all handled with great
verve . . . Don't miss'   *Irish Independent Weekender*

'What a scorching debut this is . . . A rattling good thriller'
Peterborough Evening Telegraph

The Judas File

Rebecca Tinsley

First published in 1995
by HEADLINE BOOK PUBLISHING

First published in paperback in 1996
by HEADLINE BOOK PUBLISHING

A HEADLINE FEATURE paperback

10 9 8 7 6 5 4 3 2 1

ISBN 0 7472 5068 5

Typeset by
Letterpart Limited, Reigate, Surrey
Printed and bound in Great Britain by
Mackays of Chatham PLC, Chatham, Kent

HEADLINE BOOK PUBLISHING
A division of Hodder Headline PLC
338 Euston Road
London NW1 3BH

Dedicated to the memory of my mother,
Ruth Carmichael Bryan,
a Unionist by birth,
a Republican at heart.

I have taken the liberty of mentioning real people in this novel in order to make the background as realistic as possible. My plot and main characters, however, are all completely imaginary and no reference is intended to the real people holding their offices at the times in question, nor to any actual happening.

Prologue

The John F. Kennedy Library stands on Columbia Point, a lonesome tip of land that juts out into Dorchester Bay. From this gusty promontory the tall, stark, white wedge of modern architecture looks back at Boston, the city that gave birth to the Kennedy political dynasty.

As he approached it on the bus, Bill Anderson reflected that Boston was now better known for its notional paternity of the 'Cheers' bar. Certainly he had seen more tourists clamouring to take home a 'Norm and Cliff' beer mug from the Bull and Finch on Boston Common, than there were pilgrims here at the Jack Kennedy shrine.

When Bill left the bus at the Kennedy Library stop he lingered outside for a moment, his khakis flapping in the bracing breeze, a rucksack over his anorak-clad shoulder, and he studied the cleanness of I.M. Pei's design as it pierced the clear, blue February sky. It resembled the hangars on Cape Canaveral that had housed the giant *Saturn V* rockets. It was a fitting analogy, given that JFK had prompted the moon-race in the first place.

Grafted onto one side of the Library was a rectangle of glass, an atrium eight storeys high, that looked virtually black in the sun. Inside hung an enormous American flag, like the battle

1

colours of a conquering, but now fallen, prince. The banner gave a solemn and dignified touch in an already solemn, dignified place.

Bill paid his money at the admissions desk, and filed into the auditorium with the other visitors. He blended anonymously into the crowd; a neat, middle-aged man of average height with bland, regular features. It was not Library policy to ask visitors to leave rucksacks in the cloakroom. Bill had already ascertained that when he had come here last week.

For the next twenty minutes he watched the introductory video presentation on JFK's youth, although he didn't take much notice because he had seen it so recently in the company of his wife. The only reason he sat through it again was that it might arouse suspicion if he did the exhibition too quickly. It was unlikely that anyone at the Library entrance would have subconsciously noticed Bill Anderson in particular, but he couldn't take that chance. He sat quietly in the auditorium, and mentally rehearsed his plan of action.

Bill's day had begun rather earlier than normal, at a quarter past five. The upside of this unwelcome start had been that he had showered, eaten breakfast and left the house before his two teenaged daughters were up and hogging the bathroom, shouting at each other and their parents. They were in the most offensive stage of adolescence, and although the Reverend Patterson had assured him that they were only going through a phase, Bill was nevertheless concerned that they would become as undisciplined and irresponsible as their peers at school.

His eldest daughter was altogether different; she had graduated last year from Inverkirk University in Scotland, and now had a high-powered government job. Bill was immensely proud of her and her commitment to their cause. He and his wife hoped that the younger girls would turn out like their sister in time.

By six o'clock that morning Bill had left his pleasant Edwardian home in Rosedale, a leafy and solidly middle-class district of Toronto. He drove to the airport that had been called Malton when he was a little boy, and that was now rather grandly named Lester Pearson International, after a former Canadian prime minister. Using cash, he bought a one-way ticket for the 7.45 a.m. Air Canada shuttle service to Boston. As a Canadian, he had not for one moment considered using an American airline of any description. Besides, Air Canada had four shuttles a day to Boston and back, and they were at times that suited his purpose.

On the plane, Bill concentrated on office paperwork; he was a corporate executive with a nickel-mining company, but for twenty years before the transfer to headquarters in Toronto he had been a mining engineer. Today he was 'working from home', as he quite often did. His flight got into Logan at 9.20 a.m., and Bill was soon heading for the Commuter Rail terminal. There was nothing to delay him: he had only his rucksack, which he had stowed above him on the plane rather than checking it in; and Immigration formalities for Canadians were near non-existent. Canadians made fifty million trips a year across the border to the south, and they could do so without a passport.

Bill reached Boston's North Station by about ten o'clock, and headed for the luggage locker where he had left a suitcase a week earlier. He and his wife had taken a short vacation motoring around Massachusetts. There had been an element of risk involved in bringing in the case with them, but visitors with Ontario licence plates and skis strapped to the roof were a common sight crossing the border at this time of year.

From the case he retrieved four compact but heavy bundles,

and loaded them into his rucksack. Then he left the suitcase in the locker, and got back on the subway, this time on the orange line, to the imaginatively-named Downtown Crossing Station. He changed onto the red line that went south-east, and alighted at the JFK/U.Mass stop. By a quarter to eleven Bill was on the shuttle bus that ferried passengers from the subway station to the JFK Library via the University of Massachusetts. As he passed the campus he suppressed a snigger of contempt for these dime-a-dozen pillars of American academic excellence. But it also gave him a warm feeling of superiority over the Bog Irish locals. Bill Anderson liked to feel superior.

When the introductory video finished, Bill let the other visitors troop out before he followed them into the corridor and the adjoining rooms of the exhibits. Then he spent five minutes studying the first display, which was a map of the state by state results of the 1960 Presidential election that Kennedy had won by a whisker (and only then because his rich, bootlegging daddy had rigged the ballot in Chicago).

When Bill was sure no one from his group was going to wander back for another look, or to use the public lavatory beside the auditorium exit, he slipped into the men's room, chose a cubicle at the end and locked it. From his rucksack he pulled a pair of pliers, and within fifteen seconds he had removed the panelling that enclosed the cistern. Then he found an appropriate niche in amongst the pipes for one of the bundles in his rucksack, took a miniaturised timer out of an alarm clock, and made the final adjustments to it. It was an operation Bill had practised again and again at home in Toronto.

A week earlier he had located the easiest hiding places, and worked out how long before the next batch of visitors exited the auditorium. Now the plan had been put into action he was pleasantly surprised that there were no hitches. Within two and a half minutes he had replaced the panel, and was washing his hands triumphantly.

He wandered slowly through the rest of the exhibition, watching a minute or so of each video about different aspects of the JFK presidency, and then passing on. The final room, devoted to the trip to Dallas, was mercifully tasteful, with no gory footage from the Zapruder film of the impact of the bullets. Instead there were a few seconds of Walter Cronkite's reaction to the news he was getting through his earpiece. The veteran newscaster struggled to remain composed before the cameras, then told the nation the awful truth. Very restrained, Bill admitted as he walked out of the exhibition, into the atrium with its flag, and up the stairs to the bookshop. Among the postcards and key-fobs for sale was a poster of the late President hugging his pretty, young daughter Caroline, with the caption: *It's OK to dream again.*

No, it isn't, thought Bill as he walked into the adjacent men's room, and opened his rucksack.

Forty-five minutes later he was back in the centre of Boston at Copley Station. He picked his way along the crowded sidewalk of Boylston Street, past Boston Public Library, which looked like a Greek temple, and across Copley Square. Before him stood the sixty-two-storey John Hancock Tower, the tallest building in New England. The guidebooks admitted that the skyscraper was unloved at first because the windows had a habit of falling out, but now that this minor defect had been fixed the office block had been embraced as a worthy symbol of civil pride.

Bill took the elevator to the Observation Deck on the sixtieth floor. There weren't many tourists about at this time of year, or on a weekday, but the Canadian visitor bided his time and strolled around the gallery, studying the impressive city panorama below him. Then he slipped into the men's room, and again swiftly performed the ritual with the pliers and the timing device.

Only one small bundle remained in his rucksack now. He hovered about the lobby, pretending to consult his guidebook while carefully avoiding two elevators in a row when other visitors appeared at his side. Finally he got one to himself, and when the car was in motion he opened the cupboard that housed the telephone, and slipped his package inside.

When he emerged at the foot of the John Hancock Tower his work was finished, and he retraced his steps to the left luggage lockers at North Station. No point in abandoning a perfectly good suitcase. The waste-not-want-not common sense was typical of his Scots-Irish Presbyterian ancestors. However, it was not his meanness with money that stopped Bill from taking taxis that morning. He preferred to be unseen as he left his subtle messages to Boston.

He caught the 2 p.m. flight back to Toronto, and was at home with plenty of time to spare before supper with his wife and daughters. It was with a certain tightness in his chest that he switched on the early evening news, and sank into his favourite armchair. Like a sports fan who doesn't want to be told the result of a game that he had videoed for later consumption, Bill had deliberately avoided listening to radio bulletins that afternoon. However his fears proved unfounded: fate had not tinkered with his carefully laid plans.

The CBC news was dominated by dramatic film of the gaping, smoking hole in the side of the John Hancock Tower. Helicopters were circled around it like vultures, broadcasting the clichéd and breathless commentary of their airborne reporters. At the base of the flaming monolith a sooty-faced Fire Department official described the devastation inside the building: charred corridors, collapsed ceilings, blackened walls.

Evidently the elevator had exploded while it was on the ground floor. Not only had the blast killed the dozen or so tourists who were inside it at the time, but scores of homebound office workers were also caught as they exited into the lobby from the elevators. The lucky ones were now sitting on the pavement holding bandages to their glass-scarred faces, too shell-shocked to perform for the network microphones. Those who had been hit by flying masonry or steel were laid out in blanket-shrouded lines inside.

Swarms of ambulance crews were tending to the wounds of passers-by who had been showered with glass from the Observation Deck. The one outright decapitation, and three other 'fatalities' had mercifully been carted away before the TV crews could get to the scene.

As for the body-count inside, both on the sixtieth floor and in the lobby, the number was thirty-five and rising. But the on-the-spot reporters were too stunned to keep a clear-headed tally. Only one journalist had so far groped her way to the conclusion that the bombs had been timed to catch the pedestrian rush hour at maximum flow. The rest were gorging on incoherent eye-witness accounts of severed limbs and shredded skin. 'There was a woman lying by the elevators with her stomach open,' said one young computer programmer to the camera. 'It was like looking at the window display in a butcher's shop,' he sobbed.

There was the usual mixture of expert opinion and speculation on the extent of the fire on the Observation Deck, and its spread to lower floors; but to Bill's relief there had been no sightings of the perpetrator of this evil crime. Before he had embarked on today's mission he had been positive that his path had been free of security cameras. The dim-witted Boston reporters, from whom CBC was taking its pictures this evening, had hardly addressed the 'why' part of the equation when they were interrupted by news of another bomb, south of the city.

The John Hancock Tower had been merely an appetizer, thought Bill with a gleam in his eye. Now the Kennedy Library would be the 'main course', for the later evening news programmes. Then the plan was that his Loyalist friends would claim responsibility overnight, thus leading the morning bulletins. It was called 'news management' in the business, but for Bill Anderson it was merely the first episode in the battle to reclaim the land of his forebears.

Chapter One

Two weeks later, on a dreary, wintry afternoon, Michael Fitzgerald was at his desk in the Ministry of Defence in Whitehall, in the heart of London. At the moment, his Department was streamlining the armed forces' pension and benefit arrangements. As Under Secretary of State, Michael had been flooded with irate letters from all three branches of the services, including Guards officers of the Household Cavalry, who were outraged that his Government intended to make them pay for their fox-hunting activities, and cancel their subscriptions to the Quorn. In addition, Michael had discovered that large numbers of soldiers were still receiving five pence a week for a rifle-training course they had attended in the 1970s. It cost many times that sum *per capita* to administer the scheme, so Michael had to axe it. Naturally, the operation was causing much more controversy than would a plan to scrap nuclear missiles or invade Iceland.

Michael was forty-one years old; he had been a Conservative MP for the past decade, and had spent the last eighteen months in his present post at the Ministry of Defence. Newspaper columnists hailed him as a rising star, but Michael recalled the fate of other promising, ambitious young men and women whose careers had been blighted by such praise. He kept his head down, avoided making exciting speeches on subjects beyond his departmental brief, and worked very long hours.

On his desk there was a black and white photograph of his wife, Caroline, and their daughter, Laura, who was sitting on the back of an elephant. It had been taken two and a half years ago in India. Michael wondered if it was time to replace the photo with a more recent one, but putting the photo of Caroline away for good was a psychological bridge too far.

At ten past two his American research assistant, Mandy, stuck her blonde, big-haired head into his office. 'Time to go, Michael,' she twinkled. 'The Secretary of State's giving you a ride today.' How the petite Mandy could look so enthusiastic about Parliamentary Questions, Michael did not fully understand. The prospect of taking his turn at the Dispatch Box filled this particular Under Secretary with dread, but Mandy approached every arcane aspect of British democracy with the enthusiasm of a young palaeontologist on a dinosaur dig.

He gathered his papers and dried the nervous clamminess from the palms of his hands with a handkerchief. He could hear the booming, plummy baritone of Johnny Burleigh, his Secretary of State, bantering with Mandy in her office next door. It was obvious that his American research assistant would never surrender to the sixty-five-year-old's undoubted charms. But the craggy-faced, firm-jawed Old Etonian persisted with his campaign strategy. It made Johnny doubly hot under the collar that Michael confessed indifference to the 'firm little buttocks' and 'bewitching smile' of the history graduate from Buffalo, New York. 'And she's a damned clever girl,' Johnny protested more than once. 'How you can shun the company of such an intelligent creature?'

And there lay the secret of Johnny's success, it seemed, although he was far too much the gent to boast. The stories around the Ministry were legion, however; their Secretary of State was a witty rogue, and had no time for dull men. But he couldn't resist smart women, and it was to his credit that he remained chummy with his conquests long after they had pushed him out of their beds.

As Michael walked through the Ministry of Defence corridors side by side with Burleigh that afternoon, the older man went suddenly quiet, as if he was mulling something over. Johnny had been answering Parliamentary Questions 'from peasants and idiots on both benches of the Commons' for many years, so he didn't suffer the nerves that caused Michael such misery. But when they emerged from the back door of the MOD building and climbed into the waiting ministerial Jaguar, the reason for his gloom became apparent.

'I s'pose this'll be your last Question Time with me,' Burleigh grumbled as he flopped back into the leather bucket seats. 'Some self-important turd at Downing Street told me I'm losing you to that ghastly man Grace.'

'That's highly unlikely,' Michael responded quietly as the car pulled out into the traffic on Whitehall. 'Grace can't stand me.'

'Trevor Grace won't have any say in the matter. You're moving up.'

Michael made modest, 'Oh, nonsense, it's just idle gossip,' noises, but his Secretary of State hushed him.

'Balls, Michael. The Commons is seething with chatter about this bloody reshuffle, and you're mentioned more than anyone else. The word is you're going to the Northern Ireland office.' Burleigh glared out the window at the elaborate gates to Downing Street. 'Looks like the entrance to Auschwitz, doesn't it? By the way, the silly little fucker who lives there can force Grace to take you, whether that frightful oik wants you or not.'

'And he doesn't want me,' Michael said firmly, but without anger in his voice. 'Although God knows, I can't recall ever stepping on his feet. In fact, I can't recall uttering a single syllable on the subject of Northern Ireland either.'

Johnny Burleigh laughed with an abrupt, seal-like bark. 'You don't need to step on his feet to offend him, dear boy. All you have to do is open your mouth and you've mortally wounded a secondhand car-dealer like him. He's not one of us, Michael.'

' "Not one of us" is the kind of thing Mrs Thatcher used to say,' Michael teased. 'And by the way, I thought Grace was in the trucking business, not secondhand cars.'

'Worse!' Burleigh exclaimed. 'D'you know he married the boss's daughter? The girls in our department say he's all wandering hands and cheap bottles of Chianti. Shifty, uppity shit, with a strangulated, ersatz middle-England accent.'

'Where'd the knighthood come from?' Michael asked as the Jaguar nosed between the policemen on guard at the Palace Yard entrance of the Commons.

'Cocksucking. And if you recall, the PM put him in Northern Ireland as a reward for keeping his anti-European views to himself at the appropriate moment, just before the 1996 Inter-governmental Conference. Grace was the ringleader of a whole mob of Little Englanders, but he suddenly had a change of heart – I wonder why – and shut them up on cue. That's how he got Ulster.'

The Jaguar came to an effortlessly smooth stop at the portico on the right side of Palace Yard, and the Secretary of State puffed as he hauled himself out of the car. 'Trevor Grace is the last

Northern Ireland Secretary. What a note to leave on! No wonder it's such an almighty mess.'

'Come on, Johnny. I thought the new constitutional arrangements were supposed to be working pretty well. They've got the referendum out of the way, and most people on both sides of the border accepted the negotiated settlement. And the elections to the new Stormont Assembly went incredibly smoothly, considering what might have happened.'

'Yes, I'll grant you that much. They've got their regional talking shop at Stormont, and of course they're starting up all these dinky little cross-border commissions to organise a joint Tourist Authority, and a Potato Marketing Board. It's just a pity the Loyalists decided to blow up a few third-generation Irishmen in Boston, isn't it?' the Defence Secretary grumbled as they walked under the portico, and past the policeman's pillar box.

'Well,' Michael responded reasonably, 'no one expected the peace talks to produce a settlement that every single person in Ireland could subscribe to, you know. Maybe the Loyalists will calm down when they see that these cross-border commissions won't lead to a united Ireland. They're just innocent, money-wasting quangos full of the great and the good, finding harmless areas of common interest between Ulster and Eire, like agriculture and the electricity grid. And both sides have got this new Bill of Rights to protect them too.'

'Pity the rest of the United Kingdom isn't allowed one. You know, you're parroting propaganda like a Northern Ireland Minister already,' Burleigh croaked as they walked down the book-lined, green-carpeted corridor towards the Members' Lobby. Their colleagues rushed past them, heading for their offices, or waddled back from a long lunch, or scuttled to the Chamber for Prayers at 2.30. Several MPs winked at Michael as if they were telepathically transmitting, "You're on your way," or "Remember me when you get there," or "Best of luck!" from the truly disingenuous.

Johnny and Michael passed a Labour MP who had won a recent by-election, and the Defence Secretary took a deep breath. He turned to study her trim figure as it retreated down the Victorian Gothic corridor with its carved wooden panelling and second-rate paintings.

'God, this place smells of sex. There's a kind of electric charge in the air. Wonderful! Courses through the veins like cognac. I've had a political erection since 1979.'

Michael ignored Johnny's ramblings, and offered a thin smile to a blow-dried blond man of his own age, a sworn enemy, and a member of his own party. It was rumoured that the fellow was being passed over in the reshuffle, and Michael had difficulty suppressing his glee.

By the time they reached the Members' Lobby a few moments later, Johnny had almost finished a story about a handsome political journalist of his acquaintance who had slept with female MPs across the political spectrum. The hack concluded that the more extreme their views were, left- or right-wing – it didn't matter which – the more repressed they were in bed.

Before they reached the dark double doors that led from the Lobby into the Chamber, Johnny halted abruptly and grabbed his Under Secretary by the elbow.

'Michael . . .' He paused to examine the floor between them, two dark blue pin-striped suits in a pow-wow. He pulled the junior minister towards him, as if he was slightly bewildered by the rush of MPs around them, and the noise of their voices echoing in the high-ceilinged lobby.

'I'll miss you, Michael,' he fretted in a bluff, embarrassed tone. 'I know I'm a dreadful old fart to work with—' Burleigh winced and studied his shoes again, still gripping Michael's elbow. 'I told you, didn't I: Grace married the boss's daughter.'

Finally he released his grip, and the two men walked through the doors and into the Chamber, pausing only to bow their heads towards the Speaker. Then Michael followed Johnny as he threaded his way through the crush of MPs, to the green bench on the left-hand side of the Dispatch Box.

Fifteen feet above them in the Press Gallery sat Charlotte Carter. On her lap was a notebook, a pen, and this afternoon's Commons Order Paper which contained questions on defence-related matters that MPs had tabled. Her dark blue wool skirt suit and cream silk blouse befitted a thirty-year-old BBC Lobby Correspondent who had to look respectable and authoritative on screen. The neat severity of the best of Marks & Spencer was relieved only by a Liberty scarf, and a pair of pearl stud earrings.

Her four years as a television reporter, first on City news, and now at Parliament, had toned down any ambitions Charlotte might once have had to dress casually, or to wear colourful patterns. Even her shoulder-length chestnut hair was unfussy; straight and tucked behind her ears. Anything more complicated might fly about if she was filming outside. In Charlotte's ever self-critical opinion, her only on-screen attributes were her big green eyes which she could open wide when she wanted to stress to the camera that her audience should listen to what she was saying; and the wrinkles that appeared on her broad forehead when she was being told lies by whoever she was interviewing.

Otherwise, like most women, Charlotte was not particularly happy about her appearance. The reflection in her mirror was a million miles from the popular Superwoman image of the TV reporters who went to glamorous places and were rich, beautiful, clever, wore designer outfits even under attack in the theatre of war, and never spent their spare time ironing, or shaving their armpits. These fictional creatures also hung around with charismatic, handsome, powerful men – just the types who wouldn't notice Charlotte if she was having a fit on the floor in front of them. She didn't even get wolf-whistles from building workers: though other people found her attractive, this journalist so often looked too serious and preoccupied.

Charlotte leaned forward in her seat to survey the Chamber, and her eyes came to rest on Michael Fitzgerald, which was hardly surprising given the comparative ugliness of most of his colleagues. From this angle Charlotte had an excellent view of his fine mane of light brown hair. When she was bored she would study Michael's hair because it was so interesting, and utterly without structure. He never seemed to bother with a parting; she supposed that it simply fell into place when he ran his fingers through it. And it was much longer than anyone else's on the Government or Opposition front benches. It swept out behind him as if he was constantly walking into a breeze.

She liked his face too, although she could see that some people found him a touch severe around the jaw. Cartoonists exaggerated the size of his nose, and made him look like a supercilious camel. But as Charlotte had become acquainted with Michael Fitzgerald over the past eighteen months, she had looked forward to those rare moments when he allowed himself a genuine smile.

Charlotte and Michael had lunch about once a month on average, sometimes a drink in the evening, and little chats whenever they met in the corridors of the Palace of Westminster. Theirs was a typical Lobby relationship: she fed him interesting rumours she had heard, and he leaked juicy nuggets of information to her in return. In that way Charlotte was able to do stories about unattributable but utterly true embarrassments for the Government, and Michael could make life less easy for his rivals on the Tory benches.

Charlotte was skimming her way through the afternoon's defence questions when Paula Tyler sat down next to her and flashed a frenzied smile. 'Loved your piece on the Government's pollution policy,' she quipped. 'Was it on the *Six O'Clock News*, or the *Nine* last night? Can't have made you any friends, mind you,' she laughed.

Paula was a Lobby Correspondent for Independent Radio News, and at forty-seven she was much older than most of the bratpack of political scribblers. The skinny, sharp-featured journalist supplemented her income by penning a whodunit a year, and she had a devoted fan club of library-goers across the nation. She was also one half of a power marriage of sorts: Paula's husband ran Cable News Network's London bureau.

Charlotte, who had no idea how this woman found the time for both disciplined creativity *and* networking, as well as her IRN job, greeted Paula warmly. Then, as usual, Paula's eyes settled on the skin below Charlotte's neck, in the v-shape of her blouse. It was only for a second, but Charlotte felt strangely violated by the enquiring glance. Paula and her husband went to a nudist camp every year for their holidays, and Charlotte knew that the woman was just curious. If only Paula knew how little there was to be curious about – size 10, not fat, not skinny, not anything.

'My word, the rumour mill is working at fever pitch this afternoon,' Paula bubbled in her usual jolly-hockeysticks manner. 'The PM's done the knifing by phone this time to stop the cameras outside Number 10 capturing those brave but suicidal smiles of the colleagues whom he's cast into outer darkness. But it hasn't dampened down the feverish speculation.'

'That's because there's nothing else to gossip about at the moment,' Charlotte suggested. 'Everyone's so profoundly bored by Euro-bickering. Naturally every reshuffle appointment is being interpreted according to how it changes the Euro-balance in the Cabinet.'

Defence questions had started by this time, and Johnny Burleigh was on his feet, skilfully deflecting an ill-informed and gracelessly phrased attack from his opposite number. He made it look so easy, with his laconic charm and the off-the-cuff jokes that momentarily took the wind out of the Labour spokesman's sails and delighted his own side.

'God, look at them,' Paula remarked sourly. 'Jumping up and down in their seats like brats who are desperate to get Mummy Speaker's attention. "Watch me, watch me, aren't I clever?" The whole lot of them are small children playing around a swimming pool, demanding that their parents observe every dive and trick they perform.'

Charlotte giggled appreciatively and pointed out a female Labour MP who was so bursting to speak that she appeared to be on the verge of wetting herself. 'They're all the product of over-indulgent parents,' she whispered, 'and they're biologically incapable of exercising any self-criticism or being less than positive about themselves twenty-four hours a day.'

'But why are most of them here, I wonder? We have to apply the John Candy question.'

'And what, pray, is that?'

'You remember John Candy, the comedian? He made silly movies; died a couple of years ago. Well, ask yourself if anyone on those benches has done as much as J. Candy did to make the world a happier place. 'Course not! They don't believe in anything but themselves, and quite a few of them can't even read the Bills they vote on, let alone understand them.' Paula waved the Order Paper as if she was dismissing a swarm of midges.

Then she targeted a smooth-cheeked young Tory MP on the back benches. 'Look at that one – couldn't pass a Politics GCSE. Why's he bother? Lousy pay, dreadful hours, and correspondence about blocked drains and broken paving stones in The Suburb From Hell that he represents.'

Charlotte squinted her eyes and peered down at the MP in question. 'Mind you, he's quite yummy,' Paula conceded.

'Yummy? He's a dwarf!'

'Don't be so size-ist. I bet he could be quite fun in bed. Anyway, don't you think short men have a certain novelty value? You know, sort of like sleeping with manual labourers.'

'No,' said Charlotte stoutly. 'I refuse to consider that MP as a sex object.'

'But don't you see, that's the only way to approach an interview with someone excessively important,' Paula chipped in perkily. 'You have to imagine them standing there in their underwear, and after that they'll never intimidate you.'

'Yuck. Oh God, I wish you hadn't put that idea in my head. You're a disgusting woman!' she laughed.

'I thought you liked *him*.' Paula arched an eyebrow, and they both gazed down at Michael Fitzgerald, who was now standing at the Dispatch Box. 'Of course, he's rather a class act compared to this bumfluff and acne brigade. I've been preparing a potted biography of him since he's bound to be promoted in the reshuffle. His life story reads like a map of how to scale the heights of the British Establishment.'

'Oh, come on, Paula.'

'No, it's true. Ampleforth, one of the poshest Catholic public schools, then Oxford – and not just some college for rugger buggers. He was at Balliol. Then the law. Marriage to a beautiful, posh woman. A safe Tory seat, and a steady climb up the slippery pole. Michael Fitzgerald never does anything impetuous or rash. He's a prime example of how the Establishment regenerates itself by bringing in promising understudies from the middle classes. He's had it smooth all the way,' Paula concluded with a touch of irritation.

'But Michael's life *hasn't* been all that smooth, has it?' Charlotte countered. 'First of all he's a Catholic, and whilst Britain has had a Jewish prime minister, and a female one, there's never been an RC yet. I think you're underestimating the natural conservatism of the Establishment.' She gave Paula a stern look. 'And you have to remember how much Mrs Thatcher disliked Michael. She kept him on the back benches as if she was punishing him for being clever, but too sopping wet for her taste.'

Charlotte stole a sideways glance at her friend to see how she was taking this, and after a significant pause she muttered, 'And I don't imagine he found his wife's death smooth either.'

'*What?*' Paula shot back. 'When was this?'

'A couple of years ago, I think. Evidently it happened after the most recent *Times Guide to the Members of the House of Commons* was published.'

'What happened, Charlotte? Christ, I'm glad you told me or I would have made a right bloody fool of myself in my report tonight.'

'It was a car crash, I think.' Charlotte's eyes returned to their loving appreciation of Michael's tousled head. He had just finished answering some self-congratulatory question from an MP on his own benches. He looked relieved, as if he was glad to have completed his turn at the Dispatch Box. He leaned back on the green bench and closed his eyes. When he opened them a moment later he was looking straight at Charlotte in the Press Gallery, and he made a slight waving motion with one of the hands folded across his chest. She returned his brief smile, and felt her cheeks burn with fire.

To her embarrassment, it seemed that Paula had witnessed this little exchange because the IRN correspondent whispered, 'He's rather yummy. Why don't you sniff out the terrain? You do like him, don't you?'

'Oh yes, I like him,' Charlotte's eyes replied, but she shook her head as if she was a nun dismissing sinful thoughts. 'Paula, he's quite beyond my reach. Michael Fitzgerald is unattainable.'

'Why?'

Charlotte shrugged sadly. 'Why do they always make the brush in a bottle of nail polish just too short to reach the last twenty per cent of varnish at the bottom? And why would Michael Fitzgerald be interested in me? These are the eternal questions, Paula.'

'No,' her friend disagreed abruptly. 'Why aren't men's mouths like power-shower heads? *That's* the eternal question, my love.'

21

Chapter Two

At the Northern Ireland Office, a mere five minutes down Whitehall, Sir Trevor Grace was in an important meeting that same afternoon. The Secretary of State was listening intently to a Detective Chief Inspector from the Special Branch of the recently renamed NIPD, the Northern Ireland Police Department. The old title, the Royal Ulster Constabulary, had been dropped as part of the peace process because the Catholic community wasn't wild about things royal, and the word 'Ulster' was a symbol of the bad old days of Protestant corruption.

The burden of the NIPD officer's message was that 'his people' believed the remaining hard core of the Provisional IRA who were still in business were about to strike 'big time' with a massive bombing campaign on mainland Britain. It was to be in retaliation for the Loyalists' bombings in Boston, two weeks ago.

As Grace listened his blue eyes became icy and pale. In contrast his cheeks shone ruddily, like the complexions one encounters in golf-club bars. Although Grace was fifty-four, his hair was still corn blond, and he wore light blue suits in the belief that they flattered his colouring. Indeed they might have, had he not also sported a substantial paunch that hung over the top of his trousers.

At four o'clock that afternoon Grace was dragged away from the NIPD officer to take a phone call from the Secretary to the Cabinet in Downing Street. The good news was that he hadn't been sacked: he was staying put at the NIO. The Secretary of State was painfully aware that this particular PM wasn't going to promote him further, and that the post of Northern Ireland Secretary would disappear when the new governing Assembly in Belfast had an executive in place. The Assembly had already elected committees which would gradually take on the work of the Northern Ireland Office. The idea was that when everyone was confident that the committees and the executive were functioning smoothly, then London would bow out of Belfast for good, and let the locals get on with running their own affairs. But what then for Sir Trevor Grace MP?

He stood in the outer office, the telephone pressed to his ear, and received the bad news: Michael Fitzgerald was to be his new Minister of State, and Grace's deputy.

Downing Street obviously believed that putting a Papist there would send the 'right messages' to both the Dublin Government whose arse they were always kissing, and the Catholic minority in Ulster. When Grace pointed this out, he was smoothly informed that Fitzgerald wasn't really an Irishman because he was two or three generations out of the bog, and that he could bring his 'considerable talents and negotiating skills' to the Northern Ireland Office.

It was no surprise to Grace that the PM couldn't take the time to call him personally – he was used to the little weasel's high-handed indifference to his views. But it annoyed him that others in Government and the press might suspect Fitzgerald had been forced on him. Consequently Sir Trevor would have to behave as if he had wanted the man in his team all along.

When he put down the phone he tried to forget the news about Michael Fitzgerald. He returned to the meeting next door and they discussed how hard it was for NIPD to get intelligence on the IRA's movements in the new political climate.

'The Special Police Battalions of NIPD are made up of' – the Special Branch officer searched for the right word – 'former Republicans. As you know, sir, they patrol their own areas of town, and impose their version of law and order. It means we can no longer raid known IRA houses or gather information from our old sources. Basically we've turned over large parts of West Belfast to the Provos, only they wear police uniforms now. It's an impossible situation, sir.'

Grace stood by the window gazing down at the courtyard full of ministerial cars, his mind swimming with malevolent thoughts. Then he grinned wolfishly. 'Well, my good sir, take heart. I think you'll find that your patrols in the Republican ghettoes will be starting up again sooner than you'd think. You mark my words.'

When Michael finished Question Time he walked directly to his office in the Commons where he dealt with his constituency work. It was a pokey little room at the end of a rabbit-warren of a corridor, and it had an uninspiring view of the Palace's rubbish bins. Waiting on his desk were a stack of letters to sign, and a message to call the Cabinet Office immediately. The junior minister's fingers shook as he punched in the Downing Street number.

To his surprise, the Cabinet Secretary put him straight through to the Prime Minister, who told him what a splendid chap he was, and how well he had been doing at the MOD. 'What do you think about being Minister of State at the Northern Ireland Office?'

There was simply no entry in the political lexicon that Michael could have used to refuse this offer. It was a huge leap up the ladder from Under Secretary of State to Minister of State: one step away from running an entire Department: one step from the Cabinet.

'But most important of all, Michael, I'll be counting on you to be part of the team that oversees the final hand-over from Westminster to Stormont. This is the end of direct rule by London, and the beginning of home rule by Belfast. It's very historic,' the PM droned flatly.

When the call was finished Michael leaned his elbows on the desk and covered his face with his hands, thanking the spirit of his wife Caroline, wherever she might be, for watching over him. His heart thumped with joy, and he would have leapt to his feet and waltzed around the room, had there been someone there with whom he wanted to waltz. But instead he savoured this private, intense moment of achievement alone.

Twenty minutes later he left his office, and as he walked down the corridor he reflected how odd it was that the PM had bunged him into Northern Ireland. Michael had never expressed an opinion on the subject: maybe that was precisely why he was being sent there.

When he reached the crowded Members' Lobby he was immediately struck by the loudness of his colleagues' voices, in contrast with the monastic peace of his little office. He stood at the edge surveying the mêlée of dark blue suits and open mouths, and felt strangely disgusted by it all: the chattering and plotting; the smallness of their incestuous political world; the blatant attempts to outmanoeuvre each other. The scene was so familiar to him, but at the same time it was remote and alien. He was still very much the self-reliant only child who would rather play quietly with his toys than mix in with these rougher, dimmer children.

For a moment Michael hovered on the Lobby's periphery unnoticed by those who were discussing him, like Jay Gatsby, anonymously observing his own party. Then, from out of the horde of gossiping MPs, a hand waved, and a more welcome face beckoned.

'Tell me what's happened,' Edward Power demanded with a friendly nudge. Labour's Northern Ireland spokesman lowered his voice and turned his back on the Lobby. 'Come on, Michael, don't be a prick. You've got the most extraordinary grin on your face. What did you get?'

'Eddie, you know it's not out for another two hours—'

'Look, bugger that, Fitzgerald.'

'Eddie, promise not to tell?'

'Yes, yes, yes,' Power chanted impatiently as he drew his friend, and the godfather of his firstborn, into a huddle.

'Minister of State, Northern Ireland.'

'Brilliant bastard!'

'Quiet!' Michael rolled his eyes in exasperation. 'I haven't seen Grace yet, and I'm not looking forward to it.'

'Oh, you won't live that long,' Eddie quipped, and released Michael from the neck grip. 'One of these Ulster Unionists will have killed you before you can say your first Hail Mary. Hey, this is going to be great, working on the same area.' Edward Power's boyish enthusiasm faded as Michael's attention switched away from him like a radio being turned off.

'Charlotte,' Michael called after the BBC reporter who was

picking her way around the edge of the busy Lobby. 'Charlotte, how are you? I liked your pollution report last night. Do you know Eddie Power?'

Charlotte shook Eddie's hand and glanced back at Michael with a sly look on her face. 'Now, I suppose I'd be wrong to jump to hasty conclusions about why a defence minister should be talking to Labour's Northern Ireland spokesman. Nothing to do with the reshuffle, of course?' Her wide green eyes sparkled.

'Yes, you would be wrong,' Eddie interjected. 'We were reminiscing about our schooldays.'

Michael registered the disbelief on Charlotte's face. 'It's true,' he added before Eddie could volunteer any unflattering details. 'We were contemporaries at Ampleforth, and then at Oxford. And, would you believe that he never replaced my Steely Dan records? An obscure 1970s rock group,' he added for Charlotte's benefit. 'Power here spilt vodka on my LPs. You see, he had a drinking problem even then.'

Edward Power, as he was known in the Commons, and to the viewing public, was preparing an equally embarrassing response when Michael was besieged by his research assistant, prettily breathless and clawing at his arm.

'Michael, you've got to come with me!' Mandy's voice sounded as if she was selling tasteless, mass-produced, but perfectly formed cupcakes on TV. 'Now, Michael. You have to see someone. And you have to tell me something,' she added with meaning. Then Michael realised he had thoughtlessly forgotten to let her know about his promotion. But before Mandy dragged him away he turned back to Charlotte with a smile.

'How about lunch tomorrow?'

'Yes, please,' she beamed, and tried to ignore the poisonous glare from the small but perfectly formed blonde at Michael's side.

Charlotte and Eddie watched them leave the lobby, each with their own cruel remarks about the American research assistant on the tips of their tongues.

'She hasn't got a chance there,' Eddie commented tersely. 'There's only one woman in Michael's life, and she's a thirteen-year-old tyrant.'

'I'm a reporter with the BBC.' Charlotte wanted to change the subject before she heard any more to depress her.

'I saw you demolish the Government's environmental record on last night's news. Shame you did the same to several Labour councils, but I guess that's journalism.' Power offered her his camera-dazzling grin. Unfortunately his teeth were appalling; they ruined his otherwise regular features. It was generally accepted that Power was handsome and charming and tele-visual, but this journalist found him just a bit too baby-faced. His hair was frizzy, too, and whenever she saw him she had the urge to whip out her comb and sort him out. If only Michael would share the secret of where he got his tresses cut . . .

'Wouldn't it be amazing if Michael really did get the Northern Ireland job?' she mused innocently. Charlotte was aware that Eddie probably knew the truth, and she hoped to trick him into confirming her hunch. 'The Loyal Unionist Party MPs have already got a whiff of something because they're stalking the corridors demanding blood sacrifices and the desecration of the monasteries.'

'I don't understand why they're so excited about it, frankly, d'you?' Power crossed his arms across his chest as if he was rather annoyed. 'Michael isn't exactly a ticking time bomb, is he? He's hardly going to arrive at Stormont and declare that he's always been a secret Republican. In fact, it's hard to find a more cautious, moderate, sensible person on the Tory benches. And he'll be doubly careful not to upset the charming Reverend Scott and his temperance brigade.'

Charlotte nodded thoughtfully, pleased that her suspicion about Michael's promotion had been proved correct. 'He's hardly going to screw up his career at this stage.'

'Precisely. Michael's very clear about his ambitions – he wants to go to the top, so he'll toe the line with all those fire and brimstone nutters in Belfast, even if it chokes him. They just don't appreciate how self-controlled Michael is. Caroline was the only person who could make him relax, and now she's gone I reckon he's grown an even tougher hide. Believe me, he'll do the Northern Ireland job competently and quietly, because he knows that's the fast track to promotion.'

'Well, he'll need a tough hide in the months ahead,' Charlotte muttered, and surveyed the increasing numbers of MPs who were arriving to join in the frantic rumour-swapping activity. 'I hope they won't go on about his Catholicism.'

'Who? The Loyal Unionists?' Power asked caustically. 'Oh, Michael can take care of himself. Actually, his biggest obstacle at school was that nose. Everyone called him Hymie. He had to throw a lot of punches to lose that label.'

Charlotte's eyes opened wide. 'But you were all Catholics at a Catholic school.'

'We were all beastly little bigoted boys who picked on each other,' he chuckled. 'If Michael survived "Hymie" he'll survive those cavemen in Belfast. Look, Charlotte, I've got to go, but let's keep in touch.'

The television reporter nodded distractedly, and watched the Labour Party's Northern Ireland spokesman disappear into the scrum of feverish networking. But before she could digest Power's words she was surrounded by Paula Tyler's force field of mental energy. The IRN hack had appeared from nowhere, and her sallow cheeks looked flushed.

'Nigel Swinton's dead,' she whispered hoarsely. 'This morning. London Hospital. They're saying cancer.'

'Let's hope they keep saying that,' Charlotte commented with a meaningful glance at her friend. 'Poor man. He was only thirty-eight or nine, I think.'

'With a bit of luck the ratpack'll concentrate on what it means for the Government's majority, and how bloody the by-election'll be.'

'Now that's a damned good angle. Paula, excuse me, won't you, but I've got to run. I'm going to write the Swinton obituary myself and send it to the *Six O'Clock News* now. That might at least keep the BBC on the right track,' Charlotte gabbled. Then she glanced at her watch and grimaced.

She had enough on her plate already this afternoon: she would shortly have to prepare her TV piece on the Government reshuffle. Once she got the official word from Downing Street she would be interviewing backbenchers and 'senior Party figures' to get their reaction to the new Cabinet team. Then she needed Opposition comment, and photographs and graphics explaining which ministers were 'in' and which 'out'. The whole thing had to be sewn into a neat two-minute package by the time the title sequence for the *Six O'Clock News* began to roll. It was fingernail-destroying stuff.

As Charlotte battled through the crush of suits in the Lobby, her competitor from IRN hared off to her own word processor with the same hectic agenda in mind.

Chapter Three

The Reverend Robert Scott, who was an MP and the leader of the Loyal Unionist Party, was not at Westminster that evening. Nevertheless he was on his feet, declaiming and denouncing in his forthright manner. Reverend Scott, or 'God Bob' as he was known to the press, was addressing the new governing Assembly at Stormont, in Belfast, to which he had recently been elected. God Bob represented the good people of County Down in the Stormont and Westminster Parliaments; and when he wasn't doing that to the best of his God-given ability, the ginger-haired, forty-five-year-old was preaching the gospel of the True Presbyterian Church of Christ the Protester.

The previous speaker in the debate in the Stormont Chamber that evening had been a Sinn Fein Assemblyman, who was also a former IRA hunger-striker. These days his image owed more to designer stubble and Calvin Klein than to the faeces-covered blankets of the H-block protests.

The Sinn Fein Assemblyman had just warned that unless more progress was made towards a united Ireland, the bombing might begin again in earnest. His fellow Assemblymen wondered if this was a not-very-subtle threat to the Protestants present, or whether it was entirely for the benefit of the other

Sinn Fein members who were demanding results from the so-called 'peace process'.

Whatever the truth might be it was not really relevant as far as the Loyal Unionist Party (LUP) leader was concerned. God Bob hauled himself to his full five foot six and glared around at the pseudo-Classical splendour of the Stormont Chamber.

'I am surprised that the Assemblyman from Ardoyne does not believe there has been much progress towards a united Ireland,' the high-pitched, metallic voice spluttered. 'I would say that we are on the verge of handing the keys of Belfast to the Tea-shock himself.' God Bob's pronunciation of the Irish Prime Minister's Gaelic title was calculated to annoy the Catholics present, and it did.

'So far, the Royal Ulster Constabulary has been renamed with the American-sounding NIPD, and the Royal Ulster Regiment is now the ugly-sounding Northern Ireland Regiment. The Crown Courts have become the Northern Ireland Justice Commission, and British Telecom and British Gas have been persuaded to call themselves NIT and NIG – surely, not a change for the better! Now we are told that UlsterBus must become NIB. And why have these clumsy, alien and improbable titles invaded our language?' he asked with a disbelieving shake of his mop of flame-coloured curls.

'Because it has been decreed by the Brussels bureaucrats who administer the Regional Funds for Specially Sensitive Areas of Ethnic or Religious Diversity.' His disgust and amazement was all too apparent as he quoted from the document in his bony hand. 'The European Union has dictated that Ulster must submit itself to thousands of debasing and offensive changes if this Province is to qualify as a specially sensitive regional area worthy of Euro-handouts. This is the price of the devil's gold!'

he yapped like a furious Pekinese. 'I say to you that the cloven hoof is upon them. What next will they demand of Ulster? Must we have the Pope's head on our coins and stamps? This is the shape of things to come!'

God Bob swivelled his head around to take in the circular chamber, his dog collar wedged like some surgical appliance. 'The Pope's ambassadors in Brussels have demanded that our traditional parades and marches must stop, which means it is now illegal to be Protestant in a Protestant country. And these messengers of the Papist anti-Christ have another trick up their sleeves,' he announced, with a dramatic rustle of the papers in his hand.

'This very night the British Government has kowtowed to Brussels yet again. Yes, London has appointed a Roman Catholic Irishman to be the new Northern Ireland Office Minister of State. Is it not enough that Euro-money goes exclusively to create jobs for the Catholic minority in Ulster, and build homes and hospitals and leisure centres for people who have bombed and murdered policemen and soldiers in Ulster for thirty years? Now we have a Roman Catholic being sent across from London to oversee the devil's work,' he concluded with a fierce and vigorous nod, as if he heartily agreed with himself.

'But the loyal people of Ulster have a message for Mr Michael Fitzgerald and his friends in Brussels. No surrender!' The elfin God Bob sat down in a steaming fury as the Loyal Unionists around him roared their approval.

To one side the Official Unionist Assemblymen, who were the more moderate representatives of the Protestant community, looked painfully embarrassed by the Reverend Scott's outburst. The other elected representatives sniggered, or looked bored. Most of them had heard it all before, and knew God Bob was performing for the television cameras that recorded every utterance in the Chamber. In that respect his speech achieved its purpose: the clip of Reverend Scott suggesting that Brussels had told London to appoint Michael Fitzgerald, was used on every news broadcast for the rest of the day. Inevitably, no one was interested in the other subjects that might or might not have been debated at Stormont that day. God Bob was dictating the news agenda, as usual.

It took Charlotte Carter ten hyperactive minutes to write her obituary of Nigel Swinton MP, and send it flying on electronic wings through the BBC system to the desk of the editor of the *Six O'Clock News* at Television Centre in Shepherds Bush. Charlotte was working at a terminal in the BBC's cramped cubbyhole of an office just off the Press Gallery. Around her were seven other equally frantic reporters, tapping away at keyboards and making phone calls.

Without warning the door swung open violently, and a short, fresh-faced young man with vacant eyes swept into the cubbyhole. 'Hold the presses, everyone, I've got the scoop of the week!' he announced in a piercing Liverpudlian whine. No one acknowledged the arrival of Dave Bower, or even looked up from their screens, but Bower was unaware of their reactions. 'Who's doing the piece on Nigel Swinton?' he demanded with the same cheeky grin he employed in front of the TV camera whenever he got the chance.

When Charlotte owned up he scuttled over to her screen and started to read her copy. 'Eh, this is crap!' he said loudly when he was two sentences in. 'I've got the scoop that no one else has!' he continued, and tried to wave Charlotte out of her chair so that he could get at the keyboard.

'It's already gone to the *Six*,' said Charlotte stoutly. 'And it's not crap.'

Dave turned to the office at large. 'This is total shite, Charlotte. I've got the real story and it's brill. Really great,' he added, rolling his 'r's in the distinctive Merseyside manner. 'Nigel Swinton had AIDS: it wasn't cancer at all. And I've got someone at the London Hospital who's going to say it on screen too. Swinton was gay. Thirty-nine, unmarried, all the rest.' He leered triumphantly.

'We don't put stories like that on the *Six O'Clock News*,' Charlotte remarked with as much authority as possible, but Dave Bower wasn't listening. He stood in the middle of the room, and undid the top button of his shirt and rolled up his sleeves ostentatiously, as if he was settling down to some vital and demanding task. His eyes were constantly on the move, flicking from one colleague to the next, although he was unaware of their lack of interest.

'You can't write a piece suggesting that an MP's just died of AIDS,' Charlotte persisted. 'First of all it's tasteless, and secondly you don't have proof.'

'I've got some pharmacist at the London Hospital who's been giving AZT to Nigel Swinton for weeks.' Bower grinned. 'Now move over. I've got work to do.' The word 'work' came out as 'wake', and it had a strangely jarring effect on Charlotte who remained anchored to her word processor.

'It's not responsible journalism to start throwing accusations about before the corpse is cold,' Charlotte tried again. 'And anyway, what d'you think you're going to achieve by dragging up the fact that Nigel Swinton was gay? Quite a few people around here suspected that, Dave, but Swinton didn't choose to come out, so we should respect his choice. And his family and friends won't want us having a bloody tabloid-style orgy over this.'

The minute the words 'family and friends' were out of her mouth she regretted uttering them. Bower's eyes lit up, and he ran his stubby fingers through his closely-cropped blond hair. How soon before he started to pester Swinton's parents, Charlotte wondered. 'Go and talk to Rodney about your so-called scoop,' she said firmly, and pointed him in the direction of the cafeteria where the head of the Parliamentary Unit was known to be holding court.

When Dave Bower's short little legs had taken him off to the cafeteria, one of Charlotte's colleagues sniggered: 'That boy wants to share everything, from his exclusives and bursts of wisdom, to his farts.' No one else laughed.

Charlotte was expecting the reshuffle announcement from Downing Street at any moment, and she knew she should really stay by her news terminal, but she logged out and went to the Press Gallery telephones where she could make a call in privacy. The reporter balanced a dog-eared directory on the shelf and searched for a number for the London Hospital, her fingers shaking with nerves. What she was about to do could get her into a great deal of trouble if she was found out. But that was a chance she had to take.

Chapter Four

Michael hurried up Whitehall to Trafalgar Square, and turned left beneath Admiralty Arch. It was mid-March, and still cold and damp in London, but he didn't have a coat over his dark blue pin-striped suit: a life of ministerial cars had conditioned him to forget to take one. Politicians who had fallen from favour and been relegated to the back benches always mentioned the loss of their car and driver as one of the perks they missed most.

Michael showed his Commons pass at the front door of Admiralty House and followed the policeman's directions, up the impressive staircase towards the office of the Northern Ireland Secretary. Only an optimist, or someone who disregarded human character, would expect Grace and Fitzgerald to get on well. Michael was not a blokey kind of chap, and he did not easily mingle with the 'hail-fellow-well-met' sort that increasingly populated the Tory Party. Grace, on the other hand, was definitely in the 'prop up the bar and entertain the boys with some good stories' camp. If he was honest, Michael would admit that he preferred talking to his thirteen-year-old daughter about the morality of vegetarianism, or whether the CIA had conspired to kill President Kennedy, to take but two of Laura's current obsessive interests.

To Michael's relief Grace got down to business immediately, after the obligatory display of the glories of the office, which had been used by Churchill during World War I, when he was the First Sea Lord. From Grace's desk Churchill had sent out a message to the fleet announcing simply *'Winston is back.'*

'Welcome to the final shift in Ulster, Mike. As you know, our job is to devolve everything to this new Assembly at Stormont as fast as possible. Then we have to make sure their Assembly committees take over all the functions of the Northern Ireland Office. And then we get the hell out.'

'I see.'

'Anyway, my advice, for what it's worth, is to keep your head down. Don't try anything innovative or inspiring, because no one will thank you for it. Oh, and these commissions we've set up with the Irish Government. You know the routine – Dublin has half the seats, while representatives from the Stormont Assembly take the other half. Between you and me, this is where the real power's going to be: in these commissions. Not at Stormont.'

Michael sat in silence as Grace continued the 'voice of experience' lecture. The younger man reckoned he didn't understand much about Northern Ireland, but one thing he did grasp was that the Protestant majority weren't going to buy anything that smacked of giving the Irish Government too much influence over Ulster. For that reason the cross-border commissions had to be handled sensitively, and given uncontroversial areas to examine, such as the creation of a joint Tourist Authority for the north and the south. It concerned Michael that the Secretary of State envisaged the commissions as being all-powerful.

'We've been hurling money at Ulster for decades, just to stop it turning into Yugoslavia. And still all these damned Irish go on about is history, bloody history. Best not to know anything about Ireland, I find. Then it all washes over you. Stick to making sure the social security scroungers get their benefit payments on time; and believe me, half the bloody Province is on the dole, or claiming invalidity, or whatever.'

After a pregnant pause that Michael was at a loss to fill, the Secretary of State kicked his feet up on the desk and sighed. 'I'll tell you about history. The IRA have done more harm in three decades than the British did in centuries. 'Course, the Americans don't help. Take a look at this. Now where is it?' He picked through papers on his desk and handed Michael a yellowing leaflet, clearly brittle with age. The picture showed a small, sad-eyed child standing behind a barbed-wire fence, and the caption read, *This child's father is in a concentration camp in occupied Ireland.*

'They're still producing this kind of rubbish in Boston, you know,' Grace rasped. 'Mind you, there was a shipment of Yankee arms arriving somewhere on the Irish coast, and an IRA chappie was supposed to stick them in his lorry and drive them across the country to the IRA arms dump. Anyway, it took this Paddy two days to make the journey because he was so afraid of getting spotted by the police. And when he finally reached his destination, his boss was furious with him because it turns out his road tax disc was out of date, and he could have been stopped by the Garda at any point. Very Irish.' The ruddy cheeks reddened further as Grace chortled.

Michael was surprised to be told that IRA money was still being raised in Boston because the generally accepted view of the US media was that the Loyalist bombs there had effectively dried up donations from the Americans. The good people of Massachusetts were unaccustomed to having their objects of

41

civic pride torn apart by terrorists, and evidently when they were put to the test they didn't like bombs this close to home. But the new Northern Ireland Minister kept this observation to himself.

His new boss wiped his eyes and sighed. 'Well, enough of my stories. Back to business. I can tell you this in strictest confidence because you're one of us now. I had a meeting with the RUC this afternoon. Sorry – I keep forgetting we're supposed to say NIPD. Whatever. They're bracing themselves for the big one from the IRA. A real end-of-the-world event. I hate to think what they'll do.' Grace's sudden thoughtfulness struck Michael as insincere.

'Anyway, you'll be getting the relevant intelligence reports by the boxload. In fact, the first boxes should arrive at your house this evening, I'm afraid. Oh, I just remembered. We're having a Departmental bash tomorrow night,' the Secretary of State said with a rubbing together of the hands. 'So do come along, and bring, er . . .' Grace waved his hands feebly as he recalled that Michael was a widower. '. . . bring whoever.'

'Thank you.' Michael noticed their 'meeting' was over. 'I do have a question.' He spoke tentatively, and Grace's comradely grin collapsed like curtains falling to the floor. 'I have a very bright research assistant, an American, and I'd like to bring her with me to Stormont. She's already been through the MOD security clearance.'

'Fine, fine,' replied Grace like a benign despot with hands raised in benediction, as if anything was in his power. 'So long as she goes through the normal vetting procedure. Oh, by the way, have you heard about Nigel Swinton?'

Michael nodded slowly and felt a wave of dread wash through his system. 'Thank God it's over.'

'Yeah,' Grace said absent-mindedly. 'What was it he had?'

For a moment Michael thought he saw what looked like a mischievous light twinkling in Grace's eyes. 'Cancer,' the new minister replied firmly. 'Nigel had cancer.'

Two minutes later Michael was back in the cold, early evening air. The windows of the MOD building up ahead shone out of the darkness, and Michael felt sad that he would be leaving that fine 1920s ocean liner moored majestically at the end of Whitehall Place. He would miss Johnny, and the dry humour of his civil servants. But career progress meant moving on, and getting to grips with new problems – in other words, proving himself to the PM and his Cabinet. The Northern Ireland Office was another step on the way, he thought, as if he was delivering himself a pep talk. And if he had to keep his head down, then that was exactly what he would do. Promotion came to those who prevented embarrassments for the Prime Minister, not prima donnas who screwed up.

Michael did not reflect further on Sir Trevor Grace's sermon about the state of the peace process, which seemed about as insightful as a *Sun* editorial. He still felt guilty about forgetting to share his good news with Mandy, so he decided to invite her to Grace's party the following evening. It sounded ghastly, of course, but it was *de rigueur* that Michael should turn up. He assumed that Mandy would already be busy tomorrow. After all, his assistant was a popular, gregarious honeypot who attracted many bees. But she might at least appreciate the thought, and Michael was conscious of never fussing over her enough.

Mandy was still at her desk, diligent as ever, bright-eyed, and full of innocent excitement about Michael's promotion. He sat down on the edge of the desk opposite hers, feeling slightly awkward under her admiring gaze, and mentioned the party. She was indeed busy, but she would try to join him later, after she had seen her friends. Then Michael suddenly remembered the most important question of all.

'Mandy, you've done a wonderful job here, and I'd like you to come to the Northern Ireland Office. Maybe you'd consider it if you stayed here, rather than traipsing over to Belfast with me every week. I understand if the idea doesn't appeal.'

'Oh, I know I want to do it, Michael. Really.' She beamed. 'And I'd be missing the whole point if I didn't do the stuff in Belfast. It'll be completely fascinating, won't it?' She leaned forward as if she was trying to lasso him with her words.

'That's marvellous. Thank you. It'll be much less intimidating for me, you know, learning a new job and everything, if you're there to sort me out.' He hesitated as she grinned her perfect, white smile. But instead of a smile in response she got a grimace from her boss as he scurried into his own office.

'Oh Lord,' she heard him wail, 'I forgot to call Laura. I want to tell her before she sees it on the news. And my mother too,' he added as he punched the first memory button on his phone.

Five minutes later Mandy could hear him saying, 'And could you please video *Channel 4 News* too, as well as the *Six O'Clock*. I want to see what Charlotte Carter does to me . . . Yes, I should be home for *Nine O'Clock . . . da, da, hvala vam mnogo . . . da . . . zbogom dovidjenja.*' Sitting in the adjoining office, Mandy frowned. Michael's conversations with his daughter were littered with words from another language. Perhaps it was simply a private lingo, but it irritated her a bit.

Mandy was not to know that since the arrival of the Fitzgeralds' Bosnian Muslim housekeeper soon after Caroline's accident, words and phrases from the southern Slav language had crept into every exchange, primarily because Laura had decided it was a smarty-pants thing to do. Michael resisted at first, since he would have preferred her to learn a more cosmopolitan language like French or German or Spanish— 'or Finnish,' he had suggested to Laura with a hard stare some months before. But his daughter gobbled up every fragment of Serbo-Croat that Delva, the housekeeper, unintentionally muttered. And she made a strong case for the connections between northern Slav languages like Russian and Polish, and their southern relatives.

'I'll be able to make myself understood anywhere from Prague to Vladivostock,' was Laura's sales pitch.

'Very useful,' her father had countered, 'if you're planning on a career dismantling faulty nuclear reactors or SS20s.'

'Fascist!' Laura had hissed in response.

When Michael was off the phone he called through the open door to remind Mandy not to work too late. Then he dialled his mother's house in Hampshire.

Mrs Fitzgerald, a widow for five years, and the staunchest Mrs Thatcher fan Michael had ever known, had heard about his promotion on the radio. She proceeded to berate him for agreeing to waste his energy and youth on 'that cesspit of bandits and graft'.

'The Northern Ireland question is not about terrorism or religion any more, Michael,' she said vehemently. 'It's about who controls the building contracts and taxi firms, and who bribes whom. It's in the hands of the Mafia now. I've read all about it in the *Telegraph*.'

At that moment Michael realised Mandy was standing in the doorway, waving goodnight. She was wearing white training shoes for her journey home, rather than the spikey-heeled black things she tottered around in at the office. Apparently it was the American way, and it seemed perfectly sensible, except that the black-stockinged legs and bulky shoes made her look like Minnie Mouse.

45

After another five minutes his mother had blown herself out on the duplicity of the race she had happily married into, and in the intervening nano-second of silence Michael invited himself and Laura and Delva down to Hampshire for the weekend. Suddenly the hardened right-wing fanatic mother was transformed into the cooing grandmother who couldn't wait to see her hardened left-wing fanatic granddaughter.

'I need a chance to go over the files and acquaint myself with—'

'Yes, yes, yes.' His mother sounded as if she had no time to hear about her only child's problems; she was much more diverted by the prospect of hours with Laura.

Michael did not bother to mention that he intended to give himself a crash course in Irish history while he was staying in Hampshire, because he could imagine Mrs Fitzgerald's caustic reaction. Despite Sir Trevor Grace's advice, the new Minister of State thought that ignorance of history had never aided any politician's understanding of the present, nor his ability to avoid previous balls-ups in future. There were already too many in his line of work who thought that history began the day they were born . . .

At that moment, Charlotte Carter was also confronting the awesome prospect of getting to grips with Irish history. She was having 'dinner', if that was the word for it, in the Commons Press canteen. Sitting opposite her was the head of the BBC Parliamentary Unit, Rodney Davis, 'journalist twenty-five years, man and beast, mostly beast'.

Rodney had reached these exalted heights via the *Dagenham Evening News* and then local radio, and he was proud of his well-honed newshound sense of smell. As he expanded on his current hunches, Charlotte studied him over a plate of lasagne that would have had Italians committing suicide at the indignity it brought unto their honour. Rodney might indeed have sampled every corner of the journalistic universe on his way to Westminster, but wherever he had washed up during the Seventies, it had obviously made a lasting impression on him. He wore trousers that were too tight and which never quite coordinated with his baggy-pocketed tweedy jackets, thick-knotted wool ties, and the kind of shirts that had white collars and blue bodies, known throughout Westminster as 'David Steel shirts'. Rodney also had the bouffant hairstyle that Dustin Hoffman had sported when he played Carl Bernstein in the film about Watergate. All in all, Rodney Davis fitted right in with the rest of the BBC crowd at Parliament. Charlotte reckoned the only male journalists who were handsome, bathed regularly, wore suitable clothing and had good haircuts were invariably gay.

'I've got this instinct about Ulster,' Rodney was saying, chewing enthusiastically at a mouthful of greasy sausage. 'I reckon it's going to be *the* sexy political subject.'

Charlotte gave up on the lasagne; only Rodney could describe three and a half thousand dead bodies as 'sexy'.

'No one's really taken a look at the new Assembly at Stormont from a purely political point of view yet,' he continued. 'No one' meant 'no journalist from the BBC'. 'Most of our reports are reactive. You know – "a bomb's gone off here" or "such and such a politician is pissed off with the Government". But there's no context.' Rodney stopped and sipped his coffee as he savoured that most favourite of words.

'So I want you to go to Belfast, and look at the political process at Stormont. Now, the appointment of young Fitzgerald means another sop to Dublin, although the PM'll never admit it.

So let's start off with a profile of him. You follow him around Belfast as he learns the ropes. How do the politicians react to him? How will the old dogs deal with a Minister who's from an emerging generation of leaders who don't carry any historic Ulster baggage? And how do they feel about the fact that he's a bloody Catholic!'

Charlotte had been having her own private bet about how long it would take Rodney to mention Michael's nominal religion; true to form, her boss hadn't let her down.

'But Rodney, Fitzgerald's religion doesn't necessarily mean he's in favour of a united Ireland. In fact, I was checking through the *Hansard* database this afternoon, and there's no record that he's ever expressed an opinion on Ulster. And he once told me he doesn't go to church. And he married a Protestant in a C of E ceremony.'

Rodney slurped down the last of his coffee. 'Well, you see it's because you understand Fitzgerald that you'll make a good job of it.'

If looking up a few facts amounted to knowing someone, then Charlotte felt that she was fairly intimate with Hitler too, but she let Rodney's comment pass. She was exhausted after rushing about all day, preparing for the reshuffle statement, then filming an appropriate last-minute package for the *Six O'Clock News*. But she had got it done, watched it being broadcast, and then collapsed into the nearest bar with her colleagues. That was where Rodney had tracked her down for their little chat.

Charlotte did not mind the intrusion: she had nothing else to do after work. She wasn't rushing off to a dinner party with her witty, sophisticated friends; and there was no adoring boyfriend anticipating her arrival home any more. She had split with him last year after a disagreement about what their priorities should be. No one had come along since then to fill the space in her heart or her home.

In fact, home was her new flat in Bayswater. It was impatient for an application of paint, and resentful that it was still unadorned by paintings. It probably felt dejected because its new mistress hadn't even got around to unpacking her belongings. And she'd been there three months already. All work and no play in the life of a media woman. And they call it a glamour profession, she thought wistfully. It was about as glamorous as a pack of sanitary towels.

For a moment these gloomy thoughts hung around her head like stormclouds pregnant with rain. Then she took a sip of wine, and tried to look on the bright side. Here was her chance to do an in-depth feature on Michael Fitzgerald, and she was getting a trip to Belfast, a city she had never before visited. Then Rodney's last comment punctured the reporter's wall of preoccupation.

'Did you say you want me to add Northern Ireland to the list of policy areas I cover? Or are you removing one from me to make room for it?' she asked simply.

Something about the furtive way Rodney looked down at the coffee cup, and then fiddled with the spoon in the sugar bowl, set off an alarm bell in her head.

'Well, let's just say I'm reorganising who covers what within the Parliamentary Unit, Charlotte,' he said with a nervous cough, and avoided meeting her eyes. 'You've had six months doing the high-profile stories like back-bench rebellions, Euro-rows, and Treasury matters. So, I think it's time you had a change.'

'What does that mean?' she persisted with a tense but polite little smile. 'Who's getting my stories? What am I taking over?'

'You're going to swap places with Dave Bower. You'll take Transport and Northern Ireland and Social Services and, er, Wales I think.'

'But what have I done wrong? Dave Bower's virtually a trainee.' Taking on Ulster was a demotion: despite the lip service, London did not really care what happened in Belfast. Charlotte had the feeling that she was being sucked down into the disposal unit of a sink, and that she was powerless to swim against it.

'OK, there is a problem with the stuff you're producing,' Rodney said with a casual shrug. 'I've been meaning to have a word with you, and I suppose now is as good a time as any. Take that piece on pollution you did last night. It lacked bite. The viewers didn't know what the hell to think of it. First you make the Tories look like liars, but that's fine: they're the Government. Then you ask the Labour bloke what he'd do about toxic waste, or whatever it was, and he slags off the Government. Fine. And then you interview some Friends of the Earth type who says that actually there are some Labour councils who are the worst offenders when it comes to toxic-waste dumping.'

'The point was that a couple of Labour councils are allowing dumping in the rural areas under their control, but they only do it where the Conservative voters live,' Charlotte explained patiently.

'Yeah, but what's the sense of complicating the story like that? The viewer wants a good bit of knockabout from a TV report. Tory says this, Labour says the opposite. Bang, bang. That tells both sides of the story quickly, and without confusing them at home.'

'But what happens when there are three sides to the story, Rodney? Surely we shouldn't assume the viewers are too stupid to understand that sometimes both sides aren't being entirely straight.' She leaned across the table, fists clenched, and eyes flashing, as if she was pleading with her boss to see her point of view. But Rodney continued to avoid her gaze, and poked mercilessly at the sugar. This appeal was getting her nowhere so she switched tack. 'And how can you give Dave Bower my policy areas? He's not ready yet.'

'Dave's got what it takes to be a good journalist. It's in his guts. You're far too, you know, up here,' Rodney said with a vague wave toward the region where his brain should have resided, in theory at least.

Charlotte felt as though the veins in her neck were about to burst, and she was tempted to yank the damned sugar spoon out of Rodney's grasp so that he might actually look at her. 'Oh, come on, Rodney. Dave regurgitates Government press releases without asking questions. And he always uses the same Labour rent-a-mouth to put the boot in. D'you know, I overheard his Labour chum breathlessly turn up at an interview with Dave and say, "Remind me, what am I angry about today?" He's dim, Rodney, and he's an ambulance-chaser.'

'He's keen and he's enthusiastic,' her boss countered with a decisive dig at the sugar bowl. 'That's what you don't understand, Charlotte. Dave's part of a team. He wants to tell everybody about the story he's doing. He's excited about his work. He doesn't just hide in a corner and burrow away at it like you do.'

Charlotte took another swig of wine and tried to calm her racing heart. What Rodney meant, of course, was that Dave behaved like a bloke: he boasted, and bullshitted, and kept the boss company in the bar.

'Anyway, we'll see how you get on in Belfast,' Rodney

continued, like a doctor recommending gentle exercise and early nights. 'Hopefully it'll sharpen up your news values.'

Charlotte managed to restrain herself from telling her boss precisely what she thought of his news values, but it took phenomenal self-control to remain unruffled. When Rodney returned to the Press Gallery Bar, Charlotte headed back to the BBC cubbyhole alone. Her pride was hurt, her feelings were bruised, and she was frightened that her so-called career was on the rocks. 'Well, it's only a job,' she told herself with mock bravery as she logged into her terminal. 'The pity of it is that my job is the only thing in my life.'

Then she swallowed hard, and studied the electronic wires services to find out if the lid had been kept on the Nigel Swinton story.

In Belfast that evening a chilly mist rolled down from Cave Hill and settled over the city. In the stark suburb of Finaghy, on the south side of town, anyone with any sense was indoors. The residents of Garron Crescent seemed to have the right idea, because the street was quiet and deserted. Curtains were drawn, and only the occasional chink of light or television flicker penetrated the gloom. It was not surprising then that when the unfamiliar van turned into Garron Crescent from the Locksley Park end it went unnoticed. It cruised along for twenty yards, then pulled over and idled at the kerb.

A young man, tall and lithe, got out of the passenger side, and went around to the back of the van. He opened the doors and pulled out a crude, primitively-drawn For Sale sign attached to a stakepost. Then he wedged a bottle into the pocket of his leather jacket, and grasped a hammer in the other hand. The young man shut the van doors quietly, and went up the garden path of the house ten yards further along the Crescent.

A couple of swings of the hammer was all it needed to push the stakepost into the soggy ground. The noise brought the owners to their sitting-room window, which was unfortunate for them because they caught the full force of the flaming bottle as it crashed through the glass. The woman, who was in her sixties, was drenched in petrol which immediately ignited and scorched off her hair, eyebrows and lashes as if they were vapour. She fell backwards onto the floor and rolled across the carpet, flailing her arms and legs, but the dress was alight and her frantic movements had little effect.

Her husband, also in his sixties, got more glass than petrol on his face. One shard punctured his right eye and sliced open the lid further every time he blinked. Within seconds his face was awash with blood, and he staggered blindly around the room, gasping for breath.

The young man in the leather jacket hurled himself into the van, and a moment later he and his driver pulled into the busy Upper Lisburn Road, heading back to the centre of the city. They had successfully delivered their unsubtle message to the only Roman Catholics in a respectable, lower-middle-class and predominantly Protestant road. The For Sale sign would give any other 'Taigs' in the area a wake-up call, and they might take the initiative to move out before another vanload of dissatisfied Loyalists came calling. And they *would* come calling again – until they were satisfied that the new Assembly and its cross-border commissions were dead and buried.

News of the attack on the couple in Garron Crescent reached the Catholic neighbourhoods of West Belfast by midnight. By then it was known that the woman was unlikely to survive the burns, while her husband had lost one eye, and was lying in an oxygen tent, his feeble heart straining to fight off a terror-induced asthma attack.

Two young men, determined to balance the equation, stumbled out of a West Belfast pub, got in a car, and drove along the M1 to the Finaghy turnoff. But instead of going left towards Garron Crescent they went right, and drove to the Suffolk council estate. They double-checked the address, and delivered a similar message to the inhabitants, who happened to be one of the last remaining Protestant families in the area. At the start of the Troubles there had been almost three thousand Protestant families here: now there were about four hundred left. After tonight's IRA visit, there would be one fewer.

The war had begun again.

Chapter Five

The previous evening's tit-for-tat ethnic cleansing in south Belfast occurred too late for any reports or pictures to make the newspapers the following morning, but the new Northern Ireland Minister heard the unsavoury details (three dead, one fading fast) on the radio. Nor had the quality papers questioned the cause of Nigel Swinton's premature demise. However, one of the tabloids was threatening to 'reveal all' about the wretched former MP in tomorrow's edition. That meant they were still waving their chequebooks around, searching for solid 'proof', Michael thought with a mixture of disgust and sorrow.

His breakfast was further interrupted by the delivery of a large envelope emblazoned with the House of Commons portcullis. He recognised the scrawl immediately – it had been familiar to him since he had copied pages of school science notes written in this distinctive script by someone who had understood the subject rather better than Michael.

Fitzgerald opened the package without a second thought, and was examining the contents when his daughter, 'Tsk, tsk, tsked!' him, in between spoonfuls of muesli cereal.

'Call yourself a Northern Ireland Minister?' she drawled

sarcastically. 'That could have been a bomb in there, and you gaily ripped it open, endangering my life, and Delva's, and your own too. I hope you realise that a couple of years of so-called "ceasefire" doesn't make a peace. As we know from last night.'

Michael stared across the breakfast-table at Laura's knowing, elf-like face; it was pale as the undead, and framed by long dark hair. Her brows arched into suggestive half-moons above her dark eyes; every inch her mother. For once Michael did not argue back because Laura had a point. From now on, opening the front door to strangers, and ripping open envelopes, were things of the past.

Last night, when he had returned to his home near Westbourne Grove and confronted the first of his boxes, Michael had waded through a spine-chilling security brief on all the ways in which his family might be blown sky-high by crazed Irishmen. There would be no more jumping into the car and roaring off, without getting out the mirror device first to check underneath. And no last-minute trips to the cinema down the road at Whiteley's. No more doing anything on a whim, so it seemed. The Fitzgeralds would soon be accompanied everywhere by a security detail.

'What's all this?' Laura was peering at the books and pamphlets that slid out of the envelope. Michael examined the note that had come with them.

'It's from Edward Power MP.' He glanced up at her frowning face. His daughter hated it when she was in a position of ignorance. 'You remember, my school chum Eddie? He's the Opposition Northern Ireland spokesthing. He's sent me some stuff about Irish history, and Amnesty International reports concerning the British Government's conduct in the Province.' He picked through the pile of publications. 'And most

56

important, here's a boxed set of Steely Dan CDs. My God, all six albums. What a lovely man Eddie is.'

'Oh no!' wailed Laura. 'Pop music from the Dark Ages!'

'Get used to it, Morticia. You're going to be hearing lots of it. Here, read some of this Trotskyist propaganda on British imperialism.' He tossed her a badly-printed pamphlet about the SAS's alleged shoot-to-kill policy.

'Trotskyist?' Her neat nose wrinkled in disapproval. To Michael's relief she had inherited her mother's snout, not his. 'What's Trotskyist?'

'Trotsky was a Russian revolutionary who fell foul of Stalin, and he had to leave Moscow for Mexico. But Stalin dealt with him in the end, just like he liquidated everyone who upset him. An assassin put an ice-pick in Trotsky's head.'

He watched his daughter biting her lower lip, wondering what was coming next, and how to make some smart riposte, no doubt.

'You'd like Trotsky, my little angel,' he went on. 'He thought the revolution should be spread everywhere in the world. Switzerland, Basingstoke, everywhere.' Michael finished his croissant, and watched Laura's hackles rise. 'And since you insulted my taste in music, try this on for size: if you're going to be frightfully politically aware, you should know about Trotsky. You're thirteen years old, and your brain's rotting already.'

There was a sharp snort of breath through teenage nostrils, and a little grunt of displeasure as his daughter exited the kitchen, muttering, '*Odjebi.*'

'What did that mean?' Michael enquired of Delva, who had just walked in with a fresh pot of coffee. She shrugged her shoulders, and filled his cup.

'You don't want to know. I'm just sorry she has picked it up.

You must think I'm a foul-mouthed woman, Michael. But she makes me explain these things. She is a highly manipulative child.'

Delva pushed a few strands of grey hair out of her eyes, and tucked them back into the slightly chaotic bun at the nape of her neck. Then she sifted through the morning papers, clucking her approval at the favourable mentions her employer had merited.

Delva had been a maths teacher in the ancient city of Mostar until the war. When her husband and sons were tortured to death by Serb soldiers there was nothing to stay for any more, so she had used the family's savings, and bribed her way to Germany, and then to Britain. A friend of a friend had put her in contact with Michael when he had been searching for a housekeeper, after Caroline's death. As far as the MP was concerned, he knew immediately that Delva was right, and he prayed that she didn't decide to take up teaching again before he had packed Laura off to university, embalming classes, or whatever she finally settled on.

Delva accepted the Fitzgeralds' strange lifestyle without question. The odd hours that politics dictated did not phase her. Nor did the migration between Michael's cottage in his North Yorkshire constituency, and London. Even the prospect of spending weekends and the summer in Northern Ireland didn't perturb her. 'A quiet backwater,' she'd quipped, and suggested to Michael that it would be good for Laura's education to see a part of her own country that most British people preferred to ignore.

Compared with Delva's experiences, Belfast was indeed a quiet backwater. Michael's only concern was to see his house-keeper put on some much-needed weight; it was difficult to ask if she had always been thin as a rake, or whether her boniness was a consequence of being starved by Serbs. She had a hooked nose, and heavy eyelids which made her look sleepy or vague. But Delva was neither, and so good was her English that she was constantly correcting Laura's sloppy grammar.

From the hallway came the crash of a small human body hurling itself down the stairs, then a hurried farewell in some foreign tongue, and the slam of the front door. Kisses from Laura were a rare event, as were hugs, but Michael felt he had more of his daughter's precious time than many parents, simply because they argued so much: about whether she could have new wall-paper and curtains for her room; about whether she should have to do games at school because it was 'so tedious'; about Aborigi-nal land rights. Michael hated the expression 'quality time', but that was probably what their fights amounted to.

Her departure for school, possibly the last trip she would make unaccompanied by a policeman, reminded Michael that he too should be getting ready to go: he had a nine-thirty meeting at his new office. As he was selecting a tie he pondered the day ahead: a briefing from Army Intelligence, then another briefing from an NIPD officer who was in London at the moment, a dozen boxes of turgid documents to read and absorb, and a gruesome party with his new colleagues. He knotted the tie and scrutinised his reflection unhappily. Then he recalled that he was having lunch with Charlotte Carter, and he reconsidered the tie. A minute later he had a much nicer one around his neck. A day that brought him Steely Dan, and Charlotte Carter, couldn't be so bad after all.

'Thanks very much for seeing me at such short notice,' Charlotte said as she took a seat across from Edward Power in the MP's Commons office at ten o'clock that morning. She reached for her pen and notebook instinctively, but noticed that Labour's Northern Ireland spokesman winced slightly at the sight of them. He was happy to pass on his expertise on Ireland, just as any politician likes to have journalist acquaintances who are in their debt, but he didn't relish being quoted on what he was about to say.

'I promise this'll be off the record, but you see I never remember anything unless I write it down.' Except the lyrics to annoying songs by Barbra Streisand, she might add. And why does she spell her first name like that, anyway? However, Power looked like the kind of forty-something who wanted Streisand deified, so Charlotte curtailed this pointless line of thought. There was no better place to start her background research on Michael Fitzgerald in particular, and Northern Ireland in general than with Edward Power, lifelong friend of the new Minister, and expert on Irish politics.

'Assume I'm a total idiot. Give me an A to Z for the mentally subnormal.'

Power grinned, and Charlotte realised why she found him less than sympathetic. It wasn't just the frizzy hair: it was the sneering upper lip. He leaned his elbows on the desk in a businesslike fashion. 'OK. Basically it's inevitable that Ireland will eventually be one country again because even though the Catholics in the North are in the minority at the moment, you have to understand that they're breeding their way toward becoming the majority early in the next century. Now, bearing that in mind, you'd think the Protestants, who are in the majority for the time being, would do a deal fast, before they become the minority. But sadly they don't see it like that.' Power sounded as if he was rattling off a five-times table, and Charlotte duly took down his words of wisdom.

'By the way, when I say "the Protestants" I mean the voters who are represented by the Official Ulster Unionists who are sensible, and who get most of the non-Catholic votes. There's also the Loyal Unionist Party, God Bob's loonies. Naturally these two parties have been at each other's throats for years.'

Charlotte nodded and scribbled away like a diligent student as Edward Power continued his lecture. 'The Catholics in Northern Ireland vote for the Social Democratic and Labour Party, the SDLP, who made their name campaigning for civil rights in the late Sixties. I should mention that a small minority of Catholics vote for Sinn Fein, the political wing of the IRA.'

'What's a small minority?'

'About ten per cent. Less than vote for the Alliance, which is the only party in the whole Province that isn't sectarian. All the others are based on one religion or another.'

'And I suppose the class who vote Alliance are the nice sensible middle classes.'

'Got it in one. Now, a lot of the Catholics are nationalists, which means they want the six counties of Ulster reunited with the twenty-six counties of Eire, the south of Ireland. They're called nationalists, by the way, because they believe Ireland is one nation. And if they carry Armalites or Black and Deckers about in their handbags, they're known as Republicans. OK?'

Charlotte nodded and kept scribbling.

'The Protestants don't want a united Ireland because they don't want to be ruled by the Church of Rome via the Government in Dublin. They think they're British anyway, not Irish. So they're loyal to the Royal Family, God love 'em, and they call themselves Unionists. A few of them carry sophisticated weaponry too, and they've killed more people than the IRA during the Nineties. They're called Unionists because they want to retain the Union with Great Britain, not because they want a united Ireland. When they're really wound up they call themselves Loyalists. Confusing, eh?'

Charlotte rolled her eyes heavenward in response. Then she glanced down at her notes. 'Remind me why six counties of Ulster were separated from the rest of Ireland in the first place.'

'OK. In 1920 the British Government finally bowed to the inevitable and decided to let the Irish run their own country. Remember we'd occupied the place for several hundred years, and taken their land, and kept them in poverty: all the usual run-of-the-mill imperialist stuff. But the Protestant population of Scottish descent who were concentrated in the north-east of the island made such a fuss about it that London had to give them their own province, which was supposed to remain British.'

'Why didn't London tell them "tough luck"?'

'Well, World War I had just finished, and thousands of Ulster Protestants died fighting for King and Country. There was a feeling that their loyalty to the Crown should be rewarded. At the time, everyone conveniently forgot that thousands of Roman Catholics from the north of Ireland also fought and died for Britain.' Charlotte tried not to notice the sneer which accompanied that last remark.

Power got to his feet and paced the room, hands in pockets, like a lecturer. 'Anyway, since the current Troubles began in sixty-nine, a bucketful of Government investment has improved the living conditions of the poor Catholic communities. They were pissed off because the Protestants hogged the best jobs and houses and fixed the elections. But that's changed, and oddly enough these days it's the working-class Protestants who feel they're slipping behind in housing and education and community facilities. Unemployment is *the* big problem that affects both sides. In some parts of Belfast, eight out of ten men are on the dole. So now you've got angry people sitting around feeling bored, and feeling betrayed.'

'And have they been betrayed?'

'Oh yes. And to make matters worse, their middle-class brethren have done very nicely working for the Government directly or indirectly on building contracts or whatever. Now the lumpen, downtrodden Protestants see London asking Dublin to help the British sort out this mess for good, and not surprisingly, they reckon they're being well and truly shafted.'

'Are they?'

'Yes, and they always will be, because they're working class, and too stupid to realise that they have more in common with the unemployed Catholics in the next street than with the middle-class Protestants in their ponderosas in pleasant parts of Antrim and Down. Which are very pleasant, by the way.'

'Spoken like a true socialist,' the reporter observed with a wry smile.

'These Protestants are like the Habsburgs – or was it the Bourbons?' His performance faltered for a moment. 'You know, they remember everything, but they learn nothing. They can't admit that the old Protestant regime was foul to the Catholics. They're in denial, and not surprisingly the Catholics reckon that given half a chance the Protestants would behave just as badly all over again. They're primitive, these Unionists.'

Eddie shook his head in dismay, and continued to pace around his cell. 'Of course, both the Catholic and Protestant communities have been let down by their politicians. None of these old gits have ever actually run anything, or taken responsibility for so much as a municipal cemetery.'

He laughed mirthlessly and glared down at Charlotte's conscientious note-taking. 'And that's why so many of the Northern Ireland politicians are unhappy about this new Assembly at Stormont. They have to start managing the affairs of the Province themselves,' he added with a puff of annoyance.

'So presumably they'd prefer to let London run everything, and write them a big cheque every year.' Charlotte consulted her notes. 'Four point four billion pounds a year, to be exact.'

Eddie nodded and sat down again, satisfied that his pupil had grasped the point. 'So, what d'you reckon Michael can do in his new job?' she asked.

The Labour spokesman picked up a biro and doodled in the margins of a letter on the desk. As he did so he pursed his lips thoughtfully. 'Well, he rang me this morning, just after you did, and we've having dinner tonight, so I'll be sharing this same cynical analysis with him.' He put down the pen and studied the reporter's face, as if he was searching for a reaction. She desisted from telling him that she was first in line for nosebag with the new Minister of State.

'So what's your advice to him?'

'Off the record, right?'

'Absolutely.'

'Nothing.'

'Nothing?'

'Yeah. The Unionists are half-hearted about this Assembly because they think it's allowing the Catholics a share in the power, and they're dead against that. And the Sinn Fein people don't really want the Assembly to work because that would give a certain legitimacy to this entity called Northern Ireland that they don't even recognise. They want a united Ireland, and that's it. And they'll get it eventually, so we should just leave them to

64

it, and get out as quietly and quickly as possible.'

'But the Protestants won't accept that, will they, even when the Catholics outbreed them?'

Power shrugged and looked genuinely mystified as Charlotte made her point.

'I mean, you can't just force nine hundred thousand very suspicious people to surrender everything they have to Dublin.'

He snorted in annoyance and sat back with his arms folded across his chest. Then the frown was replaced with the television sneer-smile, as if a buzzer had gone off in his head, and reminded him that he was being a persuasive politician talking to a journalist. 'Listen, Charlotte, London doesn't care about them any more. And what's more, Reverend Scott and his henchmen are ridiculous remnants from our imperial past.'

'But not all Protestants in Northern Ireland are like God Bob, are they?' Charlotte persisted. Eddie was unmoved by her analysis. 'Tell me, Mr Northern Ireland spokesman, why don't you ever express these opinions on the record?' the reporter asked when she realised that her lecturer was not interested in any alternative point of view.

'Because I want to be a front-bench politician, not a back-bench eccentric who is regarded as a national security risk,' Power said simply. 'There are lots of MPs in both parties who share my views about the inevitability of a united Ireland, but we all understand that it's unacceptable to the status quo to voice our opinions.'

'Well, you've given me a lot to ponder. Thanks very much. Can I come back to you with more dumb questions?'

'My pleasure. We should keep in touch.' He seemed to be chewing over his next words. 'Maybe we should have dinner soon? I mean, we could escape from this place to somewhere less oppressively political and public. Would you like to go out some time?'

Charlotte fixed a polite smile on her face, and thought of the *Who's Who* entry for Edward Power: married with three young children. She stood up and backed her way towards the door, the smile now causing her physical pain. 'Perhaps lunch would be a better idea,' she responded firmly and opened the door. 'Thanks for the help.'

As she walked along the narrow corridor past the offices of perhaps twenty other MPs, she wondered how many of them handed out such invitations on a daily basis. Did their wives realise, or care about their behaviour? Or had these MPs deliberately married silly cheerleader/doormat-types who provided their famous husbands with continuous, uncritical adoration?

Charlotte descended the spiral staircase, thinking dark thoughts about the male ego. How could so many plainly unattractive MPs believe they were worthy of sexual favour? Perhaps many tried, but few succeeded. If Charlotte conducted an anonymous poll of women who worked in the Palace of Westminster, it might reveal some interesting tales of arrogant offers and horrified rebuffs. There was great potential in this for blackmailing MPs for Government secrets in return for destroying the evidence of their pathetic scoring records.

She emerged from the staircase into the Members' Lobby which was deserted at this time of the morning. 'Hi, Charlotte!' She spun around on her heel and waved at Paddy Ashdown who was striding out of the Liberal Democrat Whip's office. He disappeared down a corridor at full speed, as usual. Now *there* was one of the few MPs who would never have to chase a woman . . . Her chum Paula from IRN had bumped into Ashdown once as he left the Commons' gym after a workout. 'Beautiful. Utterly beautiful,' was all she could mumble afterwards.

Charlotte descended to the lower corridor of the Commons. Here the dining rooms overlooked the Thames, and there were function rooms that were hired by MPs for receptions in aid of the Third World dictators and arms' manufacturers who paid them 'consultancy' fees. Of more interest to Charlotte right now were the women's loos, which were a special rarity in the Palace of Westminster.

She retreated to the privacy of a cubicle and contemplated Edward Power once again, or more accurately, his poor wife. She had three young children to take care of, all the rubbish and boredom that living in 'the constituency' entailed, and she probably hardly ever saw her husband who was in London from Monday to Thursday, then touring the country to speak to assorted cretins every weekend. Perhaps the wretched woman was so tired from changing nappies, and nights interrupted by screaming babies, that she was beyond caring what her husband did.

As Charlotte washed her hands she recalled the marital bliss of two of her friends who had packed up journalism to have babies. One of them recently confessed that she simply had no love left over for her husband, such was her emotional and physical commitment to her small daughter. The other ex-colleague admitted that she would be positively relieved if her husband were having an affair because it would get him out of her way. Both women were miserable by anyone's standards, yet the yearning for brats had been overwhelming.

Charlotte scrutinised her face in the mirror, and in particular the zit that was threatening to erupt on her chin: too many chocolate bars, as per usual. So what about this biological clock?

she demanded of herself, and not for the first time either. When would it start ticking, and knock out Charlotte's normal rational system of logic?

She resisted the temptation to squeeze the zit, and instead turned her attention to her chestnut locks. As she brushed her hair she slipped further towards gloom: biological clocks, and babies and David, the man she had left because he wanted to breed and she simply wasn't ready. That had been not much more than a year ago. And she had been so certain that he was The Right One. Perhaps he was, but evidently wasn't part of a matching pair: she had been twenty-eight, and on the verge of a major career take-off. But he was ten years older, divorced, and the father of a beloved child who had died. His needs became apparent all too quickly, and Charlotte still had so many things to do before she immersed herself in baby shit and talcum powder.

Anyway, if she was totally honest (and she never was in this case because people didn't understand), she wasn't keen on babies. Ugly, noisy things. The idea of breast-feeding one made her feel sick to her stomach. She could never think of anything to say to people's children, so she ignored them. This proved a wonderful way of infuriating the little sods, especially when they were used to being constantly applauded.

Charlotte had only to stand in a supermarket check-out queue to be reminded why she had left David. There always seemed to be dozens of stupefied young mothers, staring blankly into space while their little monsters screamed and performed dances of rage until they were given 'sweeties'. Invariably their tantrums were successful, and their mothers gratefully rammed junk food and sugar into their children's gaping mouths as fast as they could. The prospect of being reduced to that myopic state made Charlotte tremble with fear.

Predictably, her chums had assured her that she would feel different about her own sprog. Indeed. And if she didn't warm to it, she had eighteen years of desperately trying to make sure it didn't turn out as dreadful as its schoolfriends. No thanks. She would wait for the biological clock to toll.

She put away her brush and attempted to expunge David from her mind. After all, here was Charlotte Carter in the middle of the exciting career that she had wanted so much. All alone. 'Alone again, naturally': the words of some depressing song from when she had been little during the much-despised Seventies. She had a foggy childhood memory of Gilbert O'Sullivan wearing a terrible hat and sitting awkwardly at a piano on *Top of the Pops*. He played the instrument as if it was a drum-kit. Whatever had happened to the poor fellow? Yet another great Irish contribution to popular culture, along with a batch of glib, irritating, cheeky game-show hosts and DJs who were omnipresent on TV and radio. What would James Joyce make of it? she wondered. Then she admitted to herself that such a rhetorical question was pretentious, especially as she hadn't yet managed to finish a James Joyce book. She gripped her handbag under her arm, and headed out to do battle in the BBC reporters' office upstairs.

Another relic of the Seventies' pop scene was being discussed that morning, at the Northern Ireland Assembly at Stormont. A Sinn Fein Assemblywoman was taking particular delight in reminding the Loyal Unionist Party members present that they had just lost a council by-election in rural County Down because their councillors, who controlled the local town administration, had banned Gary Glitter from performing at the Civic Centre. Being devout, God-fearing members of the True Presbyterian Church of Christ the Protester to a man (and they were all men), the LUP councillors took the view that sex, drugs and rock and roll were evil. So were dancing, betting, drinking, the cinema, television, and virtually anything except reading The Good Book. The voters evidently preferred to go and see Gary Glitter, and the LUP had lost the by-election to the Official Unionists.

When the Sinn Fein Assemblywoman had finished crowing over the LUP's misery, she turned her attention to the more serious events of the previous night, the ethnic cleansing attacks in south Belfast. 'It's back to the days when the Catholic community in the North of Ireland has to keep the bath filled with water, and blankets standing by in case the Loyalist terror gangs rampage down their street hurling petrol bombs at the houses of innocent people.' She spoke with an angry shake of her over-moussed head. 'And it has not gone unnoticed that the leader of the LUP is more passionate in his denunciation of the IRA than he is in his condemnation of the activities of the Loyalist terror gangs who provoked the attack last night.'

At this, the diminutive Reverend Scott sprang to his feet and intervened with a fist already raised in fury. 'I condemn the use of all violence, unlike the party the Assemblywoman represents.'

'Then why do you persist in using the language of violence?' the Sinn Fein woman countered as she bobbed up from her seat.

'Your church is founded on blood and sacrilege!' God Bob shot back, and this time he stayed standing. 'We have heard enough from the representative of the IRA, and we have also seen enough of her hypocritical handwringing for one morning, thank you.'

Suddenly his tone changed, and he launched into his set-piece speech. 'For on this day I bring to this Assembly proof that the double-dealers in London and Dublin are conspiring to undermine the very security of this Province.'

Having got everyone's attention, God Bob produced a piece of paper from his jacket pocket with a flourish and scanned the Chamber dramatically. 'Every day, the tentacles of Dublin close in on us, while London meekly turns the other cheek. As we sit here, both Governments are plotting to allow the United States Air Force to build a military base on the outskirts of London-derry. We are told that the United States of America can no longer afford to keep its forces in Germany, and that it will consequently be moving thousands of men and airplanes and helicopters and missiles to this Province. And we are supposed to be grateful to the United States of America for bringing us employment opportunities and building contracts. This, appar-ently, is the help we were promised when the so-called peace process got under way in 1994.'

Both sides of the Assembly Chamber were listening to the Reverend Scott in intrigued silence now, for this revelation was news to every member there. 'So we will have thousands of military personnel from a foreign power on our soil; an alien power that makes no bones of the fact that it supports the Republic of Ireland and wants what it calls "the will of the Irish people". This is the same alien power that has supplied the IRA with arms and money for decades. Now they will be right here on the soil of Ulster with their arms and money. How convenient it will be for them to further "the will of the Irish people",' he concluded, his falsetto voice squeaking with anger.

When he sat down, the Assembly session disintegrated into mayhem. Every journalist in the place headed for telephones and laptops, preparing TV cues and first paragraphs of scoop stories in their heads. A civil servant from the Northern Ireland Office who had been observing the debate from the public gallery, rushed for the exit. He was rather less thrilled by God Bob's dramatic announcement because it would involve him in considerable work for the rest of the day. Finding the source of these leaks was never easy.

On the other side of the Irish Sea, at the Palace of Westminster, Dave Bower was encountering a similar problem that morning. What had happened to the source of his leak? Yesterday the pharmacist from the London Hospital had been prepared to stand in front of a BBC camera and tell the word that Nigel Swinton MP was being treated for AIDS when he died. Today the pharmacist refused to even take Dave's phone calls. The super scoop was turning into ratshit, as the young reporter admitted to his boss, Rodney.

But Dave was not easily deterred. He badgered away at the pharmacist's equally reluctant colleague until finally the truth emerged: 'Look, it's been decreed from on high, OK?' the junior technician explained in a conspiratorial whisper. 'The consultant in charge of Swinton's case got the tip-off from someone at the BBC. A woman rang here yesterday, and said my mate was going to give an interview or whatever. And of course the consultant went wild and came down here and tore him apart. So just don't call back, OK?'

Dave put down the phone, and doodled thoughtfully on the notepad in front of him. Then he swivelled around and reached out a hand to tap Rodney on the shoulder. His boss was hunched over his receiver, and engaged in management-speak with someone god-like in the newsroom in Shepherds Bush, so Dave turned back to his notepad. On second thoughts maybe it would be better to keep his latest discovery to himself, until it came in handy.

Chapter Six

Michael's new office at Admiralty House was an improvement on his claustrophobic shoe box at the Commons: it had high ceilings and fine plaster cornicework. There was also a big window, but the view was of no interest unless you cared about ministerial cars. Nevertheless it let in what light there was on such a drizzly March morning.

He started the day by meeting his new staff and touring the building. It was very much the 'first day at a strange school' experience that he recalled from childhood, but sadly his mother would not have a special tea with all his favourite cakes ready this afternoon.

His secretary, Esther, who was a young version of Barbara Cartland, had hair like pink cottonwool, and pearls roped around her neck. She was distinctly cool towards Michael at first which disturbed him because he knew how much he would have to depend on her to protect him from tedious, time-wasting people like other Tory MPs.

Esther explained quite sternly that he should put a lock on his computer files immediately, since everything he was likely to look at from now on would be highly classified. The new Minister of State wondered if he should use *Laura* for his identity code, as he had at MOD. But as he sat at his enormous and unfamiliar mahogany desk his daughter's name seemed far too obvious. The Northern Ireland Office had really serious information in its files, unlike the MOD, where Michael had floppy disks full of statistics on how many sugar cubes the British Army of the Rhine used.

Inspiration came to the new Minister in the form of the mail delivery. A shambling, bleary-eyed man who looked nearer eighty years old than seventy, appeared in the secretary's office next door and launched into what was obviously a daily performance. He warbled, 'If you can't find a partner use a wooden chair,' then broke off to cough up a lump of lung (or so it sounded to Michael who was eavesdropping through the open door). When the bronchial rattling subsided, he did a further verse of *Jailhouse Rock*.

'That's one of your best, Bert,' Esther remarked. 'Mind you, it's a wonder you can even hum with all that post you're lugging about today.'

'Yeah, Elvis's got tons of letters this morning. Stupid ponce.'

'Shush!' Esther hissed. When Bert the mail 'boy' had shuffled off, Michael wandered next door and spent the next two minutes bullying the woman until she revealed who 'Elvis' was. At length a blushing Esther explained that Sir Trevor Grace was known throughout the Ministry as Elvis because of the amount of grease he used on his hair.

'Marvellous,' Michael laughed, weak-kneed and watery-eyed. Esther obviously approved of his reaction, because she became far more helpful and friendly. And he had a code-name for his system.

Once Michael had set up mission control on his desk (the photo of Laura and Caroline, some highlighting pens for picking out relevant passages in documents, post-it notes, and the phone and PC positioned where he liked them), he emptied his ministerial boxes and quickly re-read a report that had been of particular interest to him.

Brigadier George Rowbottham was Director of Army Intelligence in Northern Ireland. He had flown over to London this morning especially for his eleven o'clock meeting with the new Minister of State. They knew each other already, albeit superficially, from Michael's tour of duty at MOD.

When the Brigadier entered Michael's office he appeared to be all chest and torso, like a perfect square under the uniform and gold braid. His legs were an afterthought, and there wasn't much of them since he only came up to Michael's shoulders. His head had a mere scraping of grey hair around the edges, and his features seemed to have been stuffed and overcooked.

They sat down at Michael's conference table and helped themselves to coffee.

'So, welcome to the Northern Ireland Office. I was delighted to hear of your appointment.' Michael's smile was professionally non-committal. 'No, I really mean it,' the Brigadier said firmly. 'You made a good impression at MOD.'

'You're very kind. I've still got a lot of background reading to do before I can be of any use, I'm afraid.'

'Well, you let me know whatever you want, and I'll do my best to help. Shall I run through—'

'Yes, please.'

'Our feeling is that this is easily the most exciting and hopeful period in the last three decades in Northern Ireland. Granted, the sectarian killing continues, which is bloody awful; and of course there are too many hard men out there who bear a grudge. We don't kid ourselves that they'll go home and watch Noel

Edmonds just because Gerry Adams says so.'

'Especially after last night's ethnic cleansing . . .'

'Yes, but what matters is that most terrorists on both sides have hung up their balaclavas, and are biding their time, withholding judgement on the constitutional settlement for the moment. That means the onus is still on the British Government to make this peace work. And we can start by ensuring that the new Assembly and Executive and Committees are all given a fair chance to succeed.'

Michael tried not to let his surprise show, but he sat up a bit straighter. He had expected to hear the same story from Rowbottham as Grace had spouted yesterday; keep your head down and sign the cheques. But the good Brigadier was enthusiastic by contrast: he was leaning forward again, punching the air with his hammy fist, and his weathered face was animated.

'It's ironic, really. The IRA strategy in the Seventies was to sustain a Long War, the idea being that they'd sicken the British into giving up. But the truth is they've sickened themselves instead. The British shrugged off the bombs and violence, because most of it was happening on another island, and that's the way we are anyway. That's where the IRA miscalculated. In the past three decades the Republicans did their best to drive business and jobs away from Ulster, and they were left with a garrisoned city. If you'll forgive the vulgarity, Michael, the IRA crapped in their own nest to make a political point and to get the world's attention. Then they found they had to live with the stink.'

'So you reckon the grassroots were fed up and couldn't face another twenty-five years of discomfort and inconvenience?'

'And the hum of the ministerial car beckons them: they want to stop being rebels and start being respectable politicians. It turns out they rather like chairing committees and meeting world leaders. Upwardly Mobile Provo, I call it.'

'What about the forthcoming IRA bombing campaign on the British mainland?' the Minister asked through narrowed eyes. Earlier on that morning he had been briefed by the same Detective Chief Inspector from the Special Branch of the Northern Ireland Police Department whom Grace had met the day before.

Rowbottham nodded impatiently, as if he were bored with the story. 'The 14th Intelligence Corps, based at Lisburn with the rest of Army Intelligence, has been tracking Republican thinking throughout the peace process. Even before the ceasefire in the summer of '94 we were trying to gauge their reactions to the changing political mood, and we've continued monitoring them through the recent referendum on the negotiated settlement, and then the election of the Assembly.'

'It sounds like the opinion polling done by Tory Central Office,' Michael mused.

'No, it's more accurate because we'd never come up with an idea like the poll tax,' Rowbottham retorted with a good-natured wink. 'Anyway, we believe the masked men are still giving the constitutional settlement a go. And remember, the American and Irish Administrations won't allow the IRA another chance if they screw this up.' The Brigadier paused to draw breath. 'Certainly they'll retaliate when Loyalists petrol bomb Catholic homes, but we're unlikely to see a return to a failed IRA strategy.'

Michael tried to choose his words carefully. 'You see, I had received a . . . different impression.'

Rowbottham sat quietly for a moment. 'I'm not surprised. As you'll soon learn, not everyone around here wants this to succeed.'

'But what you've said is most encouraging.' Michael was as cautious as an elephant tip-toeing across a skating rink. It helped that Rowbottham was an expert at decoding carefully-phrased sentences, and pursuing the real meaning through this elaborate charade of not mentioning Grace by name. 'I do have one question.' Michael waved the report he had recently re-read. 'The so-called ethnic cleansing—' he began, but Rowbottham cut him off.

'No. It isn't so-called, Minister. It *is* ethnic cleansing.' The Brigadier pushed a blank piece of paper between them and drew a rough map of Northern Ireland. 'Here, here and here are the sites of recent attacks. And here and here are where most of the other Loyalist atrocities have been. Notice anything?'

'They're all in the eastern side of the Province.'

'Within four counties, to be precise. Our intelligence reports lead us to believe that the Loyalist paramilitaries – and by that I mean the small minority who are still active terrorists – are trying to purge these four counties of Catholics. It's as simple as that. They're preparing for a Doomsday scenario when the British give up and hand over to Dublin. Then the Loyalists will demand that the country is repartitioned, giving Eire the two Ulster counties with the higher Catholic population, and leaving a smaller, purer Northern Ireland that's fit for the Protestants.'

Michael studied the map and groaned. 'This is just what we need. So, what can the Government do?'

'Both communities in Northern Ireland, the Protestants and the Catholics, must be reassured that they aren't losing out to the other side in the peace process. So it's up to us to ensure that some symbolic changes are made, so the masked men on both sides can go back to their people with results that prove there are dividends to be had for laying down their guns.'

'Like renaming the Royal Ulster Constabulary the Northern Ireland Police Department?'

'That pleases the Catholics. The Loyalists also need their symbolic victories, and these are harder to deliver because the Unionists tend to think that every time a Catholic street gets its paving stones repaired then a Loyalist district is losing out. Personally, I reckon bringing employment to the Protestant areas of the Province would be a good move. How about relocating a Government Department from London to Belfast, for instance?'

'That's quite a symbol,' the Minister remarked with a crooked smile.

'But Michael, the sooner one realises and appreciates the importance of symbols to both sides of the community, the nearer one is to understanding them. For years the British Government said, "Well, only thirteen people died on that Sunday they melodramatically call Bloody Sunday. What's all the fuss about?" You see, we failed to appreciate that these points in time are terribly significant. The individual incidents stick in the imagination, as opposed to the unrelieved vale of tears and the thousands of deaths.'

Michael sat back under this barrage of psychology, and felt duly chastised. 'Point taken.'

'Anyway, since we're talking about sensitive areas, there's something you should know.' Rowbottham grimaced as if he was in physical pain. 'Top-secret security information is being passed to terrorist organisations. God knows how, but we're certain there's an established route. Part of the problem is the way we store intelligence: terrible mistakes are made in putting too much guesswork on paper. That's why we're using a new codified system, with different categories of intelligence, so the men who are ninety per cent likely IRA cell members aren't on the same lists as old women who once gave Gerry Adams a cup of tea.'

Rowbottham cleared his throat loudly. 'Our Military Reconnaissance Force are on to it as we speak, but pinpointing the pond-life responsible for the leaks isn't particularly easy. We're also creating a special category of terrorists and former terrorists who are calming their more restless brothers – you know, urging them to give the peace process a chance. We call this the "Judas File", for obvious reasons. Frankly, these are the people we should be protecting, and we need more resources to do it.'

So that was the punch line. Michael nodded thoughtfully. 'Presumably this new "Judas" codification is utterly secure.'

'As secure as anything can be in a country where half the locals are mad or brilliant or psychopathic. I'm sorry,' Rowbottham said, flushing. 'I'd forgotten you have Irish antecedents and—'

'No, don't worry,' Michael reassured the older man. 'My grandmother once told me that most of Ireland checked into the insane asylum every winter, and the rest were drunk. And no, I'm not being sarcastic. Because it's an Irish revolution it has to include drink, poetry and humour.'

Rowbottham shook with laughter and slapped his paw on the table. 'I'm looking forward to working with you, Minister.'

When Rowbottham had gone, Michael found himself humming *Jailhouse Rock*; it had been going through his mind all morning. The meeting with the Brigadier had stuck a bit of adrenalin in his system, and he was determined not to lose sight of the fact that he might be able to do something useful and creative with this job. When he turned into Esther's office she looked up and smiled at him.

Things were getting better already.

Chapter Seven

At eleven-thirty that morning, Classic FM was broadcasting one of Neil's favourite pieces of Mahler, the slow *Death in Venice* movement of the Fifth Symphony. He sat at a modern pine table in his kitchen with a map of Belfast spread out before him. He had lived in the city all his life, so it wasn't that he needed to orientate himself: he was searching for unemployment benefit and social security offices in Roman Catholic neighbourhoods. Somewhere like Ardoyne was as alien to him as downtown Casablanca.

Neil had a modest three-bedroom, semi-detached 1930s house in Ravenhill Parade in Ormeau, south-east of Belfast city centre. It was a quiet area, populated by respectable Protestant families, and he had lived here with his wife Jane and their two sons for the past twelve years.

His origins, however, were in working-class East Belfast. From the bottom of the street where he grew up, the schoolboy Neil could see Samson and Goliath, the huge yellow cranes looming over the Harland & Wolff shipyard, where his father had been convener of the engineering shop stewards.

When the Troubles began in 1969, the able-bodied men in Neil's street formed a defence association to protect themselves from IRA attacks. They met regularly at the local Orange Lodge to drill and prepare for the fight. Neil's father had joined them, not to take the law into his own hands, but because he shared his neighbours' concern that the police and Army were doing nothing to safeguard 'their' people against the rebels. The Government at Stormont had 'gone soft' on the mutinous, disloyal Roman Catholics or 'Taigs', and were giving in to every Provo demand. East Belfast men like Neil's dad didn't for a minute believe the Catholic campaign for civil rights was sincere. Their demonstrations were the beginning of the end of Ulster, and the Papists wouldn't stop until they had a united Ireland. Even if their Protestant Government at Stormont was going to stand idly by, the Loyalists of East Belfast were not about to surrender. They armed themselves, and they taught the Taigs a few lessons too, on occasion.

By the time Neil was seventeen he was in the Ulster Volunteer Force, although even at that tender age he wasn't too impressed by their sloppy set-up. Too many members were ill-disciplined and wasted their lives in pubs. Neil was a plump, short boy – never strong or macho – and he wasn't interested in Western-style bar fights with yobs, when there was serious work to be done in defeating the Catholics. Despite his physical disadvantages he was soon ordering his dim-witted comrades about.

The turning point in Neil's career as a terrorist came in 1974 when the Protestant people of Ulster decided to demonstrate to London just how unimpressed they were by the Government's plans to hand power to the Catholics. The trade unions and Loyalist paramilitaries came together to organise a strike that brought the Province to its knees. The people who made the Ulster Workers' Strike a success were condemned as scroungers by the British Prime Minister at the time, Harold Wilson.

The very same word, 'scrounger', was uppermost in Neil's mind that morning as he studied the map of Belfast. He was planning a little exercise to punish unemployed Taig scroungers and welfare mothers. It had long been an IRA tactic to bleed the British Exchequer by getting its feckless, lazy supporters to sign on for every benefit they could. The priests aided the Republican cause by making sure the scroungers produced dozens of children who would also become leeches. Then the honest, hardworking, tax-paying Protestants had to support them.

Not that Neil had much personal experience of honest hard work or tax-paying. Soon after the Ulster Workers' Strike in 1974 he was arrested, interrogated at the RUC Castlereagh Station (where, to his own amazement, he was brave enough to keep his silence), and done for illegal possession of firearms. He spent the next two years in prison, reflecting on what was happening to Ulster, and wondering what to do with the rest of his life. He had left school at seventeen expecting to go into the shipyard, just as his father had, just as every man in his street had. But the decline in shipbuilding cancelled that option. More important to Neil, he had realised he was much smarter than the other men in his neighbourhood, or in prison.

He started studying accountancy, stuck with it when he came out of jail, and qualified. Now he was a 'freelance accountant', which meant that he took care of the books of drinking clubs, building companies, taxi firms and other legitimate-sounding businesses, all of which kept the UVF in guns and butter. He was, in effect, the Managing Director and Chief Financial Officer of a large protection racket in East Belfast. Which was why he and his family could afford to live in a pleasant house in another part of the city.

Neil was also the UVF's top Brigadier, the unchallenged

leader of those Loyalist terrorists who were still engaged in a death-or-glory struggle for Ulster. The days when he personally clubbed people to death were long behind him, but he had passed the traditional murderous initiation and proved himself in the accepted fashion when it mattered, in the Seventies. Now nobody expected this unlikely figure to get his hands dirty when his brain was so much more useful to the struggle.

He pushed the huge spectacles that looked like television screens up his neat, owlish nose and peered at the map. His face was still chubby and moonshaped, and at forty-two his short, curling hair had already turned salt and pepper. When he was working from home he usually wore a baggy grey tracksuit that coordinated with his hair colour. It also covered his middle-aged spread.

'Here we are, King Billy.' The prize-winning terrier at his feet looked up as his name was mentioned. 'It's party-time,' Neil told the dog gleefully. He had located an ideal dole office in Ardoyne . . .

Charlotte's working life was divided between the BBC's cubby-hole off the Press Gallery in the Commons, and the Corporation's more elaborate Parliamentary Unit headquarters in a grand Edwardian pile on Millbank, just five minutes' walk from St Stephen's entrance to the Commons.

Legend had it that during the 1980s, a BBC lackey in charge of planning the Queen Mother's funeral had found the place while looking for good camera locations to shoot the procession. The BBC immediately leased as much of the pompous grey stone building as they could, and promptly spent thousands of pounds of the licence-fee payers' money making it as splendid as possible. The cream-coloured corridors looked down on an elegant atrium, and the entrance hall was dominated by a Busby Berkeley staircase. BBC apologists justified the cost because MPs and other VIPs needed to give their interviews in pleasant surroundings. (Apparently no one recalled that Boris Yeltsin's greatest television moment had been on top of a tank.)

It was to this newsroom and studio complex that Charlotte and her colleagues repaired to edit video tape, write scripts for their reports, do radio interviews, and listen to proceedings in the House on TV monitors. Only print journalists, who had all the time in the world to put together their reports, could afford the luxury of sauntering over to the Press Gallery to watch debates on a regular basis. If you were a TV or radio hack you worked to rather more demanding constraints: if a minister resigned at a quarter to five, you were expected to have something ready for the hourly bulletin at five.

On the BBC reporters' desks, which were formed into long rows across the office, there were TV monitors and the Corporation's in-house News and Current Affairs information system that provided wires service reports from around the world. At dull moments, when MPs were debating Sunday trading or fisheries policy, Charlotte could check out the weather in Laos, or the price of pork bellies in Chicago, or follow court cases in Chile; all the time looking as if she was hard at work.

Apart from the TV studios which lured MPs into the building on Millbank, there was also a restaurant in the basement. Its tables spilled out into the leafy atrium, giving the impression of *al fresco* dining beneath the attractive fan-shaped glass roof. The restaurant had become a scene of frenzied daily power lunches, and it was there that Charlotte was meeting the new Northern Ireland Minister today.

It took Michael a couple of minutes to make his way across

the restaurant to where Charlotte was sitting because he had to pass several tables of politicians and journalists who yelled friendly abuse at him about his promotion. The more dangerous characters congratulated him with approving nods of the head.

'How many knives have I got sticking out of my back?' he asked Charlotte. 'Reshuffles really do bring out the worst in people, don't they?'

His hostess raised her glass of mineral water and gave him a knowing wink. 'What a clever fellow you are. But for God's sake don't look down, or you'll lose your balance and fall off the ladder. Just keep your eyes on the stars,' she advised, but he shook his head as if dismissing the flattery, and picked up the menu.

'My feet are firmly rooted on the ground. God, I'm starving. What do you recommend?'

Charlotte was studying his hair, and the way it swept off his forehead and lay in perfect layers. Even when it flopped towards his eyes it looked fetching. 'Well, the black noodles with three types of mushroom are fairly irresistible, and so is the Japanese vegetable tempura. You still vegetarian?'

Michael nodded without his eyes leaving the menu. 'Mmm. Laura claims she can smell meat on me, and she makes such a fuss about it that it's easier to abstain. The little harpie gives me unspeakable descriptions of abattoirs.'

'By the way,' Charlotte frowned, 'why do people come to decent restaurants and pay lots of money to eat pigeons and rabbits? I mean, if they eat vermin like pigeons then why don't they eat rats?'

'Or squirrels? I don't know. These are important considerations, but first we should order, because I'm fading fast.' He put the menu to one side and craned his neck to find a waiter. Then he noticed that Charlotte was studying his tie.

'Very nice,' she smiled, and watched him blink with embarrassment.

'Jerry Garcia. You know, the Grateful Dead? He used to design limited edition ties. Al Gore has one,' he grinned proudly. 'And the only other person I've seen wearing one here is the Lord Holme of Cheltenham. We try not to clash,' he added.

When the food was safely on its way Charlotte got straight to the point and asked Michael if she could follow him around Belfast, doing a profile of him and the politics of the Assembly.

'I'm grateful for the free publicity, but I have to ask Grace's permission.' He took a swig of water as if he was washing a bitter taste out of his mouth. For a moment he seemed preoccupied; then he leaned forward and started to laugh.

'Oh, I must tell you about Trevor Grace, but first you have to promise that everything is off the record.' He rolled his eyes because he knew it sounded pedantic, and their lunches were always off the record, but the ritual must be respected. Charlotte gave a perfunctory nod.

'Everyone at the Northern Ireland Office calls him Elvis, because of the gunge Grace rubs into his hair. Think about it, it's perfect – the Las Vegas swagger when he's doing his cabaret act at the Dispatch Box, the "Great I Am" routine—'

'—and the blubber,' Charlotte added.

'Precisely. The whole place is known as Graceland, and Belfast is Memphis, and everyone's in on it except the man himself, and his equally oily cronies.'

Charlotte grinned as Michael rattled on, becoming more and more acid about his new boss, and their first meeting. 'I can see that if I want to learn anything I'll have to dig it out myself.' He hesitated and ran his fingers over the white linen of the tablecloth. 'And God, Charlotte, there's so *much* to learn. Could I borrow some old *Panoramas* and documentaries from the BBC tape library, do you think?'

'Leave it to me,' Charlotte beamed, and they both became rather animated because the food had arrived. Charlotte, who respected a man who liked his food, did not want to distract him, so she allowed him three mouthfuls before she asked him more about his new job. He told her about his encounter with Brigadier Rowbottham and offered her a mushroom.

'Mmm, that's good. Have some of this.' She passed him a slice of aubergine.

'Thanks. Now, Charlotte, the important news is that I had a look at the *Good Food Guide*, and the Ulster restaurant scene sounds promising.'

'Haven't you been there before?' Charlotte asked as she speared another of his mushrooms; she was not a woman to push food around her plate, let alone anyone else's.

'Certainly not. I had Irish grandparents, so I was brought up believing Ireland was a primeval swamp full of starving, miserable, downtrodden, simple folk – all except for Dublin. According to them, Belfast was the dullest, most dreary provincial town in the world.'

'Why'd they leave?'

'They wanted the chance to make it, and that meant leaving Ireland in those days.' Michael shrugged. 'To a lesser extent it still does now, I suppose. Anyway, even when my grandparents had made their modest pile, they never lost the chip on their shoulders about the poverty they'd grown up with. They wouldn't eat bread or potatoes, you know, because they said that was peasant food.'

'And they never went back?' the reporter asked.

'They wanted to forget all that, and so they set out to construct a lifestyle straight out of a Barbara Pym novel. Consequently they became so English it was almost comic – you know, vicarage tea parties and evenings at whist drives.' He glanced up from his plate and noticed that Charlotte was examining him carefully. For a moment he wondered if he'd slopped food on his chin, but it seemed that she was listening to him in her serious manner.

'How's the prep going?' she asked as she performed oral sex with a roasted pepper.

'Better than you'd think. I started reading about the IRA last night, and the next thing I knew it was two a.m. You know the Maze Prison – they used to call it Long Kesh, then they renamed it, like Windscale. The IRA boys referred to it as "Lazy K", and the prisoners had the most elaborate system for communicating with the IRA leadership outside on a daily basis. They printed their messages in miniature writing on cigarette papers and hid them in unmentionable places. During visits they'd slip them to their chums who'd come to see them. And at one point in the Seventies Republican prisoners had dug so many tunnels under the Maze, the Government seriously thought the buildings might collapse.'

Michael shook with laughter, hardly the appropriate reaction for a Tory minister. When he was at the Dispatch Box in the Commons, or being interviewed on television, Michael was the authentic article; grown-up, serious, and sharp as a razor. But away from the political stage he was refreshingly different from the other pompous, self-obsessed ministers that Charlotte had interviewed in her time. Michael was one of the few who occasionally had an original idea, yet he was clearly riddled with self-doubt. Charlotte warmed to that because she was afflicted with the same disease.

'And the prisoners organised "the Republican University", modelled on what happened during the Vietnam War. You recall how the Viet Cong used to teach themselves astrophysics and accountancy while they sheltered in those tunnels? That's when they weren't shooting down B52s, of course. Well, Gerry Adams made his chums read agit-prop books all day long in their cells, and if they hadn't absorbed the correct political lesson they were made to read them again.'

'Perhaps that's why the ordinary IRA footsoldiers have been so committed to their cause? They've had their history rammed down their throats.'

'Quite. But I tell you what's odd, Charlotte; the IRA leadership made a fatal assumption. They thought the British Army would be as feckless as the Americans were in Vietnam. Our boys have stuck it for three whole decades, whereas the US just didn't have the stomach for South East Asia.'

'No, well, I guess they preferred the peace and quiet of their homes in Harlem, or Washington, or Detroit.'

Michael studied her impish expression for a moment and considered telling her she reminded him of the young Audrey Hepburn. But it sounded like a corny pick-up line, so he kept the observation to himself, and asked her about her work. That was as personal as he dared to get.

Neil was at his habitual position at the kitchen table, mobile phone in hand, dictating instructions to his minions in less pleasant parts of Belfast.

'Just tell bloody Ken that I want the Sinn Fein councillor for the Falls, and that solicitor they use whenever they get caught sawing someone's knees off. You know the one – Lennon? McCartney? Tell Ken to find out.'

Neil wasn't too impressed by the non-committal reply he received from his caller. He sighed like a patient saint who was often tempted to stray from the straight and narrow path, and strangle the lesser mortals around him, but resisted with super-human resolve. 'I thought you told me this psycho Ken has a direct link right to the centre of things. Tell him to fucking well use his brain and get the damned files out! He's not going to get in trouble. We've still got the ear of the someone near the top. Understand? There won't be any inconvenient enquiries.'

Apparently his caller finally understood, and left the boss in peace. Neil switched the radio on once more, but *The Blue Danube* induced a swift negative reaction from the Loyalist Brigadier. He sat in thoughtful silence for a moment, then reached for the mobile phone. It was time to talk to someone influential.

The Press Gallery Bar in the House of Commons has all the charm of a 1960s British Rail cafeteria, but Dave Bower, the BBC's up-and-coming investigative reporter, had no aesthetic objections to the place. In fact, he graced its gloomy portals daily, most often in the company of his boss, Rodney, who preferred to spend his spare time there rather than at home with his wife and children.

That afternoon, Dave looked in for a swift half of alcohol-free lager after lunch, and joined a group of print journalists who were familiar to him. They stood in a swaggering clutch around the bar, beer mugs in one hand, while they jiggled the coins in their pockets with the other hand. As usual they exchanged wisecracks about the day's news topics, and gently abused each other for employing purple prose in their articles.

Today, they were collectively less interested in the political

implications of yesterday's Cabinet reshuffle than in Nigel
Swinton MP's demise. Dave Bower, who was still searching for
an original angle on the story, fixed an eager grin on his face,
ready to laugh at the wit of these more experienced hacks, and
pinned back his ears.

'It's only a matter of time till Tollmarch cracks, isn't it?' one
reporter quipped. 'He's got half Fleet Street parked on his
doorstep at Dolphin Square. And the *Sun* are going ahead with
those holiday snapshots of the two of them together on some
trade junket to Morocco.'

'You'd have thought they'd have been a bit more discreet,
wouldn't you?' another seasoned scribbler remarked.

'Yeah, but you know what Tollmarch's line'll be, don't you?
He'll say lots of MPs share flats in Dolphin Square, and the fact
that both he and Nigel Swinton were young and pretty is just
coincidence.'

'And he'll say he was a bit drunk on the Morocco trip, and it
was all good clean fun. And he'll get away with it—'

'—until those nasty little abrasions start ruining his complexion, eh?'

Dave Bower made a pretence of examining his watch and
gulped down the rest of his lager. Back in the BBC's Press
Gallery cubbyhole he grabbed the House of Commons guide
that profiled each MP, and looked up Tollmarch. Thirty-seven
years old, married, with a seat in Kent. It even gave his constituency address. Dave's nostrils flared and his eyes widened, as if
he had just caught the scent of his prey on the breeze. Then he
scuttled off in search of his boss, Rodney.

Chapter Eight

Nine hours after his lunch with Charlotte Carter, Michael Fitzgerald was having a much blunter conversation over a considerably less distinguished meal in the Strangers' Dining Room at the House of Commons. 'I suppose I'd better be going, Eddie. I've got this bloody NIO party.' Michael checked the bottle of Gevrey-Chambertin to make sure there was nothing left, then he waved at their waiter.

He and Edward Power had drunk their way through one and a half bottles of "Geoffrey" as they called it. They were confined to base tonight because of a three-line whip, but the ten o'clock vote had come and gone between their discussion of the current situation in Northern Ireland. Normally the old schoolfriends would have ventured beyond the Palace of Westminster to somewhere that served better food in a less club-like atmosphere. And where they weren't surrounded by fellow MPs.

'You're really planning to take Laura to Belfast for the summer holiday?'

'Why not?' Michael asked with outstretched hands. 'The security for ministers is probably much better there than it is in London. And you can get murdered walking around Banbury or

Harrogate after dark these days. Anyway, Grace never goes there, and that looks bad.'

Eddie nodded. 'Even the worst imperialists and colonialists used to be vaguely acquainted with their despotic kingdoms, but your Northern Ireland Secretary seems to think it's beneath him.'

'And, let's face it – getting first-hand experience of the Falls Road is something for Laura to bullshit her friends about.' Michael grinned and shook his head. 'Delva pointed out that the kind of people who look askance at living in Belfast are the ones who take their families to Florida for their holidays.'

'Get a nice big house so I can come and stay. Then we can have a Steely Dan weekend.' Power gave an enthusiastic clap of the hands. 'I s'pose you haven't had time to suss out the market for Thai-stick in Anderstown?'

'Let me get the bill,' Michael insisted when it arrived at their table. 'I asked you here tonight, and I've pumped your little brain all evening.'

'I gave Charlotte Carter a similar performance this morning. She's quite something, isn't she?' Power's otherwise red eyes sparkled.

'What d'you mean? She's smart, yes. And she's a good journalist,' Michael retorted, poker-faced and icy.

Power leaned back and hooked an arm over the back of his chair. 'Oh God, Michael. Loosen up,' he drawled, with a click of the tongue. 'I meant, she's attractive, is all.'

'That's rather obvious, I should have thought,' Michael sniffed. Then he noticed his friend's raised eyebrows. 'Oh no, you're not going to try it on with her, are you? You leave her alone. She's not like that, and she's certainly not your type.'

'What's that supposed to mean?' Eddie was enjoying every

second of Michael's discomfort.

'She's a nice young woman, and she'll tell you to go to hell.'

'She already has.' Power savoured the effect this had on his dinner companion.

'You imbecile. Have you no judgement whatsoever? It's so obvious she's not the kind to mess around with one-night stands or married men. You're just a staggering prick on legs, Eddie, and you leave a nasty, slimy trail behind you.'

'This is interesting. No, bear with me,' Power persisted as the Minister scrunched his napkin up on the table with finality. 'Why are you annoyed at me, Michael? Because you think I'll damage my political career by screwing people who'll blab about it if I ever get a decent spokesmanship? Or because you don't want me breathing all over your little friend?'

Michael looked disgusted and signed the bill. 'You're a moron.'

'Well, if you like her why don't you try her, and see what happens? Jesus, you've got to get out of this sanctimonious widower's exile.'

'I can't believe you made a pass at her. What did you do? Whip it out and plonk it on your Order Paper?'

'Lighten up, Michael. She isn't a nun, and she was pretty self-assured in the way she put me down.'

'What did she say? That she'd prefer to go out with a rabid three-legged dog, no doubt. Or she'd rather spend an evening in Sarajevo?'

'Why don't you ask her out? It'd do you good, and she's your type.'

But Michael shook his head. 'Why in God's name would she be interested in a widower with a thirteen-year-old daughter, and more work than he can handle? I'm hardly an appealing proposition.'

'I expect she's already got a man in her life. She gave me that impression.' Power watched Michael's reaction.

'Quite,' the Minister remarked, and turned his attention back to the bill as if he was indifferent to this news. 'And you made a bloody fool of yourself with someone who could be more than useful to your career. And you don't even feel ashamed of yourself, or dented by the refusal, I suppose.'

'I work on the principle that if I ask enough women to shag me the law of averages means a certain percentage will say yes, so the more I ask, the better I'll do. Anyway, back to your virginity complex. When are you going to emerge from purdah? You can't mourn for ever. I know loads of women who'd like to get their teeth into you.'

'I find you more and more crass and insensitive and primitive as time goes by. You were an animal at school, but I expect we all were.'

'Ah, but you were a gazelle while the rest of us were wart-hogs. Come on, Michael, seriously. Laura isn't going to fall apart if you start seeing a few women. And it'd do you good.'

'Eddie, I'm not interested in "seeing a few women". I was never a bed-hopper, if you recall.'

'How could I forget? You always got the most gorgeous girls and kept them for a long time.'

'You talk as much crap at the dinner-table as you do at the Dispatch Box, which is quite an achievement. Look, Eddie, I haven't got the time to get tangled up, not with this move to Northern Ireland. But I don't expect you to understand that because you'd happily fuck a plate of ravioli.'

'As long as it's shaved its armpits.'

'Speaking of armpits, I have to attend this shindig of Grace's.' Michael reluctantly got to his feet. 'Are you going to find a park bench, or can I give you a lift home?'

When Michael's ministerial driver had dropped Power at his flat in Dolphin Square, they doubled back to the Northern Ireland Office. Considering how much wine the Minister had consumed, he felt more tired than drunk. When he and the driver pushed open the doors to the conference room in the basement of Admiralty House they were hit by a wave of smoke and heat and the smell of spilt beer. Michael's headache took a turn for the worse.

'You come and get me when you're through, sir,' said the driver, who had spotted the fluffy Esther holding court in one corner, and was already edging her way. Michael watched him disappear into the crush of civil servants and MPs, a heaving mass of shirtsleeves, open collars and perspiring foreheads. The women's make-up had gone shiny and sticky, and the men were whiskery and crumpled. Michael wondered if he couldn't just slip upstairs and get a taxi back to Bayswater. Then he remembered that he'd promised Mandy he'd be here. He slipped off his suit jacket, draped it over his shoulder, and headed across the crowded room to look for her.

Perhaps his research assistant had decided to stay with her friends, rather than return to this steaming pit of aliens – and who could blame her? As Michael threaded his way between sharp elbows, he narrowly avoided having red wine spilt on him by an Under Secretary of State who was licking Bulgarian Cabernet Sauvignon off his secretary.

Mandy was in the little kitchenette, carefully wedged between the wine boxes and two departmental principals, who were leaning towards her like jackals sniffing meat. She was wearing what appeared to be a black bodystocking with a frilly little skirt that could have come from the wardrobe of the Royal Ballet.

Either Mandy had been there for a while already, or she'd arrived drunk. The moment she glimpsed Michael she gave him a blinding smile and brushed her admirers to one side. 'Michael, just in the nick of time.' She slipped her arm through his and led him to the source of alcohol. 'These fascinating gentlemen were about to explain the British Civil Service pay structure to me. Now, where have you been?' She stamped her foot in mock annoyance. The gesture wasn't wholly successful, however, because she swayed slightly and grabbed Michael's other arm to steady herself. 'What'cha want to drink?' her ruby red lips asked.

'The beast of Bulgaria'll be fine, thank you,' Michael said awkwardly. The two principals who had been salivating over Mandy were now watching the new Minister in unconcealed admiration. Their prey had attached herself, limpet-like, and was gazing up at Michael through her thick lashes as if he was Apollo, rather than a tired mortal who felt out of place and embarrassed by her attention.

'My, what strange people inhabit these subterranean cultures,' she drawled in her oft-employed imitation of Blanche Dubois. 'I do declare, they haven't formed any noticeable acquaintance with mouthwash or toothpaste. My dear Mr Fitzgerald, would I be out of place in suggesting a pan-ministerial memo to the effect that oral hygiene is desirable in circumstances such as these, where we must associate in confined spaces?'

'Have a draft on my desk in the morning. Would you like to sit down?' Michael asked as Mandy swayed into him again, and renewed the grip on his arm.

She shook her head defiantly and glanced about her with disappointment. 'No music. We'll have to teach these people a thing or two about partying, Michael.'

Partying was not something Michael felt qualified to offer any opinion on. He forced himself to be gregarious at functions in his constituency or at MOD receptions. He could supply serious conversations by the yard, or even a ping-pong game of witty abuse, but not trivial small talk or partying.

Through the fog of booze Mandy perceived that she wasn't holding his attention. He had also wriggled out of her grasp. 'So, are you going to Belfast tomorrow?' she asked.

'Just a day trip for some house-hunting. It's St Patrick's Day tomorrow, so Stormont will be closed, but I thought it might be a good opportunity to get a feel for the city. I'm going to save the meetings with windbags and masked men until I know what I'm talking about.'

'Hello, young Fitzgerald,' the Secretary of State bellowed behind him, as if he had just shot a hole in one. Michael jumped in shock, which made Sir Trevor Grace laugh. 'Touch of the jitters, eh? Glad you could make it.'

Michael winced and then gestured towards his research assistant. 'This is Mandy, sir.'

The Secretary of State grabbed her paw and ran his icy eyes all over her body. Michael noticed that she didn't even attempt to smile in response. Drunk or not, she certainly knew swamp slime when she encountered it.

'No wonder Mike was so keen to have you by his side. I can't say I blame him.' Grace smacked his moist lips; the red cheeks had taken on the appearance of plastic moulding that a clown might stick on his face.

'He's Michael, not Mike,' Mandy glared.

'And I'm sure you know better than anyone, my love. Now I've got to remove him from you for a moment, if you'll forgive me.' He pushed Michael before him, and gave Mandy a final leer.

'I bet she's a handful! I suppose it must keep you on form, though. Why do they wear these black legging things that show up every curve? It's torture to have to admire them from afar all day.'

Michael let himself be manhandled through the room to the cluster of Under Secretaries of State with whom Grace had been drinking. The new Minister did his best to engage the men and women in conversation, but he was sober so he was at a disadvantage. However, they roared with laughter at Sir Trevor's stories about the dreadfulness of Eurocrats, and Michael discovered that the best policy was to stand there quietly. Occasionally he was distracted by the rather public fondling occurring between an Under Secretary of State and a young woman from the Accounts Department. If Michael's majority had been as slender as was that MP's, he thought he might have paid more attention to his constituency business, rather than rubbing himself against other people's thighs.

Fitzgerald was planning his escape when someone tapped on his shoulder. 'Your young lady isn't looking too hot. I think you'd better come over here.'

Michael excused himself and fought his way back to Mandy who was sitting in the kitchen, bleary-eyed, and as white as a sheet.

'Come on. I'll give you a lift home.' Michael helped her stand up. 'It's terribly hot in here.'

'I don't want to ruin your evening,' she mumbled as he eased her towards the doors.

'Don't be silly. I can't wait to get away. Oh, I'd better find our driver.' He was about to turn back when he noticed that his research assistant had turned green.

'Do you need the loo?' He pushed her down the corridor and

into the women's lavatory, then he held her hair out of her eyes as she brought up the evening's consumption. It took several regurgitations to empty her stomach, and between each session Michael wiped her face with a wet paper towel, assuring her that it was nothing to feel humiliated about, because it happened to everyone at sometime or other. When matters stabilised, he left the weeping Mandy to clean herself up while he fetched his driver.

Ten minutes later, the ministerial Rover was cruising through the empty Central London streets, heading for Mandy's flat in Kentish Town. His tearful assistant had shrunk into a corner, overwhelmed by the awfulness of her performance. She was soon asleep, and when they reached her home, Michael had to support her up the stairs, and into her bedroom.

'God, I'm so sorry, Michael. I'm just not used to drinking so much,' she gurgled for the twentieth time. 'I really wanted to have fun with you this evening, and instead I did this.' She sighed and lay back on the pillows. For a moment her boss wondered irrelevantly why her accent had become markedly Scottish. It was obviously the product of three years at university north of the border. 'Please forget it happened, Michael. We never get any time to really talk. And I—' she ran out of words and pulled him towards her.

'Get some sleep.' He gently unclenched her fists from his jacket lapels.

'But I wanted us to have fun together,' she protested sleepily, and took his hand. 'You're always so busy,' she sobbed tragically.

'Come on, I've got to go. Will you be OK?'

'I wish you'd stay the night with me.' She gave his hand a plaintive squeeze.

Michael pulled himself loose. 'What you need is sleep, not a minister in your bed. I'll shut the lights off as I go. Good night.'

When Michael was back in the Rover he tried to read some papers but his brain was thick with a roaring headache. And he felt shaky and unsettled after Mandy's clumsy, drunken pawing. She was pretty and entertaining and she seemed to be devoted to him, but there wasn't the slightest response in his brain or his balls.

Perhaps Eddie was right. Had he become emotionally neutered? Did it matter? Probably not, except that he had never felt so lonely in his life. Until very recently he had comforted himself with the knowledge that he was in love with his wife, and that there had been twelve wonderful years together, which was more than many people had in a whole lifetime. But in the past weeks he had realised that he could only really love Caroline as a memory. That left a yawning, aching gap that he filled with work.

Michael gazed out of the window at the empty, dark streets of London, and wondered what the future held in store. Years of ministerial boxes interspersed with years on the Opposition benches? What a prospect. Then he realised that he was too tired to consider his empty heart further, and filed such thoughts away in a locked room in his head.

Back at Westminster, Dave Bower was putting the finishing touches to his report on Peter Tollmarch MP, former flatmate of the late Nigel Swinton. Between frantic bursts of tapping at his keyboard he absent-mindedly spooned chilli con carne into his mouth. As Charlotte watched him from across the Millbank newsroom, she thought he resembled a mechanical toy proving the durability of batteries, rhythmically scraping his spoon evenly around the styrofoam container without his eyes once leaving the words on the screen in front of him.

The smell of chilli filled the already stale office air, and Charlotte struggled not to heave. Dave regarded eating as a waste of time: food was just fuel that must be consumed to keep the show on the road. His practical approach could not have been further from Charlotte's philosophy. In a world where men searched for their mothers in your bed, and films were often half an hour too long, good food never failed to satisfy.

Charlotte was on the late shift tonight, and she was monitoring a debate on fisheries policy that threatened to go on into the small hours. Until Rodney had decided to play musical chairs with his reporters, Dave Bower would have been struggling to make cod sound interesting, but now that was Charlotte's privilege.

As Dave wrote, Rodney scuttled to and from the editing suite where he was putting together the film for Dave's package. Charlotte could not recall her boss ever giving her such assistance when she had been working to a tight deadline, but she kept that sour observation to herself.

'We've got shots of Mrs Tollmarch coming out of her house – oh, remember to say it's a luxury country cottage—' Rodney remarked over Dave's shoulder as they read his script. 'And she puts the baby in the car and drives off. So you need to say something about how long she's been married to Tollmarch and how old she is, right? Then we go to the supermarket.'

Charlotte, who hadn't really been paying attention to matters aquatic in the Chamber, pulled off her headphones and peered at Dave in disbelief. She knew she should shut her mouth, but after a whole evening of the Dave and Rodney Show she was bursting with annoyance.

'You actually followed this woman around a supermarket and asked her if her husband had been having a relationship with Nigel Swinton?' she asked Bower.

'Yeah, it was great,' Dave bubbled with a dizzy flush of adrenalin colouring his cheeks. 'No one else thought of going to see Tollmarch's wife. They were all outside Dolphin Square, waiting to doorstep him. But he's not stupid, is he? They're not going to get anything from him.'

'So you went to see his wife?'

'Yeah, she was brill. Tollmarch and Swinton were "very close friends" and "Peter is devastated by Nigel's death",' Dave paraphrased with a bad attempt at an upper-middle-class accent. 'Of course, she's sticking with this crap about how Swinton had cancer, but no one's going to believe it tomorrow morning when the *Sun* publishes those holiday snaps of them camping it up with little Arab boys.'

Charlotte shook her head and clicked her tongue in disgust. 'What does harassing Mrs Tollmarch achieve?'

'She's fair game. She's in the public eye because of her hubby's profession.' Dave shrugged.

'So you've proved that Peter Tollmarch is confused about his sexuality. I wish the press would be as terrier-like when it comes to uncovering financial corruption in this place. But of course it's more difficult to investigate MPs on the take, rather than sniffing people's knickers.'

At this point Rodney wrenched his attention away from Dave's script and turned towards Charlotte.

'This is a good story, and it's *your* news judgement that's at fault, not Dave's. This catches the public's imagination.'

A quiet, cautious voice of sanity inside Charlotte told her to shut up at this point, but her temper got the better of her, and she shook her chestnut locks again.

'It's not a story, though: it's a tragedy for this family, and we should leave them in peace to sort it out.'

'Look, Tollmarch is spoken of as future leadership material, and the public has every right to know if he's not up to the job.'

'And has the public also got the right to ask Mrs Tollmarch if she and the baby are HIV positive?'

'The public has the right to know the truth.'

'Then why don't we give them the truth about the crime statistics in London, eh? Why don't we reveal that people of Afro-Caribbean background account for a disproportionately large number of convictions?'

'Because the public would jump to racist conclusions,' Rodney snarled. 'It's too complicated for them to grasp because we'd have to explain the whole social background. It's irresponsible and racist to—'

'No, it's statistics, and I would submit that a person's private sexual preferences are also complicated and—'

'Well, I wouldn't have had to doorstep Mrs Tollmarch if Charlotte hadn't silenced my contact at The London Hospital,' Dave chipped in with the skill of a well-practised grenade tosser. Rodney's attention was instantly rooted on the young hack as Bower continued: 'A woman from the BBC called Nigel Swinton's consultant physician and warned him that someone in the Hospital's pharmacy department was going to give me an interview.'

For the first time in days Rodney's eyes met Charlotte's directly. 'Is this true? Was it you?'

Charlotte took a deep breath. 'Yes. I thought what Dave was doing was—'

'I don't give a fuck what you think!' her boss barked. 'That was totally unprofessional behaviour, and I'm astonished at you. Maybe you should go back to being a City reporter. I mean, do you really want to be a journalist? You can regard this as a formal warning. You'll get it in writing tomorrow. Now, we have work to do if we're going to get this on *Breakfast News*.'

Charlotte was left to study his back rather stupidly. A formal warning, she thought as she slipped on the headphones and found that they were still discussing fish in the Commons. A warning meant she was running out of lives. Was it back to using twenty different words to describe how shares move up and down? Perhaps Rodney had a point: maybe she wasn't cut out for this line of work. Whereas Dave Bower was an appropriate crusading moral guardian of the public interest!

She ground her teeth in fury and drew a picture of a big fish on her notepad. Then the gravity of Rodney's words struck her: it wasn't a wrap over the knuckles this time. It was a written warning, and in an organisation like the BBC, that was deadly serious.

Charlotte's career had been so important to her that she had sacrificed her boyfriend, David Stone, in order to work at Westminster, rather than settling down. Was this really the same career, the most precious part of her life, the burden of dreams and ambition that got her out of bed every morning? If she didn't have her work, then what was she left with? That harrowing consideration was too appalling to dwell on, so she side-stepped it, and drew a large shark, open-mouthed, approaching her unsuspecting fish.

Then for the first time she realised that her boss was more than just an irritating and pedantic bureaucrat sent to try her. Rodney Davis, head of the BBC Parliamentary Unit, had the power to destroy, and from now on he would be watching her, and waiting for her to stumble again. She would have to make her Belfast report a dazzler, she thought with a sinking heart. Otherwise Charlotte Carter might be looking for a new career.

Chapter Nine

It was 17 March, St Patrick's Day evening in Belfast, and it was raining – typical British Bank Holiday weather. Mac didn't feel like standing around at the bus stop in Malone Road so he waited in the car with Vince. The bus wasn't due until ten past six, which was in another quarter of an hour, so he turned on the radio. After a couple of bars of a Mozart piano concerto Vince, who was slouched in the driving seat, groaned.

'You can tell who's been using this car, can't you? Switch that crap off, will you?'

'Shut up, bonehead,' Mac grumbled at his brawny nineteen-year-old driver.

'There,' the florid-faced Vince announced as he fiddled with the tuning dial. 'This is more like it.' He nodded approvingly as the speakers pulsed with the computer-generated thump of drums.

But Mac's fingers were on the dial within seconds. 'I hate that dance shite. I'm not having that.' His authority was not often challenged by a fat, spotty errand-boy like Vince. 'Now this is proper music, this is. The Kingsmen. You've probably never heard of them,' he laughed. 'Before your time.'

Louis, Louis was also before Mac's time, but the pale-skinned, gaunt, twenty-five-year-old prided himself on his vast

109

musical repertoire and superior taste. He was also proud of his experience in the field, and the medals that a skin-headed idiot like Vince could never earn. All Vince had to show the world was a conviction for theft at the age of twelve.

Mac sat back in the passenger seat and glanced at his watch; two minutes past six. Then he checked in the car's rearview mirror, not that he could see much since their breath had clouded up the glass, and the outside was dappled with rain. The last watery light of a feeble spring afternoon was disappearing fast, and the cold crept in for the night like a cloud of damp death. Mac hunkered down into his donkey jacket and pulled his black baseball cap over his eyes. In one earlobe was a small, silver earring; he had two days of bluish stubble on his cheeks, and his dark brown hair was so short that it was all but hidden by the cap.

Louis, Louis was having an agreeable effect on him; it was unwinding the knots of tension that felt like steel rivets driven into his skull. Nevertheless he remained ashen-faced and twitching with nervous energy. The Kingsmen were followed by something more modern. Mac snapped the radio off fiercely, and reached for the battered plastic sports equipment bag on the back seat. Then without a word to the beefy-necked Vince he got out of the car. His driver saw Mac pull the donkey jacket collar up, then walk around the corner into Malone Road.

When the cream and maroon-coloured Citybus appeared, Vince started the engine and eased the car forward and around the corner after it. He paused twenty yards from the bus stop and watched his colleague climb on to the vehicle.

Mac still had the strange, droning chorus from *Louis, Louis* doing circuits in his head as he paid the driver and went to the back of the bus. He placed the sports bag on the seat beside him and unzipped it. The bus juddered forward and picked up speed, and Mac glanced over his shoulder, out of the back window. Vince was a hundred yards behind, side lights on, windshield wipers swishing away the waves of rain. Mac turned his attention to the other passengers, who were old women mostly, returning from a holiday visit to their friends, careful to get home before dark. There was also one old man, and a young woman Mac had noticed at the bus stop. She was quite pretty.

Three minutes later Mac spotted the landmark: the entrance to Windsor Park on the right-hand side of Malone Road. He sat up straight, and his hand rested inside the sports bag. Fifty yards further along on the same side of the street was the Roman Catholic church, and as the bus whooshed past it, several passengers blessed themselves, predictably the elderly women he had been watching, but also one of the old men and the attractive young woman. The cautious habits of twenty-five years had so quickly and carelessly been forgotten.

Mac eased the Webley revolver out of the sports bag, got to his feet, and braced himself against the seat in front. After the first two shots the bus came to a shuddering halt, and the passengers were pitched forward. They were surprisingly quiet as Mac walked down the aisle, picking off the old women one by one; then he reloaded and took out the old man, and the young woman. Their screams were more like whimpers, but he could hardly hear them anyway, what with the ringing noise in his ears.

The bus driver was heading for the door, but Mac cut him down before he had made the first step. He crumpled as though his legs were made of gelatine, and Mac had to pull him into the bus on his way out. With the revolver back in the sports bag, he walked away at an even, normal pace to the car which was idling in neutral a few yards behind. He got in, and they turned right, down Cadogan Park, not so fast that they would attract attention, but not too slowly either. An hour later, an NIPD patrol found the burnt-out shell of the car behind the Avoniel Leisure Centre in the Loyalist part of East Belfast. The first part of Neil's plan had been completed.

On that same drizzly March evening, there was a deadly fight taking place in Grasmere Gardens, in North Belfast. Donny Lennon was pursuing an alien down a corridor as it twisted and turned, but he seemed unable to catch up to it. Finally he blasted it and it screamed horribly, and blood spurted out of it. Nevertheless Donny's score was useless.

As usual, he was being soundly beaten at Doom, the computer game favoured by his ten-year-old son. Donny had observed more than once that all his solicitor's training came to naught at the hands of his sharp-witted, computer-literate only child. 'My so-called agility is as fearsome as a bucket of jelly when it's put to the ultimate test against our offspring,' Lennon had told his wife earlier on that Bank Holiday. So much for the glib performances before the local magistrates.

When it was Donny's turn again he stabbed furiously, but ineffectually at the joystick. Once more the grinning masked alien won.

'You're a dead man,' his son commented with relish as he took the controls.

Three of Neil's associates parked their car several doors down from the Lennon house, carefully avoiding the street-lights. They had to peer up each garden path to see the house numbers through the rain and the gathering dusk. These were nice houses; not the kind whose doors open straight onto the streets.

One of the men stayed in the car, but before the other two got out they consulted a piece of paper to remind themselves of the layout of Donny Lennon's house. Then they scanned Grasmere Gardens, which was empty of pedestrians. It was hardly ideal weather for dog-walking.

They slipped up the garden path of the Lennon home, and around the side to the kitchen door. It was much easier to kick open than the imposing slab of wood at the front of the house. They had pulled on balaclavas even though they weren't leaving witnesses, and the silencers on their handguns muffled any sound that might have alerted neighbours. They shot down Donny and his wife in the hallway by the kitchen, and they found the ten-year-old boy cowering under the dining-room table. But unlike the alien in Doom, these victims didn't make much noise, or produce virtual blood. Within five minutes the three men were on their way back to the part of Belfast where front doors open straight onto the street.

At that moment, another jigsaw piece was being slotted into Neil's master puzzle. Two of his 'men' were in a less salubrious section of town: Crocus Street, just off Springfield Road in West Belfast. They were sitting in their van, waiting for a Special Police Battalion of the NIPD to move out of their way. The Special Battalions were made up of former Provos who patrolled 'their' communities, keeping an eye on things.

At the top of the street was an ugly concrete building that looked more like a public convenience than a school. It would be a quick job: a couple of incendiary devices and a bit of petrol spilt around the place. They didn't expect to find anyone inside, but if some misguided man or woman was working there they would be dealt with. As far as the two Loyalists in the van were concerned, they would deserve what they got for volunteering to help in an Adult Literacy Centre that boasted non-sectarian roots and integrated classes.

The Special Battalion Patrol disappeared bang on time, and just as the two colleagues suspected, the building was empty. They were in and out in less than two minutes, before anyone could peer through their net curtains and wonder who owned the unfamiliar van. But as they drove away to a spot where the van would meet a fiery end, the two men agreed that although they'd done a good job, they'd been faintly disappointed to find the place deserted.

The tidal wave of Neil's Blitzkrieg moved on. Half an hour later, and half a mile away, in Donegal Street, the offices of the *Irish News* were also empty. The Nationalist paper was housed in a brick building that looked as if it had once been a pub, with big windows and blue woodwork outside. This part of the city, just north of the centre, in what might be described as the commercial district, was like a ghost town on St Patrick's Day. There was no one about, except for a Northern Ireland Regiment soldier, who happened to be on patrol on that side of the street when he heard a thudding, smashing sound nearby. He gestured to his mate who was on the other side of the road, and indicated that they should have a look around the back of the building, where it seemed to him that the noise had originated.

They went past the Belfast Training Centre, and turned right down the lane to a service alleyway. Their route took them past a betting shop which had an empty car parked outside it, and a Catholic bookshop which displayed clerical vestments in the window. There was no street lighting, so the soldiers didn't notice what had happened to the back entrance to the *Irish News* building until they were almost on top of it. Then they stopped in their tracks and squinted at the mess that the Landrover had left when it had rammed its way through the steel doors.

Instead of gripping their Tommy guns across their chests, the soldiers pointed them into the darkness ahead. Both young men strained their ears, and blinked away the raindrops that were clinging to their eyelashes, but it was impossible to see much. Then suddenly there were hurried footsteps in the darkness, and before the soldiers could issue a challenge or a warning they were caught in the beam of powerful flashlights.

'You're not supposed to be here,' a voice said wearily. For one surreal moment neither the intruders nor the soldiers moved. Then the men with the flashlights fired two or three times each, and stumbled over each other as they ran up the alleyway to the car that was now idling outside the bookie's. A moment later the car had pulled into the empty, rainswept Donegal Road.

'They weren't supposed to be there,' one of them huffed testily like an indignant child sent to bed as a favourite TV programme began. 'Someone should be shot for making a fuck-up like that.'

'OK. Point taken. It wasn't very clever. I'll look into it,' Neil assured the man with the voice of a petulant youngster who was on the other end of his mobile phone. 'Otherwise it was a brilliant day's work . . . Yeah . . . Bye.'

Neil switched off his mobile phone and returned to the list in front of him on the kitchen table. As each unit called in with their report, he ticked off another accomplishment: a bus full of Taigs, a Sinn Fein solicitor, the Ardoyne dole office, a school, a Sinn Fein councillor, and now the *Irish News* office. All the while Neil kept one ear on BBC Radio Ulster's news updates to confirm that the bombs had actually detonated, and to check his tally of dead and wounded.

He mentally switched off when the programme went to Republican politicians for their shocked and outraged reactions. Apparently the IRA had decided their cause was better served by allowing the Loyalist killings to go unmatched tonight. Then all the sympathy and attention would be focused on the victims of the evil Protestants. Good tactics, thought Neil with grudging respect. He wished his boys were capable of exercising the same logic.

None of the Loyalist units would visit his house: too risky. Their business was better handled from public call-boxes and on mobile phones. Anyway, he didn't particularly want his kitchen filled with skinheads in dirty jeans and Doc Martins who didn't bathe often enough. They were a scruffy, meat-headed, tattooed lot; not an aquiline nose or a neatly turned phrase amongst them.

When Neil heard his wife moving around in the next room, he looked up from his list. 'Hey, what about a cup of tea in here, eh, Jane?' He did not wait for a reply because he had issued an order, not a request.

While she filled the kettle and washed a few plates there was a live broadcast on the radio from the integrated school. Neil could sense his wife straining to hear the news. So much for her stupid plans to attend 'Irish history' classes there.

When Jane placed the china cup and saucer in front of him she didn't even receive a grunt of appreciation. Her husband was diverted by the latest, breathless on-the-scene radio report. The new Minister was on hand to condemn the senseless and brutal events, and to demand an end to the 'ethnic cleansing'.

Barely five hours since the operation had begun, and they were already calling it 'the St Patrick's Day Massacre'.

Chapter Ten

The next morning, 18 March, it was cold but clear in London, and Charlotte Carter was contemplating her William Morris curtains. It was 8 a.m., and even though the reporter had a day off work in lieu of all those late-night shifts, she had been unable to sleep in. Her internal clock was working in league with her brain to deprive her body of the sleep it needed. Whose side are you on? she demanded of herself as she lay in bed. Of course she knew the answer: You're awake because you've got to get to grips with this flat. It's like a refugee camp on the Gaza Strip. Time to sort it out, rather than spending the morning browsing in clothes shops. Or passing the afternoon at the cinema, falling in love with Tom Hanks all over again, and then feeling cheated that you never bump into him at the Marks & Spencer sandwich counter in Whiteley's Shopping Mall down the road.

She abandoned Alfred the Rabbit, her battered and much-mended lifelong companion, to the luxury of the double bed, and stumbled into the kitchen. As the kettle boiled she spooned a yoghurt down her throat and listened to the end of the eight o'clock news summary on the *Today* programme.

'And Loyalist areas of Belfast are reportedly bracing themselves for a possible IRA retaliation after yesterday's attacks on the Catholic community. However, Sinn Fein says former members of the Republican Army are committed to the peace process and will not be drawn back into violence. Unionist politicians have condemned what they call "rogue elements" in the Loyalist movement for breaking the ceasefire.'

Charlotte would usually register the horrors in Belfast and tune out, because for the past three decades, bombs in Northern Ireland had been like wallpaper music to someone sitting in London W2. But now she had a picture of Michael's face dancing in front of her eyes.

Charlotte stood over the brewing tea, wondering if some crazed Fenian or Loyalist would organise a welcoming present for Michael Fitzgerald. The Provisionals were famous for their own goals, but rubbing out a Catholic politician would show exceptional dimness. Of the three hundred and fifty 'volunteers' that the IRA admitted had died during the Troubles, it was reckoned a hundred had blown themselves up. And when the IRA had started bombing Britain in the Seventies, one of the first people to die was a Catholic cleaning lady at the Army barracks at Aldershot. That must have been well-received in West Belfast. Another subtle message from the men who brought you Enniskillen.

As she showered, then pulled on her jeans and sweatshirt, she realised that for the last twenty minutes she had been totally preoccupied by the welfare of the Minister of State for Northern Ireland. A touch irrational, perhaps, considering he had very probably forgotten her existence, until they next bumped into each other in the Lobby.

Charlotte dismissed that miserable thought and turned to the task at hand: her flat. It was beautiful, but it needed paintings, or whatever it was that people put in their houses to express their personal essence. It was at the top of a five-storey terraced Edwardian house in a square with a garden in the middle. There was a balcony where she imagined she could lounge on summer evenings, sipping wine and listening to Sade CDs. Quite who she would be lounging with was another matter. Alfred the Rabbit quite probably.

After two hours of finding spaces for battered old handbags that might one day be useful, Charlotte was bored beyond belief. She sat in the middle of the wooden floor, savoured a cup of coffee, and tried not to think about the size of her mortgage, and how hard it would be to find a job if she was given the bum's rush by the BBC. Rodney's ultimatum plunged her into gloom once more. Then with a little shiver of joy she realised that the St Patrick's Day Massacre had pushed Dave Bower's fearless political exposé onto the backburner.

She switched on the radio for the eleven o'clock 'heads', as they were known in the trade. The resumption of bloodshed in Northern Ireland was still leading. What was it like reporting from Belfast during the worst of the Troubles, she wondered – like the day of Bobby Sands's funeral, when the hotels were so full of journalists from around the world that they were editing film in the corridors . . .

Did reporters become hardened or blasé? A boy she knew said you never forgot your first bomb. Tim Horn. He had been on Charlotte's course of 'induction into the Corporation' when she had joined the BBC, after her stint in the City with another network. Together they had done their drill practice at Television Centre, sworn the oath of allegiance to 'the finest broadcasting organisation in the world', and promised to fulfil their mission to inform. In reality, Tim and Charlotte had sat at the back of the propaganda sessions making each other giggle with irreverent observations; and they had disrupted pep talks by asking the Corporation's gauleiters why Radio 1 couldn't be sold off; or getting them to explain how advertising had corrupted Channel Four's news values.

At the end of the course Tim had returned to his native Belfast, and Charlotte had gone to Parliament. They kept in touch through the BBC's electronic mail system, and with weekly late-night phone calls when both were on duty in empty newsrooms. Tim was just the man to show Charlotte around Belfast. She immediately looked out the BBC Ulster newsroom number, wondering why it had taken her so long to think of him.

Belfast referred her back to Television Centre in London where Tim was apparently over for a meeting. Charlotte fully grasped the pointlessness of such BBC News and Current Affairs gatherings, and within five minutes she had tracked him down and persuaded him to have lunch with her. The bad bit was that they would be confined to Shepherds Bush because he had to be in attendance that afternoon.

When he appeared in the foyer of Television Centre an hour and a half later, Tim was wearing his usual bewildered expression.

'This is an extraordinary organisation,' he said by way of greeting. 'They've just found out that the fellow who runs the N'Rooda section of the World Service has been giving free advertising to his uncle's business interests back home. But since no one else here understands N'Roodese he's been getting away with it for months.'

They walked out of Television Centre and down to the desolate traffic island known as Shepherds Bush, but they were too absorbed in conversation to take in the urban decay. Charlotte knew from experience that prolonged walks with Tim hurt her neck because he was six foot five, and she was at a ten-inch disadvantage. It was easier to concentrate when they were sitting opposite each other, even if it was in a pizza restaurant. Pizza was not the greedy, *gourmande* female reporter's first choice, but it was the best on offer in this cultural desert.

'You look like Parliament's suiting you,' Tim remarked when they had secured some Budvar beer. 'Is it fun?'

'Like a course of chemotherapy,' she could have responded, but she wasn't up to confronting or sharing her problems. 'You look fine yourself,' she evaded, 'despite the burdens of responsibility on your broad shoulders.'

'Promotion is all very well, but I'm not looking fine. I'm even balder, aren't I?' He gestured at his thinning blond hair. Charlotte was rather more diverted by the enormous proportions of his hands. He had a shambling way of walking and moving that suggested a tree in motion.

'Calm down. No one can see up there.' The affection in her voice made Tim smile. His eyes were slightly sunken into his round face, and he looked as if he was perpetually brooding.

He glanced at the menu. 'Well, at least we'll be able to manage better than this when you're in Belfast. You know you'll have to take everything I say with a pinch of salt, don't you? I've become warped by reporting all this bollocks, and naturally I was slightly twisted when I started anyway.'

'Because of your background?'

'No, because of my *reaction* to my background – which is suffocatingly Presbyterian. My parents are respectable, lower middle class; blunt, law-abiding and quick to judge. So I grew up thinking it was quite normal to call nuns "the whores of Christ". And whenever we took tea with friends we hadn't seen for a while we'd say "God bless you, and to hell with the Pope."

And all the bloody hypocrisy, Charlotte.' He waved his splendid paws in distress at the memory.

'My father told me how backward and wretched the priest-ridden Irish country people were, living barefoot in their shacks with their animals, and all their superstitions. He said the Catholics believed in the Little People and knitted clothes for them, and left them out at night.'

Charlotte's jaw sagged. 'Did they?'

'It wasn't as widespread as my old man reckoned. Once I went to visit some of our family who'd stayed in the country – good Presbyterians, of course. They were a bunch of inter-married, illiterate morons living in sheds. But they felt this incredible superiority to the RCs. They lived in just the same squalor, with just as many bloody children, but they were supremely comforted by their conviction that they were better.'

Charlotte held up her hand to slow him down. 'Is this why the working-class Protestants in Belfast believe they have a natural right to all the jobs, and the Catholics down the street don't?'

Tim nodded. 'They've been Loyal to the Union, and they deserve better than those rebellious Taigs. But listen: one of these damned cousins of mine is completely wild. Dickie. He'll go on terrific drinking bouts, and disappear for days at a time, on walkabout. While I was staying there, Dickie emerged after about ten days off God knows where, and I asked him what he'd done. He said he'd found himself by a large lake, and gone to sleep. And when he'd woken there'd been a fine fat pig standing looking at him. And the pig had said, "Jump on my back, Dickie Dasher, and I'll ferry you over the water." Honestly, Charlotte, that's what he said!'

His audience of one laughed, incredulously, but as Tim

122

continued his face got redder. 'And the other thing about Presbyterianism, apart from all the tight-lipped disapproval, is the prudishness and anal retention. They used to lock up the swings in the playground on Sundays so children wouldn't be tempted to enjoy themselves. I mean, Christ! And I had a maiden aunt who believed it was sinful to look at her body, so she used to bathe in a darkened room. And she got breast cancer, but because she would never have touched them or watched out for lumps, she died. I overheard my mother say my aunt's breasts were as hard as rocks. I can remember that so clearly, because I was about five at the time, and my mother took me to view her corpse which was laid out at her sister's house. I can still feel my mother lifting me up under the armpits, and holding me so I was right beside this cold, waxy, white face and making me kiss her cheek. And all I could think about was her breasts as hard as rocks.'

'Well, I wasn't really enjoying this pizza anyway, Tim. But thanks for sealing its fate,' Charlotte snorted as she pushed her plate away.

'This one really is from Chicago.' Tim prodded a bit of pepperoni. 'There's a finger in it. And if there was any more oil in this salad dressing we could apply to join OPEC.'

Charlotte sighed and ripped the label off her beer bottle. 'I'm looking forward to visiting Belfast. To be honest, I'm in a bit of trouble at the Parliamentary Unit, and I get the feeling this is my last chance.'

'Are you serious? What's wrong with your stuff? I really liked that thing on pollution you did. It made the Labour guy look like a real prick.'

'Ah, but my work is all shades of grey, Tim, whereas my boss Rodney Davis believes the world is black and white.'

'Well, he wouldn't get very far in Belfast. He sounds ridiculous, your boss.'

'One of the things I like about your accent is the way it sounds as if you're asking a question at the end of every sentence.' Charlotte saw that Tim had taken it as a personal compliment, rather than an observation on the Belfast-style of speaking, so she added, 'It's such a shame that what you have to say is such a load of balls.'

He abandoned his pizza to a fitting fate, and sighed melodramatically. 'I see you've still got all the charm of Stalin's granny. Well, don't hold your breath for a shit-hot political story out of Belfast. Politics is dying, if not dead.'

Charlotte smiled bravely.

'What's wrong with this chap?' Michael asked Margaret, his secretary at Stormont Castle, where part of the Northern Ireland Office was housed in splendour. She screwed up her little nose like a piglet who was reluctant to divulge where she had hidden her supply of truffles.

'Who, James?'

'Yes. He seems rather over-qualified to be my driver and bodyguard. What's the problem?'

Margaret, who was sitting opposite her new boss, moved her head in a figure of eight, as if she was combining a yes with a no. Michael raised his eyebrows to accompany his question, and studied the woman's closed, nervous face. Too much make-up for Michael's taste, presumably because she had a poor complexion. Her dark eyebrows were plucked into a severe thin line which made her look harder and older than her thirty-five years. But the eyes were warm and kind when she smiled.

'He had a drink problem, did James,' she conceded after a bit more probing from Michael. 'His wife was dying of cancer, and poor James went through a rough patch. But he's all together again now.'

'But he was an Inspector.' Michael looked through the man's NIPD file. He liked the sound of James best of all the potential candidates for bodyguard. He wanted someone mature and dependable, not young and macho. 'Can I meet him?'

Margaret smiled and tossed her long, dark hair over her shoulder as if she was pleased by his decision. 'I saw him about ten minutes ago in the staff canteen.' She got to her feet, and glanced down at the notepad in her hand. 'By the way, Sir David Mackay is arriving soon.'

When she had gone back to her office, Michael walked across the room to the large map of Northern Ireland that was pinned on one wall. The names of towns and villages triggered the release of recently acquired information, and more familiar memories in the ministerial brain: Enniskillen, where the IRA killed eleven on Remembrance Sunday in 1987; Londonderry, where it all began with the civil rights march in 1968, and where the Army blotted their copybook in 1972 with Bloody Sunday; Greysteel; Warrenpoint, each with a catalogue of horror and suffering.

Michael found the River Bann and ran his finger along it. To the east the majority of the population was Protestant; to the west they were Roman Catholic. Then he traced the border areas to the south, where the IRA had intimidated Protestant farmers into moving out. Would the whole Province end up in two distinct ghettoes, with virtually no integration? What a terrible testament to man's inability to find solutions to such problems.

Among the notes and papers on his desk was an ancient copy of the IRA's weekly paper *An Phoblact*, and he re-read the editorial with a heavy heart: '*Our rules are taken from history.*

We remember the famine. We remember the Fenians. We remember 1916 and the executions. We remember the Loyalist pogroms of the 1920s. We remember and are most proud of the small band of Republicans who down the years carried the torch of freedom.' Etc.

So much memory, and so little idea of what future they wanted, the Minister reflected. Then there was an old report from the US Defence Department: between 1971 and 1974, the IRA and its American friends stole enough arms from US military bases to arm ten battalions. How much hardware was still in hidden arms caches around the Province, and south of the border?

'Minister, Sir David Mackay is here,' Margaret announced in her tight Belfast voice.

Michael came around the desk and extended his mitt to the Chief Constable of NIPD with as much geniality as he could muster. Sir David looked at him as if he were a wild animal about to pounce, and Michael stiffened his back accordingly. Mackay was a neat, grey, tidy man with small dark eyes, and a toothbrush moustache that bristled over thin, colourless lips. The Chief Constable had a slight frame, and as they sat down opposite each other at the conference table, Michael wondered irrelevantly how long ago the police had abandoned their height requirement for recruits. As a little boy, bobbies had seemed massive and intimidating creatures to Michael, but Mackay, who was probably in his mid-fifties, couldn't have stopped a shoplifting granny.

The Chief Constable launched into his performance and it soon became apparent that he had nothing to add to the now familiar 'we're expecting an IRA spectacular' story that Michael had heard from the NIPD Special Branch officer who had briefed him in London. The Minister studied the inscrutable face, and his mind wandered. Why did Sir David's good lady allow her husband to grow such an untactile moustache? Surely no woman would want to kiss those bristles . . .

When the routine about the IRA bombing campaign was finished, Michael thanked the Chief Constable for his words of wisdom, and then diverted the man's attention to the St Patrick's Day Massacre. Army Intelligence, in the form of Brigadier Rowbottham, had already suggested that the address and layout of the houses of both the Sinn Fein councillor and solicitor who died had been leaked by NIPD officers to Loyalist paramilitaries.

Now Michael had to persuade Sir David Mackay to investigate his own men to get at the truth. From what he had already heard, the Minister was confident that the Chief Constable was an honest, decent man who had made a sincere attempt to root out the 'rotten apples' inside NIPD. But it seemed that 'collusion' had been a persistent problem which would continue to undermine NIPD's neutrality in the view of many Roman Catholics in the Province.

'I appreciate the amount of work you've done in the past to plug the leaks, Sir David, but our aim has to be to remove the basis for the support and protection the terrorists still receive in some cases. I know that you fully understand that, and I hope we can work together to prevent any further leaks. We can't allow the IRA to have these propaganda victories.'

The Chief Constable's back stiffened, and he perched on the edge of his seat, as if he were bracing himself for an earthquake at any moment.

'So I'd like to see a full investigation into how the St Patrick's Day event occurred, please. Of course I've read this report,'

Michael remarked evenly as he indicated the document that explained NIPD's internal investigation into the massacre, 'but there are still a few matters that don't quite add up.' That was about as subtly as Michael could put it.

The Chief Constable's dark eyes flashed in silent response, and when their meeting concluded he departed as formally and coldly as he had arrived. Michael wondered if anything at all would happen as a result. He doubted it.

Sir David Mackay was in a sombre mood as he travelled the short distance from Fitzgerald's office at Stormont Castle back to NIPD headquarters. He immediately summoned his Assistant Chief Constable, and waved the St Patrick's Day report under his nose.

'This wasn't acceptable to our new Minister, so I suggest you produce something of a bit more substance,' he barked. 'Fast!'

Then he sat back in his chair and stared out of the window with a ruminative frown. He too had been less than satisfied with the report, and the whiff of NIPD collusion that it had failed to expunge from the atmosphere. Mackay had instigated a thorough clean-out of the ranks since the ceasefire in 1994, but his instincts told him there were still a few battle-hardened Loyalists secreted in the bureaucracy, passing on Intelligence. But where should the Chief Constable begin, in a renewed clear-out exercise that would be both time-consuming and bad for morale?

'By the way,' he called after the departing Assistant Chief Constable. 'I suspect we may be about to see even more changes around here.' His deputy, hovering unhappily on the office threshold, took note.

Chapter Eleven

'Quite a party Spock's having,' the sergeant remarked. 'Must be twenty people in there by now.'

'Hope he's got enough jelly and ice cream,' his colleague muttered. It was Saturday afternoon, and for the last twenty minutes the two plain-clothes soldiers had sat in their Escort, which had faulty heating, and watched the comings and goings at the home of a man whose codename was Spock. 'Do they still have jelly and ice cream at parties?' The corporal deferred to his sergeant who was married with two children.

'Yeah. It's the cost of the presents that's changed from when we were kids. Look, here's more wise men bearing gifts.' He nodded towards a man, woman and two children who were approaching Spock's house on foot from the other end of Norglen Crescent, in the Turf Lodge area of Belfast. In his arms the man had a large box wrapped in coloured paper, with a bow on top. When they reached the neat, semi-detached house, they passed through the white wrought-iron gate, and walked up the path.

'There he is,' the sergeant said as Jack Heaney opened his front door and welcomed the visitors. 'He really does look like a Vulcan too.' Then his voice changed suddenly. 'Hey, who are these, here in the Volvo?'

'Shit! They can't have been there long. Have they seen us, d'you reckon?'

'Not from where they're parked. Something tells me they're not the kind of people Spock'd invite round. I think we should give it a minute, then we'd better call.'

The soldiers sat as still as statues and watched the men in the Volvo who were in turn watching Spock's house. A VW Golf came slowly down the road, and paused while a woman and a child got out of the back seat. Like everyone else who had arrived on that damp March afternoon, they were carrying presents. Once again the front door swung open and revealed a tall thin man in jeans and a cream Aran jumper. His face was long, chiselled, and pale. Even from the Volvo, thirty feet away, the man's ears were visible, and remarkable for their size and whiteness in contrast to his dark, wiry hair.

As Spock's new guests were ushered inside, the men in the Volvo started moving. The sergeant grabbed his radio while his colleague reached onto the back seat for their rifles.

'Come in. We're in Norglen Crescent near the Falls Park. Request immediate armed backup at Spock's house.' But before he had time to describe the three men or give the registration number of the Volvo, his partner hissed at him to get out and hide on the other side of the Escort.

By now the strangers were out of the Volvo, machine guns in hand, half-crouching, half-running towards Spock's house. The two plain-clothes soldiers rested their rifles on the roof of the Escort, and shouted out a warning at Spock to get inside and shut the door. The men from the Volvo swung around and fired at them, and the soldiers bobbed down and squatted behind the wheels of the Escort as the car's windows shattered in the spray of bullets. Then they pivoted back, one at each end of the car, and took aim at the men at Spock's front door. Two more shots pierced the muffled afternoon silence of the sleepy street, and one man crumpled. The other two scuttled past the door and made for the alleyway at the side of the house.

The sergeant picked off another Volvo man before he could disappear around the back, but the third one returned fire and sprayed the Escort. The corporal, the one who had asked for clarification on children's party food, was hit in the chest and thrown back into a hedge by the force of the bullets. His sergeant fired at the remaining intruder but the shot ricocheted off the alleyway wall and smashed a neighbour's window. His next shot caught the third Volvo man in the leg, and he sank down to the ground by Spock's dustbins.

Inside the house, twenty-five adults and children were lying on the floor under food-laden tables, or behind the sofa where flying glass would not reach them. When the shooting was over the children started to cry on cue, like a chorus in a tragic opera. The sergeant yelled through the sitting-room window for someone to call for an ambulance. Then he stood over the wounded Volvo man until the Army backup he had requested arrived. He was later glad that he had not followed his first impulse, which had been to finish off the remaining intruder. It might not have been a very shrewd career move.

That Saturday evening Michael received a phone call from Brigadier Rowbottham, the Army's Director of Intelligence in Northern Ireland, who gave him the edited highlights of the afternoon's shoot-out at Spock's house. But when the Brigadier rang again the following morning with more information, he requested a face-to-face meeting with his Northern Ireland Minister.

Michael's heart sank: he and Laura were staying at his mother's house in Hampshire, a good hour and a half from London even on a Sunday, and even further from Belfast; he was reluctant to interrupt this much-coveted break. He had spent the last two days reading books on Ireland, watching the videos that Charlotte Carter had arranged for him to borrow, and catching up on the sleep he'd missed since his elevation to the NIO.

'Where are you, Minister? Did you say Petersfield?'

'Yes, my mother's house is in Steep. It's a village—'

'I know Steep. It has rather a good pub, if I recall. You see, I was stationed at Borden for a couple of years. Lovely countryside round there. Would you mind if I popped down to see you this afternoon? I'm in London at the moment.'

Michael returned to reading about the Falls Road curfew but his daughter broke his concentration yet again. 'What on earth does this mean?' She scrutinised the lyrics sheet that accompanied the Steely Dan CD her father was playing. ' "I stood up on the platform/the man gave me the noose/he said 'you must be joking son/where did you get those shoes?' ".'

'That's what's known as irony. What do you think of the music?'

Laura, who was bundled up in several layers of woollen jumpers, sat at one end of the sofa, feet beneath her, curled up like a cat. She shrugged. 'Supermarket muzak. But the words are so strange.'

'Well, it kept Eddie and me busy when we were at Oxford. We'd lie around in each other's rooms half the night, driving the neighbours mad, no doubt, playing these records and striving to decode the inner meaning. We thought it made us intellectually superior to our peers because we liked music that was more complex than, for instance, 'Lay lady lay, lay across my big brass bed'. That was Bob Dylan. Couldn't go anywhere at college without people playing that rubbish at you, and worse, singing along.' He grimaced at the memory. 'So Steely Dan was our revenge. Here.' He joined Laura on the sofa. 'This one kept us guessing for weeks. Where is it?' He flicked through the lyrics booklet. '*Chained Lightning*. This is it. Turns out it's about Berchtesgaden, which was the town in Bavaria where Adolf Hitler used to go for his holidays. Bizarre.'

Laura was reading a biography of Hitler when Delva showed Brigadier Rowbottham into the sitting room and then went back to her game of bridge with Mrs Fitzgerald and her friends. The Brigadier, as cube-shaped as ever in a lovat-green tweed suit, exchanged weary remarks with Michael about how horrible the Sunday papers were being to Peter Tollmarch, MP. Then Michael led him into the kitchen which was the only warm room in the house, and they sat at a large wooden table eating crumpets and drinking Earl Grey tea.

'The incident in Belfast yesterday needs more clarification than I could possibly give over the phone, Minister.' This prompted Michael to wonder about these mythical line-tappers; and not for the first time. Every Department of State revelled in its own melodramatic version of the alien eavesdroppers, although no one had explained to Michael precisely who they were.

'It wasn't a Loyalist attack, although that's what our two plain-clothes men assumed at the time. As well they might,' Rowbottham grunted defensively. 'They were keeping an eye on the house of Jack Heaney, who's the big IRA banana. Works out tactics, strategy. You won't see his face on TV because he doesn't hold press conferences like Adams or McGuinness. He's not interested in getting elected to things, and he probably doesn't believe in democracy anyway. But he was instrumental in getting the original ceasefire in 1994.'

The Brigadier paused to smear a bit more butter on his crumpet.

'We take a casual interest in him, just as we do the other leading Republicans,' he went on. 'This isn't by any means a twenty-four-hour watch, and of course he often has his own bodyguard, but yesterday afternoon we happened to have two men there.

'So did NIPD Special Branch,' he continued after a bite. 'They had a Mobile Support Unit there, but sadly their Divisional Commander hadn't thought of letting us know they were running an undercover surveillance operation on him. They had three men there.'

'And two of them are now dead,' Michael volunteered. 'And you lost one of yours.'

Rowbottham snorted angrily and helped himself to some of Delva's raspberry jam. 'NIPD said they had every reason to believe Heaney was having a senior pow-pow of active IRA units. This is from their E4A undercover surveillance unit, by the way. And they classified their information as A1, which means top quality, rather than F7, which is what it turns out to have been. Spock was—'

'Spock?'

'Codename for Jack Heaney. Looks like a Vulcan – you know, *Star Trek*,' Rowbottham explained with a vague wave of his square, sticky fingers. 'NIPD thought he was taking delivery of some fuses and detonators that've been floating round town all week. They staked out the place, and saw people arriving with boxes wrapped up like presents, and they swooped.'

Rowbottham held up a finger before the puzzled-looking Minister could interrupt. 'That's their side: now here's ours. Spock has twin boys, eleven-year-olds, and it was their birthday party yesterday. The people who were delivering presents were the parents of the boys' schoolfriends and neighbours. We knew what was happening because we've got the date of the boys' birth in our records, as well as everything else you ever wanted to know about Spock, like how often he hires videos. He likes Bergman and Bruce Willis, by the way, which explains a lot. Of course, the giveaway was the bunch of balloons tied outside the house, and the fact that all these hardened, bloodthirsty IRA volunteers turned up with their children in tow.'

'I'm going to ask a question that reveals just how little I've absorbed so far. Why didn't your men know about the NIPD operation? And vice versa?'

The Brigadier sat back in his chair and rubbed his hands across the grains of the wooden table. There wasn't even the slightest note of apology or embarrassment in his voice.

'In theory, we pool intelligence and let each other know what we're up to. But in practice, well, in practice this is the second such mix-up in the last twelve months. And three years ago there was an equally regrettable . . . let's just say there have been other mishaps.'

'Who is supposed to coordinate the two intelligence-gathering operations? I thought it was Sir David Mackay of NIPD? And what happened after the last "incident"? Wasn't some action taken to prevent this happening again? Leaving aside the apparent trigger-happy impulses of NIPD Special Branch, why aren't your people talking to each other?'

'That's one of the reasons I thought it might be better to meet here, Minister. We have reason to believe that some of the intelligence gathered by NIPD is—' Rowbottham left a significant pause, and the theatricality of it annoyed Michael even more, 'unreliable. And we're reluctant to pool intelligence because there's evidence that NIPD is leaky, as you know very well. Somewhere within their organisation there is a bad apple who's passing information to the Loyalists. We're unhappy

135

about sharing our most confidential material if it's going to end up plastered on walls in the Shankill Road.'

'I'm sure the Chief Constable of NIPD would wish to do everything he can to stop these leaks.' Michael watched the Brigadier's overcooked face contort as his words sank in.

'Minister, I've come to you on good advice – Johnny Burleigh's advice. Frankly, it would be much better all round if the Army was in sole charge of all intelligence-gathering in the Province. I'm sure that would win the support of the Nationalist community, who have their reasons for believing NIPD are less than even-handed as it is. We all know that just because they got rid of the name RUC, it doesn't change the fundamental attitudes of the people who work there.'

'But there's been a whole retraining programme,' Michael countered. 'Catholics have been recruited, and several dozen officers with a questionable past were retired.'

Rowbottham shrugged as if to say, 'Mackay's cosmetic changes don't convince me.'

'What does my boss say about this?' Michael wanted to make this as difficult as possible for the Brigadier.

'Sir Trevor Grace is of the opinion that NIPD should remain in charge of intelligence-gathering *and* the coordination of all surveillance operations.'

'But you and Johnny want me to go into battle for the Army?'

'Incidents like this, and the St Patrick's Day Massacre, are destroying any chance we have to preserve the ceasefire, such as it is.'

Michael peered into his empty tea cup at the dregs of Earl Grey. He had initially thought better of the Brigadier than to try such an obvious ploy. Now he felt rather disappointed that the purpose of all this candour had been to manipulate him. It was just like the good old days at the Ministry of Defence when the Army chaps attempted to get Michael 'on side' against the Air Force and Navy. Now the enemy was NIPD.

'Well, I'm grateful to you for coming here to brief me on this, but if my Secretary of State has full confidence in NIPD then I doubt whether my arguments will make any impression on him. It's much more important to get Military Intelligence and NIPD Special Branch working together in so far as possible.' Michael could have added something less polite about soldiers playing spies, and their amateurism in the face of an increasingly professional terrorist threat from both the Protestant and Catholic paramilitaries. But he metaphorically bit his lip, and allowed the Brigadier to draw his own conclusions. This would be the last cosy chat Rowbottham would initiate, for Michael was having none of the Army's little games.

When Rowbottham had gone, Michael tried to reach Sir Trevor Grace on the phone, but his boss's Rottweiler-like Parliamentary Private Secretary assured him that Army/NIPD shootouts did not merit frantic Departmental activity. The PPS's message to Michael was, 'Don't worry, there'll be a news blackout on this screw-up and their relatives'll be told they died in training. Sir Trevor has seen it all before.'

How comforting, Michael thought as he returned to his homework. The Army is plotting against NIPD, and the Secretary of State is too busy to interrupt his golf game. His initial advice to Michael had been more an order than a suggestion: keep your head down and get on with the ministerial boxes. When in doubt, drown your new ministerial appointment with paperwork – that was the rule.

Michael tried to purge his mind of the present; he focused his attention on his book, and the Falls Road Curfew.

Chapter Twelve

The following morning, Charlotte Carter received a more immediate kind of history lesson in Beechmont Avenue, just off the Falls Road. Her friend Tim, the BBC man-mountain, pointed out a faded gable-end mural that read *Gerry Adams brings us peace, the Unionists have no desire, we salute the IRA for calling this ceasefire*. The tribute was about as poetic as the mean little Spar store on the corner. It didn't look like it would stock hearts of palm, balsamic vinegar, or even avocados.

Tim and Charlotte had spent the morning strolling up and down the residential roads of West Belfast where battles had been fought and petrol bombs had been hurled for the last quarter of a century. And on and off for several generations before that, but there were no TV crews around then to record events, so no one in 'the media' made programmes about those previous Troubles.

Charlotte had been expecting West Belfast to look like the opening shots from *Coronation Street*, but the brick terraced houses were much neater and better maintained than any council estate she had encountered on the mainland. There were window boxes and hanging baskets, and the area had a tangible pride in its kinship and self-reliance. But as a nearby mural reminded her, *The weaponry has changed, but the cause remains the same*.

Tim and Charlotte continued their walk down the Falls Road, past streets with kerbstones painted in the gold, white and green of the Irish flag, and where shops and pubs had grilles over windows and wire gates over doors. The Public Library looked like a set from a *Mad Max* movie, but it was open for business, and there was a steady stream of visitors, as Tim pointed out.

'In 1970 the Army sent a regiment of Scottish Presbyterian soldiers into the Falls to restore order, which is a bit like letting the Ku Klux Klan police South Central LA. Five civilians were killed. Then the house-to-house searches began, and the Glaswegian Jimmies had a field day ripping crucifixes off the walls, and smashing pictures of the Virgin Mary. Great way to win the sympathy of the Catholic community.'

Charlotte gazed around her, trying to imagine riots in such an unremarkable setting. It was familiar the way any working-class district in the British Isles was the same as another: chip shops, launderettes, bookies, pubs, overpriced convenience stores. It was definitely Britain, albeit 1950s Britain, but extraordinary, savage events had taken place in these streets.

The odd thing was that these atrocities had occurred in Charlotte's lifetime, a few hundred miles from where she lived, and involved people who also shopped at Boots and M & S, and watched Morecambe and Wise at Christmas when they were young. But the drama had made no impression on Charlotte, or on anyone she knew. Whereas no one here was untouched by recent events. So many streets, houses and flats had been uninhabited for years, since Loyalist thugs set fire to them to drive the Catholics away.

'It isn't the Army that comes out of all this badly, incidentally,' her teacher continued. 'They've had a shitty job because the politicians in London never really told them what they were supposed to be doing here. You'd be surprised at the number of Home Secretaries and Northern Ireland Ministers who've basically said to the Army, "You boys get on with it and try to beat the IRA. Just don't pester us for a political solution, OK, because we're busy dealing with the miners or inflation".'

Tim looked around and shook his large head like a bemused bear whose honey supply had been stolen. 'If you set out to turn a population into terrorist sympathisers, you couldn't do better than to follow in the British Government's footsteps. Take internment for example: in 1971 there was a round-up of suspected IRA men, most of whom were amateurs, or totally innocent. Once they'd been locked up for a while they began to think about what was happening to their Province, and having been angry Catholic blokes when they went in, they were violent, politically-aware IRA volunteers when they came out.'

Tim gestured at another IRA mural of a phoenix rising from the ashes, and the slogan *Tiocfaidh ar la*. 'That means "our time will come",' he explained. 'Anyway, no one in London was seriously looking for a solution because they thought this would just blow over.'

'And nearly thirty years later . . .' Charlotte dug her hands deep into the pockets of her overcoat and thought about why none of this had impinged on her. What had she been doing in 1971? She'd been a little girl, living in Hertfordshire with her brother, who was now a barrister, and her father, who was a smalltown solicitor, and her mother who was a busybody then, and a magistrate now. And a Labrador called Caesar whose eventual demise under the wheels of a lorry had meant more to her than any number of dead Ulstermen.

When they returned to the car in Clowney Street, Tim drew

her attention to a weather-worn but impressive mural that declared *The people arose in '69, they will do it again at any time. Maggie T. think again, don't let brave men die in vain.*

'That's about the hunger-strikers. The people in this community couldn't believe Thatcher would allow Bobby Sands to die. It really hadn't occurred to them that she'd call his bluff.'

'Then they must be naive, sentimental people,' Charlotte remarked without malice as she got into the car. 'I'm sure it never crossed Mrs Thatcher's mind to pay any attention to Bobby Sands. She wouldn't have lost a wink of sleep over it. Hand-wringing wasn't her style.'

'So they discovered. Did you notice the way the people in this street looked at us when we arrived? It's an unfamiliar car, you see, and they were obviously worried we're Loyalists come to stiff a Taig or two. I'm serious. That's still the reality here.'

As they cruised slowly down the Falls Road, Charlotte noticed the Gaelic Culture Centre, and the street signs in both Gaelic and English. Then suddenly the car was crossing the Westlink, a modern dual-carriageway that conveniently separated the Falls district from the city centre like a medieval moat that kept troublemakers at bay. They turned left, and left again, and within the blink of an eye they were cruising down the Shankill Road, where Union Jacks flew from lamp-posts, and kerbstones were painted red, white and blue.

'I can't believe it's such a small place,' Charlotte muttered, then screwed her nose up as the smell of cheap frying fat reached her nostrils. 'I'd envisaged a huge battlefield, but they're all living on top of each other. Protestants here, and Catholics just over there.'

'That always surprises visitors to Belfast. Most of this city is pleasant leafy avenues that've never seen so much as a plate

142

hurled in anger. But here—' he shrugged at a Loyalist mural of King William of Orange '—even in the Thirties these streets were a shooting range. Now it's like Chicago or Palermo; ganglands controlled by malevolent godfathers. When one of their own steps out of line they're found with a bullet through the head in a ditch out in the country. And they'll have torture marks all over their bodies.'

Charlotte shuddered at Tim's words, and turned away to examine the modest dwellings they were passing. Was a modern Don Corleone sitting beyond those net curtains, issuing orders to his mobsters, putting out contracts on his enemies, demanding honour and respect from colleagues? Did these creatures spend the afternoon plotting to dismember close associates, then settle down for an evening watching *Emergency Room* with the family?

Charlotte observed a mother pushing a pram along the street, struggling with a plastic carrier bag of shopping and a demanding child. She was as downtrodden as the women on the other side of the peace line, but Charlotte kept that banality to herself. They all looked like miserable, working-class people who ate a bad diet, wore manmade fibres, and needed a holiday. Near the Shankill Historic Society a group of tattooed, skinheaded young men were hanging around drinking cans of beer. 'Enough to turn a dog from a gut wagon,' Tim quipped. 'There – that's my favourite.' He was pointing at a mural that read: *What do the Irish not understand about FUCK OFF?*

Charlotte gazed out of the window at the cheerless, grey, oppressive streets, and felt claustrophobic, as if she were in a prison. She caught sight of another mural that reminded the errant, but absent Catholic population, that the Ulster shooting team had won gold medals at the Commonwealth Games two years running. Should she laugh or cry?

At that moment, the Parliamentary reporter could imagine herself saying, 'Well, Tim, thanks very much. I reckon I've got the basic idea. Now I'm going back to my lovely, culturally diverse corner of London where I can yell, "the Pope is a poof!" at the top of my voice from my balcony, and no one will care.' But she didn't say anything, because Tim was pointing out new attractions, explaining more of the ghastly recent past, trying to make sense of the savagery.

Charlotte steeled herself to concentrate and empathise, and felt ashamed of her moment of weakness. 'Not a very professional reaction for a journalist,' she could imagine Rodney quipping. She didn't have to live here, after all, and it was only a few hours out of her life. And what was more, she had to prove herself with this assignment. She turned her attention to a mean-looking chapel, offering one of the twenty-six varieties of Protestantism to be found in Belfast. What a daft thing to die for, she thought idly, as they left the car for more earnest pavement-bashing.

'It freaks you, being here, doesn't it?' Tim's observation was like a fairly accurate poke in the eyes with a kebab skewer.

'Look, my angel, I feel jittery just going south of the river for an evening in London,' she sighed. 'So what's on the agenda this afternoon – a cemetery or two?'

'I have an artist friend whose work is being exhibited at the moment at Malone House. I thought we'd visit, after lunch,' Tim retorted with a slightly arch air, and led her off to the most extraordinary pub Charlotte had ever fallen into or out of: the Crown Bar, in Great Victoria Street in the centre of the city. They sat in an oak-panelled snug that was guarded by carved wooden dragons and griffins, beneath mosaics of crowns and grapes; and they ate oysters, accompanied by glasses of Beamish. Entirely what the doctor ordered. Visions of Dave Bower sitting perkily at her desk in London soon receded to the back of Charlotte's mind.

The rest of the day disappeared into an alcoholic mist of galleries, and quick-fire conversation with arty friends of Tim's who wrote plays and stage-managed operas. Charlotte didn't know anyone like that in London; while such people were sipping mineral water at the Chelsea Arts Club, the hackette and her fellow Lobby Correspondents were munching peanuts and swigging beer with half-dead national newspaper columnists in the Press Gallery Bar at the Commons.

But this evening in Belfast was of a different timbre. The BBC reporter savoured roast courgette and asparagus salad with parmesan shavings at Nick's Warehouse in Hill Street, where rundown industrial buildings were being yuppied into advertising agencies. Then Tim and his friends took Charlotte around the corner to the Duke of York for a bit of live Belfast/New Orleans jazz. After a couple of Bushmills, the oppressiveness of the Shankill Road was the last thing on her mind.

At about the same time, on the other side of the town, two NIPD officers were finishing their shift at Castlereagh Station. They had both put in several hours' overtime, that much-loved Belfast institution that ensured them a salary of £30,000 a year and three foreign holidays. Immediately after the ceasefire in 1994, overtime was discontinued, and RUC officers (as they then were) had groaned in collective agony as their earnings shrank. But the renewed bout of ethnic cleansing had remedied that, and they were booking their spring breaks in the Canaries once again.

As the two officers walked towards their cars, one told the

other about a conversation he had overheard earlier in the day. Apparently the Assistant Chief Constable had warned his underlings that the new Minister at the Northern Ireland Office wanted a more comprehensive report on the St Patrick's Day events than he had received. 'Reckon we're in for a right witch hunt,' he said.

'Come on, it doesn't mean a thing,' Ken McTaggart objected. 'A new idiot arrives at Stormont and thinks he'll start shit-stirring. But you know how it is; they soon get bored and go away again.'

'I'm just saying this Fitzgerald's going to breathe down our necks, Ken. That's what I'm saying. Even our friend in London's concerned.'

'Right,' his colleague remarked thoughtfully, and pulled out his car keys. 'Point taken. See you tomorrow.' Ken McTaggart walked on to where his car was parked.

When he exited the gates of the high security Castlereagh compound he turned right, leaving the watchtowers and corrugated-iron siding behind. He had worked at the Castlereagh interrogation centre for fifteen years now, since he had joined the RUC right after he left the Army. As far as Ken was concerned he was still a member of the RUC, but just like his colleagues he kept his views to himself when the name was changed to NIPD. It was pointless fighting about such a petty political sell-out, when they still had the war to win.

There was a good chance that Ken wouldn't survive the next wave of redundancies, or the lily-livered vetting of officers whose association with the Loyalist paramilitaries was considered 'worrying' by that spineless timeserver Sir David Mackay. Meanwhile, their gutless Chief Constable had allowed brigades of IRA men to form 'Special Battalions' to 'serve the nationalist communities'. Ken knew the logic: that it was better to have them inside the tent knee-capping their own people in the name of law and order, rather than outside the tent hurling in grenades. But the explanation didn't make it any more palatable to men who had spent their lives fighting the IRA.

Ken turned right into Ladas Drive, and at the intersection with the Castlereagh Road he went left towards the city centre. He was going for a drink at the King Richard in the heart of Loyalist East Belfast. The odds were he'd find his friend Mac there; the young fellow who had so distinguished himself in the bus on St Patrick's Day. Ken thought it was time for Mac to move onto more ambitious goals.

Tim had a tastefully decorated flat in a house in a leafy street off the Malone Road. It was south of the city centre, and an enviable ten minutes' drive from work. By the time they got home that evening Charlotte was too tired for more boozing so she made her excuses and went to bed in Tim's very Laura Ashley spare room. Poor Tim, she thought as she snuggled under the duvet like a dormouse. Halfway through the evening she had realised what it was about his shirt that had been distracting her all day: it was brand new, and still had the folds from its packaging. Had it been in her honour? She dismissed this arrogant assumption.

But her radar was sending a contradictory message. Today he had gone out of his way to show her an unspeakable time journalistically, and a great time socially. And he did give her those odd, uncritical looks that were blind to erupting zits on the forehead, or bad hair days. When they were on the BBC induction course together, Tim had followed her around like a love-sick puppy. Charlotte noticed that a rather attractive woman on the course was taking an interest in Tim, but when Charlotte had chummily asked him if he was going to move in on her, Tim had looked bewildered. 'Ach, not her,' he'd blushed. 'She's beef to the ankles like a Mullingar heifer.' With that obscure insult the young woman was banished to oblivion, and he had resumed his attentive but ineffectual pursuit of Charlotte.

God help him, she thought from the security of her bed. I'm not worth the effort. Was he really interested in her, but too gentle a gent to make the lunge? She squeezed her eyes shut and tried to imagine screwing him. No. Nice guy, funny, great company. But not her type. How many decent, amusing, sensitive men wilted and died at the phrase 'not my type' or 'I want to stay friends'?

How unfair, thought Charlotte, who was not currently inundated with offers from what she considered to be appropriate sources, such as Michael Fitzgerald. Instead she was stalked by shits like Eddie Power, or good, steady victims like Tim. She wriggled in the bed and turned over violently, trying to dispel an image from her mind. No, it was back. Tim was simply too earnest, too keen to please. She could imagine an awkward scene in bed, when she was explaining that she needed a bit of stimulation with a finger or tongue before the pummelling bit. He would be understanding and treat what followed like a science lesson, giving the clitoris a tentative prod as if it was a slug under a rock. Charlotte would inevitably lose concentration and lie there wondering if she had remembered to pay the gas bill. Oh, horror. Mercifully sleep overwhelmed Charlotte before more humiliating images could torment her.

The mysteries of the female orgasm were not on Ken McTaggart's mind tonight as he entered the King Richard, a fake Tudor pub with a Union Jack outside, and the sturdy metal grilles on the windows that accompanied such a declaration of patriotism. The off-duty NIPD officer found his long-time friend Mac at the bar, and they settled themselves at a table away from the noise of the gaming machines, with pints of beer in front of them.

'We can expect the new arrival from London to tighten up ship a bit,' Ken said tersely.

Mac licked the froth from his upper lip, but it was hard to tell if the warning had penetrated his wall of preoccupation. 'I'll pass that on,' he said at length.

It was in the back room of a pub like this one, a few streets away, that Mac had participated in his first 'romper room', seven years ago. A group of them had been drinking, discussing the latest IRA outrage, and wondering what they could do to hit back, to defend their community. As the night wore on they decided to do a job, and drove into West Belfast where they picked up a drunken Taig stumbling out of a bar – the Laurel Leaf in Gilbert Street. They stuffed him in the back and drove like shit. Then in the back room of their pub, the 'romper room', they all had a go at him. Afterwards they dumped the body on a patch of waste ground in Hornby Street, behind a parade of shops. No one found it until the next day. It wasn't human anyway. There had been several other non-people through the romper room since then too.

Mac sensed that Ken was in a gloomy mood tonight. Like everyone else, he knew that NIPD had been retiring the men who lived in the twilight world between the paramilitaries and the forces of law and order. 'So is the axe getting nearer?' Mac asked in his usual sensitive, comforting manner.

'It's this cleansweep regime. NIPD's got to be seen to be starting afresh, clearing out the old sectarian attitudes.' He mimicked Sir David Mackay's clipped way of speaking. 'But our men won't stand by and let everything through this fucking Assembly. Or these cross-border commissions. They're the fucking end, they are.'

'What d'you mean about "our men"? The politicians?' Mac countered. ' "Our men" are a bunch of fucking cowards who turn up when there's votes to be had so they can get elected to these cushy committees, and all. And then "our men" tell the world how bad we are for giving the Paddys a bit of rough. But we're useful enough when there are fucking Taigs running down the streets chucking petrol bombs. Then the people love us, all right. It's just at elections they want some respectable wanker in a tie with a bit of breeding.'

'Reverend Scott's bloody popular here. And he's the nearest thing we've got to a leader,' Ken countered apathetically.

'I don't know how you go for all that shite God Bob spouts. He's a fucking tool, he is; and so's his Loyal fucking Unionist Party. Scott says he doesn't like this Assembly, but he stood for it, didn't he? And he takes the money too, thank you very much!'

The NIPD officer shrugged and took a mournful slurp of his beer. Mac left Ken with some friends playing a game of darts; he was too angry to stay and hear the NIPD man's whining about how tough life was on £30,000 a year. Instead he fetched his car, and drove out on the Castlereagh Road into an altogether nicer part of town. On Cregagh Road he stopped to use a public phone, and rang Neil to check that it was OK to pay a visit. Two minutes later he was sitting in Neil's kitchen, while the ever-silent Mrs Neil made him a cup of tea. Her husband was issuing orders to the troops via his mobile phone, like a Wall Street *arbitrageur* dealing in the Japanese market in the middle of the night.

When Neil was finished, Mac passed on the hearsay about the new Northern Ireland Minister and his crackdown on passing sensitive information. Neil stroked King Billy, who was sitting on his knee like a canine Sphinx, and listened to his lieutenant. The report was a regular event, an essential part of the link between Neil and their friends in high places.

'I suppose it was to be expected,' he commented vaguely. 'Now, I want to try out an idea on you, lad. You know how the IRA used to plant one bomb to flush people into the path of a second bomb? Well, I've come to thinking that we should be planting Bomb One to attract the police and squaddies away from our real targets. Think about it; it means we can plant devices where there's normally high security. Neat, eh?' His eyes sparkled with child-like pleasure.

Mac agreed. 'So who's our real targets?' he asked.

Neil grinned enigmatically. 'That depends on what we want, and from whom we want it.'

The next morning, Tim took Charlotte for a drive around the city to see the sights before she got down to work: Queens University, the imperious City Hall and Donegal Square, the Albert Memorial that was a miniature version of Big Ben, and the hills that towered over the metropolis. Charlotte was equally interested in the small things that marked it out as a war zone: the tannoy in the multi-storey car park that constantly played pop music to ensure that the sound system was always working in case they had to broadcast a bomb warning; the yellow barriers that could be brought down at any time to seal off some part of the town; the vast number of BBC Outside Broadcast vehicles parked at Television Centre, ready to speed off to wherever news was breaking.

Then it was down to business: Charlotte collected a crew and headed south to Stormont, where she was to interview the

Reverend Robert Scott in his offices at the Assembly. She had been dreading this encounter because, like any normal English person, she found his fire-and-brimstone rhetoric vulgar and disturbing. The Celtic passion was embarrassing, particularly when he was protesting his very Britishness. Yet, as he stumbled to his feet to shake hands with the young reporter, he was smiling as benevolently as might a favourite uncle. He was even shorter than she had imagined he would be, and his hand felt delicate, as if his bones were like a bird's, that could easily be crushed.

The crew set up their gear and Scott asked Charlotte some benign questions about her assignment. But once the tape was rolling, and the first question was out of her mouth, she remembered why the good Reverend frightened her.

'This Assembly may limp on, but one thing is for sure,' he stated prophet-like, with a dramatic quiver in his high voice. 'There will be no discussion of a united Ireland; and unless that is understood there is no point in pussyfooting around the Irish Government. The people of Ulster have had enough of surrender, surrender, surrender, and they will go no further,' he added with an indignant shake of his ginger curls. Just to complete the picture, the eyes bulged and the lips were distended. 'Nor will we debate constitutional niceties with terrorists who leave the negotiating table to bomb innocent civilians. Moreover, Dublin must drop its threats and imperial fantasies.'

'But in the referendum, the Irish people voted *in favour* of the negotiated settlement that respects the will of the majority in Ulster,' she retorted mildly. 'And opinion polls south of the border consistently show that the Irish don't want unity with Ulster today or tomorrow.'

'All part of their cunning game. They're just trying to lull the people of Ulster into a false sense of security. But we will not be fooled. They have only one thing on their agenda, and that is the disembowelment of our Province. Just look at what they're doing with these cross-border commissions. You mark my words; those commissions will bring us a united Ireland through the back door.'

Charlotte's eyebrows arched in amazement. There was no need to prompt him to continue because he was clearly on automatic pilot. The thin, squeaking voice had expanded like a balloon to fill the office, as if to compensate for his physical shortcomings. 'It is a sorry day when the craven Government of the United Kingdom engages in a courting ritual with an alien power,' he raged at some unseen point in space just above Charlotte's head.

'This is treachery, and the British Government are traitors. Dublin is just biding its time, and waiting for the British to leave Ulster to the whims of the men of violence. They have been bought off by the promises of gold from the corrupt demagogues in America.'

During the sermon Charlotte sat back and studied God Bob's body language; tense, pale-lipped, retentive, constipated, but oddly theatrical and charismatic. Charlotte was intrigued by the way he pronounced 'British' as if it had no 't' – 'Bri'ish'. All his words emerged as if he had just broken a tooth, or his dentures were slipping down his throat. Here was the man of God who believed that only 'the chosen' could be saved by being reborn, and the rest of us were damned for ever, no matter what good we did in our daily lives. If his Protestant Ulster was Eden, then Charlotte reckoned she'd rather go down to the hot place: at least Hendrix and Duke Ellington would be there.

When the Reverend Scott had puffed himself out on Dublin's

duplicity, and the homosexualist, child-abusing Church of Rome, the reporter asked him for his solution, but rather confusingly, God Bob did not appear to have registered her question. He steamrollered on about blood 'n' guts like the Alice Cooper of politics. Charlotte tried again, but her words bounced off his wall of sound, and disappeared.

However, when the interview was over the Wrath of God suddenly switched from A.C. to D.C., and was all charm and warmth. He had done his turn, and hadn't disappointed the crowds, and now he could sip his tea and remark that his wife was trying to get him to give up sugar but that he was rather a naughty fellow and kept slipping two cubes into his cup when her back was turned.

Charlotte and the crew crawled out into the corridors of Stormont, dazed from their verbal battering. She had failed to extract anything of interest, and in the interviews that followed every politician she spoke to played their part predictably. By the end of this fruitless morning, the reporter despaired of getting an original angle on the emerging politics of the new Stormont Assembly.

That afternoon she settled into the seat of the British Midland shuttle to Heathrow and contemplated the abyss: it was sporting a 1970s Dustin Hoffman haircut, and it had already given her a formal warning.

Chapter Thirteen

At the headquarters of the Northern Ireland Police Department, a stone's throw from Stormont, Irene Taylor was puzzling over the photocopier records during her lunchbreak. Mrs Taylor, a wiry, grey-haired woman in her fifties, had been an administrator there for the past five years, and one of her duties was to allocate the costs of photocopier use between NIPD's various sections and departments. For this purpose a notebook was attached to every photocopier in the building, and whenever someone used it they entered their departmental code number, how many copies they had taken, and when. Since the machine had its own counter, it was possible to keep a tally of how many copies were actually made, as opposed to registered. Naturally not everyone was strictly honest, nor did they remember to fill in the details when they were in a hurry. But by and large the system worked.

This afternoon, Taylor was pondering three different dates over a two-week period on which anonymous photocopies had been made on the same machine, in the Records Section of the Special Branch. They were anonymous because no one had recorded them or signed for them. Yet the machine's counter testified that they had been made. Mrs Taylor was acquainted with the people who used the photocopier in that part of the building, and they were usually scrupulous and consistent in their entry of details in the little book. That was why the three phantom photocopies were interesting; all had occurred on the same dates as another irregular series of events in the same department.

One of Irene Taylor's additional duties was to monitor the records of who took out which secure files, and when. This system had been instituted two years before, after a leak of documents embarrassed the top RUC brass, as they then were. Taylor could not recall the minutiae, but she thought the fuss was about a list of informants that had gone missing. Since then there had been another notebook dedicated to recording who pulled out which files in Special Branch. The notebook was held by the secretary who had access to the files, and who ensured that every officer who made a request also recorded who he was and when he looked at the file. And, equally vital, when he returned it.

What interested Taylor that lunchtime was the coincidence; on the three occasions in the last month when an unfamiliar signature appeared in the notebook, there were also three phantom photocopies. Taylor walked upstairs to ask the secretary if she remembered anything about who had made the strange and as yet unidentified signature in her book. The woman raised her eyebrows and squinted at the scrawls in question. At first she was defensive because she could not recognise the signature. Only three or four officers regularly took out these specific files, and their initials were easy to identify. She glared at Taylor over the rims of her half-moon spectacles and assured her that she'd know if someone new was asking for access.

Then she sniffed triumphantly, and reached for her pocket diary: she had been away on all three occasions on a two-week holiday to Menorca, and a temp was working in her place, she announced with satisfaction. Yet again it had been confirmed to her that she was irreplaceable. Look what occurred when she went away.

Taylor thanked the secretary for her trouble, and obliged her by promising to buy some of her raffle tickets for the Ulster Hospital kidney machine appeal. Then she returned to her department, and flicked through the other photocopying records looking for another example of the mystery signature so she might learn his identity. Nothing. She walked around the building surreptitiously examining the noticeboards in case her mystery man had signed up for the soccer team or the office outing to *Sunset Boulevard*. No such luck. She made a photocopy of both notebooks, and naturally, she registered the facts afterwards in the photocopying notebook.

That evening, Irene Taylor showed the photocopies from NIPD HQ to her husband, Brian, who was a schoolteacher at the Methodist College. When she had explained the relevance of the three dates, and the secretary's absence, they sat at their dining-room table, wondering whom to tell. Mrs Taylor didn't want to lose her job, and her very act of leaking might be regarded as a hostile act by some members of her own community.

They had a cup of tea, and discussed it a while longer. Then Brian Taylor recalled a young reporter who'd done a very sympathetic piece on the Methodist College's attempts to offer non-sectarian education. A giant of a man, and since then Brian had seen him on the box every week. He told his wife he would try to remember the fellow's name. Then they settled down to watch the news together.

The following morning, Charlotte was in an editing suite in

the News and Current Affairs wing of The Spur at BBC Television Centre. Like all such suites it was tiny, and stacked with expensive video-tape editing equipment that generated so much heat that the claustrophobic cells had to be cooled, even in winter. Somehow the air conditioning never quite removed the smell of the crisps, pizza, and coffee that its inhabitants consumed in industrial quantities.

Charlotte was reviewing and editing the interviews from her trip to Belfast, and they made boring viewing. The party spokesmen were actors whose overfamiliarity with the role made their performances stale. More depressing still, there was no point at which their different lines converged. The politics of Ulster seemed destined to remain static, unlike Charlotte's career which was going down the drain.

Her editing was interrupted by a phone call from Tim. She assumed that he was returning her earlier message in which she thanked him for taking care of her in Belfast, but he was uncharacteristically abrupt.

'I had an interesting conversation last night, after our regional news programme went out. On my way home I went to see this nice couple who live near me, as it turns out.'

Charlotte grabbed a pen and took down notes as Tim explained the woman's findings. 'This phantom photocopier was doing his business in the two weeks before St Patrick's Day. Now, it's impossible to prove which files were involved, but this has to be more than a coincidence.'

'What are you going to do now?' Charlotte asked breathlessly. What she meant was, 'This is the scoop I've been searching for: will you let me run with it, dear Tim?' Here was the story that would leave Rodney and the hateful Dave Bower gnawing off their fingers in jealousy.

'You mean, what are *you* going to do,' Tim corrected her. 'I'm not on first-name terms with the new Northern Ireland Minister responsible for security in the Province. You are. So you go and tell him.'

'Does this mean you aren't running this?' Charlotte asked, incredulous.

'Oh, for fuck's sake, Charlotte! This is the real world, and the woman who gave me this information could have the men with the Black and Deckers arrive at her front door if anyone knew what she'd found. This is really serious. It's not about getting a scoop story. It's about making NIPD plug the leaks in their security machinery. To save lives!' Tim added testily. 'You don't achieve that by embarrassing them in a wanky little exposé on TV.'

Charlotte's ears and cheeks burned, and she wanted to crawl under the desk to hide. 'So what do I tell him?'

'Don't explain the source any more than you have to. Just suggest that Special Branch should tighten up their procedures for borrowing this certain category of files. And while we're on the subject of security, it's obvious someone inside the Northern Ireland Office is leaking sensitive documents to God Bob. How else did he know about the US Air Force coming to Derry? It's as if someone is deliberately trying to throw as many spanners into this new Assembly as possible. Tell Fitzgerald about it, Charlotte. He'll think of a way to stop it. That's what these cretins are for.'

'Right,' Charlotte croaked meekly. 'Will do. And thanks so much for all the nannying. I'll return the favour one day,' she stumbled on, still cowering and chastised. 'I'm looking forward to the arrival of my artistic purchases, by the way. Come and inspect them when you're next in London. I might manage to hang them on the wall by then.'

'Got to go. Call me if you hear anything I should know.' And he was off the line, leaving Charlotte feeling like a small child who had wandered into an adult world by mistake. Then she was overwhelmed by a bitter wave of self-disgust. Rodney had frightened her so much that she was beginning to react like Dave Bower.

She leaned on the editing desk, buried her head in her hands, and tried to clear her mind. What price is too big a price to pay for a bloody mortgage? she wondered. Who the hell are you, and what do you want to achieve in your silly little life? I want to be true to myself, she concluded simply. Sod Rodney and his job. She reached for the phone.

Five minutes later she had failed to penetrate the protective barrier of Esther and Mandy in Michael Fitzgerald's office, but she did glean that the Minister would vote in the ten o'clock division tonight. So if Charlotte loitered around the Members' Lobby she should be able to catch him. What did it matter that her shift this week was theoretically 9 until 7 p.m.? What else had she got to do this evening, apart from hanging around the Commons like a desperate tart? Nothing. Zip, as Tim would put it.

'Look, I'm not doing auditions for a stage version of *Reservoir Dogs*, so how would you gentlemen like to remove the sunglasses? You look ridiculous.' Neil waved at the chairs around his kitchen table, indicating that his visitors should sit down.

'This meeting is long overdue,' Neil said as a preface to their discussion, but he stopped when he noticed that one of the five men had pulled a pack of cigarettes out of his pocket, and was about to light up. 'Not in here,' their host snapped. 'You can gas yourself for all I care, but in this house we care about our health.'

His pale lips settled back into a hard line, like a slash in his chubby face.

Neil disliked these extremely rare occasions when he had meetings in his house: too many of the comrades dragged in mud on their boots, and left an unpleasant smell in the air when they had returned to their natural habitat in East Belfast and the Crumlin Road. This batch were of a slightly better caste. Some were considered thoughtful compared to the likes of Mac the bus conductor. Others present served a commercial purpose; they facilitated the legitimate front businesses like pubs and clubs.

The IRA were always much better at thinking and raising money because they attracted more middle-class help: accountants, lawyers, tax specialists and bankers to help them do their money laundering. Neil was thankful when he found colleagues who could spell, or stand in an enclosed space without farting.

This afternoon they were considering strategy. That meant Neil told his deputies 'the line' which they took back to their people as if it was written on tablets of stone. Any serious grassroots dissent was usually communicated back to this unlikely Moses in his baggy grey tracksuit. He in turn would consult the Loyalists' friends on high.

After the success of Boston, Neil wanted to turn their attention south of the border, to Eire. His political associates believed the Irish would begin agitating for the cross-border commissions to take on more executive powers, thereby usurping power from London and Stormont.

'We've been losing out to those Irish bastards for the past thirty years,' one colleague jabbed the air. 'But they'll soon back off when they know what it's like to have the heart ripped out of their city.'

'So d'you think this'll be OK?' Neil asked. The assembled

company nodded emphatically. Giving the Irish a shot across the bows would be popular in the Orange Lodges and pubs frequented by their supporters. Neil rubbed his pudgy fingers over his pale, closely-shaven chin. 'Hey, can we have some coffee in here?' he called out to his wife, Jane, who was sewing in the next room. 'Oh, that reminds me, she needs to go to the shops. Can one of your drivers take her there this afternoon, while we're debating whether Krzysztof Kieślowski sold out when he stopped making films in Poland and moved to France?'

There were blank faces around the table, then one of the guests cleared his throat. 'Sure, she can take mine. Are you having trouble with yours?' he ventured.

'No, but I wouldn't let my wife drive,' Neil said proudly. 'I don't think driving is feminine. Now, let's have your report from Dublin. Which of my targets will work?'

When the coffee had arrived Neil pulled himself up straight in his chair. 'Now, you gentlemen should get used to drinking this. This is decaffeinated coffee.' He enunciated each word separately and clearly as if he were teaching English as a foreign language. 'Caffeine puts far too much stress on your heart and circulatory system—'

'—as opposed to membership of the UVF, for instance?' one of the colleagues suggested. No one else dared to smile under the weight of Neil's cold, baleful glare.

Charlotte was killing time in the Commons before Michael arrived to vote. It was eight o'clock and she could have murdered a bottle of bubbly, but the newshound needed someone appropriate with whom to drink it, so she could charge it to expenses. Perhaps a wander into the Lords might produce a suitable victim?

She found the perfect candidate emerging from the gentlemen's lavatory with a shocked expression on his distinguished, wrinkly features, as if he had just been beamed down from a more rational world. Here was the man to tell her what she wanted to know about Sir Trevor Grace.

'Lord Bolton,' she said pleasantly as she approached the six foot three scarecrow, a man renowned for his passionate pro-European views ('I fought through a world war, and I have every reason not to want another one'). In other words he was a hero to half the Tory Party and a headcase according to the rest. 'How are you these days?'

He squinted his eyes to focus on the young reporter, and when he realised it was Charlotte, he smiled and revealed years of dental neglect. Lord Bolton was a little unsteady on his feet, and his baggy, threadbare suit was crumpled, as if it had been slept in, but Charlotte knew the hereditary peer well enough to overlook his dishevelment. It was due to age, not alcohol.

They headed for the Pugin Room, one of the Palace of Westminster's more pleasant bars, with a bay window overlooking the Thames. It had inviting leather armchairs and sofas, and above its oak panelling, the walls were hung with the vigorously patterned paper that Pugin himself had designed. Charlotte adored the camp Gothic grandeur of the place, which was vastly preferable to some of the other bars in the vicinity where you had to fight to stay standing.

'I need your help to make sense of something concerning your great party,' she began when the old boy had gulped down half a glass of champagne, and sunk back in a sturdy, comforting chair.

He snorted. 'My dear, there are many things about my great party that I can't make sense of myself. Still, I suspect you're using your usual technique to get me to tell you more than I should.' He crossed one long, thin, arthritic leg over the other and his face registered pain. What could a healthy young woman say to comfort an old man whose body was collapsing? This evening she would keep her platitudes to herself.

'Why is the Conservative Party still committed to the Unionist cause in Ulster? You know, the official name is "The Conservative and Unionist Party", but I don't really get it.'

Lord Bolton ran thin, blue-veined fingers across his forehead as if he was reading Braille. 'They believe in the constitutional entity called the United Kingdom of Great Britain and Northern Ireland. That's it, put simply; it's God-given. That's why the same cast of characters hate Europe. It threatens their vision of our sovereign nation. And of course the Unionists hate Europe because it's full of Catholics.'

'So if someone's anti-European there's a chance he's also pro-Unionist? Take Trevor Grace, for instance.'

'No, Charlotte, *you* take Trevor Grace, by all means.'

'Grace fought a long, tough anti-Brussels battle. Would I be correct in thinking he's probably sympathetic to the Unionists?'

Bolton nodded. Then he took a sip of champagne, and lingered over his next sentence. 'I doubt whether he really cares one way or other about Ulster, though. Trevor Grace has his eye on becoming Foreign Secretary.'

'*What?*'

Bolton held up a shaky finger to indicate that there was more to the story. 'He wants to be the leader of a new model anti-European Conservative Party. You must remember that no one cares a fig about Ulster, whatever they tell you. The real issue is Europe, the Achilles' heel of my splendid party. And don't write Grace off. He's a very ambitious man who's biding his time to stir up anti-European backbench feeling once more.'

'How?'

'Well, haven't you noticed how often he tells his own side of the Commons that the Eurocrats have made the Northern Ireland Office do this or that? You know, abolish pints of milk in Belfast, or whatever. He's always using it as an excuse to do something that annoys the Unionists. He says, "Don't blame me, this is what the monsters in Brussels have dictated". But the point is this.' Lord Bolton lowered his voice conspiratorially. 'When you get him behind closed doors with the people who decide how to dole out Euromoney, Grace never puts up a fight. He doesn't even ask for more than he knows he's going to get.'

Charlotte pursed her lips thoughtfully. 'So he doesn't behave like a proper negotiator who would naturally start by asking for a hundred while knowing he'll have to settle for fifty? Is that it? Grace asks for fifty, and ends up with only twenty-five?'

'Quite. But why should he care, because it's only Ulster. In reality he's letting the Europeans dictate the terms attached to these whopping great cheques we get. You know, abolishing quarter-pounder cheeseburgers, or putting the Pope's face behind Post Office counters throughout the Province. Apparently the Eurochaps are amazed he never asks for more.'

'What's he up to?' Charlotte asked, although she had guessed, and was more interested that Lord Bolton knew about quarter-pounder cheeseburgers, when most Lords hadn't heard of Paul McCartney, let alone fast food.

'I'll tell you what he's up to, my dear. He's running his bloody election campaign from the Northern Ireland Office. And one day he'll turn around and say, "Look at the Euro-interference we had in Northern Ireland. That was a test-market for the muscles of Brussels. Given half a chance, these Belgians and Spaniards will tell us how to run our own country in the same way". That sort of nonsense. Pure opportunism. Heaven knows if he even cares about Europe, for that matter. Grace is simply taking a gamble that the Party will be frothing at the mouth for an anti-European leader.'

Charlotte bit her lower lip, and watched a new indignation animate Lord Bolton's otherwise exhausted demeanour. 'Let's have some more champagne,' she suggested. Now she had even more to tell the Northern Ireland Minister.

Chapter Fourteen

Michael Fitzgerald got back from Belfast that evening at about
eight o'clock, which meant that he had time to check in at the
Northern Ireland Office before the ten o'clock division. As
usual, he found signs that his civil servants had combed Admiralty House for obscure documents requiring immediate action
to stick in his ministerial boxes. What intrigued and irritated him
was that discussion papers on the role of badger tunnels in
Northern Ireland remained in his in-tray, when such weighty
political matters would have been perfect material for the new
Assembly and its committees to get their teeth into. Instead of
which the contentious and explosive issues went to the Assembly, and Michael was left with the rules and regs for the making
of goat's cheese in the Province.

At ten to ten the Minister and his driver, and their security
detail, drove the short distance from Admiralty House, down
Horse Guards Parade, right into George Street and across Parliament Square to the Palace of Westminster. Michael left the two
men playing cards in the car while he hurried in to vote.

The Members' Lobby was swimming with chattering suits,
and the decibel output of each mouth was in ratio to the volume
of House of Commons's subsidised wine consumed with that

MP's subsidised dinner. The subject on everyone's moist lips this evening was the announcement that Peter Tollmarch MP wouldn't be standing at the next election: another victory for truth. Michael narrowly missed being drawn into conversation by a cheeky young fool of an MP whose ambition was greater than his talent or ability. Then he spotted the back of a familiar chestnut-coloured head. Charlotte was being talked at by a notorious proportional representation fanatic, so Michael politely butted in and extracted her.

'Would you like a drink after this division?' His expression communicated both his exhaustion and thirst. By contrast she looked pleased that he had sought her out, rather than the other way around. While he voted and warned his driver that he would be longer than expected, Charlotte returned to the Pugin Room, where she had lately been gossiping with Lord Bolton.

Five minutes later Michael sank into a generously padded leather seat, and was handed a glass of champagne by his saviour from the BBC.

'I had a bizarre meeting with the Reverend Robert Scott and his cronies this morning,' he said. 'Oh, by the way, this is off the record, as per. Anyway, he told me that all the previous Ministers of State were closet Fenians, and at least this time the Prime Minister had stopped the pretence and appointed a representative from the Vatican to the post.'

'Wait – don't tell me. He then delivered a speech with all the spontaneity of a metronome, and didn't hear a damned thing you said.' When Michael nodded, Charlotte told him about her interview with God Bob the previous morning. The Minister laughed wearily.

'The only variation on your encounter is that he literally read his speech from a piece of paper. His eyesight isn't so good, and he kept losing his place. I asked him if, after all these years, he had reconsidered any of his political positions, or ever re-examined his strategy. Being compared to Chairman Mao didn't please him, or his MPs, who don't like people to assume that they're under God Bob's total control.'

'Do I surmise that you're going for a bit of divide and rule?'

'There were definite signs of tension on the faces of those fine, upstanding defenders of Ulster. By the way, they turned up looking like an undertakers' convention.' He mimicked their clipped Belfast voices, and Charlotte laughed louder than she'd intended. She covered her mouth with her paw as demurely as possible, then her eyes narrowed as she considered Michael's strategy. Here was the man who was going to keep his head down and wait for promotion to a more suitable ministry.

'So you're trying to do a deal with one of God Bob's deputies?'

'I haven't got that far but there's one chap who interests me, McKinnley. He's the Clint Eastwood type; strong and silent, hard as nails. For a start that means he's had much more hands-on experience of the struggle than the rest of these wanky politicians.'

'Is McKinnley the one who the Army picked up one night on the border in the company of some shady, but well-armed men?' she asked.

'McKinnley makes Enoch Powell look like Mother Theresa. But he's basically a pragmatist, he wants power, and I suspect he might be up for a deal. I've got to check him out.'

'Careful, Michael. I'm serious. And I meant to tell you something I heard about your beloved Elvis: he's probably a closet-Unionist. He's certainly still courting the anti-European, pro-Unionist part of the Party.'

Michael looked sceptical. 'I get the impression he thinks all sides in Ulster are scum. You know, the "curse on both their houses" philosophy. "Let's pull out and let them get on with it".'

'Anyway, *has* God Bob ever reconsidered his song and dance?' Charlotte asked with a teasing smile.

'Certainly not,' Michael barked in a fair imitation of the Reverend Scott. Then he gestured at the waiter for another half bottle of champagne. 'Betrayal, retreat, surrender-all because London is pussyfooting around the Papists,' he growled, and watched Charlotte giggle appreciatively.

'I made the point that I knew rather better than he did what it was like to be ruled by Rome, having had ten years at Ample-forth where there was an unhealthy preoccupation with prevent-ing pubescent boys from masturbating – which is nothing if not ambitious. Well, at this point there was a spark of light in the eyes of the undertaker's apprentices, but God Bob just chugged on, pre-programmed to rave. Hadn't heard a word I'd said.'

'Pity they keep re-electing him.' Charlotte made her point gently.

'And it's strange his voters don't demand more from him. He always has a new excuse for wrecking peace initiatives, and yet no blame attaches. It's a mystery. All my predecessors have indulged his whims and done this elaborate dance around him, trying to keep his temper sweet, as if he's a greedy, monstrous baby,' the Minister muttered as he refilled their glasses.

'But I heard in Belfast that Scott is actually a pretty good MP. If you've got a blocked drain, or your street-lights don't work, then God Bob's your man. Well, can you imagine how the local council maintenance department must react when they pick up the phone and it's God Bob on the other end, screaming about eternal damnation unless they fix Mrs Narg's leaking tap.'

'And threatening to send the Archangel Gabriel and the boys around to kneecap them,' Michael commented between swigs. 'I asked God Bob if there were any local issues he wanted to raise, and he hadn't a clue what I was talking about. So I mentioned the fact that the eleven-plus exam results in the Shankill area are the worst in Northern Ireland; but he just stared at me as if I was fondling a rosary right there in front of him. Then I asked what he wanted the Government to do about the extraordinary levels of male unemployment in the working-class Loyalist areas of Belfast. No interest,' Michael said in disgust.

'He probably thought you were trying to trick him, or deflect him from his mission.'

'Silly me.' Michael waved a self-mocking limp wrist. 'There is only one political subject on God Bob's agenda, and it's God Bob. And Charlotte, my dear, the language these people use! During the meeting, the Boss went to the lavatory to drink the blood of Jesuits, or whatever it is he does to top up the battery. When Scott was out of the room, McKinnley told me that Ulstermen were British to the very tips of their fingers and core of their bowels. It was very aggressive, clenched-fist stuff.'

'But the irony is that only a Celt would use language like that.' Charlotte shook her head in dismay. 'Except that the Celts like Gerry Adams MP go to image consultants to iron out that sort of thing.'

'I met him yesterday as well. Did you know that in Dublin they call him Armani Adams?' The Minister sniggered. 'He reminds me of that revolutionary poet in designer sunglasses who used to run Nicaragua. What was his name? Daniel Ortega. The one who made very boring speeches that sounded like a sociology textbook. Anyway, my conclusion is that we should send everyone in Sinn Fein and the IRA to the States on a junket because it really gives them the taste for constitutional politics and respectability. They'd realise what fun it is to do lecture tours, and meet Oprah, and do *Larry King Live*.'

'And Richard Attenborough or Steven Spielberg could make a movie about their struggle,' Charlotte chipped in. 'Then they'd get to go to the Oscars and make a daft speech.'

'They're dreadful people. D'you know, I've only encountered one grown-up in Ulster politics: John Alderdice who runs the Alliance Party.'

'And he's a psychiatrist, which explains it, doesn't it? Now, to change the subject entirely, I have something important to tell you. But please, please, don't let me down by revealing the source, or there could be awful consequences. You're taking a rocky path now, not the one that's going to enhance your career. I'm serious, Michael.'

She stared hard at him, until his indulgent grin vanished.

Chapter Fifteen

Two days later, Michael was back in Belfast for a 10 a.m. session with Sir David Mackay, the Chief Constable of NIPD. The Minister asked Mandy to sit in because she was often insightful, and she noticed nuances or side glances that Michael never picked up because he was, by his own admission, too busy talking.

'So, let's begin with the shoot-out at Jack Heaney's house,' Michael prompted. 'Remind me why your men invaded a kiddies' party. Granted, Spock is a deeply evil man with blood on his hands, but is he silly enough to have an arms dump in the garden shed?'

The Chief Constable perched on the edge of his chair, and his dark eyes narrowed into Brazil-nut shapes as Michael persisted: 'I'm new to this job, but I'd have to be a simpleton not to notice that the Army and NIPD seem to spend considerable time and energy plotting against each other rather than the terrorists.'

The Chief Constable made a sportsmanlike display of shock at Michael's analysis. 'I'm afraid I don't understand how you've come to that conclusion, Minister.'

'Military Intelligence are itching to grab overall responsibility for intelligence-gathering in the Province. They've told me – well, you know what they say about NIPD: unreliable information, sloppiness, deliberate leaks of sensitive information to Loyalist paramilitaries through a handful of your officers who live in a twilight world where they fancy themselves as James Bond commandos. Actually they remind me more of the Watergate burglars. Gordon Liddy. You recall him? He used to set his arms on fire to prove that he was tough.'

The Police Chief had begun to flush, but he managed to reply through clenched teeth. 'I will not deny that there are a few rotten apples in the barrel, but in the past two years we have taken action to weed them out, and to ensure that the leaks you refer to do not recur. And of course I should add that officers from the Roman Catholic community have joined our ranks now.'

'Then why did the St Patrick's Day Massacre occur? Has anyone been sacked as a result of your internal enquiry?' pressed Michael.

The flush grew darker. 'The St Patrick's enquiry is continuing, Minister. But may I remind you that there is no evidence whatsoever that any information was passed to the paramilitaries who conducted those attacks.'

'That's not what Military Intelligence says. Remember, Chief Constable, you're up against the Army, and they're the Napoleons of plotting. Now, you have to convince us, the politicians, that you deserve to maintain the lead position in Intelligence.'

The Chief Constable was looking very uncomfortable, his back ramrod straight, and his eyes bright as marbles. Michael wondered how often his predecessors had instigated these blunt conversations with Mackay. Perhaps they had beaten about the bush a bit more. Maybe they hadn't bothered at all because they were busy following Grace's advice to keep their heads down. Michael pushed that depressing conclusion to the back of his mind.

'The only thing I'm interested in, is stopping the Republicans getting sympathy and support from the minority in this Province. It's just like the bad old days when your patrols did 5 a.m. house searches for no particular reason. It turned people against you.'

'Can you provide examples of this alleged behaviour? I'll have every incident investigated.' Mackay's voice was clipped and tight, like a disrespectfully plucked violin.

Michael slumped back in his chair and waved his hands as if he was shooing away the Chief Constable's words. 'When the IRA finds its support has evaporated, then they'll stop throwing bombs. And that support will only evaporate when Roman Catholics stop believing they're victims, and that the police are above the law. So, I propose we try something different.' Michael plucked a sheet of paper from the closed file on his desk. The Secretary of State's initials at the foot of the page signalled that he approved of the idea, or wasn't particularly interested, which Michael suspected was more likely.

'I'd like a programme of community meetings where you and your officers are seen to be listening to people's concerns. Police forces on the mainland have been imaginative and innovative in integrating themselves into urban areas where the population is hostile to them. Perhaps you should send some of your better people to study what's being done in Toxteth and Tottenham and the East End of London. Then they might learn how consultation and sensitive community policing has begun to reduce tension. I'll need your proposals by the end of the week, you know, names of officers who would benefit from—' the Minister decided against saying 're-education' '—a trip.'

Michael smiled frostily at Sir David, who ducked his head and made a note on his notepad.

'And finally, a trifling matter, Sir David. You'll need a new system for protecting the security files in the Special Branch Records Department at NIPD HQ. At the moment there's a fairly primitive arrangement in operation. From now on, two or three officers will be responsible for monitoring which personnel look at those files. And only a certain restricted category of officer will be allowed access. I suggest you invest in some simple electronic security system, so that only those officers with the correct code can get into your files. A proper record of who examines sensitive material will be kept by officers themselves, not the administrative staff. The records will be reviewed regularly.'

Michael closed his file. 'I'd like to know what you've done about this by the close of play tomorrow,' he concluded pleasantly but firmly, like a doctor whose five-minute consultation time is up.

But as the Chief Constable gathered his belongings, Michael continued in a more tentative voice. 'Incidentally, I'll fight quite hard to keep the responsibility for intelligence-gathering with NIPD.' He watched the Chief Constable's eyebrows knit together in confusion. 'I happen to believe that the problems of Northern Ireland should be solved by the *people* of Northern Ireland – which in this case means NIPD. You must be aware that a Labour Government would probably disband NIPD completely. So the more progress we make now in dealing with these problems, the less likely it is that a new government will have grounds to bury you. I look forward to your cooperation, and I hope you'll see that I am fighting your corner.'

Mackay was clearly baffled, but his eyes flashed with cold fire, and the two men parted with equally icy formality.

'Well, that was about as diplomatic as the Soviet invasion of Afghanistan,' Mandy laughed when they were alone. 'You sure you weren't a bit soft on him, Michael?'

'Oh, I can't be bothered to piss about any more.' The Minister stretched his arms above his head and yawned. 'I was looking through my predecessor's notes yesterday, and he spent too much time gently manoeuvring these people about, as if he was rearranging fragile china ornaments. Well, I'm going to set them some objectives, and make a few threats.' He yawned again and got to his feet. 'So I've already made enemies of Mackay, and Rowbottham in Army Intelligence. Not bad going, eh?'

'I hope you're prepared for their rearguard action,' Mandy warned him as they walked through the building to the waiting ministerial Range Rover.

Michael gave a humourless laugh as he held a door open for her. 'If any of this lot tried to blow me up they'd probably bomb the house I lived in five years ago. Or get the wrong Michael Fitzgerald, probably one with black skin.'

Mandy nimbly hauled herself up into the back seat of the Range Rover and slid toward her Minister who was glancing at the rest of the day's schedule. 'Or they'll raid a synagogue, thinking it's a Catholic Church,' she smirked. 'Did you know CID burst into a house in North London a few years ago, and arrested this very middle-class young couple, and kept them in a police cell all night, because they suspected they were IRA. And the couple kept saying, 'But our name is Cohen, look at our driving licences and credit cards, we're the Cohens. We're not even Irish.' And the CID guys ignored them until finally the

Cohens' lawyer arrived, and they realised they'd raided the wrong address.'

Michael clicked his tongue and rolled his eyes. 'I can't bear it.'

'So what's next?' Mandy peered at his schedule. 'Stewartstown Road Community College to see Mrs Dee of the Adult Literacy programme; the Windsor School, to see the headmaster. That's an integrated school, isn't it? Then the St Xavier Retirement Home, and the Belfast Action Trust's workshop on youth training. God, you can't get enough of this stuff, can you, Michael? You do several of these every time you're here.'

'It's useful for me to listen to people at the sharp end, and maybe it helps if they know someone in Government wants to hear what they have to say. The citizens of this Province can't rely on their MPs or their Assemblymen to represent them, after all.' He added through clenched teeth: 'Oh, and by the way, Mandy, we've got a camera crew from the BBC following us around today. D'you know Charlotte Carter? She's doing a piece on the politics of the Assembly, poor woman.'

'What politics?' Mandy sneered in a manner that she obviously assumed was attractive.

'Oh, Charlotte has a pretty good idea what it's like. And this afternoon we're off to Armagh to see the massed ranks of the Catholic Church. I hope they're not expecting me to kiss their rings,' he muttered with an absent-minded scan of his typewritten speech. 'Christ, this is mealy-mouthed crap. Who wrote it?'

Mandy ran her eyes over the first couple of paragraphs. 'Oh, that's Kirk Douglas. You know, the principal who looks like Kirk Douglas.' She pointed at her chin, as if that explained everything, which it did.

'Well, he writes more like Captain Kirk than Kirk Douglas.'

Michael skimmed the text of the speech he was supposed to deliver to the Northern Ireland CBI that evening. 'And this one's pointless too. These platitudes about how the recession hasn't hit Ulster as badly as the mainland. Businessmen here'll see through that in a moment. It's their real position they're concerned about, not how well they're doing in comparison with Rwanda. Honestly, do they really expect me to spout this rubbish?' He glared out the window at the Upper Newtownards Road, and his eyes settled on the hills that appeared to be floating in the middle distance above Belfast. 'I suppose the idea is to keep me busy bullshitting harmlessly, while they carry on with the same old game. You know, I thought the Ministry of Defence was a giant wanking machine, but this is even worse.'

'Do you want me to have a go at them?' Mandy pointed at the two speeches.

'Don't bother, my celestial wordsmith, save your energy.' Michael looked away at the nondescript villas they were passing, the hideous modern library, and an ugly new Presbyterian church. He also made a mental note of the Castle Hill Chinese Restaurant, thinking it might come in useful one evening if he was working late. 'No, Mandy, I began today living dangerously by pulling Sir David Mackay's ears, and I think I'll carry on that way. I'm going to wing it with these speeches. Grace never reads the drafts, so as long as I don't invent policy I guess I'll be OK.'

'Now, Michael, don't be naughty. You know there isn't any policy.'

The Minister snorted softly in response. 'Perhaps these bloody priests would like to know about Laura's latest theory. First of all, she's polytheist, but it's more complicated than that. She reckons God is present in all whales, because they're the cleverest creatures on earth. And she thinks the dolphins are their angels.'

'Oh, that's so cute,' Mandy gushed.

'That means the Japanese and Norwegians and Faroe Islanders will die in hell. Which sounds reasonable to me. Just in case Laura's theory is correct, you should jolly well make sure you eat dolphin-friendly tuna,' Michael warned Mandy with a jesting wag of his finger.

In the event, the Minister stopped short of sharing Laura's vision of heaven and hell with his audience of Roman Catholic clerics from all over Ireland. He was addressing their annual shindig of Eminences and Holinesses in the Cathedral City of Armagh, and he had an uneasy feeling from the welcome they gave him that afternoon that they regarded him as 'their' boy.

Charlotte, who was standing at the back of the hall with her crew, couldn't suppress a broad smile when she saw how embarrassed Michael was by this adulation from his fellow Catholics. She, and her camera crew, had been beside him all morning in Belfast as he had shaken hands with old ladies, and met voluntary community workers, and asked intelligent questions of teachers at each stop in his tour around the less salubrious parts of Springmartin. He was treating his ministerial post like a permanent by-election, but if people expected meaningless, jolly small talk from Michael, they soon realised they were going to get one hundred per cent of his attention.

Michael lacked personal warmth in the conventional sense because he didn't press flesh and breathe all over people like a double-glazing rep. But he did let each individual know he was interested in what they had to say, and that he had an open mind. It was plain to Charlotte he was leaving a sea of converts in his wake. And when he insisted that his security detail stayed outside the school, or community centre he was visiting, he instantly dispelled the heavy atmosphere that normally attached to these jaunts.

After what must have been a tiring morning, Michael still had time to listen to a young mother who stopped him as he walked into the hall in Armagh where he was meeting their Reverend Fathers. She told him it was impossible for women with children to go out to work with so little nursery or crèche provision available locally. As usual Michael asked Mandy to take the young mother's name and address, and he promised her that he would get back to her.

When Michael had been applauded by the Irish Catholic hierarchy, he stepped up to the lectern and glanced around the hall. 'Sitting amongst us are some of the most important opinion leaders in Northern Ireland. You share a tremendous responsibility because in so many senses you are the moral caretakers of the communities where you preach and teach. Many of you are serving God in parts of this beautiful Province which are nothing better than ghettos; places where people feel afraid, and frustrated because they don't have work, and where society has been frozen for almost three decades. The vacuum in which you work makes your considerable achievements all the greater, in my view. Roman Catholic communities have discovered a tremendous self-sufficiency and brotherhood through these Troubles, and much of the credit for that goes to people sitting in this room.'

Heads were nodding, and Charlotte felt a perceptible glow of warmth rise from the audience as Michael continued. 'But I believe that you have a new responsibility, and that is to encourage your flock to be more confident and outward-looking; and to start behaving like citizens of this Province of Ulster.'

The word 'Ulster' was as warmly received as a handful of

crushed ice down the back of their dog collars. 'There has been a good deal of lip-service to the wider Christian interest in finding a solution to the Troubles, but we have to face the fact that the cultural divide persists in part because the Roman Catholic Church allows it. You gentlemen have held your flock together to protect them, but now you must help them to shoulder the burden of living in a country made up of people of all faiths, and not in exclusive ghettos. There is a new role for this Church in initiating contact with the Protestant community. Both sides are ignorant of the other's history and beliefs. Nothing is more symbolic of this ridiculous divide than the fact that Protestant and Catholic children in Northern Ireland who have a hearing impairment learn an entirely different form of sign language.'

Charlotte glanced from the audience up at Michael and noticed he had no notes in his hands. 'I suspect there is much to bind people together here – such as unemployment, which now affects both communities on a scale unknown in the rest of the British Isles. We can look to Liverpool for inspiration. Cardinal Warlock and Bishop Shepherd stood shoulder to shoulder in their Herculean efforts to revitalise the economy of that great city. *Why not here?*

'Better schooling is another area where the Church should have a voice. But this Church continues to discourage integrated education, if not in word then in practice, because it fears it will lose its grip on its flock – not a very positive or self-confident view of the future. This Church even refused to give First Communion to children who attended integrated schools – I'm glad that has now stopped.

'Equally, the Church must dispel the Roman Catholic community's view of itself as a victim of the imperial British

Government. Of course there has been insensitive policing, and blundering behaviour from the security forces here. But things are changing for the better, and at some point the past has to be accepted for what it is. How long can people stay angry, or keep alive some fantasy that the minute Roman Catholics make up fifty-one per cent of the population, then somehow Northern Ireland will become an Elysian meadow? Who can deny that Protestants are worried because they fear they will have to bow the knee to Rome?'

His questions hung in the air, and Charlotte noticed that the audience's warm glow of a few moments ago had become a nervous frost. If it was possible for silence to be hostile, then this was it.

'How long is it morally correct to make it difficult for parents in mixed marriages to bring up their children in a non-sectarian environment? How long can the Church comfort its members with the promise of a united Ireland that we will probably not see in our lifetime, if we're honest? And how long can the Church put off facing this fundamental decision: is a united Ireland so important that it is worth a continuing war against the Loyalists, and a ghetto-life for its community? Or is justice and reconciliation a more realistic goal? The point is *not* to discard the chapters of Irish history, but rather to turn to a fresh page.'

There was a shifting of bottoms and a few shaking heads. Charlotte quietly slipped out of the hall, into an empty corridor, and dug out her mobile phone. She called Tim in the BBC Ulster newsroom and told him to alert the *Six O'Clock* newsdesk in London that she had film of the new Northern Ireland Minister making a corker of a speech. 'You know the way they said only Richard Nixon could go to China and make peace? Well, tell them only a Roman Catholic politician can tell the Roman

Catholics to forget about a united Ireland.'

'I'm sending a despatch rider there immediately to get the tape,' Tim gibbered. 'By the way, you should tell our friend Fitzgerald that people who make remarks like this end up with bullets in the back of their heads. I thought you told me he was just another careerist?'

'It seems he's annoyed with the politicians here, so I reckon anything could happen now. We're into uncharted territory with this particular careerist,' Charlotte explained.

When she returned to her position by the camera, the audience was growling its displeasure, but there was some scattered applause too. Her camerawoman, pink in the cheeks from excitement, leaned over and whispered, 'Fitzgerald just told them their stance on contraception and divorce is at least thirty years behind the Roman Catholic Church in Eire. And that it's no wonder it scares the shit out of the Proddies when their image of contemporary Papacy is scandals about priests wandering the land abusing children, and then leaning on the Irish Government to cover everything up.'

Charlotte registered the anger and enthusiasm and disbelief on the previously blandly pious faces in the audience. Then she noticed Mandy, Michael's research assistant, who was standing to one side near the back, a cloud of fury disfiguring her normally simpering face. Surely she had known what the Minister was going to say? Why would she care anyway? Then Charlotte wondered irrelevantly, and rather uncharitably, if Mandy went about knickerless, like Sharon Stone in *Basic Instinct*.

When Michael wrapped up there was a surprising amount of applause, and although there were clusters of agitated disapproval, the Minister was immediately enveloped by chattering priests. Charlotte phoned Tim again and gave him instructions for editing the piece. An assistant producer would make a start on it while Charlotte travelled back to the BBC's Belfast studio. Then the package would be fed to London, and the *Six O'Clock News* might give it a place in its running order this evening if some touching human tragedy didn't hog the headlines. 'Here we go, here we go, here we go,' she sang to herself when she hung up.

As she left the meeting with her crew, Charlotte was alarmed to find several dozen people outside who were carrying banners and posters demanding that someone should *Save Ulster From Sodomy*. There amidst the picketers was the small but perfectly formed Reverend Scott, vigorously denouncing the whores of Christ. Her crew hastily set up just in time to tape Michael emerging from the hall and greeting God Bob as politely as if they were at the Queen's Garden Party.

The crew clambered into their Renault Espace, and they chugged back to Belfast. This was newsmaking the way Charlotte liked it: real, unplanned, and not just a string of soundbites from a stuffy Chamber full of MPs who protested too much about how honourable they were.

At a quarter to five she arrived panting and flustered at her editing suite, and shortly after, Tim poked his head around the door. 'You're heading the *Six O'Clock News* tonight. There isn't much happening, so you're it.' Charlotte suppressed a little squeal of delight and terror, and got working.

An hour and a half later, Sir Trevor Grace was turning beetroot red with anger. He had just watched Charlotte's report on the BBC bulletin, and was still staring at the television screen in furious wonder. Then he realised that he didn't care about the story on riots in the Middle East which had followed, so he switched off the remote control and stewed with anger.

'What the fuck does he think he's up to?' Grace demanded of his PPS who was slouching in a chair on the other side of the office. 'I thought he was supposed to be all smells and bells? You know, one of them! A bloody Papist!'

'He didn't actually contradict a word of Government policy.'

'That's because there isn't any fucking Government policy,' Grace snapped. 'That was the whole fucking idea. Now he's sounding like a bloody Unionist.' He chewed the side of his index finger as if it was a Chinese spare rib. 'Next thing you know, he'll be telling them to drop their "right to life" stuff.'

The PPS cleared his throat. 'Er, bad luck.'

'What?' the Secretary of State barked.

'Fitzgerald always votes for the most liberal abortion bill amendments. He's on record as being in favour of a woman's right to choose.'

Grace let his head rock back against the chair, and stared at the ceiling. 'Bloody marvellous. Why didn't someone warn us about this? I suppose there must be other ways to flush him out. Snotty little Bog Wog. What's he going to do next?'

'What was it Thatcher said about Gorbachev when she met him?' Neil mused aloud as he switched off the news that evening. 'She said, "I could do business with that man." Yeah, that was it.' He stroked King Billy's silky ears and glanced across the sitting room at his wife who was mending some socks. 'Pity Fitzgerald's a better spokesman for the cause than our own politicians,' he grumbled, and reached for King Billy's grooming brush.

The Reverend Scott was back from his demonstration in Armagh in good time to see the local Ulster news which was largely devoted to Michael's performance. Scott sucked his lower lip for five minutes, then the phone rang and interrupted his miserable rumination. 'This was not what we had in mind,' he rasped at his caller.

At seven-thirty that evening, the ministerial Range Rover collected Mandy from her flat in Fitzwilliam Street in the university area of town, and continued to Michael's modest new abode not far away, in Ireton Street. The Minister emerged from his terraced Edwardian house wearing a dinner jacket and bow tie, but without the speech that he had despaired of earlier.

When he climbed into the back beside Mandy he remarked on her evening dress. His research assistant took that as a great compliment because he had never before passed comment on her clothing. She didn't realise that he thought her tight skirts, low-cut tops and body stockings were tarty, rather than alluring. Since the night of the party in the bowels of the Northern Ireland Office Mandy sensed that Michael had moved further out of her grasp. He had never mentioned her barfing performance, but she still felt his reserve.

On the other hand, she consoled herself, he was friendly, quick to tell her what was happening and he involved her in most meetings. Whenever he was in Belfast he took her out to dinner or lunch, and pumped her for ideas on what he should do, and who he should talk to. It was hardly a consolation for Mandy, but there was clearly no one else on the horizon. She had to bide her time, and hope that he would eventually relax.

When they arrived at the Grand Ballroom of the Europa Hotel, the television cameras were waiting. This time the other networks weren't going to miss out on what the new Minister had to say. Charlotte, among the crush of journalists

and cameras, noticed that Michael's poisoned American dwarf
was wiggling along beside him, looking every inch the proud
wife in tow. If Charlotte's eyes could have sent death-rays,
Mandy would have been a heap of steaming meat on the
carpet. Instead the reporter swallowed hard and watched
demurely as Albert Morrison, the Chairman of the Northern
Ireland CBI, greeted Michael as if he was an astronaut returning from a moon landing.

Cameras flashed and reporters yelled questions, but the Minister shook his head and smiled. The CBI boss was on the point
of shepherding his celebrated party into the Ballroom where the
annual dinner was being held, when Michael hesitated and
turned around. Then his eyes settled on Charlotte and her crew,
and he motioned for them to come with him.

'I thought you were supposed to be profiling a day in the life
of a new Minister?' he winked as she caught up. 'Charlotte, meet
Albert Morrison, CBI. Charlotte and I had some fun with a room
full of priests this afternoon.'

'There's an American Senator here, by the way.' Morrison
sounded as if he was warning them not to drink the water. 'He's
on a mission to study civil rights violations in the Province.
Anyway, someone invited him to attend. I thought I should warn
you because he's not— Ah, here he is.'

Charlotte glanced over her shoulder at the camerawoman.
'Keep the tape rolling, please.' The CBI man tried to move them
into the reception and away from the youthful Senator from
Massachusetts, but his manoeuvre failed, and a moment later the
Senator was pumping Michael's hand.

'Mr Fitzgerald, it was great to hear about your promotion,'
the American said with a terrifyingly toothy smile. 'I hope
you're aware that there's concern in the United States that

your Government is moving too slowly to secure social justice and peace here,' he lectured loudly. Everyone within twenty yards had fallen silent, and looked on in horrified embarrassment as the Senator puckered his lips self-righteously.

'Perhaps we could make peace last if you and your friends in the States would stop supplying the murderers and psychopaths here with bombs and guns.' Michael smiled back brightly and raised his voice so that it carried around the room. 'And speaking of peace, did you realise that any large US city has three or four times the rate of death by violence as did the whole of Northern Ireland at the worst point in the Troubles? What are you doing about bringing peace to the streets of American cities? Perhaps the British Government should send over a Human Rights delegation to see how you treat people in East St Louis, or Harlem, or Philadelphia, or South Central Los Angeles?'

'That's totally unrelated—'

'While you're here in Belfast, why don't you visit the chip shop in the Shankill Road that your IRA friends blew up in 1992, killing nine completely innocent people? *Then* you can report back on Human Rights abuses!' Michael pushed past the Senator and started to work the crowd of dinner-jacketed businesspeople. Suddenly everyone started talking again, and the tension was broken like an elastic band snapping. The Senator hesitated, the veins on his wide forehead bulging, then he swept out of the room.

And Charlotte had it all on camera; she nearly skipped to the nearest phone. The BBC newsroom organised another dispatch rider, but Tim was off-duty, so she alerted the editor of the day that she had an interesting clip of the new Minister which they might want to offer to *Breakfast* in London, and the *Today* programme. The *Nine* might even bung it in at the end of the bulletin, if they could turn it around in time. Then she went back to her camera crew, hugging herself in celebration at her second scoop of the day.

When Albert Morrison, the Chairman of the CBI in Northern Ireland, introduced Michael, he addressed a few remarks of his own to the audience of 300 businesspeople seated at large round tables in the Europa Ballroom. Morrison stood at the microphone at the top table and checked his notes rather uncertainly. Michael, who was sitting to the right of Morrison, noticed that the man's hands were shaking. He guessed that Morrison was a few years older than he was, but his round, plump face and angelic blond hair gave him an air of innocence and vulnerability.

Yet once the man overcame his nerves he spoke with intelligence, and Michael got out a piece of paper to jot down some of the points Morrison made about Ulster's top-heavy bureaucracy, and the death of the apprentice system. The statistics he quoted were familiar: Ulster's economic success ranked a very inglorious number 126 out of 171 Euro-regions; every year 8000 young people came onto the Ulster job market, yet there were only half that number of places.

Then Morrison blinked nervously, and threw a perfunctory glance down at Michael. 'Lastly, Minister, we have a message: the businessmen and women of Northern Ireland are keen to open up commercial links with the South. There is a four-million-person market for our products and services just across the border, and the sooner we can do business there freely, so much the better. You could start by giving us a decent road and rail link to Dublin. Northern Ireland is open for business in Europe and with Eire.'

Morrison sat down to a roar of approval from his audience,

who were seventy per cent Protestant, Michael reckoned. So much for religion, he thought as he joined in the applause; let's get on with making money. Here was the great force for peace that he had overlooked. Middle-class Irishmen unite! You have only your bank accounts to consider.

Michael began his speech by praising the business community in Ulster for carrying on in less than favourable conditions since 1969, and promised he would pursue the points that Morrison had raised.

'But this evening I'd like to talk to you about politics, and the deafening silence of the centre in Ulster. I'm referring to the middle classes, the successful businessmen and women, the professionals, and the suburbanites. In other words, the people of Ulster that you represent.'

As Michael spoke, again without notes, Charlotte noticed that the rather buoyant mood of a moment ago had gone. Instead the audience was silent and still.

'You and I are kidding each other if we think that a few road-building projects, or industrial parks are going to sort out this region's economy. The investment that's necessary to rebuild Ulster isn't going to happen until there is real, permanent peace. And the brain drain won't stop either. How many young graduates do you know who have left Northern Ireland? Too many.'

He had touched a raw nerve, and heads started nodding. 'Now I understand why many people in this room will think that getting involved in the community or in politics is a waste of energy, and that their time is more usefully spent in running successful businesses and providing employment. Of course I understand that, but sadly too many clever, capable, well-organised people have come to the same conclusion. The result is that Ulster is not getting the quality of political representation it deserves—'

Michael had not intended to stop, but he was interrupted by applause and a few, 'Hear, hears!'. 'You may be interested to know that in the state of Nevada, they have a special category on every ballot paper at elections which allows voters to cast their ballot for *none of the above.*'

They were clapping again. 'Or perhaps we should go straight to the root of the problem and bring in term limits for all elected representatives.' The audience thumped their tables. 'Well, you've made your feelings fairly clear, so next time I have a group of politicians around my table who refuse to cooperate with each other, I'll know what to threaten them with.' More laughter and applause.

'Seriously, I understand that some of you with experience of work in the community may have found yourselves in a frustrating vacuum. Others have simply fled to the leafy suburbs and switched on Classic FM to drown out the noise of what's happening down the road. But we both know that nothing will be solved until people like you put pressure on your elected representatives to accommodate the other people who live in this small but beautiful Province. Better still, you should get involved in politics.

'Your sensible, calm, rational voices must be heard above the bigotry, and narrow-minded ranting that characterises too much public debate in Ulster. I believe that it is only when the parties stop spouting the most extreme view on any subject, and stop challenging each other's patriotism or purity, that there'll be hope. And when the politicians realise that they must embrace the grown-up politics of compromise and reconciliation if they are to hold their seats at elections, then there'll be hope. But while there is silence in the centre then all we'll hear are the accusations of treachery from the fringes. And there will be no hope.'

Michael sat down without another word, and the audience froze as if they were too stunned to react. There were no merry whoops or cheers this time, but the burghers of Belfast got to their feet as one, and clapped their guest speaker.

As Charlotte drove the short distance across Belfast city centre to the studio, she too was soberly appraising Michael Fitzgerald. As the reporter wearily trudged her way up to the newsroom, she wondered if Sir Trevor Grace had also underestimated him.

The next morning, Neil was on his hands and knees on the sitting-room floor, rigging up his new CD player. 'Why do I have to spend so much of my time sorting out other people's problems?' he grumbled as his wife brought him the mobile phone. This was the latest in a series of ridiculous interruptions that had distracted him from mastering the graphic equaliser. He took the phone, sighed dramatically, and slumped back in an armchair. 'Yeah?' His briskness was meant to convey how busy he was.

'Mac here. Sorry about this, but we're having a territorial dispute, and we could do with a few words from on high to bring the Avoniel Road boys into line. They're a bunch of fucking spastics, and someone's got to get them off our patch.'

Neil removed his big square glasses and rubbed his eyes as his lance corporal described the ongoing battle for possession of the lucrative streets of East Belfast. They were worth fighting for: protection money from shopkeepers and taxi outfits, graft from building firms, and a clear run at the local drug market. But as one mob got too big for its Doc Martens it squeezed onto another's ground, and the ensuing arguments were time-consuming to sort out, as Neil knew only too well.

'No one goes south of Castlereagh Road. Tell them to get back to the borders we agreed in November, or we'll cut them out of the next shipment. Then they can see how amusing it is to spend ten hours with a coffee grinder and a bag of fertiliser just for one bloody bomb,' Neil decreed.

As Mac rambled on about the insult to their honour, his boss slipped the heavy glasses back on his neat, owlish beak, and reached for the incomprehensible instruction manual that accompanied the CD player. Would he ever set the digital clock on the display? Perhaps his sons could sort it out when they came home from school.

By now he was bored by Mac's hymn of hate. 'Yeah, well, you tell them we've got better things to do than argue with them, and they're traitors to the cause for getting obsessed with their commercial operations while we have outstanding military objectives,' Neil whined. 'This isn't much of a bloody war if our soldiers are more interested in lining their pockets. Just imagine what would have happened if Genghis Khan had hung around the bazaar in Samarkand, hoping to make a few quid out of the illicit trade in yaks' testicles, rather than pushing on to conquer the rest of Asia Minor?'

Neil knew he'd lost his lance corporal pretty early in that sentence, but it served to remind Mac who the Goebbels of this movement was. Not that any of his young fools knew about the German doctor with the bad skin and the club foot.

'You know, I've been thinking we should hire a PR company so we can have a charm offensive on this Fitzgerald guy,' he said suddenly, with total disregard for Mac's tale of woe.

'A what?'

'A public relations consultant. Everyone's had them – Papa Doc, General Noriega, that lot in Indonesia, Peter Lilley. That way we could put across the kinder, gentler side of Loyalism. You know, working for the community, pavement politics, family values, helping old ladies across the street,' Neil mused.

'Yeah? Well, Ken reckons it'd be more to the point if we just stiffed Fitzgerald. He's making NIPD tighten up the procedures for getting out secure files, and Ken says it's going to be bloody difficult.'

'Oh, that Ken is a fucking paranoid headcase,' Neil said with an angry grind of his teeth.

'It isn't just Ken who thinks we should wipe him out. There's people higher up agree with him.'

'Well, we're not wiping out Fitzgerald. He's good value, and he's got style. I like him. No, I'll tell you who our real enemy is: it's bloody traitors like that cunt who runs the CBI. They're in such a hurry to get buggered by Dublin they're bending over already. It's the same old story, Mac. It's the enemy within that's our problem.' He threw the CD instruction manual on the floor in disgust.

That morning Charlotte was in Belfast, working on her next report on the politics of the new Assembly. She interviewed a political science lecturer at Queens University, and a well-respected journalist from a local radio station. Then for contrast she took her camera crew into the shopping streets just north of Donegal Square, and into working-class areas that were either very obviously Protestant or Catholic. No one she talked to believed the Assembly had a chance of success while the paramilitaries continued to slog it out. The politicians were held in low esteem by all and sundry.

Charlotte had to refuse Michael's offer of dinner and the opera that night in Belfast because she was supposed to be on duty at Parliament first thing the next morning: Rodney's wish was her command. So instead of admiring the Minister's beautiful hair over an orgasmic meal at Roscoffs, and then fighting the urge to hold his hand all through *La Bohème*, she went straight to BBC Television Centre at Shepherds Bush for an evening of video editing. If that wasn't enough to drive a girl to chocolate bars, masturbation and self-pity, then what was?

When Charlotte was closeted in her editing suite with a mercifully competent video-tape editor, they skimmed through some tape of Michael at the meeting in Armagh in search of an establishing shot of the Minister and the priests. Suddenly Charlotte noticed something curious, and made the VT editor spool backwards. 'There. Run that again, please.'

The next four seconds of film did not make sense, and it took Charlotte two viewings to register why. Mandy, the research assistant, was on the edge of the throng around her boss when Michael emerged from the hall to find the Reverend Scott and his anti-buggery brigade. The Minister smiled and extended his hand amiably, but something else happened first, something Charlotte hadn't spotted at the time.

Instead of making a beeline for the Minister, Scott had walked up to Mandy. It was obvious he knew her well, because he was smiling like the indulgent uncle that Charlotte had witnessed before. The horrified expression on the midget Mandy's elfin features was even more interesting; she narrowed her eyes and said something through clenched teeth that sent God Bob reeling back.

What was going on there? How did these two know each other, and why didn't the poison dwarfette want anyone to see

196

that she was acquainted with the Dalai Lama of County Down? Charlotte stashed these queries in the back of her mind, and tried to ignore the other question that lurked there; was Michael sleeping with Mandy? Was he taking her to *La Bohème* in Charlotte's place this evening? That was a vile thought with which to torment herself. 'Back to work,' the reporter muttered sternly. Then she fished a chocolate bar out of her handbag for a little consolation.

Chapter Sixteen

Sir Trevor Grace read from a briefing paper and guffawed loudly. 'Here's an IRA classic. Remember the bomb they let off in Hyde Park in 1982? It killed eleven soldiers, and lots of horses. Suddenly there was a cooling of relations with Dublin, and the IRA wondered why. I mean, if there's one thing that we have in common with the Irish, it's our love for bloody horses, isn't it? So what do the IRA do? Kill them. Almost as clever as blowing up Harrods or bombing Heathrow Airport. I mean, why don't they just drop a SAM missile on the American Embassy if they want to annoy their paymasters?'

Grace's ferret-like PPS chortled appreciatively as the Secretary of State shook his head and leaned back in his leather upholstered chair. 'I don't know, Mike. These Paddies are a dim lot, aren't they?'

His Minister of State sat in studied silence on the other side of Grace's desk. It was Monday morning, and Michael had returned from Belfast at 7 a.m. especially for this meeting with his boss. So far there had been nothing but 'stories' about IRA members who believed the priest in their village could fix horns to their heads if they misbehaved, and the tale of an IRA fund-raising trip to Moscow that ended in disaster when the

Russians told them to come back when they'd started killing priests.

Michael stifled a yawn. It reminded him of a lounge bar on a Sunday morning, with the local gin and tonic know-alls chipping in their 'and that's another thing' observations about the human condition and the state of the nation.

When Michael had received the summons to London he had expected to be beaten about the head for his outspoken and much publicised speeches. But Grace hadn't even mentioned the press coverage, perhaps because it had been ninety per cent positive in Belfast, Dublin and London. Save for the *Catholic Herald* and the *Universe*, of course.

'Well, I suppose we'd better get on.' The Secretary of State searched around his desk for the memo he wanted. 'Right, here it is. Sir David Mackay of NIPD has been muttering in my ear, Mike.' Grace fixed his X-ray eyes on his Minister for an uncomfortable five seconds. 'The Chief Constable says you're cracking the whip and it's going down badly in the ranks. You're seen as too partisan, you know – biased against them.'

Michael bristled. 'Why would I be biased? And why would the Chief Constable be telling the ranks, as you call them, about a series of measures that should be taken to protect sensitive intelligence?'

Grace put his head back and laughed without humour. 'You can't be surprised they think you're biased when you come down on them like a ton of bricks. You told them what kind of locks to put on their filing cabinets, and threatened to disband NIPD. Then you told them you'd hand over the keys to your old chums in Military Intelligence.' Grace shook his head like a disappointed schoolmaster.

'I didn't threaten; I told Mackay that a Labour Government

will disband NIPD, and that the Army is agitating for the lead role in intelligence-gathering in the wake of St Patrick's Day, and the fiasco at Spock's house,' Michael shot back. 'That's common knowledge. What's more interesting is why Sir David Mackay is misrepresenting my words to everyone at NIPD HQ, down to the tea ladies. *That's* biased behaviour, wouldn't you say?'

'You're letting your personal prejudices influence the way you handle NIPD—'

'What personal prejudices?' Michael stared at him, incredulous.

'Oh, come on, Mike. You're putting the boot into NIPD and—'

'No. You tell me what personal prejudices I bring to this job,' the Minister persisted. 'The one prejudice I have is that I want us to stop giving the IRA these propaganda victories like the St Patrick's Day Massacre; I want to root the terrorists out of the communities that hide them and pay for them, and that the IRA craps on in return. The hard men pray for this kind of ammunition so they can say to moderate people, "Look what your conciliation gets us. Nothing".'

Grace glared at him coldly, and rubbed his bottom lip with the side of his index finger, as if he was sharpening a knife. 'Get off NIPD's back. They're doing a good job in bloody awful conditions. If you carry on like this, Mike, you'll cause a strike.'

'We're Conservatives. We don't let policemen strike,' Michael reminded his boss with an imperious glare down his nose. 'Look, there is a security problem at NIPD Special Branch. Someone removed sensitive files on three separate occasions in the run up to the St Patrick's Day event. Sir David's security system is about as reliable as a British weather forecast.'

Grace blinked as if a circuit inside his head had shorted. 'I see.' Then the ruddy mask broke into a sneer. 'Well, I'll look into it.'

Michael swallowed the lump of anger that had risen in his throat. 'Thank you. Have you got time to look at a few suggestions?'

The Secretary of State seemed surprised. 'Sure. What have you got?'

Michael removed a sheet of typewritten paper from his document case and passed it to Grace. 'The big item is one we might try to get Dublin to co-sponsor with us in an application to Brussels; a high-speed rail link between Belfast and Dublin, maybe one between Belfast and Derry too.'

Grace scanned the sheet of paper. 'Fine. Infrastructure stuff.' He sounded perfectly reasonable. Even the colour of his cheeks had returned to their normal feverish pink.

'Then a programme to expand the provision of nursery schools and crèches. I'm sure we could get a more flexible and skilled labour market if there were more women free to do part-time work. For instance, the Japanese are happier employing women rather than men in electronic assembly plants. We've still got that microcircuit manufacturer from Osaka sniffing round Ulster, looking for a site, and this might interest them.'

'Good. Ideal for Brussels,' Grace commented.

'Now the next idea tackles the criticism that the civil service at Stormont is too remote. What about a scheme to allow the secondment of administrators from Dundonald House and Stormont Castle to various approved voluntary organisations such as the Belfast Action Team? I think that would serve two purposes: it feeds some administrative skill into worthy groups that are amateur and overstretched by their very nature; and it gives public employees a taste of how policies are implemented on the ground.'

'Check. Go ahead. Good idea. Fine by me. Just fill out the European whatsit form,' the Secretary of State elaborated.

'The next idea uses the same principle, but it puts graduates who've just left university into Government offices and bodies like the Fair Employment Commission. Incidentally, it also removes a wadge of graduates from the unemployment statistics.'

'Yup. Fine. Ah, that reminds me of a story. Dicky Thingey, that Labour MP who represents that dump in south London. Some chap came into his surgery, black as the ace of spades, going on about how he'd been sacked from his job because he was coloured. He told Dicky he was a carpenter in a theatre in the West End, and he was the only black there. Of course Dicky looked into it and it turns out they didn't sack him because of his colour at all; he was the only one in the whole place who wasn't queer!'

The PPS barked his approval while Grace shook with laughter and slapped his knee. Michael waited for the hilarity to subside. Finally, when the tears had been wiped from the corners of Elvis's eyes, he asked his Secretary of State, 'Aren't all these Euro-initiatives going to annoy the Unionists? They dislike the idea of taking Euromoney because it makes us beholden to the bureaucrats in Brussels.'

But Grace waved his hands as if it was of no consequence. 'Where else can we get the cash for your schemes? Certainly not the Treasury. Got more on your wish list?'

'How about a common history course in all secondary schools in the Province? Everyone keeps saying that ignorance is the greatest hurdle to mutual understanding—'

'No, Mike,' Grace interrupted. 'I can't go with this. There'll be a bloody riot if we try to push *that* through the Assembly. Next idea?'

Michael raised his hand like a cop directing traffic. 'There are already several adult education colleges running common Irish history courses, and they're immensely popular.'

'Then why'd you need this?' Grace asked and pointed at the sheet of paper. 'Next idea,' he repeated brusquely.

Michael bit his bottom lip, and wondered if he should argue his ground. But the set of Elvis's jaw made it clear there would be no further discussion.

'OK,' he said, 'how about a rolling devolution of power and responsibility to local councils across the Province who prove themselves capable of sharing power.'

Grace sighed and sat back in his chair. Then he looked at the ceiling for a moment and clicked his tongue. 'Mike, stop trying to do politically sensitive things. You're rocking the boat enough as it is. Just avoid the politics, and leave it to the Assembly.'

Michael had been under the impression that politics was their business, but he knew truculence when it was staring him in the face. 'In that case, my next suggestion is probably completely out of order.'

'I don't see anything else here.' The Secretary of State glanced at the sheet of paper.

'I didn't put it in writing. I want your permission to re-open dialogue with the Loyalist paramilitaries. I'm talking about going direct to them, to find out what it'll take to stop the bombing and ethnic cleansing.'

'They refuse to have a united Ireland or any powersharing,' Grace shot back.

'No, with due respect, that's what the Loyal Unionist politicians say. I think we should find out what the paras themselves say.'

'Hmmm. Can you do this quietly? I mean, utterly untraceably, without using the usual Military Intelligence route?'

Michael shrugged. 'I've no idea. I wanted your permission, and your opinion.' He hoped that his boss's ego would screen out the blatant insincerity in his Minister's voice.

'All right. Keep me in touch. And don't give away the shop.' Grace sniggered. Michael noticed that every time Elvis grunted his belly shuddered and wallowed like a sack of little piglets strapped to his chest. 'OK, Mike. I'd better get on with all this rubbish,' he announced, and Michael got to his feet, knowing he'd been dismissed. 'We're working out a few ideas for moving some of the armoured personnel strength away from the base at Crossmaglen.'

Michael stopped in his tracks. 'Where to?'

'Back to HQ at Lisburn, probably at the end of next week. Their presence is making the nationalist community there unhappy, so it's a gesture to build confidence. It'll take them a couple of days to do it, and they don't want too many masked men taking pot shots at them, so it's got to be carefully planned. Anyway, keep in touch, Mike.'

The Minister nodded absent-mindedly, and retreated past the ever-present and mysteriously invertebrate PPS. Michael returned to his office and worked for the rest of the morning, stopping once to call Johnny Burleigh, at the MOD. The Defence Secretary agreed to meet him at Boodle's in St James's. When Michael returned to his desk three hours later, and rather the worse for claret and port, he reflected that it was fortunate that he had stayed on Johnny's good side while he'd been his underling at the MOD. The old boy had just set him straight on something rather important.

Chapter Seventeen

Two days later, Charlotte Carter had a day off work, which was small compensation for working until midnight most of the time, trying to make interesting reports out of boring debates.

This morning she had a pencil tucked behind her ear, three nails clenched between her teeth, a tape measure jabbed into the back pocket of her jeans, and a hammer in her hand. All that was missing was the check shirt and hard hat. Mercifully, this Village People cabaret was being performed without an audience in the privacy of her sitting room, where Charlotte was hanging the pictures she had bought on her first trip to Belfast. Both canvases were big, still-life oil paintings of flowers and vases, nothing that would cause shooting pains to the eyeballs when viewed first thing in the morning.

When they were up, Charlotte stood back and congratulated herself. The fledgling collector had broken the spell, and introduced some life into her new lair. This called for a celebration: Rain Forest Crunch ice-cream, just half a pint. She had to leave room for tea later on with Michael Fitzgerald.

As she shovelled in spoon after spoon of Ben and Jerry's, she glanced absent-mindedly at the cork noticeboard on the kitchen wall. On it was pinned a calendar from the World Wide Fund for Nature featuring a splendidly lazy panda reclining like a Roman emperor and chewing a stick of bamboo; next to it were invitations to dinner parties that she knew she would regret turning up to half an hour after she had arrived; and there was a picture of her brother, looking handsome and suntanned.

She and Jeremy had both been at a loose end last summer, so they had rented a small villa on the Algarve together. Brother and sister shared a love of sunbathing, eating seafood, and reading whodunits, which had guaranteed a week without many arguments. Jeremy was more interested in Portuguese men than Charlotte, so she had left him to his nocturnal bar-haunting, while she had early nights with P.D. James and Ruth Rendell.

Now Jeremy had found the man of his dreams, so he wasn't available for a trip abroad this summer. Charlotte had yet to confront the grimness of what to do with her holiday quota. Could she face a week lazing around her parents' house in Hertfordshire, listening to them discuss their respective legal work? At least Jeremy was following the career path that was genetically required of him, unlike Charlotte who had mystified her parents by shunning the law. Even if their son was gay, at least he was a gay barrister. But their daughter? Something to do with the frivolous world of television, and not worthy of serious consideration. And what would be their reaction if she lost her job at the BBC?

Charlotte shrugged off these unsettling thoughts and put the ice cream away. Then she showered and changed into more respectable trousers, blouse, scarf and jacket. Half an hour later she was crossing Queensway and walking down Westbourne Grove, where there was always a tantalising smell of curry in the air. It was enough to drive a hungry young woman quite mad.

It was curious that Michael lived a short walk away from her square, yet he had never mentioned it, even when he had dropped her home one night last week after they had been drinking at the Commons. So near, and yet so far, Charlotte reflected as she almost collided with the fruit and vegetable stall spilling out onto the pavement. Little Lebanon, Little Teheran, and Little Athens, all crowded into a faded but lively corner of W2. Political refugees had been coming to this area ever since the Russian Revolution. Most recently the Hong Kong business élite was arriving, which meant some excellent restaurants and grocery stores had sprung up to cater for them. Bring us your huddled masses, but be sure to remember the cuisine too, please.

Michael's house was a white, three-storey Georgian terrace in a gentrified, quiet side street jammed with Mercedes, BMWs and Volvo Estates. The door was answered by a young man, presumably part of the Minister's security detail, and a friend of the chaps sitting outside in the ministerial Range Rover. He pointed Charlotte towards the source of the Carly Simon.

The Minister was in jeans and a grey 'Opera North' sweatshirt with the sleeves pushed up in businesslike fashion. He was in an armchair surrounded by papers and those hateful red boxes, and he appeared to be absorbed in his work. Charlotte hovered on the threshold for a moment and took in the room, as if it might tell her something more about its occupant; two sets of French windows letting in a lot of light; plants; and the type of delicate old Regency furniture that was inherited, not purchased. One entire wall was bookshelves, floor to ceiling. The other walls were sagging under the weight of modern art. On the floor were Persian rugs, worn, and no doubt insulted by being covered by boring Government papers.

'Hello,' Charlotte said brightly, and then felt unaccountably foolish and awkward. Michael leapt to his feet and made room for her to sit down, then subdued Carly Simon, and asked the policeman to please make them a cup of tea.

'Ms Carter, I've come to the conclusion that what Northern Ireland needs is a unifying symbol, some role model that brings both sides together. For the amount of money we spend in the Province every year I reckon we could probably buy a world-beating soccer team. If only there was a brilliant Jewish diva from Derry, or a Hindu athlete from County Tyrone whom everyone could be proud of. Or a non-sectarian symbol that was important to everyone, some logo that expressed a common aspiration . . .' His words trailed off into a preoccupied silence.

'How about the balaclava and the Black and Decker?' Charlotte suggested with a twinkle in her eyes.

Michael tried to look disapproving, but it wasn't successful. 'You're such a bad woman,' he laughed. 'Thank you for coming round. I'm afraid I can't feed you until Laura returns. She and Delva have gone out somewhere, but they shouldn't be long. Anyway, Lobby terms, blah, blah, blah, OK? Now, Grace dragged me in for a reprimand yesterday morning. NIPD are going wild over that leak you mentioned. Apparently I'm causing "a bad feeling in the ranks". I'm the Catholic bastard in London accusing them of incompetence, and I've got it in for them. Which I haven't. I honestly believe the Chief Constable is a decent man; just a bit limited, and blind to his rotten apples, as he calls them.'

'How many rotten apples are there?'

'Very few, I suspect. But it doesn't take more than one or two well-placed Loyalist sympathisers to cause problems. There have been a dozen or so caught red-handed over the past twenty odd years. Naturally the nationalists say they've not yet been rooted out. Several cases got to court, and a few have resulted in prison sentences, but you can never satisfy the Republicans.' He sat back in the armchair as if he was exhausted by their lust for blood. 'Anyway, I'm up shit creek with Elvis, although I did get a commitment out of him to tackle the problem you brought to my attention.'

Charlotte arched an eyebrow. 'As long as the contact at NIPD doesn't get in trouble.'

'I don't see how it can be traced. Don't worry. Now, what's bizarre is that Grace is quite happy for me to go off and start talking to the Loyalists, on the quiet.'

'That's extraordinary. Is Grace setting you up?' she asked tentatively.

Michael seemed to be in two minds about what he was going to say. 'Johnny Burleigh reckons he's already tried to set me up. Grace told me about some Army manoeuvres that have been planned in Crossmaglen. I thought it sounded crazy, and Johnny says it's not happening. It's never even been mooted. But Grace made a point of telling me about it. I still don't understand why.'

'This sounds horrible. Watch out for him, for goodness' sake, Michael. You know what I've been told about him. Be careful. Oh by the way, does your—' she groped around for the correct term '—assistant, Mandy, know God Bob?'

'No. Except that she was introduced to him when he met me at Stormont,' Michael said without interest. 'I think you're being a tad paranoid about Elvis, but I do appreciate the warning, and it's all the more reason why I need to be cautious with those charming Loyalist paramilitaries.' Another significant silence, and a rub of the ministerial forehead. 'This is a big favour to ask, Charlotte, and you must tell me to go to hell if you don't want to be involved, and I'll understand it. But when you were planning your piece on the politics of the

Assembly, you said you might interview the UVF?'

Charlotte nodded. 'But my boss stopped me, because apparently it's OK to be a terrorist if you get a couple of councillors elected, but it's not OK if you're just a terrorist. I do know how to get at the UVF, though. I'll have a word with my friend at BBC Ulster, and ask him if he'd sound them out.'

'Thanks, that's a relief. You see, I'm reluctant to use the path that's been taken before by the Government, through MI6, because I think it's bound to be leaky as hell.'

'That's OK. I'll be your go-between.' Charlotte grinned cheerfully. Then she wondered what the Minister's chest looked like beneath the Opera North sweatshirt. How she would love to push him down on that Persian rug and investigate. 'I like your paintings,' she remarked.

He seemed pleased by her interest, and she followed him into the dining room where the walls were also crowded with richly coloured pastels of tropical plants and flowers.

'This is Jenny Webb. Famous for her campaign to free the Ambridge One. Do you listen to *The Archers*?' the Minister asked, and saw his guest shake her head bashfully. At that moment the front door slammed shut, and there was a high-pitched screaming noise. As it got closer Charlotte realised someone was attempting to sing the Queen of the Night's aria from *The Magic Flute*. The shrieking stopped abruptly when it reached the dining room.

'Laura, this is Charlotte Carter, from the BBC,' Michael explained without taking his eyes off a painting. 'And Charlotte, this is my beloved daughter, Madam Mao.'

Charlotte smiled weakly at the pale, heart-shaped face framed by long, dark tresses. Although Laura had not inherited her father's de Gaulle nose, she had the Fitzgerald technique of

212

glaring down her snout disapprovingly. She employed it to equal effect, and Charlotte withered under the icy blast.

'I'm starving,' Michael commented. 'I'll give Delva a hand in the kitchen.' And to Charlotte's distress he left her alone with the monstrous five foot four of malevolence that stood before her in its black jeans and jumper.

'Hey,' Laura called after her father. 'Don't forget you said we could go to see a film at Whiteley's. They all start at around six, so we have to get a move on.' That was a pointed remark, thought the television reporter; just letting me know she wants me gone.

Laura studied her for a moment, muttered, '*Picka ti materina*,' and then walked out of the room. Charlotte heard her call out something else, and it brought a swift rebuke from the kitchen. Then Michael returned with plates of cucumber sandwiches, crumpets, onion bhajis and vegetable samosas. 'They appear to have bought most of M & S on their little outing. Ah, Delva,' the Minister exclaimed as the housekeeper brought in the tea, and a large carrot cake, 'please say hello to Charlotte Carter, who's helping me plot the downfall of Sir Trevor Grace. Charlotte, this is Delva, who's going to be our ambassador to the Balkans, when I have any say in these things.'

Delva complimented Charlotte on her journalism, and asked her to sit down. Laura reappeared and perched on a chair at the other end of the table, like a frog who might leap away at any moment.

'Actually, we prefer *Channel Four News* in this house,' she said in a matter-of-fact manner.

'We watch all of them, when we have time,' her father corrected.

'*Jebem ti majku*,' the child responded with another burst of

213

incomprehensible venom. This time Delva snapped at Laura in this mysterious but robust language, and the room went silent. As Michael and Delva retreated to the kitchen for plates and cutlery, Laura turned a hideous broad smile at Charlotte.

'*Va te faire foutre*,' the television reporter said clearly but quietly.

'What does that mean?' Laura shot back with burning eyes.

'It's French for "go fuck yourself".'

'Brilliant,' Laura said in admiration. 'Will you write that down? I'll get some paper.'

When Michael returned to the dining room he noticed a sudden change in the atmosphere. 'So, is it the Harrison Ford or the Tom Hanks?' Laura was asking their guest. 'Charlotte's coming to the cinema with us,' the thirteen-year-old announced. 'We're deciding which of these old men is the yummiest.'

Michael rolled his eyes and poured the tea. 'Please join us, Charlotte. Unless you're already doing something?'

Oh, I'm very busy making my flat pretty so I can share it with no one at all, the reporter thought as a wave of melancholia washed over her. 'I'd be delighted. Thank you.'

As Michael, Laura, Delva, Charlotte and several gentlemen from Special Branch were taking their seats in Whiteley's multiplex, Albert Morrison was packing his briefcase with work to do at home in Belfast that evening. The Chairman of the Northern Ireland CBI was the last person in the office to leave, and he went from room to room switching off lights, and turning on answering machines.

At ten past six, Morrison locked the front door of Fanum House, crossed Great Victoria Street, and went down Windsor Street to the car park where he had left his BMW. The orange sodium glow of the street-lights illuminated his passage through the murky evening air. A couple of paces from the car he pulled the automatic locking control from his coat pocket and turned off the alarm system. Then he put his briefcase in the boot, and opened the car door. Morrison was crouching to get in when he heard footsteps behind him. As he turned around he was hit by five bullets, delivered at close range, into his well-padded chest. The force of impact made him bounce back on the car, and by the time he had slithered to the ground his assailant was halfway across the car park. Morrison was dead before Mac's car had reached Great Victoria Street. Another clean, fast job from the man who was responsible for a busload of dead Catholics on St Patrick's Day.

When the film at Whiteley's was over, Charlotte left the Fitzgeralds and returned to her flat, pleased with the way her friendship with Michael was developing, but wary of pushing her luck, or overstaying her welcome. The Minister was also in a good mood for the same reason, until he heard the news about Albert Morrison awaiting him at home.

Sir Trevor Grace's PPS wanted Michael to make the usual statement of defiant outrage to the media; and the television camera crews were henceforth directed to Michael's house for a doorstep soundbite. Then the Minister called NIPD for more details. Morrison had been forty-four, the father of three children, and had run a successful dry-cleaning business which his wife managed while he did his stint as Chairman of the CBI.

At 8 p.m. the Ulster Volunteer Force claimed responsibility for the hit: Morrison was targeted because of his speech about trading with Eire. He was a traitor to the Loyalist cause, and had therefore been executed.

Michael poured a glass of wine and sat quietly in the kitchen, trying to collect his thoughts. In his head he had the image of Albert Morrison's hands shaking as he had stood at the microphone, clutching his notes. It was ironic that a man who feared public speaking had been so brave in the forthrightness of his message.

When the media had clustered on the path outside his house, and the arc-lights were blazing, and the sound men were satisfied with the levels of noise their equipment registered, Michael launched into his set piece. There was no need to pretend to be shocked and saddened, because he was, and it showed. He did the normal condemnation of mindless violence, and restated the Government's determination to continue its search for a lasting peace. Then he talked about meeting Albert Morrison recently, and about the courage of his message.

'It's such a terrible, bloody, pointless waste. It's self-evident that these murderers are evil, but they're also stupid. They're wasting the Province's best people for the sake of a warped, bitter, fanatical lunacy. Events like this will make their own supporters despair of them. The paramilitaries should remember that, because one day the people will demand that they account for all this waste.'

Michael and Laura watched the interview broadcast on both main evening news programmes, and then the Minister sent his daughter to bed. Half an hour later when he went upstairs to say goodnight, she was unusually quiet and subdued. It was rare that she pulled him onto the bed for a leisurely embrace, but tonight she held him in a tight grip. He lay beside her while she drifted into sleep, and as he listened to Laura's steady breathing Charlotte's earlier warning did laps around his mind: *This is a big boys' game – be careful.*

216

Chapter Eighteen

The next morning, Ken McTaggart paid a visit to the Records Section of Special Branch at NIPD.

'It's about who has access to the files,' he explained to the secretary with the fierce half-moon spectacles. 'I'm following up on the security stuff – you know, the notebook you keep of who looks at whatever.'

The secretary nodded and handed him the relevant notebook from her top drawer.

'Remind who spotted this first?' Ken asked.

'Irene, down in Administration.'

'Of course,' Ken nodded and examined the pages.

'I was away on holiday at the time, so I don't know who took out the files,' the secretary added pointedly. 'Is this serious? What's going to happen?'

'Nah, it's just red tape. You know, the usual. It doesn't matter.' Ken flashed her a grin. Then he flicked through the notebook until he found the randomly picked initials that he had scrawled on three occasions in a two-week period when the secretary had been away. 'Here.' He handed the book back and smiled again. 'Thanks for your help.'

★ ★ ★

Charlotte was in her nest in the Press Gallery at Westminster. It provided her with rather too good a view of a fat and unprepossessing Conservative MP who was savaging his own Government for subsidising the arts. Heaping abuse on opera-goers united the philistine element on both sides of the Commons. But Charlotte's attention was elsewhere: her boss, Rodney, had just queried her latest expenses claim and given her a hard time about the amount of champagne she bought the likes of Michael Fitzgerald and Lord Bolton, 'with no obvious results to show for it'. Evidently he was unimpressed by her reports on Belfast.

At that moment, Paula from IRN took a seat beside her. 'So why is it OK to use my taxes to subsidise dim, feckless people with ten children, and nuclear reactors that don't work, but not opera?' she enquired. 'Ug. I bet he's a child-molester. Hello, Charlotte,' she added brightly.

The IRN Lobby Correspondent was glowing from a suntan acquired at some Mediterranean nudist colony, and Charlotte tried not to think about sagging, sunburned bottoms.

'Oh God,' Paula groaned, 'look at that one. You know, I've been thinking. The standard of English usage in this country is sinking to deplorable levels, and the grammar and accents one hears on television must set an awfully bad example to the young and impressionable. So I have a solution. You recall the way the Government's broadcasting ban on IRA members meant that an actor spoke Gerry Adams's words?'

'Yes, it was rather funny.'

'Well, we should employ actors who speak proper, old-fashioned BBC English to read and correct the words of anyone on television or radio who uses Estuarial English, or has an ugly regional accent—'

'Or who uses clichés and bad grammar?'

'Exactly. Take this cretin who's holding forth right now. Always the same tedious, ill-educated, self-serving remarks delivered in a grating voice. He's bound to suffer from premature ejaculation,' Paula commented loudly.

'I don't want to know what grounds you have for coming to that conclusion, if you don't mind.'

'Speaking of premature ejaculation, have you heard what happened to the Prime Minister first thing this morning?' Charlotte shook her head and leaned forward to catch the gossip. 'When he got to the kitchen, he found that his lady wife was wearing a rather revealing evening gown, and standing by the cooker, waiting for a pan of water to boil. Naturally the PM was nonplussed, as he so often is, and he said, "My dear, what are you doing?" And his wife told him that she wanted him to screw her immediately, right there on the kitchen table. And the PM was astonished, and asked her why. And she said, "Because the egg-timer's broken, and you like your eggs done in two minutes".'

While Charlotte and Paula tittered in the Gallery like naughty schoolgirls, Michael Fitzgerald was picking his way through the Lobby outside the Chamber. He made a brave attempt to avoid several world-class bores, but fell at the final hurdle, and was trapped by an intense old Conservative with a ludicrous silver handlebar moustache who was angry about the European Union's agricultural subsidies in Ulster. Just in the nick of time Mandy rushed up to him, high heels clattering, and grabbed his arm. Michael excused himself and allowed her to drag him away.

'Oh Michael, I've done something awful,' she moaned. 'I'm really sorry about this, but I think I've lost the costings for the nursery-school expansion programme. And that witch of a principal at Admiralty House says she's got to fax it to Brussels in the next forty-five minutes if they're going to accept it. That's when applications close,' she explained with a near-hysterical wail of anxiety. 'Have you got a copy?'

Michael shook his head, and looked at his watch. 'Oh, hell. I've got to go in now. I'm answering questions in ten minutes.' Mandy hopped about in front of him like a demented rabbit. 'Look, the original is in my PC, under the file called *Bruss.*'

'But how do I get into your PC?' she whined. 'Oh God, Michael, I'm so sorry about this.'

'It's OK. Calm down. Use my codeword, then go to *Bruss.* The code is *Elvis.* OK?'

'Great. No problem. Sorry about this, Michael,' she jabbered, and dashed out of the Lobby. The Minister ran his fingers through his hair in an attempt to bring some order to it, and headed into the Chamber, this time steering clear of the senile farming expert.

'Ah, the talent's arrived, I see.' Paula gave Charlotte a pointed smile. 'Mind you, he doesn't look like he's had much of a holiday, poor dear. Someone told me he spent most of Easter in Belfast. Is that right?'

'So I gather.' Charlotte pretended to read the Order Paper.

Mercifully, Northern Ireland questions began, and eighty per cent of the MPs in the Chamber waddled out. Sir Trevor Grace launched into his cabaret routine, swaying around at the Dispatch Box as if he were compèring a Beauty Pageant; registering theatrical expressions of shock and disapproval whenever Labour's Northern Ireland Spokesman, Eddie Power, made a sharp point; and playing to his own albeit-depleted benches with cheap shots about the Opposition being soft on terrorism. Elvis made them laugh when he explained that the forthcoming name change of the Royal Mail in Ulster was out of his hands. 'I'm just following my orders from Brussels like the good European that the honourable gentlemen know me to be.'

This was the cue for the Reverend Robert Scott, who was the MP as well as the Assemblyman for the beautiful acres of Down. A display of fury from his benches was a predictable part of Northern Ireland questions, and you could have set your watch by him. Like a model steam train emerging from a shed he puffed himself up for his normal outburst.

'Not once has the Secretary of State mentioned the appalling ethnic cleansing that is being visited upon the people of Ulster. We are seeing history repeat itself,' the ecclesiastical foghorn bellowed. 'Innocent Protestant families are being massacred, just as they were at Portadown in 1641 when bloodcrazed Roman Catholics murdered them. And then there was the Siege of Londonderry in 1689, when the courageous inhabitants declared "no surrender", even when Death looked them in the face.'

Charlotte was not the only observer to wonder if they were going to get a complete history lesson before the Speaker stepped in and asked Reverend Scott what his question was. 'The message is still "no surrender"; not to Europe, not to Dublin, and not to the IRA!' he choked dramatically.

Everyone looked faintly embarrassed by the righteous indignation, but God Bob was immune to their reactions. The faithful little steam engine had chuffed out of the station bang on time, and done his star turn.

A moment later, Eddie Power asked if the Secretary of State had ruled out any form of dialogue with paramilitary organisations. Grace hauled himself up in a leisurely fashion. 'No discussions,' he said dramatically, and slumped back onto the Government front bench.

Eddie, bristling with energy, bobbed up with a supplementary. 'Is the Secretary of State telling the House that he's ruled out any talks whatsoever?'

Grace turned to face his own side of the Chamber. 'Some honourable gentlemen don't seem to understand the Queen's English. Just for the benefit of the Member for Coventry I'll say it again. No talks with terrorists. No discussions with any paramilitaries until they obey the permanent ceasefire, and prove that they're serious and sincere.' Elvis turned back to the Labour benches and leaned across the Dispatch Box. 'Got it this time?!' he yelled. The Conservative benches erupted into laughter, and Grace plopped onto his seat. Beside him, Michael fixed a semi-smile on his face. He and Eddie made eye-contact, as they so often did, and exchanged a private look of horror.

Michael's performance at Question Time was quite different in style and content to those of his master. He was low on bombast, but thanks to his barrister's training, quick with facts and statistics to show up his questioners' ignorance. He shaped his reply according to how serious he believed the questioner to be, and when they were sincere in their concern, such as the SDLP MPs, he gave thoughtful, detailed, and usually non-partisan replies.

On their way out of the Chamber Sir Trevor asked his Minister for a quiet word, and Michael followed him into a corner, by the entrance to the Liberal Democrat Whip's Office. 'I thought you should know immediately that the PM wants to make a trip to Ulster soon.' When Michael's forehead wrinkled in consternation Grace nodded his agreement. 'Loony, I know, but the PM feels it's vital to remind the people of Northern Ireland that he has their interests at heart.' That meant politics at Westminster was sticky, so it was time to divert everyone's attention with a trip to Belfast.

'But now is hardly the moment, not with all this ethnic cleansing, and the retaliation attacks. It's much too dangerous.'

Grace held up his hands innocently. 'The PM wants to express his solidarity with the business community in Ulster, after the shooting of that CBI chap. Now, you get to work on putting together an agenda for him. Foundation stones to lay at new factories, or something like that. And why don't you get him to visit one of these nursery schools of yours? That would give the whole programme a good send-off.'

'We're not quite that advanced—'

'Just get one up and running, somewhere,' Grace suggested vaguely. The Secretary of State had trouble remembering which part of Belfast the Shankill Road was in. 'I know you'll sort it out.' Grace gave his Minister an agreeable and equally insincere grin. 'Must rush. Bye, Mike.'

The preoccupied Michael crossed the Members' Lobby and wandered into the Library Corridor. In front of him was McKinnley, one of the Reverend God Bob's apprentice undertakers, and he was alone, what was more. Michael quickened his pace and caught up with him.

Twenty minutes later, the ministerial car glided out of Palace Yard and waited for a break in the traffic in Parliament Square. In the back seat Michael took out a notepad and jotted down the headlines from his conversation with McKinnley. The policemen at the gate realised that a minister's car was purring beside them, and they stepped boldly into Parliament Square with hands upheld. As if by magic this suicidal gesture brought the traffic to a halt, and Michael swept out in front of a line of bemused motorists who didn't know why some creep in a Rover should have right of way.

Referendum still hasn't convinced McKinnley the Irish don't want to invade Ulster, he scribbled; *but open to Mercs and perks.* That meant Michael reckoned McKinnley wanted the trappings of office in a power-sharing government of Northern Ireland that included Catholics. Here was the seed of a major potential split with God Bob, who wouldn't have allowed a Catholic cleaning lady into any council building.

Michael intended to return to the House later to track down the other undead Loyal Unionist MP for a casual natter. Perhaps he too felt it was unfair that the Official Unionists would get all the prestigious jobs in the new Assembly – just because God Bob declared that it was one of the Circles of Hell. Once the Loyal Unionists had a stake in the system, they might fight to make the Assembly work, Michael reasoned.

Then he glanced at the note the steward had handed him as he left the Commons just now. *Call Charlotte Carter*. Michael would suggest dinner, although he suspected she would be busy, or seeing another of her doting MPs. Or the boyfriend Eddie Power had alluded to. Still, Michael had a good excuse to try, although he didn't want her to think he was chasing her. He would suggest Clarke's Restaurant as a way to break down her resolve. Clarke's might do it, he reflected. And he was right.

'Jack Nicholson is dead on; he's the best. It's obvious. What about *One Flew Over the Cuckoo's Nest* then?' the Garda sergeant demanded with a belligerent set of his jaw. 'Or *Wolf*. No one can beat that.'

'That's bollocks, it is,' said the blue-uniformed constable seated on his right. 'He's got that one look that he gives the camera – you know, the half-crazy leer – and that's it.'

'And what about that crap Nicholson did in *Batman*? It was useless!' The Irish policeman on the opposite side of the Garda Armoured Personnel Carrier had to shout to make himself heard above the roar of the engine.

It was the end of their shift, and they were heading home, down the N14 to Letterkenny, in County Donegal in the Irish Republic. They had spent the day keeping an eye on the border areas near Strabane, where it was thought that some of the IRA active service units who were still in business came to collect their arms.

'*Chinatown* – now that was amazing. Take Nicholson out of it, and what're you left with, eh?'

'Faye Dunaway.'

'Bollocks. Any tart could have done the part. Jack made that fucking film what it was.'

'Right,' said the first policeman with renewed vigour. 'Or *The Shining*.'

'Don't be so fucking silly. What about *Terms of Endearment*? That was fucking crap.' The anti-Nicholson thesis was being put forward by a new contributor, the sergeant sitting squashed up at the back. '*A Few Good Men*? Nicholson should have been shot for doing that.'

'Yeah, well, he's not so stupid if he gets paid five million dollars every time he flashes his teeth at the screen. I mean, driving around Donegal in an APC that smells of yesterday's farts, and all for a few punt a week – *that's* stupid.'

'I wish people wouldn't wank into empty cigarette packs and then leave them on the floor in here,' the sergeant commented flatly.

But before his colleagues could discuss this sociological phenomenon, the Armoured Personnel Carrier hit what felt like an uneven patch of road. A second later, an explosion ripped through the bottom of the vehicle, and up into the passenger compartment. None of the amateur film critics would be going to the cinema again.

'Your flat?' Michael asked in disbelief.

Charlotte shrugged, and rested her fork on the plate, the divine taste of the apricot tart and fromage frais lingering on her palate. 'Well, you can hardly ask the man who runs the Loyalist paramilitaries to meet you at the Reform Club.'

Michael's brow furrowed and he drained his glass of California chardonnay. 'You're right.' He gave Charlotte a steady, serious gaze across the table. 'But I also don't want to endanger you. You've done quite enough already, without having the UVF's own Jean-Paul Sartre round for tea.'

'Coffee, actually. The idea is that he comes to my place at 9 a.m., then you arrive at, say, nine-thirty. And when you've finished your discussion you disappear, and he'll leave half an hour after, so your security detail doesn't spot him.'

'But what if this Neil character's being followed? Special Branch is bound to put a tail on him the minute he steps onto English soil.'

'Apparently he's had rather a lot of practice at avoiding menacing shadows. As long as he's got a map of the area, he can shake any tail, so we've been told.'

'And what will my bloody armed guard think I'm up to, if I arrive at your place, then emerge an hour or two later? Or indeed ten minutes later, if we find this bugger isn't willing to make concessions.'

Charlotte gave him a sly smile. 'They'll think you're visiting the woman you dropped home one night late last week – the one you're dining with tonight. Relax. There's no story to sell to a paper. After all, neither of us is married.' She fluttered her eyelashes innocently.

'I don't think this works very well from your point of view. If the worst happened, you could be linked to me in some vile tabloid story.'

'No, Michael. If the worst happened, someone would get wind of the fact that a Northern Ireland Minister was secretly breaking bread with the UVF. As far as I'm concerned, it's no big deal that your security men can swap a few knowing winks about what their master is up to.' If only their salacious suppositions were true, she thought ruefully.

'I suppose they've seen it all before, but this is very noble of you.' Michael refilled their glasses. 'I don't want you to feel exploited.'

Charlotte sipped her wine, thinking how much she'd like him to exploit her, right here and now on the restaurant table. If only their secret liaison was for real. But perhaps he had his hands full with Randy Mandy.

Michael had changed the subject, and was talking about his new house near the Botanic Gardens in Belfast, but his audience found herself grinding her teeth in fury at the prospect of Michael bedding Mandy. Perhaps his security detail regularly passed evenings outside Mandy's house; maybe that was why he was so cautious. A tabloid might indeed be interested in the private life of a good-looking young Minister who bonked his way across London. Charlotte was having no part of that.

'I told you that your research assistant knows Reverend Scott rather better than she's letting on, didn't I?' she interrupted with a crooked, shark-like smile. 'Do your minders often find themselves waiting outside houses while you visit friends? Is that what you were getting at?'

'No, Charlotte. You of all people should know that.' He looked stung, as if she had slapped him across the face.

She wilted under his hard stare, and for something to do she poured them both some coffee from the cafetière that had just arrived at the table. 'I'm sorry. I don't know why I said that,' she blundered on. 'I'm sorry.' She checked his face again, but the cloud was still there. Regrettably the floor of the restaurant did not open up and swallow her whole.

'I put my research assistant to bed a few weeks ago. I suppose that counts, but she had thrown up on me first,' he added with a bitter little laugh.

'I'm sorry. I suddenly had visions of being Bimbo Number Five on Sexy Minister's Fun List.' She risked a feeble smile, but it was met by a wall of indignation and hurt.

'I'd never put you in that position. Surely you realise that? It's quite enough asking you to be associated with me so I can meet the masked men.'

You have no idea how much I'd like to be associated with you, chum, and that's the problem, Charlotte thought. You're concerned with protecting my honour, whereas I've got other forms of recreation in mind. But you're not interested in me, the internal monologue blubbed, and Charlotte bit her bottom lip to keep the emotion out of her voice.

Then, because she'd drunk too much champagne and wine that evening, and because she had nothing to lose she said out loud, 'The House of Commons is full of women who'd be happy to be associated with you. Me included. You have quite a fan club in the Gallery.'

She kept her eyes firmly planted on her coffee cup, and wondered what awful fate awaited her after these wildly unwise outpourings of lust.

Silence. Then a nervous clearing of the throat. 'Goodness. Well, I don't give a damn about the Gallery, but coming from you, I'm flattered. And I'm sorry I lost my temper.'

Charlotte finally steeled herself to meet his eyes, and was relieved to find that he was blushing at her bowed head. Now, maybe, he'll pick up the ball and run with it, as it were, she thought with heart palpitating.

But no, he was back to the attractions of trendy Botanic Avenue near his new home, and for another half hour they sipped coffee and talked nonstop, as was their way. When they left the restaurant and climbed into the back seat of the waiting Range Rover, it was as if nothing had happened between them; neither anger nor her expression of desire. Charlotte, who was quite confused by now, felt a gloomy hopelessness descend as the car pulled into her square. They stopped near Charlotte's building, but before the policeman in the passenger seat could get out and open her door, the Minister told him to stay put, and that he'd be back in a moment.

Michael walked her to the front door, cursing Sir Trevor Grace for his general hatefulness, while she fished the key out of her handbag. She was thanking him yet again for a delicious meal when it happened: he kissed her, straight on the lips. Then he pulled her into the shadows to one side of her front door, and kissed her again, more urgently. She wrapped her arms around his neck and kissed him back with every ounce of passion she possessed. Mutual groans and dizziness followed. She steadied herself against him and kissed him again with the full force of the surge of electricity that had tripped all her internal circuits.

Finally he pulled away from her. 'God, Charlotte, you'll have to forgive me. I lost control.' Charlotte was perfectly happy to carry on losing control, and swap more spit, and drag him

229

upstairs to her flat, and imprison him for several days. But he squeezed her hand and backed off. 'I'll be in touch. Bye.'

As she climbed the stairs to her flat she sang, 'Yes, yes, yes!' to herself. It had finally happened, although why he felt it necessary to apologise, she didn't quite understand. By the time she had showered away the evening, and the steamed-up mental frenzy, she was thinking more rationally. Perhaps a widower might not feel like hurling himself into her bed, having only just realised that he was the object of her affection. When Charlotte had wriggled down between the sheets, she lay wondering what would happen next. Would he regret the kiss? Would there be more evenings of chatter until he had got his mind around the carnal aspect of their . . . whatever it was they had?

And why was she so keen to get him into this bed of hers, when she had been appalled by the prospect of exchanging bodily fluids with anyone for the past year, since she had left David? Out of the void came a song from the early Eighties: '*Is this a love thing, or is this just a sex thing?*' It was uninvited, but it chorused through her brain in a most annoying manner.

As Charlotte lay there wondering if Michael was an on-top lover, or an underneath type, the Minister was confronting the hateful red box that awaited him at home. He took a highlighting pen, and went through the first document, colouring passages at random. It would make his officials think that Michael had read the contents carefully, when in fact his mind was less than a mile away, with Charlotte. Was it madness to try to wrestle her away from the boyfriend Eddie Power had hinted at? Would Michael humiliate himself in the process? Did Charlotte's kiss mean that she was open to persuasion, or just rather sorry for an old codger like M. Fitzgerald because she would be staying with what she had?

Michael plodded through his notes for the following day, and went to bed feeling weightlessly lightheaded, and distracted by the rediscovery of his sexual urge.

It wasn't until the following morning, when he switched on the *Today* programme, that he learned about the UVF's latest atrocity in County Donegal. It was the first attack on the Eire side of the border since the early 1970s; an ominous turn of events. Evidently the Secretary of State was handling the press himself, and was using the opportunity to repeat the Government's resolve not to deal with terrorists. The odd thing was that Grace's PPS hadn't rung the junior minister when they received news of the attack on the Garda Patrol last night. Why not? Michael pushed this disquieting question to the back of his mind, and hurried to catch the early plane to Belfast.

There was another Ulster item on the *Today* programme, but Michael was too preoccupied by Grace's manoeuvrings for the other news to register. Charlotte, however, heard it while she was getting dressed: the UVF had claimed responsibility for the assassination of two people, a husband and wife, at their semi-detached home just off the Lisburn Road, in Belfast 9. That was near where Tim lived, she recalled. Brian Taylor, a school-teacher, and his wife Irene had been shot to death when intruders broke down their back door and entered their house in the early hours. Mrs Taylor, who had worked at NIPD HQ, had been targeted for her 'treachery'.

Tim had not revealed the name of the woman who had noticed the phantom photocopying in Special Branch, but it was obvious that she worked at NIPD. Not any more. A bewildered, frightened Charlotte set out for Westminster with an empty stomach: not even plain yoghurt would have stayed down. As she swayed backwards and forwards in the crowded Circle Line carriage she

tried to convince herself that Irene Taylor was not Tim's inform-
ant. What on earth could she say to her BBC Belfast colleague if
the dead woman was one and the same?

When she logged into her terminal in the BBC cubbyhole off
the Press Gallery, she searched the wires services for details of
the double murder. Then she called Michael at Stormont, and
was promptly referred to the Press Office by his secretary. When
the reporter insisted on leaving a message, she was told that the
Minister would be out of the office for most of the day.

Charlotte groped around for something appropriate to say
to Tim. Then girding her loins she called the BBC newsroom
in Belfast. After an unhappy conversation, during which Charlotte promised to find out what had happened at the Fitzgerald
end of the story, she went for a wander around the Palace to
clear her aching head. Her excuse for this diversion was that
she was collecting the day's Order Papers from the strange
little office in the basement where bills and notices were
published. She knew of more than one sex-starved MP who
lurked at the foot of the steep staircase in the hope of getting a
glimpse of knicker.

Charlotte's brain was in such a cloud of preoccupation that
she was unaware of the click of Mandy's heels behind her.

'Hey, Michael's been trying to call you,' she announced
between cracks at the gum in her mouth. 'He's out today. You
want his mobile number?' she sneered contemptuously as she
took in the reporter's unadventurous dark grey skirt suit. Charlotte fled from the pert and pretty American, but as she scuttled
back to the Press Gallery, something about Mandy's voice stuck
rather irritatingly in her head: it was the way she had said 'out' as
if it was 'oot', like an owl, and not an American variety of owl
either. What part of the States did she come from? Charlotte

asked herself, wishing her rival would go back there on the next plane.

The day got worse; Michael was in the middle of a meeting in north Antrim, and unable to talk for long, but he promised he'd been as vague as possible about the source of the information when he had spoken to Mackay of NIPD. Then Charlotte was forced to turn down his offer of dinner the following evening because she was working on the late shift.

Just when she reckoned she had hit rock bottom, the quality of life took a further lurch downwards: Rodney went thermonuclear when Charlotte asked if she could take the day after tomorrow off work.

'Why such short notice? Has someone in your family died?' he asked with a glowering fury that could have passed for rabies in a dog.

'No, and I'm sorry about this, I really am, but it's terribly important,' she muttered enigmatically. Rodney was the last person who would understand why she was hosting a powwow between a terrorist and a Minister.

'So important that you can't tell me about it? Just like your champagne-swilling sessions with obscure Peers of the realm: you assure me you're getting vital information from your contacts, but you can never quite articulate what it is that you've learned.'

Charlotte blushed and examined the toes of her shoes. How satisfying it would be to deliver a swift but precise kick to Rodney's groin.

'Are you deliberately trying to piss me off?' her boss continued. 'I can't just rearrange the week's rota because you suddenly decide you're indisposed for some mysterious reason. You should ask yourself how serious you are about your future in journalism. I don't see your reports getting any crisper or clearer.'

Despite this unhappy exchange, during which Charlotte miraculously kept her mouth shut, she succeeded in getting the day off. Nevertheless, she was left with the crystal-clear impression that she had used up another life, and there would be no more similar stunts. However, Rodney's warnings were petty to the point of irrelevance while Charlotte had the murder of Irene Taylor and her husband on her conscience. Death had a way of putting the importance of her mortgage payments into perspective.

The fate of the Taylors had slipped Michael's mind some time ago, mainly because he had been talked at by a most interesting old man throughout a lunch that was accompanied by phenomenal quantities of wine. The Minister was the guest of Sir Edward Montgomery, whose family had been High Sheriffs of Antrim since 1603. It was like unearthing a dinosaur; a representative of the grand, landed folk who had arrived from Scotland, and cultivated the previously Catholic acres that the Monarch had redistributed to them. The Montgomerys had later built the linen factories that made Ulster so prosperous in the nineteenth century.

Naturally the weather-beaten, silver-haired Sir Edward (Eton and the Guards) spoke with an upper-class English accent, without a trace of Irish, although he continually referred to 'his fellow Irishmen' in a way that the followers of the Reverend Robert Scott would never countenance. 'My father and my grandfather were members of the Orange Order but it's a terrible load of rubbish now. Full of the most awful types. And d'you know, they have the gall to march behind the temperance banner at those dreary parades when a lot of them are paralytically drunk. And they cheer God Bob when he tells them about the damnation of man and the evils of the flesh. Well, I'm not having some midget vicar tell me how many gin and tonics I should consume.'

Then Sir Edward gestured expansively at the rolling acres beyond the dining-room window of Montgomery Lodge. 'The Loyal Unionist Party has ruined this country. They've thrown out all the decent Unionists – you know, the old breed of Ulster Unionists who would have found a gradual way to give the Catholics a say. And now we've got this civil war.'

After lunch, Sir Edward led Michael out into the lush landscaped garden which sloped down to the River Bann. 'You see that, over there?' He pointed at the rolling green fields of County Londonderry, on the other bank. 'If Reverend Scott gets his way, that'll belong to Eire before long. I'm serious. They'll renegotiate the borders and give everything west of the Bann to the Irish,' the old baronet declared in horror. 'That's the bloody stupid position Scott and all these thugs are getting us into. Then it'll be down to the grass men to hold the fort in what remains of Ulster.'

'Who are the grass men?' Michael enquired of the bleary eyes.

'The rough crowd – the UVF and the other paramilitaries. They'll eat grass to survive if they have to, but they're not going to surrender this land to Rome. The sacrifices don't matter to them, because they're not interested in a normal life. They'll eat grass to protect their little Eden. Never mind that their sort has already destroyed what was good in this Province.'

With a chilling vision in mind of the grass men sinking their teeth into the Army's Judas File, Michael was driven back through the delightful Antrim countryside to Aldergrove Airport. During the hour-long journey he tried to concentrate on work, but his brain was too clouded by wine, and Sir Edward's warnings.

Michael's mind wandered to the worst that might happen. The British would tell Ulster to sod off; the grass men would drive every last Catholic west across the Bann and then hunker down in what remained of Northern Ireland; and thousands of terrified Protestants would stream north and east to avoid being subsumed in the expanded Eire.

Battered by these nightmarish images, Michael contemplated the abyss. Then as he passed through one of the dour, grey little Protestant Antrim towns, with their plethora of satellite dishes and video rental shops and Union Jacks, the answer struck the Minister between the eyes: he would make Northern Ireland a tax haven! That would open the gates to an influx of wealth and investment.

Better still, he would insist that in order to get residency status, and thus avoid tax, the world's billionaires would have to put their money in Ulster banks, and then fulfil one criterion: they would have to buy a potential luxury apartment in the Divis blocks of flats in the most terrible part of the Falls Road. The Divis was burnt out in 1972, and had been cockroach- and drop-out infested since. The area needed an injection of investment, and of middle-class inhabitants, and this was how to attract them.

Then Northern Ireland would open its doors to all the entrepreneurs from Hong Kong who were fleeing Chinese rule. His own dear Government had decided they would only let in civil servants from Hong Kong – just the people the British economy needed. But Michael would make Ulster a haven for capitalist refugees. Then both communities in Northern Ireland could unite in their xenophobic dislike of Chinese immigrants.

Finally, the Northern Ireland Office would build a new

university in Springmartin, in the heart of Provo territory. Then the former terrorists could learn computer sciences, and financial management, and creative accounting, so Northern Ireland could become a world centre for computer processing and money-laundering. If one in every five corporate executives in the United States was Irish, then it stood to reason that business was in their genes.

Buoyed by these Trump-esque fantasies, the Minister bade farewell to James, his excellent former-detective driver, and clambered onto the British Midland flight to Heathrow.

Chapter Nineteen

'Oh, I like that,' Neil remarked when he caught sight of the painting in Charlotte's hall. 'That's a fine piece of work.'

'Thank you. I got it at a gallery in the Ormeau Road.' This information caused the heavy, square spectacles to rise with interest.

'I'll have to pay the place a visit.'

Next time you're ethnic cleansing in that part of town, Charlotte added silently as she hung up Neil's imitation Barbour. 'So, what brings you to London?' she asked conversationally, then wondered if he might be doing a recce on future bomb venues here.

'My brother and his family live in Ealing, so we're staying there. The wife's shopping with the boys this morning, and, God help me, we're going to a matinée of some Andrew Lloyd Webber thing this afternoon. Not my idea, I hasten to add. Then it's Thorpe Park amusement centre tomorrow. But I shouldn't be complaining because this is better than Euro-Disney, which was the kids' first choice.'

Charlotte was tempted to ask how someone who had spent the last twenty years living on social security when not in prison could afford to go to Euro-Disney, but she erred on the side of discretion.

'Make yourself comfortable while I get some coffee.' She pointed him at her sitting room. The brains behind the St Patrick's Day Massacre requested decaf, then examined her collection of Agatha Christies. What would she say to her mother if she called right now? 'Can't talk, Mum. I'm entertaining a man from the UVF.'

She was quite enjoying the surreal quality of this encounter, but she was relieved when Michael arrived, and they could get down to business.

'I want to hear exactly what your organisation wants from the British Government, and what it'll take to make you stop the ethnic cleansing and the bombing for good. You're obviously not satisfied that the Irish people were sincere when they voted to respect the wishes of the majority in Northern Ireland. So if a referendum won't work, what will make you feel confident that Ulster won't be sold out to Dublin?'

Neil pushed the spectacles up his nose and blinked. 'The British Government has got to start doing its job, and protect us. You can't be surprised that we're concerned about our future when you've allowed the Gerry O'Kalashnikovs into Stormont. They'll be running the Province soon, and London is washing its hands of the responsibility. The troops have been withdrawn, the IRA are in the RUC now. What next?' He shrugged, incredulous.

'But as long as Protestants and Unionists make up the majority in Ulster there can't be a united Ireland,' Michael persisted. 'And you know as well as I do that there are a sizable minority of Catholics in Northern Ireland who won't vote for unity with the south. Doesn't that make you rest easier?'

'Not while the British Government is letting Dublin in through the back door with these cross-border commissions. Next thing, London'll say, "OK, let's allow a referendum of all of Ireland, and if the majority of people on the whole island want unity, then they get it." Which means the majority in Ulster becomes a minority in a referendum.'

'Hang on. What makes you think the Irish really want a united Ireland? They can't afford to take on the financial burden of Ulster. They've got a nice little earner going on the South, what with ripping off the European Union. Why should they screw it up by taking on nearly a million Protestants who detest the idea of being Irish?'

'It's not just a question of money,' Neil retorted primly. 'The voters of Ireland have a deep, historical desire for a united Ireland. Don't underestimate that.'

'And don't you underestimate the nature of voters every-where: they care about tax, tax and tax. You're being sentimental about the solidarity of the Irish people.' Michael reckoned sentimentality wasn't part of Neil's self-image. He noticed the UVF man's eyes flash with anger behind his thick lenses.

'It's part of the Church of Rome's plan,' Neil shot back. 'They want to take over the northern European countries.'

'Oh, come on! That's just Reverend Scott's nonsense. Surely you don't believe that stuff about the Irish in that referendum being cunning and pretending to renounce their claims on Ulster just to trick the British Government? It'd be the most impressive conspiracy in history.' Michael laughed. 'Look, Neil, hasn't it occurred to you that Scott's just winding you up, egging you on to do his dirty work for him? And then he condemns your acts of violence as if it was nothing to do with him.'

'I don't take orders from anyone,' Neil fumed, but Michael dismissed his words with a shrug.

'Shall I tell you his reaction when I asked him what he wanted the Northern Ireland Office to do about schools and jobs in

Belfast? He didn't give a fuck because he doesn't live there. And he knows the working classes haven't got anyone else to vote for except him. Keep them poor and ignorant – that's his strategy. And stir them up every now and then with a bit of Stone Age tub-thumping to keep them in line.'

'Robert Scott is the authentic voice of the Unionist people.' Neil sounded like a parrot on Valium.

'When has he ever put his arse on the line, or lived in a street that was petrol-bombed by the IRA?'

Neil turned away with silent fury as Michael continued: 'I know you were involved in the Ulster Workers' Strike in 1974. Now haven't you ever wondered why the Protestant working classes and the paramilitaries and the trade unions failed to follow up the momentum, and to form a political party that really represented the people who were at the sharp end of the Troubles?'

'I s'pose it just kind of fell apart,' Neil said feebly.

'The reason is that God Bob was working very hard behind the scenes to destroy the Ulster Workers' Council. He told anyone who'd listen that you were Commies, taking money from Libya. I'll show you the bloody Intelligence reports, if you want proof. He knew he'd be out of a job if you lot got your act together.'

'Reverend Scott sees through the Irish. And he knows that we can't trust the British.'

'Hang on, I thought you were loyal to the British – well, your *idea* of "Britain", which is about thirty years out of date, by the way.'

Neil's eyes flashed. 'We're loyal to the Crown.'

'Loyal to He Who Would Be A Tampon?' Michael asked incredulously. 'Loyal to a bunch of Germans, the Battenbergs, the Saxe-Coburgs, who plucked the name Windsor off a map to make themselves sound English?'

Before Michael could reach across and grip Neil around his polo-neck-jumpered neck, Charlotte suggested maybe some ice cream would lower the temperature. The reporter was so accustomed to eating ice cream at any time of day or night that it did not occur to her that others might consider it peculiar to devour a tub or two with their morning coffee.

'Yes, please,' said the representative of Murder Incorporated with the most enthusiasm he had displayed since his arrival. 'And may I use your lavatory?'

After Charlotte had pointed him to the loo, Michael followed her into the kitchen. 'Thanks for calling half-time,' he remarked with a serious face as she pulled tubs of ice cream out of the freezer. Then they both laughed, and Charlotte handed him three bowls and spoons. 'It's good to see you,' he said quietly.

She was about to reciprocate when she noticed that his smile had vanished, and that his eyes had fixed on something over her shoulder. She swung around and saw that he was looking at the photograph on her bulletin board. 'He's very handsome,' Michael commented after some effort not to grab the picture of the boyfriend and tear it into shreds.

'Jeremy? Gorgeous, isn't he? I took that last summer when we were on holiday in Portugal,' she explained over her shoulder as she carried the ice cream to the dining room.

'Charlotte, have you made plans with him? I mean, are you considering . . . you know?' he continued lamely.

'This summer, you mean?' she asked, and wondered why Michael was wincing.

'Oh, this looks good.' Neil picked up the tub of Ben and Jerry's 'Chunky Monkey'.

'Please dig in,' cooed the gracious hostess. 'Try all of them.'

'Wonderful,' Neil said after a spoonful of 'Cherry Garcia'. 'Better than Jerry Garcia's music.'

'Steady on,' objected Michael. 'It's one thing insulting the integrity of the British Government, but I could get mean if you bring the Grateful Dead into this.'

'I went to the Eagles concert last night,' Neil said pleasantly. 'They were at Wembley Arena.'

'And?' Michael prompted.

'Marvellous. Great. I'm strictly symphonic music and opera these days, but I've still got a soft spot for West Coast rock, you know. Anyway, they were as excellent as ever.'

The Minister's eyes narrowed. 'Do you identify with *Desperado*?'

'Do you identify with *There's A New Kid In Town*?'

'Is that why you're in London?' Michael asked. 'The Eagles?'

'Right, but I'm paying the price tomorrow with a trip to Thorpe Park for my boys. Ever been?'

Michael shook his head. 'No. My daughter wouldn't tolerate an amusement park – unless she was there to watch the rides collapse and crush everyone. Then she could have a good laugh.'

'I see,' Neil said cautiously, and attacked the Chocolate Chip Cookie Dough. 'How come?'

'Laura had a strange upbringing. Caroline, my wife, thought it would be interesting to give her a toy alligator rather than a soppy old bear when she was a tiny baby, and I think that was the initial trigger.'

'An alligator?' Charlotte asked.

'Yes. A cuddly alligator,' Michael said matter-of-factly. 'And we used to sing her that David Bowie song to get her off to

244

sleep.' He looked at Charlotte, but found only incomprehension.

'Don't you remember it?' Neil sounded surprised. ' "I'm an alligator. I'm a Momma-Pappa coming for you," ' he sang. 'Very apt, when you think of it.'

Charlotte wondered what she had been doing while these men were raising their children. She and her girlfriends had idled about each other's boudoirs, listened to Dire Straits and the Pointer Sisters, and borrowed their father's cars to go roaring around the lanes near her home on their way to country pubs where they studiously ignored the boys from the local school. The poverty of her own reminiscences provoked Charlotte to interrupt her guests.

'What about an internationally enforceable declaration from the Irish Government that states they aren't interested in a united Ireland against the wishes of the Unionist majority? It'd have to be endorsed by the UN and NATO and the European Union. And the Irish would forfeit their Euro-slush if they broke their word,' she added.

'Ah, now that's interesting,' Neil said as he examined the side of the Chunky Monkey ice cream, and for a moment Charlotte wondered if he was referring to Ben and Jerry's philanthropic tendencies. He put the carton back on the table and licked his lips. 'I think there's scope for that.'

This cheered Michael a bit after the depression of seeing the photo of Charlotte's boy-friend. 'OK. What else will you consider? How about some demilitarised zones where both you and the IRA stop the ethnic cleansing?'

'Oh, so you recognise that the IRA's doing it too, eh? That's a breakthrough, I suppose. They've conned the media into giving them the credit for the peace. That's like giving the East Germans credit for how good the Dresden Opera was – it ignores a few other byproducts of Communism.'

'One of the reasons they've conned the media is that their spokesmen and women are articulate,' Charlotte chipped in, 'and they don't wallow in self-pity. Like white South Africans.'

'Thanks for the advice, but if London sells us out we'll bomb our way into Stormont like the IRA have.'

'So you seriously expect the Catholics to be second-class citizens without any rights under your ideal regime?'

'Of course not. We've always said we'll share power with them in a Regional Government. And we'll keep the Bill of Rights.'

'Hang on, Neil. Reverend Scott won't countenance any type of power-sharing. Are you daring to disobey him?'

'Oh, for fuck's sake. We're pragmatic in my part of town. We just don't want fucking Dublin involved. Bill of Rights: great. A proportional share of a power-sharing executive: OK.'

'Why not fifty per cent?' Charlotte asked. 'The Catholics'll outbreed you soon. The school population's already fifty-fifty, so it's in your interest to secure half the power before you become a minority.'

Neil looked suitably mortified, but he didn't reject her suggestion, Michael noticed. For another hour they hammered out areas where the Loyalists were prepared to take a realistic, compromising approach which was at odds with Reverend Scott. When Michael left Charlotte's flat he felt as though a terrible spell had been broken, and that possibly, but only possibly, there was scope for progress.

He returned to the Range Rover parked downstairs half-expecting his security detail to report that a UVF man had been spotted in the area. But his guards were more concerned with getting him to Heathrow in time for the next plane to Belfast.

The government wanted its Ministers and civil servants to stop wasting money on military flights around the world so they used commercial airlines whenever possible, and Michael had grown accustomed to the commuter routine. This week Laura and Delva would be following him over, and together they would decide how to decorate the new house. In other words, father and daughter would fight constantly until Delva acted as UN mediator.

Michael sat in the back of the Range Rover, notepad on knee, jotting down the important points from the meeting. But his mind kept sliding away to Charlotte, romantic fool that he was. This, surely, was the reason he had been unwise to let his guard down. Now he would torture himself trying to put a positive gloss on the fact that she had a glamorous boy-friend of her own age whom she might even marry this summer.

If he was sensible and grown-up, he would do the dignified thing, and fade into the background. He would stop pestering her with phone calls, and avoid those late-night gossip sessions in Palace of Westminster bars. Otherwise his heart and ego would be badly bruised. With suitably manful determination he yanked his attention back to the murderers and liars, and their limited agendas.

Charlotte hoped to hear from Michael over the weekend, but he didn't call. This lack of communication was both annoying and slightly upsetting, but sadly she was not privy to the Minister's resolve not to put himself in competition with Jeremy, whom he assumed was the young man in her life. She whiled away the time trying to improve the appearance of her flat, worrying about her so-called career, watching Bette Davis videos, and going to a ghastly dinner party where a City fund manager with insufficiently clean fingernails bored her into a parallel universe of daydreams where Government Ministers turned up on her door-step without warning. So much for her spare time: it was a relief to get back to the unreality of Westminster.

On Monday morning, Michael returned to London and went straight into a hastily arranged meeting with his boss at Admiralty House. Sir Trevor Grace listened as his junior minister reported on the session with Neil, and his surreptitious encounters with God Bob's deputies.

'I need more time to get enough solid commitments from each side to make sure that we could sustain talks. It hinges on isolating Reverend Scott from the more pragmatic Unionists and Loyalists who see that time is running out for them. Not surprisingly, the common theme that swings them into line is that Dublin should be excluded from everything.'

'I can just see Gerry Adams MP buying that.' Grace flashed his deputy a sceptical glare. 'I don't understand why we should allow these UVF diehards in on talks if they don't renounce violence first.'

'Because the Loyalists who are willing to compromise can't risk dragging their comrades into a ceasefire, then finding that the British Government and the Unionists shaft them. That leaves them exposed, hanging on the wire. It's about their personal survival; it's as simple as that.'

Grace was unmoved by Michael's passion. 'The British Government cannot be seen talking to terrorists who are still in the business of blowing people up.'

'Why not have pre-talks, or a caucus?'

The Secretary of State laughed uncharitably. 'Only a lawyer would think of something like pre-talks, Mike. When are talks not talks? When a barrister says so. Yeah, I get it. Very clever.'

'Just give me enough time to find some solid ground—'

'Fine.'

'And there's another matter. I'm concerned that the IRA and UVF hard men might decide to take out the compromisers to ensure that the war continues. So I'd like you to consider some type of protective arrangement for the ones who are willing to talk.'

Elvis frowned sourly. 'Yeah, but how do we know who to keep an eye on? I mean, we can't devote brigades of men to this. If anyone found out we were protecting one Al Capone from another we'd look bloody stupid.'

'The Judas File.'

'The what?' Grace asked with barely suppressed irritation.

'The Army have got a special list of the remaining IRA and Loyalist men who they reckon'll do a deal.'

'Oh yeah – of course. OK, leave it with me. Now, how are we doing with arrangements for the PM's visit?'

As Michael wandered through the corridors of Admiralty House after his meeting with Grace, he wondered why he was so neutral on these secret negotiations. Perhaps Michael was still a small boy who enjoyed the whiff of conspiracy, but the exercise left the Secretary of State neither negative nor interested. Grace treated the whole episode as if he'd been there before, and knew it was futile. Perhaps that was the case, and every other innocent junior minister had tried the same approach.

But if that was so, then why hadn't Neil told him he was wasting his time? Why hadn't the Loyal Unionist undertakers shouted him down, instead of seeking him out for quiet consultations every few days?

When Michael reached his office he found that his desk was once more besieged by the bureaucratic ammunition of his civil servants – files, memos, and legislative instruments. He looked through the strata of rubbish, but his mind went back to his boss. Michael wasn't looking for Elvis's praise, but he had no idea what he had done to arouse Grace's hostility. Mandy had told him that Elvis was jealous: a Belfast opinion poll found that Michael Fitzgerald was the most popular Northern Ireland Minister in more than twenty years. His straight talk had apparently struck a chord, as had his visibility: he often went to Belfast's restaurants, theatres, and cinemas with either his research assistant, or Laura and Delva.

Visibility reminded him of the Prime Minister's forthcoming visit: a loopy idea in Michael's view, but Grace had assured him that Downing Street was adamant. He pushed his concerns to one side, and got on with another loopy idea; redrafting the instrument that would give reparations and amnesties to former IRA men still living overseas.

At eleven o'clock that same morning, Charlotte Carter was wrapping an interview on St Stephen's Green, the patch of grass opposite the House of Lords, where TV crews set up shop to *vox pop* MPs. She jogged back to the Commons, rehearsing the cue she would put on the start of the interview before she sent it to BBC Television Centre. She had very little time to turn it around, so she waved her pass and scuttled through the Commons security barriers as fast as possible without looking suspicious.

However, her pace slackened when she realised that Sir Trevor Grace was ahead of her. He was ambling along a corridor, deep in conversation with the small, but instantly recognisable God Bob. Charlotte got within earshot and then slowed down. They were discussing the Assembly, and some by-elections. To her surprise, the Reverend Scott looked at ease with Grace, and they were both laughing. That was odd in itself

– the leader of the Loyal Unionists usually savaged Grace in the Chamber.

The two men stopped for a moment, and Charlotte pretended to be scrutinising some ancient law report on the bookshelf to her side. Grace laughed again, and remarked that this would deal with Dublin for a few decades. Then the two politicians resumed their perambulation, but instead of continuing down the corridor, they took a sharp right. Charlotte trotted after them, but found herself facing the door of the men's lavatory.

Upstairs in the BBC reporters' room, with time running out, Charlotte began to bash out a less-than-literary cue to the video clip.

'You're cutting it a bit fine, aren't you?' a familiar voice droned. She sensed Rodney's unwelcome presence behind her, peering over her shoulder at the word-processor screen.

'It'll be OK,' she said cheerfully, 'I'm almost through.'

'I don't understand why it takes you so long to ask an MP two questions and then write a bloody cue. I mean, this isn't a documentary you're putting together.'

And if you'd leave me alone I could get this done and sent to Television Centre in half the time, she was tempted to respond, but she gritted her teeth and concentrated on her script.

'What have you been doing?' Rodney persisted. Charlotte rolled her eyes heavenward and bit her lip in annoyance. 'I want an explanation.'

'OK, I'll tell you. I was eavesdropping on a rather strange conversation between Reverend Scott of the LUP, and Sir Trevor Grace. I suspect they're up to no good and—'

'Ah, so *this* is the high-minded, principled journalism you espouse. Spying on Ministers of the Crown? What a revelation!'

Charlotte smiled grimly and kept on typing. 'How's this?' she asked. 'Can I send it to Shepherds Bush now?'

Rodney read it and grunted. 'It'll have to do, I suppose, considering what time it is.'

When her boss had gone on his merry way, Charlotte tried without success to track down Michael to tell him about Grace and God Bob. Mandy was as ghastly as ever on the phone, and Charlotte wondered if the reason the Minister hadn't followed up on their moment of passion last week was because he really was entangled with the hateful troll with big hair. No wonder he hadn't wanted to know more about the unusual connection between Mandy and Scott. Not a comforting thought, so Charlotte consoled herself with a bag of cheeseywhatsits and two chocolate bars.

Unhealthy food was also the order of the day at the cafeteria at the NIPD station at Castlereagh. Ken McTaggart and his superior officer carried trays loaded with fish and chips to a quiet corner, and tried to look as unwelcoming as possible when other lunchers approached their table.

'The Secretary of State's office has been on to Mackay about some special Army Intelligence list. Grace wants to know more about it, which makes it difficult for the Chief, because he had to admit he's never heard of it. The Army's been keeping it to themselves.'

'So what the fuck is it?' Ken's mouth was full of chips, and like many Belfast natives the word came out 'fok'.

'It's called the Judas File, and it's supposed to be a directory of Provos and ours who're open to persuasion, if they're offered the right deal.'

Ken slurped at his tea. 'So what? It'd be more to the point if we could get hold of a list of touts, and deal with them.'

His superior officer sounded as if his patience was being tested, but he kept his voice down, nevertheless. 'The point is that the cunts on this list'll be given protection, if people start putting together deals.'

'What kind of deals, for fuck's sake? No one's making deals. This Assembly's already full of Provos. Why'd they need a deal?'

Ken's colleague shrugged, and pushed away his empty plate. 'I'm just telling you this, right? Now, kindly pass it on.'

'Right.' Ken nodded and attacked the sponge pudding. 'Sorry. I'm just, well . . . the way it's going, next thing you know the fucking Teapot'll have his picture on our five-pound note.'

His colleague was used to Ken's inarticulate pessimism and anger. When someone got a nosebleed Ken started measuring them up for the coffin. But in this case Ken was right; the last thing they needed was their own people going soft.

Ken would be angrier still when he realised that he was to be included in the next round of redundancies, the senior officer thought wistfully as he watched Ken go.

Chapter Twenty

At 8 p.m. Paula Tyler from IRN declared that she couldn't bear one more speech on supplementary benefit loopholes, and that she was going to buy Charlotte a drink. The BBC reporter had little reason to follow every syllable of the debate, since she had already done her turn for the day with a short piece for the *Six O'Clock News*. Sadly, her masterpiece never reached the screen because a kidnapped baby had pushed her out of the running order. Who cared what the Opposition were planning to do if they won the next election anyway, when there were blubbing relatives of Baby Wayne to interview?

Paula led the way up the steep steps to the door at the back of the Press Gallery. It opened onto a long, wood-panelled room where journalists milled about gossiping, and reading ministerial announcements that were deposited on a big table. Out of habit Paula and Charlotte skimmed the press releases from Government departments: *New Dairy Regulations Spell Good News For Farmers*, and *Four-Million-Pound Road Scheme for Marginal Conservative Seat Announced*.

'What's this about?' the IRN correspondent asked. 'Trevor Grace announces a competition to design a new flag for Northern Ireland. Winner to be picked by the Assembly.'

Charlotte glanced at Paula and frowned. 'Are you kidding? What the hell's he up to?' she muttered when she reached the end of the statement. 'It says here it's being run in accordance with the European Directive on Regional Ethnic and Cultural Diversity, Clause 4, subsection 9a. *Symbols must be found to reflect the aspirations of all sections of the community*. Good grief! Grace must have hunted through the small print to find this one.'

Charlotte bit her bottom lip and put the paper down. Then she picked it up again to check when it had been released: 4 p.m., just an hour ago. 'I'll catch you up in the bar, Paula. I've got to make a call. The usual, please,' she called over her shoulder as she bolted to the BBC office down the corridor.

There was no response on Michael's private line in Belfast, and when Charlotte tried the Whitehall office she got the ever late-working Mandy, who was about as helpful as laddered tights. The pert and pretty dwarf wouldn't even divulge where the Minister was. Then Charlotte tracked down her boss, Rodney, who was in Annie's Bar, drinking with an arse-licking BBC trainee.

'This is dynamite!' She pushed the press release beneath his nose. 'I told you Grace was up to something, didn't I? If he could pick one issue guaranteed to wind up both sides in Ulster, this is it. And he's trying to make it look like it's been foisted on him by the Europeans—'

'Belfast'll cover it,' Rodney interrupted in his flat, nasal voice, and passed back the press release.

'But this is incredibly important! The Union Jack is the most potent symbol for the Unionists. They'll lay down their lives to defend it. But to the Catholic Nationalists, the Union Jack is a symbol of centuries of repression.' Charlotte gripped the sheet

256

of paper in her fist and tried to stop herself hopping up and down on the spot.

But her boss shrugged, stifled a yawn, and sipped his pint. 'That's why Belfast should do it,' he repeated dispassionately.

A perplexed Charlotte joined Paula in the Press Bar, but as the other Lobby Correspondents nattered and drank, she retreated further and further into the mental puzzle of Northern Ireland, and the sinister games of Sir Trevor Grace.

When everyone else headed to the dining room, Charlotte made her excuses and slipped away. With the help of an internal Palace of Westminster phone she located Eddie Power, and five minutes later Labour's Northern Ireland spokesman had bought them a bottle of white Rioja in the Strangers' Bar, and was offering her his own interpretation of Grace's press release.

'This'll scupper any meeting of minds Michael might have managed to bring about with God Bob's deputies. The Loyalists'll go berserk, Charlotte, and the Nationalists'll be intolerably pleased with themselves, and start going on about putting the harp and the shamrock and a picture of Bobby Sands on their new flag. It's a recipe made in hell,' Eddie summarised. 'It'll be like a homicidal Eurovision Song Contest.'

'So why's he doing it? I don't understand.' Charlotte's brow furrowed with confusion. 'Every Minister knows you ignore ninety per cent of the Euro-rules and select the ones that are convenient.'

'I don't know what Grace is up to, but the result'll be that all varieties of Unionist and Loyalist will fall into line.' Power sipped his wine and nodded philosophically. In the moment's silence that followed, Charlotte realised that Michael must have told his old schoolchum about his meeting with Neil: true friends indeed. 'They'll tell Michael to fuck off, and they won't be too happy that he misled them either,' Eddie added.

'But it isn't his fault,' Charlotte insisted with clenched fists.

'They aren't going to know that. And as for those Loyal Unionists who established a dialogue with Michael, they won't believe he wasn't leading them on. They'll fear that someone might have shopped them to God Bob, and they won't be too chuffed. I hope Michael's watching himself.'

The journalist and the MP sat in gloomy silence for a moment. 'What's Michael say?' Eddie asked. 'Have you spoken to him?'

Charlotte shook her head, and poured them both more wine. 'I couldn't get past Randy Mandy.'

'I don't like her,' Eddie sneered, and Charlotte assented in this judgement. Then she told him about the peculiar encounter between Mandy and God Bob at the priests' meeting in Armagh. The Labour MP pulled himself up straight in the leather chair. 'They really knew each other?'

'And she was more than a little displeased that he hailed her so warmly. If looks could have killed . . .'

'I think I'll check out her records with the people here who issue Houses of Parliament security passes. They must have some background information on her.'

'Hang on,' the reporter mused. 'If she had some dubious connection with Reverend Scott, isn't it rather unlikely that she would have been given security clearance to work at the Northern Ireland Office?'

Eddie rolled his eyes at the reporter's naivety. 'Mistakes happen all the time, Charlotte, especially with American research assistants, because it takes time and effort and transatlantic phone calls to dig into their background. Anyway, Mandy came with Michael from the MOD. They will have OK'd her there, and I bet Grace's lot wouldn't be fagged to go through the whole rigmarole again.'

Eddie was scribbling himself a note when a fellow Shadow Cabinet member arrived breathless in the bar. 'Thank Christ I've found you,' he puffed. '*News at Ten* want you – *now*. All the Unionist members of the Northern Ireland Assembly have resigned – the Official Unionists and God Bob's lot. And they're forcing by-elections in their Westminster seats too. It's about the flag thing.'

'Shit!' Eddie shrieked and sprang to his feet. 'This is going to be a fucking meltdown.'

But Charlotte's mind was on more mundane matters. 'The minute you've done *News at Ten*, come to the BBC studio because *Newsnight*'ll want you, and so will BBC Ulster. Now go, quickly.' She pushed him down the corridor in front of her.

When she reached the Millbank building the newsroom was in a state of noisy chaos as journalists struggled to put together radio and TV bulletins for immediate consumption. 'What can I do?' she asked Rodney when she arrived, but he waved her out of the way and answered the phone on his desk. 'Yes, she's here,' he grunted in disbelief. 'Well, no, there are other journalists here who would be more appropriate for that . . . Oh . . . I'll put her on,' he said shortly and handed Charlotte the phone. 'It's *Newsnight*,' he mumbled tersely.

It transpired that the producer of *Newsnight* had liked her reports from Belfast, and he regarded it as a minor miracle that they had a reporter who understood Ulster politics on hand. For the next hour and a half Charlotte was fully occupied on St Stephen's Green, interviewing whichever Northern Ireland MPs happened to be around at Westminster that evening, be they SDLP or Unionists.

In between live spots on the programme, Charlotte hopped around in the cold, damp night air, and listened to the rest of the show through her earpiece. Michael was being interviewed from the Millbank studio, behind her. He had been put up by the Northern Ireland Office to deal with the flak about the flag, and the by-elections. When *Newsnight* went to Belfast for a live comment from Reverend Scott, Charlotte recalled Grace's remark to God Bob about by-elections earlier today, in the Commons corridor. And she wondered how Scott had known to get himself back to Ulster this evening in time for Grace's press release about the flag. Now Scott was perfectly placed to drum up paranoia amongst the faithful.

'These by-elections are not just a referendum on the future of this corrupt, terrorist-ridden Assembly,' he howled down Charlotte's earpiece. 'We shall be asking the people of our constituencies to deliver their verdict on the so-called peace process to date. The people of Ulster know they have been betrayed by the Government in London, and they know they'll be betrayed again. It is only a matter of months until Westminster stands back and allows Ireland to swamp us, so we believe it is time to repartition Ulster. We demand that the borders of this Province should be redrawn to give two counties to the greedy imperialists in Dublin. Only then can our four Protestant counties of Ulster remain British, and avoid the insatiable hunger of the Papists. We must sacrifice two counties to save the rest.'

Charlotte stood in the glare of the outside-broadcast lights, with the April night air eating through her jacket, and closed her eyes in horror. It was getting worse and worse. She wanted to interrupt God Bob and challenge him to admit that he'd hatched up the whole thing with Trevor Grace. But Jeremy Paxman was handling the interview, not Charlotte Carter, a damp reporter on St Stephen's Green.

Then suddenly it was eleven-fifteen, and they were off air. Charlotte accepted profuse thanks from the *Newsnight* producer at Television Centre for her last-minute heroics, and she trailed back to the Commons feeling as though she had been hit by a truck. There must be something else I can do, she thought. But there wasn't.

She collected her coat, and decided to go home via the Lebanese takeaway in Queensway. Charlotte headed for the portico where taxis set down and picked up fares within the Palace of Westminster.

Suddenly a door crashed behind her, and she turned to find Michael, files of papers under his arm, hurrying down the corridor towards her. His skin was drawn tight and grey across his face, as if he had seen a ghost. The beautiful locks were particularly chaotic, and his collar was uncharacteristically undone.

'What happened?' she asked, but he shushed her and drew her to one side. 'What's Grace doing?' Charlotte repeated in a near whisper when they were out of the main thoroughfare. 'Why did he bounce you?'

Michael closed his eyes as if he was fighting back an angry response. 'Please, don't.'

'But—'

'Yes, I was bounced. He pulled the rug out from under me. Rather an effective political move, wouldn't you say?'

'But what now?'

Michael looked down at his feet and gave a rasping sigh. Charlotte noticed that he was shaking slightly. 'I've spent the entire evening trying to convince the Loyal Unionist apprentice undertakers that I wasn't plotting their personal downfall, but guess what? They don't believe a word I say. And why should they? And I expect our friend Neil is putting out a contract on me right now.'

'Oh God, it's so—' Charlotte moaned, but Michael cut her off again.

'Please don't tell me how bad it is, Charlotte. I know. I know I've been bounced.'

'I wish you'd returned my calls, Michael. I overheard Scott and Grace plotting about the by-elections earlier today.'

'Come on – are you serious?'

Charlotte glared at him and considered getting him around the throat. 'I left you messages,' she insisted angrily. Then she registered the misery and disbelief on Michael's exhausted face. 'Look, Michael, I'm telling you Grace is behind all this. He's trying to destroy the Assembly so the power-sharing idea falls apart. And he's in league with God Bob – it's all part of his crusade for the leadership of your great party. And don't forget the link between God Bob and Neil.'

Michael rubbed his eyes. 'Come on, Charlotte, that's a little far-fetched, I think. Grace is a bumbling fool, and he can't stand Catholics, but he's not in league with the Loyal Unionists.'

'He is!' the reporter rattled back, the veins in her neck standing out. 'You've got to go to Dublin and get their bloody Prime Minister to swear on his mother's grave that Ireland has no interest in Ulster! Can't you see? This is going to lead to civil war, this idea of redrawing the borders!'

'Charlotte, it's late, you're tired, and in the words of Pete Townshend, it's fucking awful. But Grace is *not* trying to provoke a civil war!'

'Oh Michael, listen to me,' she whimpered, and put a hand on his arm, but he pulled it away from her comforting touch.

'*No*, Charlotte! The last thing I need now is to be toyed with. Not after a day like this.'

'Who is toying with whom?' She stamped her slender foot angrily. 'I'd imagined that after snogging on my doorstep there might be some follow-up, but I'm beginning to wonder if it was all for the benefit of your security detail. Just a performance to explain your next visit to my place with Neil.'

Michael gave her a withering look. 'Well, you're wrong, and perhaps you're the one who should be examining her behaviour, with the commitment you already have.'

He walked past her and got into the waiting Range Rover which whooshed out of Palace Yard and into Parliament Square. The reporter stood numbly staring after the tail-lights, wondering what on earth Michael was accusing her of. She climbed into a taxi, mystified, and heartbroken, and set off for her rendezvous with a lamb kebab and some houmous.

At about the same time, there was pandemonium in the Orange Order Hall in East Belfast. Telephones were ringing and offers of help were pouring into the Unified Anti-Assembly Unionist Campaign HQ that had been set up there at lightning speed. People were turning up out of the blue, wanting to know what they could do, and donating time and money. Posters were being printed, Union Jacks sewn, leaflets drafted. Someone was chopping up the Electoral Register and sticking it to bits of cardboard, ready to be sent out with canvassers.

Earlier in the evening, Unionists and Loyalists of all political backgrounds had been called to an emergency meeting at the Loyal Unionist Party Headquarters. The conclave was arranged by the Reverend Scott, who, rather conveniently, had returned to

Belfast that afternoon. He had proposed that petty party differences be forgotten so that resources could be pooled to launch an effective fight.

And he shepherded his flock towards the logical conclusion: there should be only one Unionist candidate in each Assembly seat and each Westminster seat. That way they would maximise their vote, and beat the pro-Assembly candidates. Within hours they had a whole organisation, with committee rooms springing up across the Province.

At midnight, Scott and his undertakers dropped in at the Orange Hall to thank the dozens of volunteers who had turned up. The Reverend Scott was no amateur when it came to motivational psychology, and he gave them a grave-faced, hell-raising speech. Then he toured the hall, shaking hands, and encouraging the workers. 'We'll get them this time, boys. We'll stand by our flag until the day we die,' he told his followers with a mournful, serious expression that implied a sacrifice that he had never personally made.

'This'll stop their cursed Assembly once and for all,' he assured the people drawing up the campaign plans. Then he left them to it, his rallying of the troops done. When he climbed into his Government-provided Range Rover he turned to his deputy. 'This'll be fun,' he said, and his face creased into what could have been a smile.

The following day, Michael went to Belfast to try to find some means of salvaging the Assembly. The same constitutional lawyers who had so enjoyed crafting the peace settlement and the Assembly with its committees and executives, were back to Stormont Castle. But the uncomfortable truth remained: without a single Unionist member, the Assembly was dead. Try putting a gloss on that, thought Michael, at the end of a frustrating and tedious day.

It was about 8.30 p.m. when he finished a powwow upstairs and trailed back to his own corner of Stormont. 'Mandy – why are you still here?' He sounded concerned, rather than curious that she was overworking again.

She was startled by Michael's sudden appearance in the office because she hadn't expected him back for a while. He was equally surprised to see his research assistant here, let alone sitting at his desk. 'What are you doing? Have you lost something?' he asked helpfully.

'OK,' she said with an embarrassed sigh. She held up her hands as if she was surrendering, and Michael noticed her blush. 'I know I shouldn't be doing this. I was going through your diary.' She hesitated and covered her face with her hands. 'I know it's terrible. I'm sorry.'

'I don't care if you go through my diary. What are you looking for? Maybe I know what you need.'

'No, you can't help,' she said melodramatically and covered her face with her hands again. 'Oh, I feel awful about this!'

'Mandy, what's wrong?'

'I was trying to find out who you're seeing. Oh, how humiliating,' she mumbled through her fingers. 'You're not interested in me, and I wanted to know who it is you're—'

Michael laughed gently. 'I'm not going out with anybody. You know that perfectly well.' He sat down on the edge of the desk and handed her a handkerchief. 'Here. Now listen, this is ridiculous for an attractive, intelligent woman to be upset over a boring politician. For God's sake, everywhere you go there are men throwing themselves—'

'—but not you.'

'No. I'm sorry. You haven't chosen very well. And you can find someone much, much better for you than me.'

She sniffed into the handkerchief, and waited for the now familiar line about how he was emotionally neutered after Caroline's death, and incapable of contemplating any kind of relationship. Michael had explained it before, when she had pushed him. But to her surprise he didn't mention his wife, or his reluctance to have a casual screw. He left it at that: 'You haven't chosen very well.'

'How about we go out to eat and see a film? What about the new Robert Altman? I think it's on at the MGM Multiscreen on the Dublin Road. I'm fed up with this.' He waved at his desk.

'Great.' She smiled bravely, and followed him into the corridor.

If Michael had been a bit more observant, he might have noticed that his entry into the office a moment ago was preceded by the clicking noise of a computer terminal being hurriedly switched off. And if he had got closer to the terminal he might have felt the residual warmth from the back of it. But what he could not possibly know was that Mandy had used his personal password to access his files on the Prime Minister's visit to Belfast.

Chapter Twenty-One

The following morning Charlotte was in an editing suite at Millbank, spooling through video tape of a recent Northern Ireland Select Committee. She needed a clip of an obscure Official Unionist MP for her report on which Parliamentary and Assembly seats would have by-elections. She had found the appropriate clip of tape, but was infuriated to find that there was something wrong with the sound level. The MP was audible, but so was someone else.

'The problem is, the prat who was doing the sound on this recording forgot to switch off the mike after the previous MP did his bit,' commented the video-tape editor. 'So we're hearing one of these other MPs rabbiting away to his friend while the one you want talks. Look – see that one with his mouth open? There, at the back. That guy's nattering to his neighbour, and his mike's still on.'

Charlotte peered at the screen. There was the florid face of Sir Trevor Grace, leaning towards his PPS. 'Could you wind it back to see if Grace was the last one to speak, please?' she asked the technician, who was still cursing the stupidity of the sound engineer.

Sure enough, Grace had been addressing the committee. Then

he had sat down, and immediately started to consult his PPS in a low voice. Charlotte strained her ears, and heard Michael's name mentioned, and something about the IRA. But the sound quality was too poor for her to get a proper sense of what they were saying.

'Can we do anything to get this background conversation any clearer?' she asked the VT editor.

'Not here, but if we sent it to Shepherds Bush, they could have a go at the sound track,' he suggested, and together they made the necessary arrangements. It was probably of no consequence, she realised, but there had been something in Elvis's furtive manner that she had found even more unsettling than usual. Michael had thought she was overreacting, but this reporter preferred to trust her instinct.

Back at her desk she debated whether or not to call Michael, then she thought about the way he had blown up at her last night. That was the end of *that* little friendship. She bit her lip to scare away the tears.

To put a stop to this inappropriate public display of emotion, Charlotte flicked through the news wires on her terminal for the latest grim tidings from Belfast. Associated Press had filed a story about Protestant families near Londonderry putting their houses on the market, with the intention of moving east into what would remain of Ulster, if God Bob's referendum was a success. And with the subtlety that was the hallmark of the Republican movement, the IRA had blown up a Presbyterian church hall in Ballymoney.

Out of the jumble of nonsense in her head where there should have been a brain came a vigorous and annoying burst of *Tragedy* by the Bee Gees. This drove her attention back to the most recent task Rodney had set her: the closure of rural railway lines due to the privatisation of British Rail.

'Charlotte, it's Edward Power on line three for you,' he called over his shoulder.

A moment later, she was hovering at Rodney's elbow and wondering how to dig herself out of an awkward little hole of her own making. 'Um, this is tiresome, I know, but do you think someone else could do the railway story, please?' she asked as sweetly as possible. 'Edward Power has something he needs to discuss with me.' The words came out as if she was a Barbie doll on speed.

'What?'

Charlotte winced. 'It's difficult to explain, but it is rather urgent, you see—'

'I can't believe it's so urgent that it can't wait until after you've done the piece on the railways. What's it about?'

'I'm afraid I can't say at this stage, but I'll be able to—'

'What's Edward Power up to? Why can't you tell me?' Rodney frowned. 'It's not very professional to withhold details of a story from your superior.' And no doubt there was a BBC regulation on the exact procedure that she should follow in the event, but Charlotte didn't have time to go by the rules.

'Please believe me, Rodney. This is vital.'

'You can go and gossip with Edward Power if you must, but you'll have the railway package ready just the same.' Rodney paused significantly. 'I hope you know what you're doing.' It was a threat, not well-wishing.

Three minutes later, and rather short of breath, she took a seat opposite Eddie Power in his office. 'Here's Mandy Anderson's security pass form. She applied to be Michael's research assistant fourteen months ago, while she was finishing her degree. Sociology – University of Inverkirk. Here's the address she gave,' he passed the papers to Charlotte, 'and the references from her tutor.'

'You know, this explains why Mandy sometimes talks with a slightly Scottish voice.' Then Charlotte glanced at her watch. 'I suppose the Admissions people in Inverkirk will be at work now, won't they? I'll give them a ring and try to find out a bit more. May I?' She pointed at Power's phone. He nodded and turned fifty per cent of his attention to his pile of correspondence while listening in admiration as Charlotte pretended she was calling from the House of Commons Security Pass Office.

Ten minutes later she had discovered why Mandy pronounced 'out' like 'oot': she was Canadian, born in Toronto twenty-three years ago. And she had studied under a lecturer whose name was oddly familiar to Charlotte.

'Duncan McQuiston. Ring a bell?'

'Christ,' Eddie muttered, and got to his feet. He scanned the bookshelves above his desk, and pulled out a battered paperback. 'He teaches at Inverkirk, and his subject is Unionism and Loyalism in Ulster.'

'So maybe the Reverend Scott was a visiting lecturer while she was studying there,' Charlotte mused.

'Let's pray that's the explanation, but it's a bit unlikely that he'd recall one student.'

'True. But why was she so unhappy to be recognised by him at the God Squad meeting in Armagh? And why did she tell Michael she's from Buffalo, New York? And why would a Canadian come all the way to Scotland to do a degree when they have perfectly decent universities in Canada. I mean, they're not like these American colleges where people do degrees in golf, and how to load a dishwasher.'

They sat in silence, minds whirring through the possibilities.

Charlotte picked up the dog-eared paperback and absent-mindedly flicked through the index. 'Toronto – several listings.' There was a pause as she turned to the relevant pages. 'Oh,' she said in surprise as she skimmed the first entry. Eddie leaned forward impatiently, as if he was about to snatch the paperback out of her hands.

'This is interesting, Eddie. You know how everyone goes on about all these Irish people who emigrated to Boston and New York? Well, it says here that apparently that's where the Catholics went, but lots of the Protestants left too, and they went to Canada – to Toronto, in fact. And they have Orange Orders there. And marches and pipe bands. Hang on, let me look at the next entry under Toronto.' Eddie slumped back in the chair, a look of agony on his face.

'Bloody hell!' Charlotte commented as she finished another paragraph. 'The True Presbyterian Church of Christ the Protester has several branches in Canada, two of them in Toronto. That's God Bob's lot.'

Eddie was already on his feet. 'Are you working on anything right now?' he asked.

'Actually, I'm supposed to prepare a two-minute piece on rural rail-lines—'

'The usual crap?' he asked as he picked up his pile of correspondence. 'One of theirs and one of ours? I'm sure you'll fit it in, but right now, you'd better do some more digging. How about ringing them in Toronto and finding out if she was a member of God Bob's Church? Why don't you use my line and work here? I'll squat next door – the MP there hardly ever turns up. Come and get me if you find something.'

Almost an hour later she poked her head into the next-door office. 'This isn't good,' she announced, and Eddie noticed that she looked pale. 'Our Mandy's family are stalwarts of the True Presbyterian Church of Christ the Protester in Toronto. And the minister is a Reverend Patterson.'

'If Mandy's in with God Bob then you can bet she's in with the UVF.' Eddie rubbed his forehead. 'We should tell Michael immediately. Shall I – or do you want to talk to him?'

'You try. I've already left a message, but Esther says he's out of the office all day.' Then Charlotte sat in quiet distress while Eddie was told exactly the same tale.

'Christ, what if he's screwing her, and everything he says goes back to God Bob and the Loyalists?' Eddie groaned. 'It would explain where the little goat gets all those leaked documents.'

'Do you think he *is* sleeping with her?' Charlotte asked as clinically as possible, and tried to keep her features from contorting.

Eddie's shrug wasn't awfully reassuring. 'He should be bloody careful, whatever he's doing.' He passed her a print-out from the AP news terminal. There were more stories of Protestant families packing up their belongings and abandoning their homes in the western and southern parts of Northern Ireland for fear that the IRA would force them out.

'I tell you, Charlotte, this is going to be like the creation of Pakistan in 1947, when that great man Mountbatten gave India's Muslims and Hindus three-quarters of an hour to move several hundred miles in opposite directions so they didn't end up in the wrong country. The result was a million dead refugees.' He sat in anguished silence for a moment. 'I suppose I'd better let you get on with your wretched railway thing . . . can I help, by the way?'

By this point, Charlotte had pretty much given up on the morning's 'real' work, and accepted that Rodney would hang, draw, and quarter her in consequence. Two minutes later, Eddie had pulled the deputy Leader of the Labour Party out of an important meeting to give Charlotte a brief burst on the iniquities of rural rail-line closures. A rather stunned reporter gabbled her thanks to Eddie and dashed off to meet her hastily assembled camera crew.

Eddie called Michael's office at Admiralty House once more. Esther assured Eddie that she would give the Minister his message, but Michael's plane from Belfast had been delayed, and he'd gone straight to an important meeting. She promised she would stand over her boss and even dial the phone for him when he returned.

Michael's secretary wasn't to know that her boss wouldn't return that day. The Minister's important meeting was at Number 10 Downing Street. He and the Prime Minister's PPS were running through the last-minute details of the as-yet secret trip to Northern Ireland the following morning. The Belfast media would be told an hour in advance of the PM's arrival, and the British networks would get their pictures from their Northern Ireland colleagues. Even the exact itinerary was only now being settled, such was the tightness of security.

Michael, the PM's PPS, and a captain from Army Intelligence huddled in an office with a map of Belfast and a shortlist of places the PM might visit. First on the agenda was a brick-laying at a building site where a new Department of the Environment office was being relocated from London.

Michael twisted his mouth as if he had eaten something sour. 'I know I'm speaking out of turn here, but this is crazy. I went for a drive round this place yesterday, the Kennedy Way Industrial Estate, and there are about a dozen places where a sniper could hide. And there's virtually no way you can search a building site for bombs. I know the PM's keen to do it, but—'

'Crap!' the Prime Minister's PPS interjected. 'Trevor Grace told us this was your idea. Great timing too, by the way. The barricades are going back up in Belfast, the soldiers are being helicoptered in to stop the place turning into Jerusalem, and we're sending them the PM to oversee the chaos. This whole fucking stupid trip was dreamed up round at Admiralty House as far as we know.'

'I've been against this all along,' Michael protested.

'But Grace says it's vital for confidence in the Province that the trip goes ahead, especially right now. I wish someone would tell us what the fuck is going on in his empire.'

Michael would have liked to know too, but he concentrated on getting the brick-laying shifted until later in the morning, so that a thorough daylight search of the building site could be made immediately before the PM arrived.

Inevitably the whole planning process took much longer than Michael had assumed, and his day disintegrated. First the delayed flight, then waiting for the PM's PPS to return from Prime Minister's Questions at the Commons, and now an over-run with people he simply couldn't walk out on by professing that he had more pressing business elsewhere.

Consequently Michael did not emerge from the back door of Number 10 until four-thirty that afternoon. Esther had thought-fully put all the papers and messages from his office in the back of the Range Rover, allowing him to go straight to the airport without wasting time by returning to Admiralty House. He worked with documents spread around him as he and his secu-rity detail made the laborious journey out to RAF Northolt through the start of the rush-hour traffic. A military aircraft had been booked for what seemed like half the Northern Ireland Office, who were travelling to Belfast in advance of the PM's visit. That was Michael's extra treat to round off a perfect day: Sir Trevor Grace would be joining him.

Michael registered the reminder to call Edward Power MP about an urgent matter, and he phoned his friend on the mobile. Inevitably Eddie was in the Chamber, and his dopey secretary was vague about when the man who employed her for her legs, not her brain, would return.

Charlotte's messages he took note of, but did not act on. All day long he had considered calling, but an apology would best be done face to face, rather than shouting down an inadequate cellular phone line with his bodyguards listening in amusement. And right now he had enough problems without depressing himself with pornographic images of Charlotte and her handsome boyfriend.

Instead he pressed on with the speech the PM would make at lunch tomorrow at Lisburn. The Leader would be addressing a select gathering of Army brass who were still blissfully unaware that they would be listening to the PM's leaden delivery of Michael's well-crafted prose.

Once the Range Rover had waded through the congestion of the A40 and reached RAF Northolt, Michael was told that they would have to wait for the Secretary of State to turn up. It was just what he needed.

It was the worst TV report that Charlotte had ever assembled: she had simply let the Transport Minister say her meaningless little piece unchallenged. Usually Charlotte would have asked the woman when she had last travelled by train, or 'what's the minimum fare on the London Underground?' – the kind of questions that politicians loathed as much as 'how much is a pint of milk?'

Thanks to Eddie she had a high-profile opposition spokesman whom she also allowed to perform as he pleased because she was seriously short of time. She needed to feed the little monstrosity to the *Six O'Clock News* within the next ten minutes, so she slung the politicians together with a simpering, trite pay-off: 'So the future looks gloomy for rural rail-users, but only time will tell.'

Then Charlotte muttered the prayer of a martyr who knows she is being led to the stake, and she called Rodney down to OK her dire bit of journalism before it went down the line to Television Centre. He settled into the editing suite chair with a huff of annoyance that fully communicated his feelings about Charlotte's tardiness. Then he watched her report in silence. When it was over he gave his chin a thoughtful scratch, and Charlotte braced herself for the inevitable detonation. Her third and final career chance was about to go the way of a used teabag and she knew it would taste just as bitter.

'Now that's what I call a proper report, that is,' Rodney remarked with a condescending nod. 'You're getting the hang of it. I tell you what, tomorrow you can do the interview with Ken Clarke. We'll see what you make of that.'

At Northolt Michael Fitzgerald was still waiting for the Secretary of State to turn up so that they could all catch the military transport plane to Belfast. He filled his time by calling the Army brass who were moving soldiers back into Northern Ireland to deal with any potential violence. They reckoned the trickle of Protestant refugees who were leaving the disputed border areas would soon become a flood.

Brigadier Rowbottham from Military Intelligence had also warned Michael to expect the IRA to step up their ethnic cleansing. The Provos had finally found something to unite them with God Bob: the repartition of Northern Ireland was the next murderous step on the bloody road to a united Ireland, and the IRA were happy to help it along with a few assassinations and bombs.

In the midst of these frantic phone calls it slipped Michael's mind to try Eddie Power again, and when Grace and his retinue were finally on board it was impossible to get any work done. Everyone had to listen to Elvis's views on a recent court case in which a convicted bomber had been released because the evidence against him had been faked fifteen years earlier.

''Course, the Guildford Four and the Birmingham Six were all as guilty as hell,' the Secretary of State sniffed stoutly.

'Isn't that just an urban myth?' Michael asked from the other side of the gangway. 'I mean, isn't that a line CID put around to suit their own purposes? It's just like the Foreign Office who spent years telling journalists that Terry Waite was dead, even though they knew he wasn't, because they didn't want anyone putting pressure on the Government to do anything about the hostages.'

Grace affected not to hear his Minister. 'D'you know, I had a letter from a real purple-ink-brigade nutter who had a suggestion for how to deal with the growing Catholic population. He said, "Sir Trevor, it's come to my notice that these Catholics all eat crisps constantly, so you should doctor their crisps with a chemical that sterilises them".' Grace slapped his knee and his belly swayed about as he shook with laughter.

'But it wouldn't work. It'd hit the Protestant proles too.' Michael spoke through tightly drawn lips.

Grace frowned. 'The who?'

'The proletariat. The Protestant members of the working

class. They eat crisps and drink Coke too. All proles do.'

Grace was grinding his teeth. 'What are you talking about?' he growled at his Minister.

'The Marxist analysis of fast food,' Michael quipped. 'It's quite useful in getting to the root of things. Marxism may be a load of crap, but the historic and class analysis employed by Marxist academics can be rather enlightening, don't you find?'

Grace's cheeks went so red they began to turn purple. For one blissful moment Michael wondered if his boss was suffering a heart attack, but this was not to be.

'You should keep your anti-Protestant views to yourself, Mike!' he snapped. When Michael began to laugh in disbelief, Elvis wagged a finger angrily. 'People are fed up with your biased attitude. When I appointed you I honestly thought you'd be able to overcome your natural prejudices. But it seems I was wrong.'

The Minister was too stunned by this distortion of the truth to answer. He tried to concentrate on his paperwork, but his heart was thumping with fury, and he wanted more than anything to stick a sharp object into Elvis's fleshy thigh. Rather than live out this fantasy Michael took deep breaths to regulate his breathing. On top of everything else, the junior Minister did not need a stroke.

Once they were in Belfast Michael was mercifully separated from the Grace entourage. James, his driver and the fountain of good sense at all times, was waiting for him. The shambling, heavy-set former detective whisked Michael away, and he had the privacy of the ride to Stormont to catch up on the latest security situation.

When he reached his office at Stormont Castle, he continued his telephoning. The Army had reports of gangs of Loyalist thugs roaming the countryside of Antrim and Down, petrol-bombing the houses of lone Catholic families. Then there was news that the Dublin Government was so alarmed by the security situation that it was going to set up field hospitals and refugee reception centres along their side of the border with Northern Ireland, to handle the expected flood of Catholics who would be made homeless if the referendum succeeded.

Finally, Michael faxed the PM's speech to Number 10, and made more phone calls until quite late. His preoccupation was such that he entirely forgot about Eddie or Charlotte. He was alone in the office, and there was no one to field incoming calls for him, so he was busy whenever the BBC reporter tried to reach him.

Before he went home to his house in Ireton Street, Michael logged into his personal computer and typed in the details of the final itinerary for the PM's visit. Then he printed out a copy, put it in his pocket, and left for the night.

Mac arrived at Neil's house at about half-past ten that same evening. Like every Loyalist worth his Union Jack, Neil was very busy, preparing for the referendum and by-elections. His duty was to raise funds.

Just before Mac turned up, Neil had completed a cute piece of business which would benefit the cause. A shopkeeper had come to him with a proposition: the shopkeeper and some fellow traders had out-of-date lines and unwanted stock hanging around their premises. Since the IRA ceasefire there had been few opportunities to burn down their shops, blame it on the Provos, and claim the insurance, in true Belfast fashion.

But this new turn of events put the option back on the agenda. For a suitable fee, Neil would arrange for a team of his boys to bomb the man's store. Beforehand, the shopkeeper would take on his friends' redundant lines for a fee, and the whole lot would be destroyed. Then they would share the insurance. And who said good things didn't come out of war?

Neil screwed up his nose as he ushered Mac into the kitchen: the young man smelled of beer and fags, and for those aesthetic reasons he would never be permitted into Neil's sitting room, from whence the sound of a recently-acquired CD of *Elektra* could be heard.

'So, I suppose you've come straight from the King Richard where you've heard some great piece of information, eh?' Neil said sarcastically as he passed Mac a mug of coffee. 'Sure you can remember it?'

'I've been drinking with my mate Ken.'

'Indeed. And what did he tell you that justifies interrupting Richard Strauss?'

Mac sipped his coffee patiently. He was conditioned to Neil's peculiar allusions to completely irrelevant and incomprehensible matters. These days he just let them pass. 'Ken swears blind the Army's got something called a "Judas File". It's a list of all the Provos they reckon are soft – you know, the wankers who want to do a deal. And our lily-livers too, mind; traitors and cowards – the lot. They've got them on this special Intelligence list. But the Army haven't been too generous in sharing it.'

'The Judas File . . . eh? What a surprise,' Neil muttered. 'Well, this calls for a bit of creative thinking.' He traced his finger along the outline of his upper lip for one contemplative minute. 'And there's no chance your friend in that fine organisation that now rejoices in the name NIPD can get a copy of this so-called "Judas File", I suppose? No, I didn't think so. What about the wee chum we have who's so close to the top?'

'My mate says the Army are hanging onto it, especially in the present situation.' Like many natives of Belfast Mac pronounced the word 'sich-eh-shen'. 'Reckon we should get hold of it?'

Neil shrugged and watched the tiny bubbles winking at the rim of his coffee mug. Mac could tell that his boss's perverse mind had already moved on to some scheme that interested him more. 'Now, I want to try out a little idea on you. I've been playing around with this for a couple of days. What d'you think?' Neil began.

Chapter Twenty-Two

When Michael woke it was with a jolt, as if several hundred volts of electricity had been pumped into him. He lay in the dark, listening to the blood coursing through his eardrums, and wondered why the back of his neck was wet with sweat. Then he remembered the dream he had crashed out of, like someone being thrown through a plate of glass: Caroline was loading the car with cases and supplies for a long weekend in the constituency, and he was trying to stop her. He kept telling her to forget the baggage, and to take the train from King's Cross instead. 'Don't drive up the A1,' he insisted. 'Leave the car here.' But she had laughed at him, and suggested that he might help her pack the car, rather than standing there arguing with her.

In his dream he had shouted and screamed at his wife not to get in the car, but she ignored him. Then finally she lost her temper, climbed in, and slammed the door. All the while Michael begged her not to leave. Caroline wound down the window and told him that he had to let her go. Then she smiled indulgently and waved goodbye. 'Just let me go, Michael.'

He checked his alarm clock: a quarter to three. If he drifted back to sleep immediately the dream might return, so he sat up in bed, and groped around for the glass of water on the bedside table, hoping to clear his mind of the nightmarish image of Caroline driving off to her death.

It hadn't actually happened like that: he had been at Parliament that Friday morning, and Laura was at school. The plan was that Caroline would drive up to the North Yorkshire constituency to get the house ready. Then father and daughter would take the train after school, and Caroline would pick them up at York Station. That was their usual routine on the weekends they visited the seat. But on this occasion his wife hadn't made it beyond Nottinghamshire, and Michael was dragged out of the Chamber to be told about the accident on the A1. Then he went to Laura's school to break the news to her.

When he was awake enough to purge his mind of the dream, he sank back into the pillows, and searched for something more comforting to concentrate on: the impending collapse of the peace process in Northern Ireland, columns of Protestant refugees being snipered by the IRA, his disastrous political career. That was unhelpful too, so he turned over and thought about Charlotte. Why had she been offended by his refusal to mess around with her? It seemed so out of character for her to be on the verge of marrying one man, and yet eager to toy with another. Then he imagined what it would be like if she didn't have this bloody Jeremy. That was much more satisfactory as a potential dream, and he drifted off into a rather stimulating fantasy that involved a lost weekend in an obscure but beautiful country house, and a lot of champagne.

By eight o'clock the next morning, chartered coachloads of members of the True Presbyterian Church of Christ the Protester were setting off from church halls across Northern Ireland. They headed for Belfast, as did minivans and buses of Orange Lodge members, complete with their bowler hats, sashes, and Union Jacks. All over the Province, Unionists were packing picnic lunches and consulting their road maps with the intention of reaching Belfast City Hall in Donegal Square by ten o'clock. That was when Reverend Scott's rally was scheduled to begin.

The Anti-Assembly Campaign was having a show of strength, and such was the size and discipline of their network that with just a few phone calls yesterday afternoon, the wheels had been set in motion. So far, no one in the Press had been told, but the Unionist organisers wouldn't have to issue invitations. It would be obvious what was happening, by mid-morning. The Reverend Scott knew something else that the journalists had yet to learn: that the Prime Minister would be in town, and that the rally would be doubly embarrassing to the British Government.

That morning's papers had made savoury reading for the leader of the Loyal Unionist Party. A rather dogged reporter had discovered that a secret attempt to stitch together a pro-Assembly slate of candidates for the forthcoming by-elections had failed. The Alliance Party, the SDLP and Sinn Fein had tried to put their differences to one side, but Sinn Fein were in two minds about the referendum on repartitioning the Province. Some of their Assemblymen saw it as a first step to a united Ireland, and others believed it would put the cause of unity back decades if not centuries, since what remained of Ulster would be Protestant.

Or so the newspaper report claimed. It was music to God Bob's ears: the pro-Assembly vote would be split, as Sinn Fein, the SDLP and Alliance fielded candidates against each other in every seat – while the noble sons of Ulster had the good sense to stand only one standard bearer in each fight. The paper concluded that it would be a landslide for God Bob.

Michael Fitzgerald wanted to be at his office at Stormont by eight-thirty in case there were any last-minute problems with the PM's visit, although the security arrangements were now in the hands of NIPD. Naturally, Grace was doing all the public greeting and touring of their esteemed visitor. The junior Minister wasn't 'on' until the brick-laying ceremony at the future Department of the Environment offices at nine-thirty; and then at lunchtime when the PM was addressing a closed meeting of top Army brass. Otherwise the Secretary of State wanted Michael out of the way, and he was happy to oblige.

When he arrived at Stormont he found the messages Charlotte had left for him the previous day; calls he had ignored because it was hard to screw up the resolve to speak to her. He must apologise for shouting at her, of course. The whole episode had been a lesson to him: keep your heart and hormones under control and locked in the deep freeze of your dreams where they belong.

Nevertheless he wanted to clear the air, so he called her number at the BBC, and left a message, since Charlotte had not yet arrived. He also rang Eddie Power, and talked to his answering machine. Then he wandered out of his room to say good morning to Mandy who arrived at the office even earlier than did he. She was not at her desk, so he collected some coffee and returned to work.

At twenty to nine Charlotte called, sounding irritated that he had been avoiding her. But before she could tell him whatever was so important, Michael delivered his humble apology for having lost his temper.

'Fine,' she said briskly. 'Did you know that your research assistant's family attend God Bob's Church in Canada? I've got video of Mandy's less than warm reaction when Scott hailed her at that Armagh sodomy demo. And she studied the sociology and history of Unionism at university.'

'And how did this information get past the Whitehall security clearance procedure?' Michael asked with only a touch of sarcasm.

'Same as Donald Maclean and Guy Burgess and Kim Philby, I expect.'

Michael was finding Charlotte's urgency a bit melodramatic. 'Are you positive you've got the right Mandy Anderson? She was at MOD with me before I came to the Northern Ireland Office, you know. Our friend Neil didn't just decide to dispatch her here last week.'

'MOD is quite a useful place for the Loyalists to have a spy, wouldn't you say? Troop withdrawals and all that,' the reporter shot back.

'And I suppose it's simply amazing luck that the hard men had a plant who just happened to attach herself to a future Northern Ireland Minister? Oh, come on, Charlotte!'

'Listen, from what I've learned recently there's very little luck in it. Both the Loyalists and the Republicans have had sleepers in place throughout the Government's security apparatus for years, at all levels, from cleaners to career bureaucrats. Sometimes they're never activated; sometimes they are. Now, you must take this seriously, Michael. Get her checked out again. Have you told her anything sensitive?' She was speaking softly, almost conspiratorially, since she could sense Rodney's ever alert aerial tracking her conversation from five feet across the room. He appeared to be reading the *Guardian*, but Charlotte was not fooled.

'Oh, for Christ's sake, Michael,' she hissed. 'Do I have to spell it out? *Pillow talk*.' Behind her Rodney was breathing heavily, presumably on the point of exploding with curiosity.

There was an irritable groan from the Belfast end of the conversation. 'I'm not screwing her, and frankly I don't see why you'd care anyway, under the circumstances.'

'What bloody circumstances?' Charlotte asked fiercely. Then, displaying mistressful self-control, she put her personal feelings to one side and persisted with more profound concerns. 'This is important, Michael. I'm talking about a Loyalist sleeper in your bed.' Behind her, the pages of the *Guardian* were undergoing protracted torture, as Rodney tried to create as much diversionary noise as possible. She imagined that he was torn between his managerial reflex to tell her not to make personal calls at the office, and his hunger to know what she was talking about.

'Unlike you,' Michael barked, 'I'm not trying to carry on two parallel relationships!'

Charlotte made a tongue-clicking noise. 'There's no one in my bed, Michael. Now listen; this Mandy thing is important.'

'What about the man whose photograph graces your kitchen? Jeremy – isn't that his name? You're getting hitched to him, aren't you?'

'Jeremy is my brother,' she snarled. 'Now, kindly take my advice and find out about your research assistant instead of accusing me of incest.' And she slammed down the phone.

Michael leaned his elbows on the desk and hung his pounding, dishevelled head in his hands. Even with his face hidden, he couldn't stop wincing at his stupid jealousy; and yet, in the middle of his embarrassment his heart was singing, 'She is free!' Then what she had told him sank in and he sprang to his feet. 'Mandy,' he called through the open door, and walked into her adjoining room. There was no one there, however, although the desk was covered in papers. His secretary, Margaret, said she hadn't seen Mandy today, and went to check the photocopying room, while Michael looked for a diary on her desk. Nothing. The Minister shrugged and returned to his office, feeling as if he was about to fall down a bottomless well.

'Time we went, sir.'

Michael looked up, and found a smartly-dressed, middle-aged man standing in the doorway. 'Hello,' the Minister said absent-mindedly. 'We haven't met before, have we?'

'No, sir. I'm Ken McTaggart, Special Branch. Your normal detail is involved with the visit. And there's some rumours about a big rally in the centre of town today, so we're stretched for personnel.'

'A rally?'

'Just rumours, sir. And now, we've got to be going to the Kennedy Way Industrial Estate, sir.'

'She's not in the loos or the photocopying room. Should I check the canteen?' Margaret asked from the doorway.

'Could you phone them, please?'

Margaret nodded, turned back to her office, and continued humming *Blue Suede Shoes*. Some wit had stuck pictures of the real Elvis on the ladies' lavatory walls at Stormont Castle and they were covered with relevant graffiti about the Secretary of State. Margaret's recent visit there had obviously triggered off the song in her mind.

'We really should be going, sir, or we won't get there before the rest of them,' the plain-clothes officer reminded Michael politely, but rather less patiently.

'It's OK. James is a brilliant driver,' Michael said as he willed the silly melody of *Blue Suede Shoes* to vacate his own confused brain.

'James?' asked Ken. 'Oh, it's OK, sir. I'll do the driving, we won't need him.'

'Well, you'll have to sort that out with James,' Michael muttered. Then he had a flash of what Californians call 'harmonic convergence': Elvis, the codeword he had confided in Mandy when she had lost some important document; and shoes, the training type, that she wore to the office and home again.

He sprinted next door and knelt down on the floor to look under Mandy's desk. No smelly old Reeboks. He pulled open the drawers, but there was nothing: no shoes, no personal effects, just Government office supplies. Back in his office, with the NIPD officer making a pointed remark about the time, Michael punched out her home number, but got no reply. With an increasing tightness in the throat he called the security men on the entrance. They were a bit vague; they knew she'd arrived at about 8 a.m., well before most of the other employees, but they couldn't be sure she had left. Michael asked them to glance at their video record of arrivals and departures from eight onwards and to call him immediately.

Then he turned to Margaret. 'Could you get someone to this address immediately – Fitzwilliam Street, near the university.' He flicked through his diary for some note of Mandy's flat. 'We've got to find her.'

Margaret retreated, looking baffled, but a moment later she returned with grim tidings – the video at the entrance revealed that Mandy had left the building at ten past eight. That was time enough to access Michael's PC and dig out the final itinerary of the PM's visit before Michael arrived. It would have been useless to her yesterday evening because it was not updated until much later, after she had left.

The Government Minister responsible for security in the

Province was staring disaster in the face: a potential Loyalist attack on the PM. If all was going according to plan (which it wouldn't be because politicians always run late), the entourage should be heading for the building site where the PM would be laying a symbolic brick in half an hour.

Michael grabbed a mobile phone, and made for the door. On the threshold of Margaret's office he hesitated and tried to bring some order to the riot of conflicting thoughts in his head. 'Please call the airport, the customs people at the sea ports, and talk to the Army about their border patrols,' he babbled.

'It's all right, sir,' the NIPD officer Ken intervened. 'I'll take care of that.'

'Good. Tell them to stop Mandy leaving, and fax them a photo of her. Right now, please. It's too late to explain why.'

Then he tried Mandy's flat again, without success. 'Come on, we'd better go!' he yelled at Ken, and they ran through the corridors of Stormont, startling office workers, and hurled themselves into the Range Rover.

'Fast as possible please, James,' he panted at his driver, who had clearly won the battle about whether he was needed today. 'OK.' Michael grabbed Ken by the shoulder. 'Use that mobile system of yours and call the Prime Minister's convoy. You've got to warn them there's a risk of an attack. They must cancel all further public appearances, and get the PM to somewhere secure.' Michael ran his eyes down the itinerary he had pulled from his pocket. 'The lunch venue – tell them to get him to Lisburn immediately.' Then the Army could defend him, thought Michael. He sank back in the seat, his chest heaving, as the Range Rover swung left into the Knock Road.

'Shit!' Ken cursed the closed mobile communications system with which the Northern Ireland Office Range Rovers were equipped. 'I can't get through,' he said over his shoulder. 'Either we've got a fault, or they're on a closed circuit among the vehicles in the convoy.'

'Let me try.' James reached out for the mobile system, without taking his eyes from the road.

'I said it's not working!' the NIPD officer shouted. 'Just bloody drive, will you!'

Michael was too distracted by the prospect of an assassination attempt on the PM to concern himself with the row between his keepers. He handed forward his own cellular phone. 'Try calling HQ and get them to route you into the system.' The Range Rover tore through the leafy suburb of Cregagh, in East Belfast, and the Minister gulped to get the dry terror out of his throat.

Donegal Square, in the centre of the city, was buzzing with activity that cold April morning. Buses and coaches had begun to arrive; pipe bands and marching bands were playing warm-up exercises; stewards were patrolling the crowds, distributing Union Jacks and placards; and television crews were setting up outside broadcast facilities.

At the Loyal Unionist Party office inside the City Hall, God Bob and his men were receiving updates from the rally organisers. At the moment, they expected 200,000 people to turn up, but hoped that as news spread, more would join in. A less talented actor would have had trouble stopping a grin of satisfaction from lightening his stormy countenance. But the Reverend Scott was equal to the occasion, and he kept his elation in check. Grave concern and apocalyptic fury were called for at the appropriate moment. There would be plenty of time for celebrations later.

'Charlotte – Television Centre for you, Line 2,' Rodney called across the BBC cubbyhole at the Palace of Westminster. His reporter, still shaken after her exchange with Michael, took the call.

'Charlotte? Hello, it's Sally at Telly Centre. I've been working on the background conversation on the Commons committee tape you sent over. Listen, I've found something peculiar on the track, but it's hard to hear every word properly. I think I'd better send it down the line for you. It's . . . bizarre.'

A moment later, Charlotte was hovering at her boss's elbow. 'Rodney, sorry about this but I've got to go over to the Millbank office for a bit of VT.'

Her boss's eyebrows twitched behind his spectacles as he watched his young reporter collect her coat and handbag. From the startled expression on his face, he evidently hadn't recovered from Charlotte's earlier phone conversation. 'You're interviewing Kenneth Clarke in forty minutes,' he said suspiciously. 'If I'm not mistaken, you were going to use this opportunity to prove to me that you're up to this job. I recall that we decided this might have some bearing on your career. So what is more important than your future in the BBC, may I ask?'

'Michael Fitzgerald and the future of Northern Ireland, actually,' her much-abused heart and conscience responded silently. Charlotte met her boss's accusing glare with a shake of her head. 'This is incredibly important—'

'You're right. Interviewing Kenneth Clarke is incredibly important. I hope you have your questions sorted out. You've only got him for ten minutes.'

'No, I meant what I have to do is more important.'

'Ah – so important that you're going to miss an interview with one of the few articulate men in this Government? Good thing it isn't the Prime Minister you're supposed to be grilling, in that case. He's in Ulster anyway,' Rodney muttered, and looked at the embargoed press release on the BBC terminal. 'But no doubt your project is so secret even your boss can't know.'

'Ulster – today? The PM – with this rally going on? And all these refugees taking to the roads?'

'Perhaps someone'll blow him up, then we can have a leadership race. That'd relieve the boredom round here. But of course, you'd probably be too busy to cover it.'

Charlotte stood with her fingers twisting eagerly at the doorhandle. 'Please send one of the others to do Clarke. How about Dave Bower? This really is utterly, utterly vital. Honestly,' she pleaded, and felt a bit sick.

'I'm telling you to interview Kenneth Clarke in forty minutes. I'm not suggesting we have a debate about it, Charlotte Carter.'

'I have to go and look at this VT that's being sent over from Television Centre. I'll probably be able to get back and do the interview, if you let me go now,' she said with an almost wild stress on the word '*now*', and a strange hopping motion that involved bending the knees as if she were skiing over to Millbank.

'Are you completely mad? Is this how you imagine a real, grown-up journalist behaves? If you screw this up, you've screwed up your job,' Rodney said with a finality that left her in no doubt that he was serious. She bolted out of the door and down the stairs, pausing only to use an internal Westminster phone to instruct Eddie Power to meet her at the Millbank studios.

Five minutes later, perspiring, pale-faced and flustered, she erupted into the VT Traffic area of the Millbank office. It took another five minutes to find both a free VT editor and a free VT editing suite. Then she had to fetch Eddie Power from the reception area. At length she took a seat in the VT suite with the MP by her side. They watched the conversation between Sir Trevor Grace and his PPS twice, and had a brief consultation. Then she grabbed the tape and the MP, thanked the VT editor, and raced for the nearest reasonably private line.

'You call him,' she instructed as she handed Eddie the phone. 'I can't seem to get on his wavelength at the moment.'

A second later, Eddie was squeaking hysterically at Michael's secretary. 'Do anything necessary, but please find the Minister and tell him to stop the Prime Minister's visit. Get the PM *off the streets!* I can't stress to you how important this is.' His voice juddered and came to a halt. 'Yes, I'll be on this number for the next ten minutes. Then in my Commons office.' Eddie covered the mouthpiece. 'Will you be here?' he asked, and with one of those split-second decisions that affect one's career, Charlotte nodded yes.

So much for interviewing Kenneth Clarke. Then on a whim the reporter scuttled off to another phone and rang IRN's office at the House. 'Paula, how would you like to ask Ken Clarke some intimate questions?'

The building site was deserted. Michael got out of the Range Rover and looked around the barren bit of ground at one edge of the Kennedy Way Industrial Estate. There were neither Army, NIPD nor Northern Ireland office hangers-on there yet. No crowds of onlookers, no TV cameras. And no Prime Minister. Just the mist rolling in across Belfast from the mountains above and setting on the adjacent Milltown Cemetery; and the drone of cars on the nearby M1.

If Michael hadn't managed to warn them, then who had, and why wasn't the media circus here? The Minister stood in the mist, and glanced around at half-constructed walls, piles of bricks and building equipment. It was obvious, what was more, that no one had been here this morning, and no preparations had been made. The itinerary must have been changed. But no one had told Michael.

He wandered towards a pallet of bricks, hands in his pockets, his mind giddy with questions. Behind him Ken, the plain-clothes NIPD officer, pulled a high-velocity rifle from the floor of the Range Rover. Ken crouched behind his door and took aim at something above Michael, and out of his line of sight.

'Get down, Minister,' he yelled. 'There's an IRA sniper!'

Michael dropped down behind the pallet of bricks, and a second later the crack of a shot made him jump. He swivelled around, and his eyes darted from Ken to his target in a half-completed building above him and to one side. The NIPD officer fired another shot, but Michael couldn't see what he was trying to hit. Then the plain-clothes officer swung his rifle around in the Minister's direction.

'*Move, Minister!*' James shouted from the other side of the Range Rover. As Ken pivoted around, Michael scuttled behind the pallet of bricks. A different type of shot followed then there was silence.

'Mr Fitzgerald, stay there for a moment. Don't move. I want to make sure the sniper's gone.' The voice belonged to his driver, James. 'Not that I think there was a sniper.' Michael heard shoes crunch on the gravel, and James came around to the other side of the Range Rover. 'You're OK now, sir. He's dead.'

The Minister straightened up, and stumbled towards James, who was standing over the inert body of the NIPD plain-clothes officer. Then Michael glanced back at the half-finished building, and opened his mouth to ask a question that his numbed brain hadn't yet formed. The ringing in his head was so loud that he had difficulty thinking straight.

'Let's go, sir,' James suggested with some urgency, and they walked around Dead Ken, and back to the Range Rover. 'As soon as we got here I tried the mobile, sir,' he explained calmly as they climbed into the front seats. 'There was nothing wrong with it. It was switched off all the time, when he was pretending he couldn't get through. I suppose he didn't turn on your cellular phone, either.'

Michael stared at James as if he were jabbering in Cantonese. Finally his brain cleared of the noise of rifle shots. 'And who the hell was he shooting at?'

James started the car, and took a deep breath. 'There wasn't anyone in the building. Our friend over there was trying to make us think there was a sniper, but he seemed more interested in you. I suppose my presence here ruined his plans.'

'You mean he would have shot me and then said it was a sniper?'

In the silence that followed, Michael sensed that his driver and protector had just been hit by the after-shock. When James had collected himself, he turned on the mobile communication set and requested an ambulance and the police. Then he called through a warning to the Prime Minister's entourage. 'Now, we'd better be getting you back to Stormont,' he concluded, and released the handbrake.

'We will not bow down in supplication to the anti-Christ,' shrieked the Reverend Scott from his platform in front of Belfast City Hall. His thin, grating voice echoed through the amplification system and blasted out across Donegal Square. Two hundred and fifty thousand faces watched him; a small man, but an enormous presence. They stood shoulder to shoulder in the streets leading up to the neo-Classical City Hall, banners sagging in the drizzle, Union Jacks aloft.

'Imagine our schoolchildren being force-fed that bloodthirsty, persecuting, intolerant, blaspheming diatribe of Papacy. Imagine the indoctrination of this Church of Rome, the mother of harlots, the abomination of the earth. This Church of Rome that buries hunger-strikers and terrorists and child-abusing priests with as much pomp as it buries popes.

'We warned the Government that if they started giving in to the Catholics they would want more and more; and now they want everything. We have nothing but our territory and our traditions left. We have been betrayed by the treacherous, evasive simpletons at Westminster. We have been betrayed by the British Prime Minister who takes his orders from Dublin and Washington. But we will fight on to save the last square foot of Ulster.'

The crowd cheered as one and their flags waved like battle colours on a field of war. God Bob nodded his grim approval, and surveyed the ocean of people stretching in every direction. 'We will let them have their precious "Derry" – it isn't fit for Protestants now.' His voice sounded like a harsh wailing machine. 'We will regroup, and defend the heart of Ulster. And even when the last Protestant family is left they will stand battered by the wind and the sea at the Giant's Causeway, and they will never give in. Because we will never surrender, and Ireland will never be one,' he screamed. The little man had sung, and the crowd howled its approval.

'Sir Trevor, a rather insistent young woman from the BBC wants to speak to you, sir,' his secretary remarked as she handed Grace

298

a note. Elvis had just returned from a walkabout with the PM in a factory, and was looking serenely pleased with himself. Now the PM, badly shaken by the siege state of Belfast, had gone off to Army HQ at Lisburn to review some troops, and hand out some medals, which gave Grace a moment to polish his lunchtime speech.

'If she calls back, tell her I'm too busy with the Prime Minister's visit,' Grace scowled, and retreated into his office with his PPS in tow.

Michael was gazing at Belvoir Park in South Belfast when the mobile warbled, and yanked him out of his confused reverie. It was Margaret, his secretary, sounding frantic and annoyed with him. 'Why did you turn it off, Michael? I've been trying to reach you for the past twenty minutes! This is very important. You must call Edward Power on this number now: right now. I've already passed his warning on to the Prime Minister's convoy. Thankfully it was a false alarm, and he's safe at Lisburn now,' Margaret snapped fiercely, and got off the line.

Michael punched in the number and looked out of the car window with unseeing eyes at the dazzling green grass. Eddie answered on the first ring, and sounded quite as manic as Michael's secretary. That made three of them, he thought.

'Grace and his PPS are trying to frame you,' he said by way of greeting. 'Charlotte Carter's got them on tape at the back of a Select Committee meeting, and it sounds—'

'Slow down, Eddie,' Michael interjected. 'It just happened.'

'Are you OK? Did they get the PM?' he gabbled.

'No. It's all right.' He sounded more normal than he felt.

'Are you sure you're OK, Michael?'

'Yes, thanks to James here. Tell Charlotte to hang on to that tape. Get a copy made or something.'

'Now listen, Michael. You're surrounded by snakes. Grace is obviously manipulating Reverend Scott, and Mandy is up to no good. Just resign and come back here now, this morning. It isn't worth it.'

'I'll stay in touch, Eddie. Don't worry about me: the worst thing that could happen in my life occurred when Caroline died. I'll cope with this somehow,' he said philosophically. 'And thanks for the help. And thank Charlotte for me. I don't think she's speaking to me at the moment, but if I make it through today, tell her I plan some suitably humbling gesture. She's rather greedy, so tell her "Bibendum".'

He clicked off the phone and glanced along Prince of Wales Avenue, which ran dead straight up the hill to Stormont. Its looming whiteness glowed out of the damp, misty morning, as if it was hanging in mid-air, rather than perched on top of a hill. Half his brain registered that he had just attended his own assassination, and that Grace was plotting against him. But the other half was wondering if Charlotte would forgive him for the misunderstanding about her brother, and for dismissing her paranoia about Mandy. As the Range Rover pulled up at the porticoed entrance of Stormont Castle Michael decided, not for the first time, that he was a romantic fool. Now he was going to be an angry fool.

'I think you'd better not join me for this,' he remarked to James. 'You've saved my life once today, and it's not even ten-fifteen – so why don't you take a coffee break for the rest of the day and lie low until I've sorted this out.'

'No, sir.' James switched off the engine and opened his door. 'Thanks, but my job is to take care of you. And that's what I'm going to do.'

★ ★ ★

'I can't fucking believe this. There is no fucking discipline in this movement, that's what really drives me mad.' Neil was squeezing the telephone so hard his sweaty hands slipped on the plastic.

'Listen, Mac, I gave no orders to kill Fitzgerald. You'd better tell me now if you've got any more mates who are planning clever little freelance fuck-ups like this one, eh? Fitzgerald is far too useful to us alive, and your bone-headed mate Ken should've known better. Him and that stupid Canadian tart. Think of the laugh the fucking Provos'll have when they find out what prats we made of ourselves.'

Neil carried on fuming as Mac rattled on, then cut him off bluntly. 'We're going ahead with our plan today,' he announced. 'Fitzgerald is completely isolated at Stormont after this, and for all we know he'll have packed his bags and gone back to London for good by tomorrow. Psychologically speaking, this is the right moment to force him to do what we want: we won't have another chance. So get hold of that skin-headed idiot Vince, and someone else you trust, and do it. *Now*, Mac!'

Chapter Twenty-Three

'Get out of here!' Michael snapped at Grace's PPS. The man looked like an old coat that had been dumped ungraciously on a chair. Michael hoisted him up by his tie, and the startled creature stumbled out of the room.

Michael gave Grace a hard, silent stare until the office door closed, then he leaned over the Secretary of State's desk like a dragon about to breathe fire. 'When did you change the itinerary, and why?'

'When we realised your little playmate Mandy was passing secure information to terrorists,' Grace chirped back, a savage grin on his ruddy face. 'In other words, my old chum, you've had a fake itinerary all along. I spoke to Downing Street late last night and gave them the real plan for today. Good thing too, in the circumstances.'

'Well, I've just had an interesting experience. A member of NIPD tried to kill me, and my life was saved by the wit of my driver. But I expect you know all about this.'

'You've got mud on your trousers, Mike. How unlike you to look so bedraggled. You should get cleaned up before lunch with the PM,' Grace said helpfully, then he frowned. 'Nobody from NIPD took a shot at you. That NIPD officer was trying to save your life,' he added testily. 'An IRA sniper attempted to kill you, and sadly a Special Branch officer died defending a Minister of the Crown. You should be grateful he was there to protect you. The man deserves your appreciation, not a stream of anti-NIPD prejudice.'

'How do you know what happened?'

'I've just had a call from Sir David Mackay's office. They were alerted immediately that one of their stalwart men had just died during a "training exercise". There won't be any publicity about this, needless to say.'

'Why would Mandy have passed the itinerary to the IRA if she was working with the Loyalists and their fellow travellers in NIPD?'

'Dear me, Mike. You're so biased against NIPD,' Grace smirked.

'The NIPD man was about to take a shot at me—' But Michael stopped mid-sentence. What was the point of this, if Grace had already decided the official line? Would the worthy James get in trouble if Michael mentioned his brave role?

'Well, you'd better resign, don't you think? This makes Profumo look quite mild – at least he didn't have a terrorist in his bed.'

Michael leaned so far across the desk that Grace eased his chair away, fearing that the Minister might bite him. 'I never told her anything!'

'Except the itinerary for the PM's visit.' Grace smiled triumphantly.

'She's got that because she had the code to my PC.'

'Isn't that serious enough, Mike? Giving the code for the Northern Ireland Office computer to the tart you're shafting?'

'I gave her access to my PC. You make it sound like she'd

hacked into the Pentagon computer.'

Grace grunted, as if Michael were splitting hairs. 'The point is you've been porking Mandy, and no one's going to believe she didn't pump you for sensitive information.'

'I did *not* have a relationship with her!' Michael protested. 'And you have no proof I did.'

Grace laughed and reached into a desk drawer. 'Look at these,' he instructed as he passed over a large envelope. 'Not exactly Lord Lichfield quality, I grant you, but they're clear enough.'

Michael flicked through the black and white glossies of Mandy and he together: coming out of a restaurant, going to an official dinner, emerging from the Range Rover. All had been taken at night to make them look as if they were up to something slightly risqué. 'This proves nothing.' Michael tossed the photos on Grace's desk.

'The tabloid press and the PM won't look at it that way, Mike. I suggest you let me have your resignation by the end of the afternoon. Say you want to spend more time with your family.'

'No. You'll have to sack me. I'm not resigning.'

'Very well then, you've got twenty-four hours to think about what life's going to be like on the back benches. Until the next election, of course, when the voters aren't exactly going to rush out to support an Independent Conservative who screws terrorists.' Grace chuckled.

'What would the tabloid press and the PM think of a Secretary of State who deliberately allows a terrorist plant to plunder his Department's secret files?' Michael mused. 'Maybe they'd be interested to know how Reverend Scott finds out about flag competitions, and American Air Force bases, and ministerial appointments, and visits by the Prime Minister.'

'I'll tell you your problem, Mike,' Grace said viciously. 'You've never understood that you're an outsider here, in this party. It's not just that you're a Catholic, or a bloody Irishman. You're not one of us.'

'Thanks for explaining the British Establishment to me,' Michael laughed, and paced over to the window. 'Interesting, coming from the scion of a grand old family of landed gentry such as yourself.'

The irony was lost on Grace who frowned. 'I warned you to keep a low profile. No one's going to solve the problems of this place. Look at these bloody people; they don't want to be helped. They're hopeless, and the best we can do is stop them blowing each other up. They're just children, and you can't let children run a Province. What you fail to understand here, Mike, is that we're not required to do any more than look concerned, and get the Europeans to pay for everything.'

'Very insightful analysis,' Michael quipped as he paced back towards Grace. 'Have you any idea what's been happening out there since you and your dog-collared friend came up with this repartition crap?' There was no response, so he leaned over the desk and bared his teeth. 'We're going to have thousands of people on the move unless we can stabilise this situation, and stop this referendum. And get the fucking Teapot in Dublin on board to solve this crisis.'

'Oh bollocks, Mike. Don't take it all so seriously! The referendum's just a tactic. It'll give the Paddys a fright and teach them not to go poking their noses into other people's countries. Nothing'll actually happen.'

'But that's the point, you moron!' Michael exploded. 'Your game has let the genie out of the bottle, and you can't put it back in. Don't you see that? Now you're going to get Bosnia!'

'You're exaggerating. This'll fizzle out when the Assembly's dead and buried. The Northern Ireland Office will take charge once more, and the children can go back to blowing up a few hundred of each other every year. Minor collateral damage.'

'Comforting thought. By the way, what if I had proof you were setting me up to get rubbed out?'

Grace laughed and rocked backwards in his chair. 'Don't talk nonsense. No one was planning to have you killed. That was some individual initiative on the part of an enthusiastic loner. Now,' said Elvis, like a Chief Executive bringing a board meeting to order, 'you've got twenty-four hours. I suggest you go and make yourself respectable for lunch. I don't want the PM worrying about this before he has to.'

'Lunch? Are you serious?' Michael snorted.

'If you don't turn up and act normal, I'm handing these photos over to the Press this afternoon. And by the way, if you don't resign I'll make sure everyone knows you met the Loyalists against my orders, a mere two days after they blew up that Garda patrol in Donegal. Nice timing, Mike,' he beamed.

At this point Michael considered mentioning Charlotte's video, but he wanted to be certain it held water before he tried to salvage his career on the strength of it. He trailed back to his office, still shaking with anger. On his desk was a handwritten note from Margaret about a bomb in the National Trust shop in Botanic Avenue. It had exploded about twenty minutes ago, and the first NIPD men on the scene said two people had been taken to hospital in critical condition. The location was more than familiar; Botanic Avenue was the main thoroughfare at the end of Ireton Street, where the Minister lived. And Laura and Delva were there at the moment, since St Paul's School in London had broken up for Easter.

'I've just spoken to the plain-clothes boys on duty outside your house.'

Michael's head jerked up. James was standing at the door of his office. 'No significant damage in your street. The NIPD boys outside say your little girl and the housekeeper haven't left the house all morning. The boys went to check out the shop when it happened,' he explained. 'There's nothing to be concerned about, sir.'

'Thanks, James. You're a hero, and it was—' His voice disintegrated into an emotional vibrato. He cleared his throat and motioned that the driver should come in and close the door. 'I'm serious, James. Take my advice and pretend this morning didn't happen, all right? History is being rewritten as we speak. An IRA sniper shot Ken is the official version. Dead Ken's friends within NIPD might take exception if they know you're offering a different version of events. This is bigger than both of us.'

As James opened his mouth to protest, Michael held up a placatory hand. 'For your safety and mine, please. And now, I'd be most grateful if you could alert the airports to watch out for Mandy, since we have to assume that Ken disregarded that instruction. And then could you go back to my house and get me a clean suit and shirt for this bloody lunch thing, please?' Michael dug a key out of the desk drawer. 'Laura and Delva ought to be in, but if they're not, use this. Thanks.'

The Minister disappeared to the loo to wash his face and hands. What on earth was he supposed to do now, he wondered as he tried to sponge the mud off his trousers. Resign quietly? Stay here and fight? Allow Elvis to give the photos to the tabloids? Or walk into another Loyalist trap? Perhaps just sit down and have a good cry, he thought, and prepared to do battle once more. When he returned to his desk Margaret announced that Edward Power was on the line, holding for him.

'I've got the Ken Clarke "int",' Charlotte announced when she rang Rodney from the editing suite at the BBC's Millbank building. Then she crossed her fingers and exchanged a silent cackle with Paula, who was beside her. 'Yes, I'll feed it straight to Television Centre now,' the BBC reporter confirmed, and hung up. She and Paula whooped with laughter and applauded each other.

'Paula, I owe you,' Charlotte said with a sincere squeeze of the IRN reporter's arm. Then she bolted out of the suite and back to the newsroom.

'Edward Power for you,' a journalist announced as she walked in. Several people stopped what they were doing to eavesdrop: Charlotte's battle with her boss had become a matter of great interest, due partly to the regular updates her colleagues received from the Dave Bower Broadcasting System. She deliberately lowered her voice, hunched over the phone, and listened carefully as the Labour MP related the contents of his second conversation with the Minister in Belfast.

'I just called him, and he's OK. I mean, he dodged the bullets and the PM wasn't there. And he knows about Grace, but the bastard's got some snaps of him and Mandy, and he has until tomorrow morning to resign, or the Press will learn that the Northern Ireland Minister was rogering a Loyalist sleeper. Which he wasn't. Michael swears it's not true, and I believe him.'

Charlotte's heart skipped a beat and a smile made a brief but joyful appearance. 'Slow down, Eddie. You sound like you've got a snoutful of Bolivian marching powder. If Michael wasn't . . .' Charlotte struggled to find a less distressing word

'. . . sleeping with Mandy, then what do these photos show?'

'Just the two of them going out on the town in Belfast, Mandy exposing too much leg as usual, and clinging onto her Minister. The point is, I'm not sure he can blackmail Grace in return, on the strength of your tape. It's not that clear, is it? I mean, they could be swapping cake recipes for all we know. It was the circumstances that led us to the correct conclusion, not the actual words.'

The BBC reporter hummed for a moment, and studied the television monitor in front of her with unseeing eyes. 'And Mandy's vanished, I take it? *Mmmm*. Seems to me that Michael can ask for much more as the price of this video. Let's think of a more ambitious goal.'

'What do you mean?' Eddie sounded wary.

'Recently I asked Michael what he'd do if he could wave a magic wand over the Province. He told me he'd make all the heavies in Northern Ireland get together, and he wouldn't let any of them out of the room until he had some sort of agreement. You know, it's the line you use with naughty children who are banished upstairs until they've tidied their rooms.'

'The constitutional parties? I don't see—'

'No, the terrorists. They're the ones who'll actually deliver peace. If they don't agree to the political deal then the whole thing's a waste of time. So why not have them in from the start?'

'Because we can't be seen to allow terrorism to win,' Eddie recited.

'But it does win, Eddie. Take the Indonesian invasion of East Timor; the Chinese invasion of Tibet; Pol Pot's overthrow of the Cambodian Government; the Serbs' destruction of Yugoslavia. And it hasn't harmed Gerry Adams's career as an international jetsetter,' she chanted.

310

'I haven't got time to put the Gandhi part of this argument. Tell me what you're getting at, Charlotte.'

'My idea is that we use the tape to force Grace to bring the masked men together for a real negotiation session.'

Eddie was about to tell Charlotte that she was naive in the extreme if she thought Ulstermen could be blackmailed by a Secretary of State who was also being blackmailed on the strength of a few unclear words on a tape . . . but she barged right on. 'Talk to Michael, and see if you can sell him this.'

'Why don't you talk to him?'

'No – you call him. My boss has just given me something to keep me busy – a package on new Government funding for the computer industry in Wales,' she added with a sarcastic click of the tongue.

'OK. But this is a mad idea and it'll take ages to fix up. Grace could have manoeuvred his way into an alibi, or—'

'Rubbish!' Charlotte interjected impatiently. 'We can have this organised by tonight. What else have these people got to do? The Province is on the edge of the abyss. Have you read what the White House Press Secretary has just put on the wires? The Americans are going berserk about this repartition thing. I tell you, these by-elections have to be stopped. You can't just put down an Early Day Motion and make a speech condemning it, Eddie. That's for wankers and wimps. Now, for the first time in your life, you have to act!'

'This is a very simplistic view of the way things work,' Eddie said haughtily. 'It's impossible.'

'Good. I'm glad to hear I've got your full cooperation, weasel-face,' Charlotte chirped. 'Call me back when you've spoken to Michael.'

Eddie Power's phone call to Stormont did not last long. He

had just explained Charlotte's Big Idea when the incredulous Michael cut him off and hung up. Margaret was waving frantically from the doorway of his office.

'I've got James on the phone,' she said, with terror in her voice. 'You must talk to him. He can't find Laura and Delva.'

Chapter Twenty-Four

Someone had forced open a skylight in a room on the upper floor of the Fitzgerald house in Ireton Street, and when James stuck his head out and inspected the roof it was clear that anyone surefooted could simply walk or crawl along the roofs from either end of the terrace of houses. What was less obvious was how you would get a child and a middle-aged woman out that way.

'What about the plain-clothes men outside?' Michael asked with a jittery voice. 'Didn't they see anything?'

'There's a note, sir. It says you're not to tell anyone. No police. No Army. I thought I'd better talk to you first, in the light of what happened earlier. It says they'll be calling with their terms.'

'James, there's no sign that anyone was hurt, is there? You know, a struggle, or—' Michael prepared himself for a description of walls running with blood.

'No, sir. Nothing like that. Just this note, saying they'll call you here, on this number, later this morning.'

'How d'you think they got out of the house, James?'

He could almost hear the brain of the former detective whirring into action. 'I reckon it was the explosion at the National

Trust shop around the corner. The UVF have claimed responsibility, and I bet while the security blokes here went to look at it and offer help, the same UVF blokes brought Laura and Delva out the front door, into a waiting car. That's my hunch.'

Michael took a deep breath. 'D'you think I should alert anybody? What's your advice?'

'Nothing'll be gained by letting the world know they've got your family. And searching every house in Belfast probably wouldn't help either.' James hesitated, and tried to find words of encouragement for the silent, fretting Minister on the other end of the line. 'Look on the positive side: they want something from you. This is a kidnapping, not a murder. It could be much worse. Anyway, I'll come and get you now. You have to be here when they call.'

Not a murder yet, you mean, Michael thought when he was off the phone. He leaned his elbows on the desk, and pushed his forehead into the palms of his hands. Then he recalled telling Eddie that the worst had already happened to him when Caroline died, and that nothing terrible could happen again. I tempted God, he thought wildly, and He's paid me back for it.

'Michael, for Christ's sake, what's happening round here?' Johnny Burleigh closed the office door and strode over to his desk. 'Is this true some IRA bastard took a shot at you this morning?'

Michael couldn't help but smile, albeit half-heartedly, at his unexpected guest. 'What are you doing here, Johnny?'

'PM wanted me along to keep Grace-face in order if he got tiresome. Uppity little cunt. So, what happened? Come on, tell me. You don't look at your most lovely, by the way.'

'It's nothing, Johnny. Just a mistake someone made. Nothing to get excited about.'

The Defence Secretary raised his bushy right eyebrow in an arch. 'If I didn't know better, I'd say you're about to pass out. Are you OK?'

'I expect it's a delayed reaction.' The Junior Minister smiled thinly. The way events had developed he wasn't sure he could trust Johnny, or the Army, or anyone. 'Where's Grace now?' he asked Burleigh.

'I left him in his office, preparing for this unspeakable lunch. My chaps are dreading it, as per. What they want to hear is that we're being given the lead role in Intelligence gathering, or that we're getting better equipment,' Johnny grumbled. 'What they don't need is another pep talk from Grace or The Gormless One.'

'No,' Michael agreed absent-mindedly. 'Look, sorry about this, Johnny, but I've got to go and shove a blunt instrument in Elvis's face, so you'll have to excuse me.'

'Come and talk to me at lunch, then. There must be some way to make today tolerable. Where's that delightful research assistant of yours?'

Michael, who had got to his feet as a prelude to shooing the sour-faced old bear out of the door, stopped in his tracks. 'Mandy's not here,' he said curtly. Then he watched for the Defence Secretary's reaction. Was this a trap?

'Damned shame.' His former boss had reluctantly hauled himself out of the chair and was stretching his back. 'Suppose I'll have to go and natter to Rowbottham and his boys. Why does it always rain here?' He glared balefully out of Michael's window at the evergreen lawns that surrounded Stormont Castle. 'I think I'll introduce myself to your new secretary – Margaret, isn't it? Seems rather nice.'

When the Junior Minister had freed himself of Burleigh, he

headed for Grace's office. As he hurried along the corridor, he wondered if Johnny had been asking about Mandy for a reason, other than boredom and lust. How much did the old warhorse know? Had he been involved in setting up Michael at the Northern Ireland Office so he could be a pawn in Grace's game? A sad smile crept across his lips as he thought of the youthful Laura decrying the fate of 'prawns in the game'. Even after he had corrected her, she and Caroline had continued to use the expression deliberately.

Grace looked startled by Michael's sudden reappearance in his office, and he quickly arranged his features into their normal sarcastic set.

'You'll have my resignation tomorrow morning,' the Minister said without emotion. 'But something's come up right now, so I won't be at your love-in this lunchtime. Don't bother me for the rest of the day, or I'll track you down and set fire to that oily hair of yours, I swear. And if I find you've had anything to do with this new mess, I'll kill you.'

Grace's forehead creased with ruddy lines. 'What?'

When the Minister reached his own office he was annoyed to find that Johnny Burleigh still hadn't disappeared: he was sitting on the secretary's desk, phone in hand, chortling away as if he was gossiping with a friend in the launderette. This place is like a fucking zoo, Michael thought.

'Ah, here he is now.' Burleigh handed the receiver to Michael. 'It's that Socialist rogue, Eddie Power. Can I have him back when you've finished with him? He was telling me something rather interesting.'

'I really can't talk, Eddie—' Michael began.

'Are you OK? You sound awful. Are you safe there, Michael? For Christ's sake get Johnny's blokes to provide you with a bit of extra heavy-duty protection,' his friend in London suggested.

'No, don't worry about me.' Michael tried not to yell what he really felt, which was: 'I'm in the middle of a waking nightmare. Now get off the line and let me go home so I can find out if my daughter is still alive!' Instead he listened as Eddie outlined Charlotte's plan to use the Grace tape to force the Secretary of State to make peace talks happen.

'Hang on,' he interjected when he realised that nothing the Labour MP said made any sense. 'I can't think about this at the moment. You and Charlotte go ahead and do what you want. Sell the whole Province to Dublin for three cases of Bailey's Original for all I care.' Then he lowered his voice in a vain attempt to stop the loitering Johnny from hearing. 'Use the tape any way you want, but don't involve me, OK?' Michael handed the receiver back to Johnny, and asked Margaret to follow him into his own office. 'I've got to go home now, probably for the rest of the day,' he explained to the bewildered woman. 'Elvis knows I won't be at the lunch, but please don't let anyone pester me at home. Don't tell them where I've gone. Just pretend I'm on a visit, or in a meeting.'

Margaret stood a few feet from him, fiddling with the wedding ring on her finger, and peering into his face with concern. 'You're terribly pale, Michael. Are you feeling unwell?'

'Yes, that's it!' he exclaimed enthusiastically, as if she had hit upon a good ruse. 'Is James back yet?'

'He's waiting downstairs. Can I help, Michael? It's Laura and Delva, isn't it? Just tell me what I can do,' she ventured.

The Minister ran his fingers through his hair, and smiled at her with all the gratitude he could manage. 'I'll call you later. Just hold the fort, please. Nothing's wrong. I've probably got that twenty-four-hour 'flu that knocks people out.'

317

Margaret watched him take a last nervous glance at his desk, as if he was leaving on a transatlantic trip, and wanted to be sure he hadn't left anything vital behind. Then he smiled again and went quickly out, past the Defence Secretary, who was still on the phone gossiping, and into the corridor.

'OK,' Burleigh said in an entirely different tone of voice. 'He's gone now. What's going on?'

Charlotte was in the newsroom at Millbank. In her stomach there was a chocolate bar, but it hadn't satisfied her hunger, and she was absent-mindedly dabbing up the chocolate crumbs from the desk with her index finger, then sticking them in her mouth. Subconsciously she knew that all manner of gruesome things might have happened on this desk top, but her greed was greater than her fear of crabs at the moment.

In theory she should have been setting up her interview with the Welsh Secretary to hear all about his whizzo plans to promote the computer industry in Wales, but that had long since slipped her mind. Instead she was concentrating on the blank piece of paper and pen in front of her. For the purposes of this exercise she was leaving Sir Trevor Grace to one side: it was awkward to admit it, but there was a strong possibility that he might not play the game. However, Charlotte was relying on the politician's first instinct, which was self-preservation. Her money was on Grace selling out virtually everything to keep his career intact – which meant ensuring that her video tape was never aired.

Somehow the reporter had to work out some way of bringing the warlords and tribal chiefs of Northern Ireland together in one room without any of the parties involved objecting. That would mean tricking some and blackmailing others. Then there were the minor details like where to meet, how to stop the security services getting wind of what was going on, and how to prevent a media stampede if news got out. Would the participants arrive with guns and henchmen in tow? Would they start shooting when they disagreed about whether they should have tea or coffee? What if no one would talk, and the whole stunt ended in a stalemate or bloodshed?

Charlotte was smoothing her fingertips over her eyebrows in an attempt to generate inspirational thought when a phone call from her boss interrupted her.

'You'd better come over here immediately,' Rodney snapped, and hung up.

Charlotte flopped back in the chair, and pressed her palms against her fevered forehead. How was a person supposed to get anything done in this organisation? Five minutes later she was climbing the stairs up to the BBC's narrow little room off the Press Gallery at the Commons. Here she was, trying to sort out centuries of problems in Northern Ireland, and the Bertolucci of broadcasting expected her to do some work.

'Good interview with Kenneth Clarke,' Rodney began when she sat down alongside him at his cramped desk. 'Pity it wasn't you asking the questions.'

Charlotte fixed a terrified little smile on her face as her boss went on to praise her artful deception. 'Had it not been for the back of someone else's head appearing on screen, you would have had me fooled,' he remarked with mock admiration. 'The interview was so good that they used two questions from Clarke, so the camera did a two-shot for the question in between his answers. It wasn't your voice asking the question, and it wasn't your head either. In fact, it looked remarkably like Paula Tyler's.'

Charlotte took a deep breath, opened her eyes wide, and rubbed her hands together as if she was about to present her boss with a delicious meal. 'There's an explanation for everything, and I have a world exclusive story too. It all begins with a VT of a Northern Ireland committee.'

But Rodney was shaking his head. 'No. It all begins with you finding another job. This Clarke thing was the last straw.'

'But you can't say no to the news scoop of the decade,' she retorted with a persuasive grin. Then she realised she was sounding like a car salesman and stopped. 'Look, you know I've been working on something to do with Northern Ireland.'

'I don't know what you've been working on. Certainly not what you've been told to do. And I'm a simple fellow. I don't want the broadcasting exclusive of the decade. I just want reporters who go out and get the dull, ordinary stories I ask them for.'

'What I'm telling you is important, Rodney. Grace is sabotaging the Stormont Assembly. He's provoked these by-elections and the referendum. He's in league with Reverend Scott because they want to destroy any chance of power-sharing in the Province.' She was babbling now. 'It's really about Grace's bid to stir up the anti-Europeans, and relaunch his political career. Don't you see?'

'And what *you* still don't seem to understand is that the BBC has several dozen excellent journalists working in Belfast as we speak. That's their job: Ulster stories. If you know something, you should ring them up and tell them. Then get back to work on what you're paid to do here at Westminster.' He glanced away from her, as if meeting her eyes had been painful. 'Now, the Welsh Office want to know why no one from the BBC's called to arrange the interview. The Secretary of State is in London for the next hour and a half, then he's going back to Cardiff.'

Charlotte sat on the edge of her chair, then crossed her legs and wound her ankles around each other tightly. 'But I'm talking about access to talks between the paramilitaries.'

'You should have written a paper on it and submitted it to management. There's a sensible, established procedure for everything here,' Rodney remarked with the satisfaction of a man who takes pride in having a well-organised sock drawer.

'I'm talking about news that's breaking right now. Is there no flexibility in the system to accommodate that?'

'Of course there is. It's called the BBC newsroom in Belfast.'

Charlotte held her head dramatically, as if her brain was about to explode. 'I give up.'

'No, you don't give up,' Rodney corrected her with a prissy smile. 'I've just fired you.'

'But I work longer hours than anyone else here. Surely you're not questioning my commitment?'

'I'm questioning your view that you're your own boss,' Rodney bristled. 'You're fired.'

'Of course. Thanks,' she snapped and stumbled to her feet. 'Do not pass Go. Do not collect two hundred pounds. Evidently I don't kiss your arse enough, or buy you drinks like one of the boys! Well, stick it up your retentive, misogynistic bum, you creep!'

'What are you doing? You can't just walk out,' Rodney said in open-mouthed astonishment.

'You fired me – I'm going,' she said casually, although at that moment she was wondering what on earth she would do for money after this defiant display of independence.

'You'll work out your notice, at least until the end of the

month.' Rodney made a neat little karate-chop motion on the edge of his desk.

'Tough shit.'

'You can't go! I won't give you a good reference, and no one else will employ you,' he sang like a taunting child. 'Anyway, you have to fill out all the forms.' Then he gave her a sly threatening look. 'Otherwise it'll affect your pension arrangements.'

Charlotte feigned horror. Then she leant over the desk and grinned at Rodney. 'Fuck off and die,' she smiled, then hesitated before adding, 'Now.'

Out in the corridor she found a Westminster internal phone and called IRN. 'Paula, I'd like to see your husband about a piece of VT that CNN might find interesting. Could you ring him now?'

Five minutes later, Charlotte was walking towards the CNN office. There was a nervous spring in her step, and frenzied thoughts were spurting through her head in short bursts of mental electricity.

What have I got to lose? she demanded of her flagging confidence. Same as Michael: nothing. He's in such a hole that what I'm about to do can't possibly damage him. I hope he'll see it that way. The never very convincing self-assurance wavered a bit more.

Michael wandered from room to room, expecting to find that the house had turned into the set of a Brian de Palma film. But everything was normal, as if Laura and Delva had just popped out on a shopping expedition. The Fitzgeralds had hardly settled in; there were boxes of books on the upstairs landing, and their curtains still had a stiff, creased, new look to them.

Now everything had been violated by unknown invaders. Who had taken Laura and Delva? What did they want from Michael? Would they kill them, or were they dead already?

He stood numbly in his daughter's bedroom and looked out at the rain and the grey sky. How could he have brought them here, knowing the danger it involved? Why did he kid himself into believing Belfast was just as secure as London for the family of a Northern Ireland Minister? How often had he sacrificed Laura's safety, and health, and everything else for the sake of his political career?

He slumped onto her bed and picked up the battered fluffy alligator that accompanied her everywhere. What would Caroline make of this mess he'd created? Would she appear before him like a furious Banquo and curse him for doing this to their only child? Was any of this ego-driven, self-deceiving political crap worth it? How many times had he convinced himself that everything he did was in aid of some greater civic cause, rather than for his personal vanity?

He sank back and lay there with his eyes closed, and his brain throbbing. The day had begun in just such a way, with the remnants of a pleasant erotic dream about making love to Charlotte Carter. Since then he had accused her of sleeping with her brother, been the subject of an assassination attempt, and been set up to look like an IRA informer. Now his daughter was in the hands of terrorists. Quite an achievement for one morning in the life of a soon-to-be former Northern Ireland Minister.

Michael was dragged from this murky pit of depression by the ring of the phone. 'I'll get it!' he yelled downstairs to James as he sprinted along the landing to his own bedroom.

Mac refused to identify himself to the Minister, or to say which terrorist group he represented, but he did allow Michael a few words with Laura to prove the child was alive. When Mac was back on the line he got down to business.

'Look, you cooperate and everything will be OK. We don't want to kill them unless we have to, because it would be bad PR for us.' He repeated Neil's oft-expressed rationale. 'Anyway, our request is simple, and no one needs to know this ever occurred.'

'What do you want? Who are you?'

'It doesn't matter who we are. We want you to go to the Army Intelligence HQ at Lisburn at two o'clock. You're to leave word on the switchboard there that you want a call from Brian Holland put through to you.'

'Brian Holland? Why is that name familiar to me?' Michael wondered out loud, but he feared his mind was too retarded by panic and fear to remember. However, there was a lifetime of trivia cluttering his brain where there should have been useful, quotable statistics. 'Hang on, do you mean Brian Holland as in Holland-Dozier-Holland who wrote all the Motown hits?'

'Good man.' Mac sounded impressed. 'Brian Holland'll call and tell you what you're going to do, once you're into the Military Intelligence database. He'll give you a number, and you'll fax us a certain document while we're speaking. And it'll be a mobile fax so don't think you can have it traced, 'cos you won't manage it. And you won't be able to tamper with this document either because we're not going to leave you any time between getting it out and faxing it to us. We'll be speaking to you all the time. No room for tricks from your end. And don't tell anyone – or else this'll be messy,' said Mac, reading from Neil's notes.

'Fine. I'll be at Lisburn at two. But when will I see Laura and Delva? Why should I believe that you'll let them go?'

'That's your problem. Seems to me you don't have much choice but to go along with what we say.'

As the line went dead Michael looked at the humming receiver and nodded his reluctant agreement. He had no choice at all.

That was also the burden of Charlotte's message to Sir Trevor Grace. Using a mixture of charm and bullying on the telephone, the reporter breached the defences of his outer office, and got through to the Northern Ireland Secretary himself. She told him straight away about the Select Committee tape. Although Grace made a feeble attempt to disown his own voice, he gave in when Charlotte played him the first few words of the soundtrack over the phone, and explained that this was a video tape which clearly showed him at the scene and in the flesh.

'It's a simple deal, Sir Trevor. I'll hand you this tape in person, when you arrange for the leading lights of the Loyalist paramilitaries to attend a secret meeting in Belfast.'

'But how do I know you haven't made a copy of it?' Grace asked. Charlotte could almost sense the perspiration on his forehead, and she was relieved to have her hunch confirmed: he cared more about his political skin than he did about the wacky political adventure she was suggesting.

'Let's say we have a gentleman's agreement. You are a gentleman, aren't you, Sir Trevor? I'm not interested in your downfall. I'm merely using all the tools at hand. You'll get your tape,' she cooed down the line from London. 'I'll call with details of the venue; you get on to your friends.'

'Oh, I'll get on to my friends, all right,' Trevor Grace muttered when he had finished the call. 'You can count on that, Charlotte Carter.'

Chapter Twenty-Five

Neil prided himself on his knowledge of Irish history. It was an interest he had discovered by reading through stacks of books while in jail. He had twice since tried to set up study groups where fellow Loyalists could learn about the roots of the Unionist people of Ulster. He was only too aware that Gerry Adams had schooled his people in Irish history, and that it had been a source of strength and inspiration to the Republicans. The Provos learned that generations of 'rebels' before them had made the ultimate sacrifice; their own contribution now, during the Troubles, was equally brave and heroic and would be remembered by future generations, just as they were commemorating rebels through Irish history.

Neil might have disagreed with the content of the IRA lessons, but the method was impeccable for inspiring the troops. Sadly, his own skin-headed soldiers were more interested in drinking than reading, but that did not prevent him from pursuing his personal amusements, one of which was coming to fruition that morning.

Dublin's General Post Office in O'Connell Street has the symbolic importance of a Gettysburg or Dunkirk to the Irish. Here their national heros tried and failed in their aim to seize

327

back their country from the British. In 1916 the poet Patrick Pearse and his small band of rebels had occupied the building, and read out the 'Proclamation of the Irish Republic'. They were defeated by the British, who overreacted to this handful of patriots, and much of central Dublin was destroyed; the rebels were shot. But their disorganised and irrational gesture at Easter 1916 sparked the beginning of the end of British hegemony: and that was why Neil had picked the GPO.

Crowds of pedestrians were pouring up O'Connell Street from the River Liffey, and the commercial centre of the city, when Neil's gauleiter, a lanky twenty-one-year-old called Gary, entered the GPO building. After the savaging of the Easter Rising, the splendid neo-Classical portico and columns had been restored to their former pomposity, and even the interior was more like a temple than a post office, with a lofty ceiling covered in elaborate plaster ornamentation.

Gary made for a large hexagonal writing table in the middle of the cavernous hall, and went about his business unobserved by the crowds and the half-hearted security guard on the door. From his big plastic carrier bag (from Cleareys department store across the road; not an out-of-place Belfast bag) he produced a book-shaped parcel, which he addressed to a fictitious address in the Republic. Then he pulled another smaller plastic bag from inside the large one, and casually put it in the rubbish bin beneath the desk. He posted the parcel, without stamps (all the better to delay its passage through the post room) and left.

In the next hour, Gary returned to his car which was parked in a lot near Temple Bar, and retrieved a rucksack and a poster tube which he had bought earlier in the National Gallery of Ireland in nearby Merrion Street. It had the art gallery's logo all over it, and fitted in with his image as the fresh-faced, backpacking student, in jeans and a denim jacket, touring the city's sights, and collecting souvenirs.

Consequently when Gary wandered through the gates of Trinity College he blended in with the crowd of Euro-travellers who were visiting Ireland's famous and distinguished university. He followed the other tourists across the courtyard, and around to the right to Trinity College Library. Inside the visitors' gift shop he bought a ticket, and waited in line to examine the old book on display. It had some pretty drawings, but quite why it merited the attention of a guard and four security cameras, Gary neither knew nor cared. He was just following his instructions, which were to spend some time looking at the book, so he didn't stand out from the other visitors.

He hovered over the illuminated manuscript in the display case, and tried to read the explanatory notes on the wall. '*The* Book of Kells *is the supreme product of the flowering of Irish art which took place between the seventh and ninth centuries.*'

Gary gathered that it was a Bible, made by a bunch of monks in a place called Kells. It seemed like an odd thing to want to blow up, but he never questioned Neil's judgement. After ten minutes, Gary climbed the flight of stairs to his left where everyone else went when they had finished looking at the book. At the top of the stairs was an anteroom filled with moth-eaten books, and to his right was a long dark hall with high wooden ceilings. It too was filled with stacks of books, and a few antiques.

The anteroom was just as Neil had described it: there was an insubstantial set of barred gates to stop tourists getting at the ancient texts. Once he was alone there was nothing to prevent Gary from putting the heavy package from his rucksack through the bars, then, with the help of the poster tube, quickly sliding it behind the nearest stack of books, just out of sight. Neil had explained that the *Book of Kells* itself was too heavily guarded to deal with, but that a well-placed explosion upstairs would bring down the roof on it.

On the way out, Gary bought several postcards of the *Book of Kells*: they were beautiful, and he thought his girl-friend might like them. Then he got in his car, and drove one hundred miles north, back to Belfast.

Edward Power climbed the steps to the BBC's Millbank news-room two at a time. He wasn't panting for breath when he reached the reception desk at the top, unlike Parliamentarians of Sir Trevor Grace's generation. The political life of some of the older MPs was one long waddle from receptions to hospitality rooms to conferences, snaffling up buffets of sausage rolls until they collapsed and died from heart attacks in their fifties (thus causing untimely by-elections which were invariably won by the Liberals . . . and just as invariably reverted to their rightful owners at the next election).

The BBC receptionist summoned Charlotte from the news-room, and a moment later the MP and the journalist were taking their places at a table in the restaurant in the atrium of the same building. They both ordered large salads and Perrier to sustain them through their plotting session.

'You know, this is an entirely insane idea,' Eddie remarked with amusement when Charlotte confirmed that CNN had agreed to cooperate. 'What makes you think these terrorists'll turn up, just because you invite them?'

'Listen, both the Loyalists and the IRA want power and influence. They're basically pragmatic people who have been forced into awkward corners because of the hardline positions they adopted, and they're looking for an honourable way to get a stake in the peace process. The IRA will be there because they're terrified by what'll happen to the Catholic community if the ethnic cleansing continues and repartition goes ahead. The Loyalists will come along partly because they've been taking orders from a chain of command that starts with Trevor Grace, and ironically they'll also get involved because their politicians are letting them down.'

'Charlotte, you can't approach these massively complex problems, embedded in hundreds of years of history, and just say to everybody involved, "Right, you bastards, no one gets out of here until you've reached an agreement." It won't work, duckie,' he sneered.

'Then why are you here helping me?'

'It's more interesting than debating dog licences, I want to get Michael out of this mess, and I've got very little to lose – just a shadow spokesmanship in a party that's been in opposition since you were about three years old.' Then Eddie adopted a patronising tone. 'You're being irresponsible, and you might end up with a bullet in the back of your head by the end of today. I suppose you realise that?'

Charlotte took a thoughtful chew of her grilled aubergine and licked her lips. 'I love sesame-seed oil. It adds so much to the flavour of roasted vegetables, don't you think?'

'And even if someone doesn't kill you, you could lose your job,' Eddie cautioned. 'What'll the BBC make of this?'

Charlotte sipped her water and smacked her lips ostentatiously, as if she was sampling vintage champagne. 'I've already been sacked.'

Eddie's fork stopped halfway to his mouth. 'What? Why?'

'Apparently I haven't got the makings of a journalist worthy of this place, and I've infringed too many Corporation bylaws. So I'm out. The reason I'm still in this building, using the BBC phones, is that it'll take a week for the administration here to find out from the BBC office across the road that I'm no longer working for them.'

'Charlotte, this is ridiculous,' he said in a low, and rather more concerned, voice. 'What're you going to do?'

'To pay the mortgage? Good point. Maybe they could do with a waitress here. I'll ask the manager when I see him,' she said matter-of-factly, and speared a grilled carrot.

'What's in this for you?'

Charlotte shrugged and looked down at her rapidly disappearing salad. 'Oh, I don't know. Like you said, it's more interesting than covering debates on the manmade fibre agreements, or writing TV packages on whether Britain will become a fascist state if people have photographs on their driver's licences.' She hesitated, and blushed. 'I think Michael's in a lot of trouble, and I'd like to help him.'

'Wherever he may be,' Eddie remarked with his hands lifted skywards as if appealing for divine assistance. 'His secretary at Stormont won't give an inch.'

'Perhaps he's still wrapped up with the Prime Minister's visit?'

'I'll keep trying him.' Eddie nodded optimistically. 'The message is on its way to my Sinn Fein acquaintances, who'll talk to their chums in the IRA. You know the rule – anywhere there's a TV camera, there's a Republican. I said we were aiming at five this evening, and that I'd get back to them with a venue.'

'Good,' Charlotte remarked, like a teacher marking a pupil's prep. 'But don't tell them about CNN cameras, because we might not get that far. I'm hoping to hear from Tim at BBC

Ulster soon. He said he'd find somewhere appropriate for the meeting.'

'Like an abattoir? Is he going to be fired too?'

'Tim takes a more positive view of this. You see, in all these years of Troubles, no one has ever made these prima donnas sit down and talk to each other, so why not try it now? For the last quarter of a century – no,' Charlotte corrected herself, 'since the partition of Ireland in 1920, Sinn Fein and the IRA have directed all their remarks at Dublin and Washington; while the Unionists have pointed the megaphone at London.'

'And does your Tim friend honestly believe this'll succeed?'

'No, but he wants to be part of it anyway. He lives there, which gives him a more urgent perspective, I imagine. He knows the Province is going down the drain in three weeks when these horrendous by-elections happen.'

'Well, you and your friend have moved fast.' Eddie dabbed his lips with the napkin. 'I'm impressed.'

'What's surprising is that everyone else moves so slowly through life,' Charlotte muttered as she waved at the waiter for the bill.

'These are the times of the London-Belfast shuttles this afternoon.' Eddie placed a slip of paper on the table in front of the reporter. 'Which one should we get?'

'Ah, so it's "we", is it?'

'Come on, Charlotte. Let me tag along. I know you haven't got the highest opinion of me, but—'

'You should get a decent haircut,' Charlotte remarked, 'but apart from that you're proving quite useful, and for some reason Michael likes you. So you must have some hidden qualities,' she said with a mystified shake of her head. Then she stuffed the bill into Eddie's hand. 'Here, you can pay for this; I haven't got an expense account any more. I'll call you when I know the venue. And let's aim for the three o'clock shuttle. If you book that and pay for it, I'd be most grateful. You pick me up here at quarter past two, OK?' she smiled and left him gazing in admiration at her retreating figure.

Chapter Twenty-Six

By one o'clock, Michael could stand it no longer: it was impossible to read the paper, work, or sit quietly trying to control his imagination. All he could think of was Laura's thin, uncertain voice at the other end of the phone. It was pointless hanging around, so Michael summoned James from the sports pages of the paper, and suggested that they go to Army HQ at Lisburn immediately. The Minister had inadvertently conjured up several nightmarish scenarios in which the car broke down on the way there, or the information he needed for the kidnappers was inaccessible. He preferred to get there early and acquaint himself with the computer system so that no blunders could stop him from taking the call from 'Brian Holland'.

The Minister and his driver had an uneventful journey into the city centre where they got on the M1, and headed south. Michael took note of the helicopters above West Belfast once more, and the armoured personnel carriers on the streets. Both of these manifestations of a country under occupation had disappeared since the IRA ceasefire in 1994. But the advent of ethnic cleansing, and the panic caused by the by-elections and referendum had made them essential once more.

As they passed the Kennedy Way Industrial Estate, Michael

wondered if Elvis had simply set him up to take the blame for a security foul-up. Or had Grace actually wanted him dead? And how far had Mandy been in league with his boss – or was her only connection with Reverend Scott?

None of this mattered, however, compared to his main preoccupation: how likely was it that he would get his daughter back alive? Why should the terrorists return her? A drop-off would involve risking their necks, which was surely more hassle than a few days of negative publicity for killing a child. And executing a Bosnian Muslim who, until now, had managed to survive the combined evils of the Serbs and Croats, and the incompetence of the UN. No one would care about poor Delva, any more than they cared for the two little boys who had been murdered at Warrington. The nation was outraged for a day; then it was back to its normal diet of the lottery, the Royal Family, and television game shows.

What type of secure information were the kidnappers after? The Army's list of touts who coughed up information for pathetically small payments? Michael shuddered to think of their fate: a horrible death after God knows how many hours or days of torture. Or perhaps they were after the names of the Army's undercover agents who watched, monitored, and sometimes participated in different Loyalist terror groups. Again, it would be a vile death for those brave officers with nerves of steel.

If only there was a way of stalling the terrorists' demands, of substituting another list of names . . . more suitable targets, such as parents who had abused their children, or vicious yobs who had received only a fine as a punishment for hurting animals. Or drunk drivers who had killed and maimed, and paid the enormous social penalty of losing their licence for a couple of years.

Michael gnashed his teeth and imagined a Mikado-like hit list of citizens who deserved to get a midnight call from the men with Armalites: drug-pushers, racketeers who bled the economic life out of their communities, and corrupt builders who constructed death-trap housing for the down-trodden classes. The trouble was, the above-mentioned were all members of the terror gangs anyway. The Minister was working his way onto thugs who destroy public flowerbeds when they pulled off the M1 at the Lisburn exit.

Over the years this grim little town had paid the price for having a massive Army presence: terrorists had menaced the local population into staying at home to get their kicks. The giveaways were the high number of off-licences, video rental shops, satellite dishes and takeaway joints.

James steered them up Magheralave Road, past leafy residential streets lined with comfortable 1930s housing, not the most likely setting for the nerve centre of the British Army. Then a watchtower appeared, and grey metal siding with rolls of barbed wire at the top, stretching up the hill as far as they could see. The trees and rugby goal-posts inside were just visible. At the entrance, where large blue signs separated the sheep from the goats, they headed towards the lane for pass-holders, and stopped at the red light. The Minister's appearance at the front gate was of no particular interest to the soldiers on duty compared to the high-security Prime Ministerial visit with which it coincided, and they were nodded through.

A few minutes later, Michael was introducing himself to the captain in charge of records, and explaining that he had called earlier, and that he wanted to access some secure files in the database. He tried to make his request seem as ordinary and uninteresting as possible, although he realised he was at a disadvantage because it was unusual that he would come in person, rather than sending a minion, or simply requesting a fax. Michael was also conscious that he looked and sounded stressed-out. It prevented him from turning his full attention on anything or anybody he encountered. Instead he felt he was floating above the earth in a powerless semi-reality that allowed him to witness what was happening, but to do very little about it.

On the positive side there were so many Army big guns and political heavyweights floating around HQ today that one Minister, obviously bored by the PM's lunchtime speech, and looking for a bit of diversion in the database, wasn't completely unexpected. Michael explained to the young captain that the current security situation demanded that he retrieve an Intelligence file. Of course he had every right to be there, making these requests, demanding access to sensitive documents, but it caused some raised eyebrows around the large open-plan room.

While James was instructing the switchboard operator to route calls to the Minister from one Brian Holland onto a certain extension, Michael tried to focus his mind sufficiently to ask relevant questions. Part of his problem was that he hadn't a clue what they wanted until the kidnappers told him, so he flannelled along hopelessly, and prayed that Brian Holland would call on time.

Most of all, Michael wished the helpful officer would just go away. Then his freaked-out brain might have a second to think up some alternative to handing over a genuine list. For a wild moment he wondered if he could get the Army and NIPD to put a guard on every name he was about to divulge, or at least warn the victims in advance. But he knew that would be impossible.

Maybe the terrorists were after detailed information about where the Army kept its weapons; or how it was bringing men and materiel back to the Province, having withdrawn them after the ceasefire; or when and where manoeuvres were planned, or how the secure gates around all compounds worked. How many soldiers might they kill with the information that M. Fitzgerald MP was about to fax into the ether?

It was ten to two, and he was still playing mental ping pong with the earnest captain, pretending that what he wanted was far too sensitive to even be discussed. Why didn't he just crank up the bloody computer and go away? Then he could retrieve whatever it was in peace, and fax it to Attila the Hun of the Shankill.

At five to two fear was becoming panic, but at least the captain had now logged in, and was showing off all kinds of no doubt fascinating windows, and clever split screens that were utterly irrelevant to the Minister. James appeared at his elbow with a welcome glass of water which Michael gulped down. At two minutes to two the officer turned to ask his audience more questions about the type of document he wanted.

'I'll be able to tell you any moment now,' the Minister promised, and the captain grinned cautiously. Somehow Michael had envisaged this operation taking place at dead of night in utter silence and privacy – just the computer and him and his treachery. Instead, people were wandering about, returning from lunch, coming over to say hello and ask if they could help. A rather cheeky young secretary in a tight skirt had asked Michael to autograph her box of Lillets. It was someone's birthday, and Michael had to politely refuse a piece of cake.

The officer sat patiently beside him, discussing their new inkjet printer, and Michael checked his watch: five past two. Had the idiot terrorists got cold feet and killed Laura and Delva? Had the switchboard operator gone off for lunch and forgotten to pass on the message about Brian Holland? Had Michael misunderstood some essential part of his instructions? Had the kidnappers meant two in the morning, rather than two in the afternoon? He gulped away another wave of terror, feeling sick and dizzy with worry. The phone call was now seven minutes late.

'What's up, Michael?'

The Minister swung around in the direction of the familiar booming voice. Johnny Burleigh was standing twenty feet away, arms folded across his chest, unsmiling, and looking suspicious. 'What on earth are you doing here?' The room had gone silent, and several officers and staff members looked from the Defence Secretary, who had never before been seen in this Department, to the equally novel Northern Ireland Minister, who was now on his feet.

'Come next door, and let's have a word,' Burleigh rapped out. Then he turned to leave, as if Michael would trot obediently after him.

'No,' the Minister croaked with what was left of his voice.

When the light on her phone began to flash, Charlotte grabbed it with the speed of a grizzly bear plucking salmon from a river.

'OK, here's the rendezvous for our VIPs,' Tim began. 'It's the Grand Opera House. I reckon it's so busy in that part of town that no one will notice this lot unless they arrive in tanks. There's a car park around the back, and a stage door that leads up a flight of steps to the auditorium.'

'This is amazing, Tim!' Charlotte squealed. 'How'd you do it?'

'You recall meeting my friend Stephen? He's the stage manager, and since there's no performance tonight, I've booked it for a private party.'

'Some party. More like the Clash of the Titans. Well, I'm staggered and impressed,' she said with a mocking, extravagant tone that was familiar to Tim from their late-night phone calls. 'But I hope you don't get into trouble.'

'What a bloody daft thing to say at this stage in the day,' he commented without malice. 'When we're both ducking the bullets at around five-fifteen I'll remind you of this.'

'I'm encouraged you now think the talks'll last for fifteen minutes before the shooting begins. Right, I'll make my phone calls, and see you soon.' She paused and ran her finger down her list of tasks to be completed. 'What else do I need to do? CNN?'

Tim's response was calm and soothing. 'It's fine with CNN. Just get yourself to that wee theatre, madam. You're in the chair, after all.'

'Not if I can help it. We're going to put the Minister in charge. If we can find him, that is.'

'Michael,' Johnny Burleigh repeated. 'What the hell's up? Let's go next door. I have to talk to you about something.'

'No. I'm sorry, Johnny.'

Burleigh's face cracked into a hundred bad-tempered wrinkles. 'Could you excuse us, please?' he muttered to the bewildered officer who had been assisting the Minister. 'Sit down,' he ordered Michael. 'You look like you're about to puke. What on earth is it? What are you doing here?'

Michael, who was beyond feeling foolish or out of place, slid down onto the chair by the phone, and closed his eyes for a moment. What could he say to get Johnny to go away? How could he explain his presence here? Then the phone rang.

'Johnny, hang on. I must take that,' Michael said with a fierceness that made his former boss sit back in surprise.

'You'll have to give me a bit of time to extract this,' he said to his caller. 'Five minutes. Then ring back with the number. OK.' He put down the phone, and turned to the incredulous Johnny. 'I need to get something out of here, I'm afraid. You can try to stop me, but I wouldn't advise it.'

This melodramatic declaration made Burleigh laugh. Michael looked away, and started tapping at the keyboard of the computer terminal.

'Would you good people mind leaving us alone here for a moment, please?' Johnny announced to the room at large. 'Tea break or whatever. Thank you so much.'

When the officers and staff had filed out he turned back to Michael, but the Junior Minister was totally absorbed by his journey through the computer's directory.

'Look, I'm quite aware that someone tried to kill you this morning, Michael. And I know it was a part-time Loyalist at NIPD. *And* I know this chap was working hand-in-hand with Mandy. So why don't you tell me the rest?' he said gently. 'I'm bloody annoyed you didn't think to ask for some help from your old fool of a boss, by the way.'

'Johnny, that was this morning. Something far worse has happened since, and trusting anyone would be too dangerous. I just have to get a document out of here.' He paused for a moment and turned a drawn, agitated face to Burleigh. 'Please let me do this. Then you can arrest me, or whatever it is you're going to do. But as a personal favour to a former colleague, please—'

'Arrest you! My God, what's this about?'

'Oh Christ, I need that computer chap to do this,' Michael muttered distractedly as he searched through the different categories of secure files. 'Ah. Oh. Here it is. Right. Now how do I print the bloody thing out?'

342

'Just tell me what's up,' Burleigh insisted.

'They're ringing in two minutes and I've got to have the right file on paper by then, because they're giving me a mobile fax number,' he rattled on, as if everything he said made absolute sense. 'Oh, what does it matter if you know now?' he groaned.

'Who?'

'The people who kidnapped Laura and Delva this morning,' Michael gasped, as if it had been perfectly obvious all along what he had meant. He leapt up and went to the printer. 'Some Loyalist paras. They want this.' He returned with the single sheet of paper and waved it at Johnny. 'And now I know why they want it so badly. It's the Judas File.'

'The what? Why didn't you tell me this was happening!' Johnny said in exasperation. Then he looked at the list. 'The Judas File? Oh, the compromisers on both sides of the paras. Ah,' he remarked without interest.

'I don't care what you do or say, Johnny, but unless you can think of a way around this, I've got to fax it to them, or they'll kill Laura and Delva.'

'Michael, the people on this list are just a bunch of fucking terrorist Irishmen. To hell with them all. They deserve whatever they get. And you can send the IRA the keys to Downing Street while you're at it for all I care.' Then he grasped Michael's forearm and tugged at it. 'Now why didn't you let me know about this? How are you going to get them back? Have you arranged the exchange? Look, you've got to make them hand her over when you give them this. Don't fax it.'

'They'll think I'm giving them a fake unless I fax this immediately. You see, there's a thing at the top of the page that says what time it was printed. They know I can't alter it. That's why they want it now. They're not stupid.' Michael pulled away from

Johnny's grip. 'And it *does* matter if the Loyalist boot boys go around and kill the people on this list, Johnny. This is our last hope of getting the more moderate terrorists to persuade their murdering friends to renounce violence. And now with this referendum and the by—'

The phone rang, and any blood remaining in Michael's face departed. Johnny planted a heavy paw on the younger man's shoulder. 'Demand to speak to Laura first. Then tell these maniacs they get half now, and half when they deliver Laura and Delva.' Then he allowed Michael to lift the receiver.

'Michael! It's Eddie. I was expecting Johnny. How are you—'

'Get off the fucking line, Eddie!' Michael snapped, but Johnny grabbed the phone out of his hand.

'Go ahead. Fast. We've got to keep this line clear,' he said precisely. Then he scribbled down an address and hung up. Michael's eyes narrowed in confusion as Johnny pushed the piece of paper towards him. 'Tell them to deliver Laura and Delva there at a quarter to five this evening, and they can have a place at direct talks with the Government, and the IRA and all the ferret-faced Irish fuckers they fancy,' Johnny growled. 'And tell them if they don't believe you, then you'll start faxing them any other lists they want until they get the message that you're on the level.'

Then Burleigh grabbed the Judas File from the Minister sweaty grasp, and in one sure movement, ripped it from one corner diagonally to the other. 'Send them that bit. And tell them they'll get the other triangle when they deliver Laura and Delva. Here.' He jabbed his finger down on the address.

'I can't play around with their lives, Johnny. What is this about?' Michael demanded in a voice that was half savage caveman and half whimper.

'This is really happening,' the Defence Secretary explained in a near whisper. 'Charlotte Carter, you know, the BBC woman. She's got a tape of Grace-Face plotting to set you up to take the rap for a lapse of security, and she's making him call a meeting here, at the Opera House, at five this afternoon. It's very hush hush. No one knows about it. Eddie's bringing the Fenians, and Charlotte Whatsit is making Grace send his colleagues in the Loyalist high command.'

'Have you all gone mad?' Michael groaned and hung his head in his hands.

'Good fun, if you ask me. And nothing to be lost, as long as no one finds out what's going on. Rowbottham's working on it right now, providing security for the masked men, so they don't think they're being led into a trap.'

'I can't believe this is happening.'

'Well, we kept trying to ring you, but you'd disappeared.' Johnny sounded personally offended. 'If you'd trusted a few of us, we might have been able to help.'

'Trusted you? With NIPD officers shooting at me?' Then Michael took a deep breath. 'I'm sorry. I've probably been a bit paranoid.'

'How did they get Laura and Delva? Did they ambush their car? What were bloody NIPD doing during all this?'

'They crawled across the roof, came into the house, and marched them out the front door while the NIPD blokes weren't watching.'

'You wait till my boys do a bit of deep interrogation of your NIPD detail,' Johnny said with a sparkle in his eyes. But before he could get too animated the phone rang again, and it was 'Brian Holland'.

Michael had lost touch with reality by this point, and he was almost faint with anxiety. He demanded a word with his daughter before the hardened psychopath on the other end of the line had time to catch breath.

Laura assured her father that she was OK, and he detected an anger and defiance that had been missing earlier on. As usual she was disguising her fears and fragility with a Little Miss Tough Talk routine: Michael recognised it from when Caroline died. By the sounds of it, his offspring was obviously making the kidnappers' lives miserable, denouncing them with her Serbo-Croat obscenities. He was terribly proud of her.

When 'Brian' came back on the phone, Michael adjusted his voice to sound hard and determined. He told the kidnapper his proposal: half the list now, the other half on delivery, and a place for his 'people' at secret peace talks that were beginning at five that afternoon. To his relief, 'Brian' sounded quite as amazed as he was, and said he would have to call back in five minutes.

'What do I do if they won't accept this?' he asked Johnny while they waited.

'As far as I'm concerned you give them any bloody lists they want. The important thing is to get an exchange of hostages for material. It'll be all right, Michael.' The Defence Secretary inflicted a comforting squeeze of the younger man's shoulder. 'God, you missed a ghastly little shindig for the PM. Thank heavens Rowbottham and I were busy organising this event, so we didn't have to listen to any of it. Grace was looking as if a goat had just chewed his nuts off, thanks to Charlotte Carter's ultimatum. PM on his usual sparkling form. People nodding off all round the room. By the way, don't you dare hand Grace any letter of resignation, or I'll strangle you.'

'Believe me when I tell you that right now the last thing on my mind is my resignation, or Grace, or his pictures of Mandy.'

'I know, old boy, but hang on. It'll be OK. While we're at it we'll fax the IRA directions to Trevor Grace's London flat, and his home in the constituency, and a few other addresses of colleagues we don't like, and we'll add a little note that says, *Dear Mick, please assassinate the following. Oh, and by the way, do you do whole ministries? There're some unsavoury types round at the Home Office.*'

Michael laughed despite himself, and he was oddly touched when Johnny leaned over and ruffled his hair as if he was a favourite son. Then the phone rang again, and 'Brian' said that his associates were interested, but how could they trust the Minister?

'I presume your chums will go on ahead and check out the Grand Opera House,' Michael countered. 'They can tell you if it's a set-up. But think about it: I'd hardly gamble my daughter's life away just to get you and your friends arrested. I'll fax you the first bit of this list now. Then you have to trust me. If you ask around, you'll probably hear that the other stars in your community are attending. Give me your fax number.'

Mac was still uncertain, and more than a little uncomfortable with this bizarre turn of events. 'Listen,' Michael continued, 'you know where I live. And I know you do, so I'm not likely to mess your organisation around when you can blow me to hell when you feel like it. This is on the level.'

Mac gave him the fax number, and Johnny took the triangle of paper and sent it through as Michael continued his hard sell. 'Have you got that list now?' the Minister asked. 'OK, I'm going to get to this theatre about four-thirty, so maybe you should arrive before the rest of the show too. Here's my mobile number, and if you get cold feet or you reckon you're being tricked, then call me. And bring your boss. I suppose his codename is Berry Gordy?'

At the mention of the founder of Motown Records Mac crowed like an excitable adolescent. 'That's a good one – I like that. OK, we'll give it a try and go along with this, but you know what the consequences are if you fuck us about.'

When Michael hung up he felt a thin thread of sanity inside his brain snap. 'What on earth am I doing?' he asked his former boss.

'You're coming with me, right now. We've got some preparation to do. And the worthy people who work in this office should be allowed to carry on with their day. Before they start gossiping about us having a lovers' tiff.'

Eddie Power and Charlotte Carter used their journey to Heathrow to call Belfast and the Army HQ in Lisburn to check on progress.

'Brilliant,' Eddie told Johnny Burleigh. 'Just keep your boys as far back from the theatre as possible. We don't want to frighten away our illustrious guests. And perhaps someone could give the place the once-over to make sure no one got there first and planted a surprise package.'

'Already in hand,' quipped the Defence Secretary, who was working from an unoccupied classroom where soldiers were normally taught how to use word processors. He and Brigadier Rowbottham had established an operations centre with a few hand-picked officers to plan the afternoon's security nightmare. They hastily assembled maps of the area around the theatre, a blueprint of the building, the names, addresses and locations of those who were invited, and of course, tea cups. They looked like small boys playing with a splendid scale-model railway.

'Look, we need a contingency plan in the event that these

negotiations turn nasty,' Johnny barked. 'So we'll be ready to move in if they start pulling guns. And if the talks fail we'll need to have them in protective custody to stop the hard-liners in their own organisations rubbing them out. They all belong in jail anyway,' he laughed mirthlessly.

'Where's Michael? Does he go along with this?'

'He's having a spot of bother in another department. Let's just leave it at that, Eddie,' Johnny said enigmatically. 'I've sent him home to have a bath and change his clothes, and give himself a face mask too. He's not at his prettiest right now.'

'But is he OK?' Eddie persisted.

'Yah, yah, yah. Got some real bloody soldiers protecting him now. You wait till we sort out NIPD over this one.' He ground his teeth with satisfaction.

'So what happened to him this morning?'

'I'll tell you in due course, Eddie. He's not out of the woods by any means.'

'Hang on, Charlotte wants a word.' The Labour MP handed the mobile phone to his companion in the back seat of the Rover. After a few pleasantries Eddie heard the reporter giving instructions for how she wanted the stage of the theatre; where the chairs should be, how to place the microphones so that none of the participants knew they were being taped, and finally, how the curtains should be drawn so that no one present would be conscious that they were actually on a stage.

'That's very important,' she stressed. 'And we need the loos nearest the stage clearly signposted, and lots of mineral water on hand, in the unlikely event they get properly stuck into these negotiations. Some sandwiches too. Can one of your people go out to M & S and get some?'

'Naturally,' Burleigh gushed. He adored smart, bossy women.

'How has Elvis reacted to the ultimatum? He's more than capable of double-crossing us.'

'Yes, I appreciate that. Grace-Face is *not* a happy man,' Johnny chortled. 'At lunchtime he hunted out a phone here, and called some little runt in Sir David Mackay's office at NIPD. It turns out this is the Loyalist contact we've been searching for; the big rotten apple is the Assistant Chief Constable himself. Would you believe it? 'Course, we listened in to the whole thing. Grace told him to send the Loyalist high command to the Opera House. Now we know that the Assistant was passing tasty nuggets of Intelligence down a line that ended up with the Loyalist supremo. Most interesting.'

'That implies that Army Intelligence has an established system for eavesdropping on NIPD. How very interesting.' Charlotte paused for one tantalising moment. 'And what a pity this conversation is on Lobby terms.'

When Johnny was breathing normally again he chipped in, 'By the way, you ought to get your Army identification words right. Grace is Fat Elvis and Michael is Young Elvis.'

'Oh dear. Have you told Michael that?'

'Yes, I think he took it as a compliment, which is how it was intended when the boys here were looking for an appropriate call sign. Anyway, if Fat Elvis lets us down, we'll just go out and round up the Loyalists ourselves.' Johnny sounded calm, almost blasé, and it steadied Charlotte's nerves somewhat.

'Thank you for everything.'

'Pleasure, Ms Carter. Our men wanted to do this years ago. I don't think it stands a chance of working, by the way, but there's nothing to lose at the moment, what with God Bob's people rampaging about the place.'

Nothing to lose except Michael's political career, thought

Charlotte as she handed the phone back to Eddie. The two politicians then discussed the agenda for the afternoon's talks, presuming they happened, and Charlotte gazed out at Heathrow's perimeter fence. 'We're almost there, Eddie,' she interrupted. 'Let him get on with the arrangements at that end.'

The Labour MP said goodbye reluctantly, and studied Charlotte's profile. 'You do know you could be dead by six o'clock, don't you.' It was a statement, not a question. For a moment he wondered if she had heard him. Then he saw her yawn.

'And I'm exhausted already,' she remarked as they pulled up at the Terminal 1 entrance.

'Aren't you the slightest bit frightened?' he asked her in astonishment.

'I'm terrified. Now get out of the car. Let's get moving.'

Chapter Twenty-Seven

Michael was shaving when the call came. He nicked himself, and grabbed a bit of loo paper to quench the blood as he stumbled towards the phone. Quite why he needed to shave before he met the masked men, he didn't know, but it was therapeutic. A fresh shirt and suit, and one of his favourite Liberty ties lay on the bed in preparation. If he was going to go down, he'd do it in style.

'Is that Michael Fitzgerald?' Neil asked.

'Yes. Who's this?'

'I'd rather not give my name, but let's just say I'm not a million miles from Berry Gordy.'

'Closer to the Eagles, I would have thought.'

'Ah, you recognised my voice.' Neil sounded flattered.

'Is Laura OK? Let me speak to her.'

'She's not here, but I promise she's fine. That's not why I'm calling. It's about this meeting tonight. What are you playing at? Have you gone soft? I mean, what the hell's happening?'

'I gather that the logic behind the get-together is this: it's pointless leaving the peace process in the hands of politicians who don't basically want to work together, and who can't stop the violence anyway. The same thinking says that the Assembly

353

has failed because the people elected to it have neither the power nor the will to make it succeed.'

'How'd you get Grace to buy this? I've been contacted by, er, well, someone in NIPD who says to turn up at the Grand Opera House tonight. What is this, *La Traviata*?'

'More like the *Force of Destiny*. Grace is being blackmailed by a friend of mine, and he has to make your colleagues attend.' Michael rubbed the towel across his wet face. 'Or else he's going to jail.'

'Nice,' Neil remarked. 'No politicians?'

'Do you need God Bob there to hold your hand? Aren't you allowed to express an opinion without him around? You never did explain why you've let Reverend Scott exploit you for decades.'

'It's not like that,' Neil tutted testily.

'Oh, really? Ask yourself this: a few years ago the Loyalist paramilitaries met with the IRA. British Intelligence knew all about it, and I've read the reports, so don't deny it.'

'I'm not going to try.'

'Your people and the IRA managed to agree on an independent Northern Ireland with just enough links to Dublin to keep the Republicans happy. By anyone's standards that was a significant breakthrough. Have you ever wondered why those talks faltered and then broke up?'

There was an unhappy silence from Neil's end of the phone.

'Maybe you were too young to remember. Well, I'll tell you. God Bob found out about those secret meetings and he realised that if the masked men got a deal, he'd be out of a job. Why should the British Government court him, when they could talk to the men who could really stop the violence, who were willing to compromise? Then suddenly a senior IRA man was assassinated and the blame was put on the UVF. End of talks, not surprisingly.'

There was more silence, then an angry sigh.

'Did Grace put you up to kidnapping my daughter?'

Neil sounded surprised. 'Nah, this is my scheme. I told you: I want that list. Anyway, who's going to be there tonight, from the other side?'

'All the IRA people who aren't collecting honorary degrees at American universities at the moment.' The Minister paused and dabbed at the blood on his chin. 'I'm afraid I can't tell you why they're turning up, because I was busy avoiding one of your bullets while this was being organised.'

Neil clicked his tongue in annoyance. 'Hey, steady on. That wasn't my lot.'

'Ah, you just kidnap children. Right – forgive me.'

'I told you she's OK. And the nanny. You do what we want and you'll see them soon. So, how can I trust you? How do I know this isn't some giant bloody sting?'

Michael swung his legs up on the bed so he was lying down comfortably. 'Christ, it's like organising a dinner party for vegetarians. I suppose I should ask you if there's anything you won't eat. Right, the Army isn't going to be there to trap you because they're basically in favour of getting the men with Kalashnikovs to confront each other. I can't answer for NIPD – surely you're in a better position than I am to know their plans. Grace's instructions are to keep them away, and give the negotiations a chance.'

'But how do I know you're telling the truth?' Neil persisted.

'I'm afraid you'll have to take my word on this. I care more about getting my daughter back safely than I do about the future of Northern Ireland, and if that means no blame attaches to you

355

and that other Motown alumni, Smokey Robinson, or whatever his name is, then I'm not going to muck you around.' He rubbed his tired eyes. 'You're not as smart as you like to think, Neil. If I wanted you arrested I would have set a trap for you in London.'

Neil sucked his teeth for a moment. 'Yeah, well this whole thing sounds really crazy to me. And I'm not sure I'm giving you the benefit of the doubt. If you'd just played it straight and gave us the fucking List it would've been OK.'

'How did I know you were telling me the truth?' Michael asked rather half-heartedly. He could sense Laura slipping away from him, and he squeezed his eyes closed in a prayer to Caroline to watch over their daughter. 'Look, none of this was my idea – not the flag competition, not today's outdoor relief for terrorists. I told you, I was busy avoiding your henchman Ken.'

'That was nothing to do with me. Ken was flying solo – with the help of your assistant, I should add.'

'Well, I guess that makes two of us who haven't a clue what our underlings are up to. Look, I'll be at the back door of the theatre with the other half of the List at a quarter to five. You let me have Laura and Delva, and I'll give you the List. Then you can decide whether you come in and join the party, or not.'

'We're going to play this by ear,' Neil said cautiously. 'If we get near this place and find anything we don't like then we're not proceeding. Right?'

'Apparently so. You'll have to call me later, and then I'll bring you whatever bloody documents you want. Perhaps you'd like the keys to a few tanks and APCs too. You'll need them in your forthcoming battles with the US Army and the Irish. That's the consequence of your stupid bloody referendum.'

Neil hung up, and Michael lay for a moment, receiver still pressed to his ear, staring at the ceiling. He had a feeling that today was going to get much worse. Laura's chances were not being helped by Charlotte's insane terrorist powwow, either. What he found so hard to believe was that Johnny Burleigh, George Rowbottham and Eddie Power were going along with her. The difference was that they could get on a plane and go home at the end of the evening. Only he had to face the prospect of a dead daughter and housekeeper.

He was easing the dried loo paper off his chin when James yelled upstairs, 'Michael, there's been some bombs in Dublin. One at Trinity College, the other at the Post Office. Don't know how many casualties yet, but the Garda reckon it's bad. Sounds like the Loyalists.'

The Minister sank back on the bed and cursed loudly. What was very bad had just got worse, as predicted.

'This is perfect. Good lighting. Lots of space. Tables laid out in a big square. TV set standing by, just in case. Comfortable chairs. And the phone's working.' Charlotte paced across the stage of the Grand Opera House towards Tim Horn, who was prodding the curtains with a finger. 'You are truly a hero.'

'And you are truly a psycho. This is a mad idea.'

'But you told me the masked men had to confront each other.'

'Yeah, but I didn't expect you to apply the Girl Guide code, and get the job done. Anyway, the people from CNN are satisfied with everything. I think I'll ask them for a job when this is over, if we survive.'

Charlotte stopped in her tracks and turned to face her friend. 'Oh hell. Did the BBC fire you as well?'

'No. This is what I call stepping out of the office for a few minutes. I said I was feeling sick. And it's true.'

'So am I.' She rubbed her hands together nervously. 'Have we got the back doors open? I hope there's enough lighting to convince our visitors we haven't got the SAS in here waiting.'

'It's as good as we'll get it, Charlotte. Now relax and concentrate on that agenda. Come on. Sit down. Get your thoughts straight. Look, they'll be here in twenty minutes.'

'Michael Fitzgerald must chair the bloody thing,' she reminded the lanky journalist. 'I'm going to be the coat-check girl: "Leave your hardware with me, gents. No semi-automatic weapons at table, please." And Michael can be Wyatt Earp, the Marshal in Tombstone, Arizona.'

'Remember to call me if you need help. I'll be at the newsroom, and I'll keep my eyes on the wires. This Dublin thing sounds grisly, by the way. Twenty bodies already, and they've destroyed the *Book of Kells*.'

Charlotte shuddered. 'Oh Lord, no. Talk about meeting in auspicious times. Well, you get back to the coalface of British journalism at the finest broadcasting company in the world.'

'But Channel Four is in London. Hey, I'm not very keen on leaving you here.' He stood awkwardly by her side.

Charlotte craned her neck to see his face. 'Oh Tim, don't get all soppy on me now,' she told him with a pained expression that was supposed to communicate affection, but no prospect of anything more personal. Then she grabbed his hand for a quick, platonic squeeze. 'See you later.'

She pretended to be writing something on the draft agenda in front of her, but actually she was listening to the sound of Tim's footsteps across the stage, down the stairs, and into the distance. When he was gone she sat back in the chair, and rubbed her forehead, but the knots of tension would not be massaged away. Then she noticed that her hands were shaking and damp with perspiration. She plucked a powderpuff from her handbag, attended to her shiny nose and dragged a comb through her untended locks. There hadn't been much time for worrying about appearances; not that kind of day.

She was asking herself quite how Charlotte Carter had ended up here when there were footsteps on the stairs that led from the back door of the theatre, up to the stage. They didn't sound like Tim's; too light and quick. But they belonged to a man. The kind of man who was never seen in polite society without a hand grenade? she wondered. Someone who had just finished killing twenty Dubliners?

Charlotte stood up – rather a pointless gesture since there was nowhere to run, and no time to hide – and waited for the owner of the footsteps to appear. It was wearing a Liberty tie.

'Michael! Oh, thank heavens. I thought the Shankill Butchers had arrived early to get in a little target practice.' She took a couple of steps towards him, but the glacial expression stopped her in her tracks. 'What's wrong?'

'Is anyone else here?' he asked curtly. 'No one arrived yet?'

'No. What—'

'You chose an extraordinary day for this bloody stunt of yours,' he snapped. 'I wish you'd picked up a sodding phone and spoken to me. And by the way, no one's going to turn up to this.'

'Yes, they are,' Charlotte retorted with a flash of the incisors, and a furious clench of her fists. 'They want to talk, these terrorists. I know they're deeply unattractive people, and murderers, and criminals. But the point is that they must be made to confront each other! And I wish you'd returned some of the dozens of calls I've made to you. This stunt, as you put it, is meant to get you out of an awkward hole. It was me who warned you about Mandy, but you were too busy screwing her to take my calls; and it was me who found out that Grace was setting you up, and—'

'Yes, and it's you who's about to get my daughter killed,' he spat back, and paced away from her towards the curtain.

'What?' she said weakly.

'Some Loyalist lackey of Neil's with a fondness for soul music kidnapped Laura and Delva this morning, and I was all set to hand over the Intelligence report they wanted when you and Johnny barged in on everything.'

Charlotte sat down stiffly. 'Oh God, Michael, I—'

'—had no idea,' he continued the rather lame sentence for her in an appropriately mealy-mouthed voice. 'No, I'm sure you didn't. All this is a bit much, isn't it?' He gave the lights and curtain a contemptuous gesture. 'Anyway, we might as well go through with it. I'm resigning in the morning, so why not get sacked for something spectacularly stupid, as opposed to something I didn't do at all, like screwing my Loyalist research assistant.'

'You didn't?' Her voice rose. She checked herself. 'Where are Laura and Delva? What happened?'

Michael checked his watch. 'They might or might not be headed here right now. It all depends on whether Neil can stand the heat. If he sees squaddies and paratroopers walking around on the roof he'll take Laura and Delva back to the stinking cellar in which they've been hidden.' He stopped pacing and glanced up at the lights and rigging overhead. 'Where are Johnny's boys? Are they going to start a riot when my Loyalist friends arrive?'

'There's no one here. Just us, and a mike that's relaying everything back to the Army at Lisburn. There's no security. Otherwise the Armalite Brigade wouldn't come near.'

Michael glared at her, unconvinced, and about to jump out of his skin with nerves. 'I'm going back there to hang about and say some prayers. Please stay out of the way,' he added, and retreated to the stairs. Charlotte buried her head in her hands.

As Mac drove towards the city centre he listened to a tape of Marvin Gaye and Tammi Terrell. It was one of his favourite albums, and he could usually count on it to relax him. Under the circumstances that was essential, because he was deeply unhappy about Neil's latest big idea. Typically Mac was the one risking his life, while Neil waited at a distance until he was sure the coast was clear. That was Neil's prerogative as the brains behind the organisation, and that was why young idiots like Gary were sent off to Dublin to do wee jobs.

But anyone with an ounce of common sense knew that this terrorist summit meeting was a daft idea, a trick, pointless at best. Mac suspected that his boss was up to no good. It also bemused him that Neil had been against shooting Fitzgerald. Not that Ken had listened to Neil, of course. Ken himself had recently voiced reservations about Neil and his unorthodox business arrangements with the Provos, such as carving up building contracts on roadworks that bisected ~~both~~ Nationalist and Loyalist communities.

Ken had ignored Neil, foolishly as it turned out, because Ken and Mandy hadn't planned the hit properly, and now he was dead. But the former NIPD officer had a point about Neil, and now Mac was putting his arse on the line, yet again, for a man he no longer trusted. The car idled at the traffic-lights, and Mac drummed his fingers on the steering wheel. 'You're all I need to get by,' he sang along with his martyred hero. Then he pulled into Great Victoria Street.

At the back of the theatre was a small car park. Michael stood shivering under the glare of a bulb above the stage door, breathing clouds into the misty late afternoon air. The best that could be said for the location was that it provided no hiding spots for terrorists or the security services. Anyone who approached it by car would see that there were plenty of getaway possibilities. And everything appeared perfectly normal; no Army patrol in the road outside, no helicopters hovering overhead. But how long would it be before NIPD or Army Intelligence could no longer resist taking a look? And what about Elvis and his chums?

Michael stuck his hands deep into his pockets and jiggled around a bit to try to keep warm. Then out of the memory bank of irrelevant items in his increasingly scatty brain came a song: '*I stepped up on the platform/ the man gave me the noose/ he said "You must be joking, son/ where did you get those shoes?"*' It was one of the Steely Dan songs that Eddie had given him. Bloody Eddie, he thought with a spurt of fury that warmed him up for a few seconds. He and his fucking chum Johnny were at the top of Michael's death list, once he got through this mess with Laura and Delva intact. *If* they got through this mess . . .

He was about to ruin a pair of perfectly good Lobb shoes by kicking at the gravel when he was caught in the glare of headlights, and a car pulled into the car park. It rocked across the uneven surface and came to a stop near the back door. A window was wound down, and the voice that belonged to 'Brian Holland' asked him to step forward.

Michael did as he was told and bent down a bit to peer into the back seat of the car. It was empty. 'Where are they?'

'They'll be along in a moment, when I've rung them to say the coast is clear.' Mac kept his head well back in shadow so

Michael was unable to make out any features. 'You got the other bit of that list?'

Michael pulled it out of his jacket pocket and held it just out of Mac's reach. 'Get on the phone first,' the Minister suggested, and felt his abdomen tighten in terror, as if someone was sticking tiny knives into him.

Mac looked around the car park, and back at the Minister. 'You're taller than I thought you'd be. Usually people on the telly are midgets, aren't they?'

'Especially if they're American actors,' Michael agreed. Then he watched as Mac dialled his mobile phone.

'Can't spot anyone here. Has Vince found anything? OK, I'll wait.' Mac clicked off the phone, and sniffed. 'They'll be along in a moment.'

'I suppose everyone who's been invited will bring a bit of their own protection, and do a recce first.'

Mac sniffed again and rubbed his nose with a sparkling white handkerchief. 'That's the idea.'

Michael shivered, and his eyes searched the street beyond the car park, hoping he might see another vehicle approach. 'I watched Laura's birth,' he said suddenly, as if he was passing the time of day. 'It was extraordinary. At the very last moment they decided Caroline had to have a Caesarean, and they told me to leave the room. But they were in a hurry to get on with it, so I just stood there like a bloody idiot while they knocked her out, and chopped her open, and pulled out Laura. I would have fainted if I'd been expecting it to happen. But because it was so quick I was too fascinated to react. And there she was. A perfect little baby.' He paused and wondered why he was rambling on at this stranger.

Mac sniffed. 'We're expecting our first next month. But I'm

not sure I'm up to watching it happen.'

'Oh, but you must. It's incredible,' Michael said encouragingly. But why would Mac blanch at the sight of an opened uterus, when he chopped old ladies' heads off every Saturday night? Before the Minister queried this admission of frailty a car approached, and followed the same slow, rocking path across the car park. Michael held his breath and watched as it came to a halt. Then he saw the outlines of four people, one of them Laura-shaped. He pushed the triangle of paper in through the window at Mac, and walked towards the car that had just arrived. By the time he got to it, the back door had opened and Laura scampered into his arms.

Neil hauled himself out of the front passenger seat. Then he held the back door open for Delva. 'I still say there's a religious element to the conflict. If your lot killed all the Catholics and the Orthodox, you'd be much better off,' he was lecturing her.

'No, no, no,' Delva insisted with a defiant shake of her grey head. 'Religion is not the prime motivating force in Bosnia. That is simplistic. Bosnian Muslims are not fundamentalists, like in Iran. And the Orthodox people you spoke of managed to live quite peaceably in co-existence for many years. It is much more complicated than that. It is an ethnic conflict, like it is here, if you're honest.'

Neil wasn't convinced, but he had had enough of this argumentative odd couple, and he was suddenly aware that he was standing in a car park making himself an excellent target. He left the Fitzgeralds to their reunion and got in beside Mac.

'Got the other piece?'

Mac handed over Michael's triangle of paper, which the Loyalist boss matched to the fax in his coat pocket. In the dim light of the dashboard he held the two together, and strained his eyes to read down the list. Most of the names were very familiar: they'd get their just desert in due course.

Then it was as if an iron claw closed around Neil's heart: there it was, his own name. He snatched the List out of the light, and stuffed it into his pocket before Mac could scrutinise it. He gestured at his bodyguard in the next car, and the man joined them in Mac's Escort.

'Call up Vince and that other idiot, and get them to hang round out here,' Neil ordered. Then he pushed his spectacles up the bridge of his nose. 'You two come in with me. Let's give it a go.'

Michael walked up the road with Delva and Laura to the corner of Great Victoria Street, where Brigadier Rowbottham had arranged to have a car waiting. As they stood on the pavement in the flow of homebound pedestrians, the Minister tried several times to apologise for their unpleasant experience, but Laura cut him off.

'It's OK, Pa, just lighten up,' she said with an impatient roll of her eyes. Laura was feeling rather pleased with herself, and her father pitied the other girls at school who would have to listen to the whole episode several times. 'Go back and sort them out now, Pa,' Laura instructed, and hugged him once more. Michael watched the car disappear into the rush-hour traffic on Great Victoria Street, then turned back to the Grand Opera House, muttering prayers of thanks heavenwards as he approached the stage door.

Chapter Twenty-Eight

By ten past five the main contestants had arrived with their musclemen in tow. Eddie, who was at Lisburn with Johnny, called Michael on his mobile phone to pass on Sir Trevor Grace's message: the Secretary of State would have nothing to do with this unwise venture, and he dissociated himself from his Junior Minister's initiative. Elvis had fulfilled the bare bones of his gentleman's agreement with Charlotte, and now it appeared that he was rewriting history as fast as a Russian Commissar.

When Michael conveyed Grace's words to the terrorists he grimaced at Charlotte who was sitting opposite. You got me into this mess, his eyes said, but I'm going to take the blame. She grinned back at him foolishly, and wondered if she would ever regain his affections. Perhaps if this afternoon ended like a Shakespearean tragedy they might be lovers in the afterlife, their bullet-riddled bodies finally joined in an ecstasy of rather bloody sex. She snapped her attention away from these gruesome but strangely erotic diversions, and surveyed the stage of the Grand Opera House.

Neil, looking particularly owlish today in a light grey suit, was accompanied by four of his fellow Loyalist leaders all in their Sunday best. Jack Heaney, the IRA strategist known as

Spock to friend and foe alike, had also brought the cream of the Republican Army with him. They sat on opposite sides of the square of tables, and surreptitiously sized each other up while Michael introduced them, and explained the purpose of the meeting.

'Please save the pointless propaganda statements, because we're all familiar with the fear and loathing bit. What hasn't been explored is what you gentlemen want. What will it take to stop you committing acts of terror, and is there any scope for compromise?' He looked from Spock to Neil, and back again.

The brains behind the Loyalist paramilitary machine cleared his throat and pushed his spectacles up his nose. 'The point is, you want a united Ireland or nothing, don't you?' He offered Spock a belligerent curl of the lip. 'Be honest: and none of this diplomatic doublespeak you hand out to the Press. Unity is the only thing on your agenda. And that's the problem, because we aren't going to be ruled from Rome, or Dublin. Not ever.'

There was an amused, almost indulgent expression on Spock's Vulcan features. He had turned up wearing jeans, an Aran sweater, and a sheepskin coat, as if he was on a fishing expedition. His colleagues looked more like Gap customers. Charlotte watched Spock doodle on the notepad in front of him, and saw his features twitch as if he was forming a smart-arsed riposte. 'Why are you content to be ruled from London by Englishmen who don't give a damn about you?' It was as if he and Neil were undergraduates in a student union debating chamber at a provincial English university, rather than two men deciding whether or not to destroy their Province.

'Look, Neil,' he went on, 'you know as well as I do that politicians in London think the Ulstermen are an embarrassing anachronism. They don't even consider you British.' Spock's attitude was that of an outsider, detached from Neil's passion and fury.

'I don't see the point of this,' Michael interjected, and got a frosty glance from both men. 'What matters is how people see themselves. The Unionists believe they're British, so they are. And the nationalists believe they're Irish. But you're on the same bit of land, and I want to know whether you can co-exist.'

'That bit of land is an island,' Spock drawled. Now he was playing the college lecturer addressing dim-witted students. 'And the island is called Ireland. He's as Irish as I am.' He pointed the stem of his pipe at Neil. 'We simply want the British Government to recognise once and for all that the people of this island have the right to determine their own future.'

Neil greeted this with silence, and Charlotte wondered if the Loyalist delegation was about to open their violin cases and get to work. When no one spoke she motioned at Michael. 'Go ahead,' he gestured, and she turned to Spock.

'Just because you live on an island it doesn't make you all part of the same nation or race or ethnic group. The IRA has to recognise that no matter how hard you try, you aren't going to succeed in making the Loyalists feel any allegiance to the Irish state.'

'Right!' Neil barked unexpectedly, like a battery-operated dog who had just been turned on.

'No one says you have to be Catholics in a united Ireland,' Spock said with a patient but indifferent shrug.

Neil shook his head angrily. 'The Catholic Church is like a dictatorship in Ireland,' he proclaimed, and the rest of the Loyalist high command nodded their emphatic agreement. 'In toyshops in Dublin they even have teddy bears dressed up as nuns,' he added irrelevantly.

'Irish society is changing,' Spock countered with a philosophical prod at the mercifully unlit tobacco in his pipe. 'Young people in Dublin and the cities still have respect for the Church, but they don't let it run their lives any more. Our society is emerging into a proper, northern-European pluralist state.'

'But you just don't get it: we don't want to be part of your Ireland. We're British. We live in Ulster, and you can pour scorn on our traditions, but it's our life,' Neil argued with a nod in Charlotte's direction, acknowledging her words of wisdom. 'You can't remake us to suit your plans.'

'But there's room in the new Ireland for everyone. It'll be an agreed Ireland.'

'And what the fuck is an agreed Ireland, when it's at home? Who agrees it? The majority of people who live on the island? Oh great, and stuff the minority who don't agree.'

'The majority will respect the rights of the minority. There'll be a Bill of Rights, and a written Constitution that guarantees the rights of religious minorities,' Spock recited, as he counted the points off on his long fingers.

'See? We're going to be treated like we're cripples, or something,' Neil spluttered indignantly.

Spock tut-tutted, and turned his attention on Michael. 'Why can't you use your position to convince the Unionist and Loyalist community that they will be perfectly safe and welcome in an agreed Ireland?'

Michael laughed, and dismissed Spock's words with an angry wave of his hands. 'Oh, Jesus, Mary and Joseph; not that old hypocritical rubbish about the British Government being a "persuader". It may work on your American paymasters, but it doesn't fool anyone here.' He laughed bitterly. 'Does Neil *look* like the kind of man who is going to be persuaded by what a

British Minister says? The Unionists and Loyalists don't trust London any more than they trust the Pope. And every time someone from Sinn Fein tells us that all it takes to achieve this blissful agreed Ireland is for London to lean on Neil and his friends, we know that they're avoiding the real issue in this conflict. Ulster doesn't want to be part of any bloody Ireland!'

Neil was nodding frantically by now, almost bursting with approval. He pointed a finger at Spock. 'And your agreed Ireland sounds like a backward, corrupt, papist regime where the IRA arrives on people's doorsteps in the middle of the night and terrorises them into doing what the State wants them to do, like vote for Sinn Fein. I mean, you can imagine the IRA's canvassing techniques – "you vote for us or we'll kneecap yous".'

'That's a ridiculous simplistic and racist view,' Spock chipped in dryly, keeping his temper.

'Racist?' Neil mimicked. 'Who d'you think you are – Martin Luther King? Don't you come on with all that smoothy-chops, international statesman shite. You were rigging up incendiary devices and scuttling around in an anorak and trainers until a few months ago.'

'Stop,' Michael said and held his hands up like a boxing referee. 'A bit more intellectual discipline, please, and get back to telling me what you want.' His words were calculated to wound: both men fancied themselves as the last word in self-discipline, and both nurtured a self-image as brainboxes. 'Since you obviously can't think laterally, let me suggest a few ideas, and we'll see how you both react.' The Minister watched them bristle, then directed his words at Spock.

'Now, think realistically, strategically. You can't get a united Ireland immediately. That's obvious to everyone, even a stuffed aardvark. So finding something better than the current status quo is a good idea, isn't it?'

'That's not on our agenda. We want the British Government to recognise the legitimacy of our aspirations for an agreed Ireland,' Spock said in a dogged and not very good-tempered manner. 'And we want the British out.'

'You sound like some African dictator who's swallowed a dictionary,' Michael commented. 'So you have no bargaining position that allows you to compromise on something less? I'm not asking you to chop off your dick, you know. Compromise does not diminish your manhood,' he quipped at the impassive, Vulcan face. 'How about an independent Ulster, or an Ulster with links to Dublin, and a promise of a full review of the situation in fifty years' time?'

'Fifty years is out of the question,' Spock snarled.

'Twenty-five years,' Michael shot back. 'And a Treaty signed by the British, Irish and American Governments. And the United Nations and the European Union and Coke and Pepsi too, if necessary. It guarantees the current status of Northern Ireland as part of the United Kingdom for the next twenty-five years, right? Then there's a referendum to ask the citizens of Northern Ireland what they want to do. And we have a simultaneous referendum in Ireland and ask them what they want.'

'And in the meantime?' Spock asked.

'We bring power back from Westminster to Belfast. We set up a power-sharing executive made up of fifty per cent Catholics and fifty per cent Protestants. The Catholics make up just under forty per cent of the population of Northern Ireland now, so *your* compromise,' Michael nodded at Neil, 'is to allow the Catholics half the power. But *your* compromise,' he said to Spock, 'is that after you become the majority in Northern Ireland, you allow

Protestants half the power so they don't feel threatened. That way you get to tell your masked men that the dream of a united Ireland is still alive. It means you'll attain your Eden gradually, and you'll have to respect the Protestants' special place in Ulster.'

Spock rubbed his pale forehead as if he was in pain. The scholarly demeanour had disappeared, and the pipe was back in its pouch like a discarded infant kangaroo.

Michael turned to the Loyalists. 'And Neil can assure his people that unity with the south isn't on the agenda for another twenty-five years.'

'And what then?' Neil asked.

'You'd better get breeding,' Michael sniffed. 'No, forget I said that. We'll have twenty-five years of peace in which to find a way to protect the future minority Protestant population of Ulster. And you'll have fifty per cent of the power until your numbers fall beneath an agreed level like forty per cent or thirty-five per cent.' Michael paused again as he waited for Neil to copy down the offer. 'This is a good deal for you.'

'But why would we want to give up our democratic claim on the six counties of Ireland?' The voice belonged to one of the previously silent IRA men who was wearing the kind of glasses that turn dark in sunlight, and look faintly sinister the rest of the time. Charlotte studied the ravaged face and imagined his finger twitching impatiently on the trigger of the machine gun he was holding at the ready under the table. He cleared his throat. 'Bombing's got us this far. The British are crumbling. My men'll say we should just push further.'

'See?' Neil chorused gleefully. 'What did I tell you?'

Michael gestured at Neil to shut up, and turned to the IRA hard man. 'So you don't want the opportunity to have power here and now? You want the referendum to go ahead, and have a civil war, and then fight a street-by-street battle for Belfast that'll compare with Vukovar or Sarajevo?'

The man in the shades looked on blankly as the Minister continued. 'What kind of country will it be when you've finished? Why would anyone want to live there? D'you think the Americans are going to give you dollars to rebuild it all? They'll wash their hands of the whole business if you pull that. And you know it. Whereas I can offer you the prospect of getting the British Army out, and as many gestures as you like to keep your people on board.'

'He hasn't got any opinion now,' Neil tittered. 'He'll have to go back to the bunker and ask his mates what they think. They're all so afraid of being rubbed out by their lifelong colleagues and brothers-in-arms, that they can't say a word,' he chortled triumphantly, and pointed at the five IRA men.

Michael, who was fed up with the Loyalist's high-pitched giggling, bared his teeth. 'So why were *you* so keen to get that list of soft men on your own side, Neil? Was your name on it?'

When the Loyalist leader had gone green at the gills, the Minister turned back to Spock. 'This is the best deal you'll get, short of all-out war. And incidentally, it's a sign of political immaturity that you can't cope with the art of negotiation and compromise. Any tosser can make a defiant speech or throw a grenade.' Michael paused to let the insults sink in.

'The Loyalists and Unionists are going to fight you to the last blade of grass. They're not going to trust a bunch of lying Papists who can kill and steal from Monday to Saturday, then ask for forgiveness on Sunday, and start all over again on Monday. You recall Neil's point about Irish doublespeak.'

The Loyalists were rocking about in their seats with laughter again. 'Only a bloody Catholic could say that!' Neil shrieked, his colour restored.

'The question for Sinn Fein and the IRA is, how many of you are realists and want to seize the chance to have power in running this Province while you can? And how many of you care only about one day having your statues on St Stephen's Green in Dublin, along with the other Irish heroes and martyrs who fought for a united Ireland. Are you more concerned with your place in history, or your children's futures?'

'Isn't the bloody Irish Government going to agitate for more?' Neil asked, entirely ignoring Michael's point.

Michael shrugged. 'We'll call the Irish Prime Minister later, and see what he says. But as far as I can gather from the elegant language and sentimental declarations, the Irish're probably content to have it on the agenda as a future goal, as long as it is seen that Irish people are gradually finding a solution to an Irish problem.'

'And what the fuck is that supposed to mean?' asked another member of the Loyalist high command, a man who had served fifteen years for slitting a nun's throat.

'It's a culture clash,' remarked Charlotte helpfully. 'Your side cannot understand the Irish subtlety of promising one thing to keep a section of the population happy, while meaning something else.'

Michael nodded thoughtfully, and turned back to Neil. 'So could you live with cross-border organisations that would co-ordinate tourism, and agriculture, and electricity generation, and water supply, and gas services, and infrastructure projects like road- and rail-building?'

'Yeah. I'll certainly think about it.' Neil gazed into the middle distance, wondering how big these infrastructure projects might be, and calculating the money he could make from his protection racket. Going respectable and getting the peace dividend might have something to be said for it after all.

'And a form of power-sharing where the Nationalist community has fifty per cent of the seats, and the Unionist community has fifty per cent.'

'Yeah.' He paused. 'Sounds like a reasonable bet. Like options trading. We offset our future risks by giving a bit now. OK.'

The Minister nodded impatiently as Neil finished his musings. 'And will the Loyalists buy an international Declaration from Ireland, Britain, and the United States, that'll be enforced by the United Nations, the European Union and NATO, that the status of Northern Ireland is to be unchanged for twenty-five years?'

Neil shrugged. 'Yeah, as long as Ireland signs the Declaration, and the world's prepared to twist their nuts off if they start to get nosy again.'

'Just hang on here,' Spock interrupted. 'Mr Fitzgerald, you seem to have forgotten our fundamental problem. How are we supposed to believe that the minute you give the Unionists power, they won't abuse the Nationalist community again? Catholics were second-class citizens before, when Protestants ran this place. Who says they've learnt a thing from the past thirty years? Look at them – God Bob'll be herding Catholics into concentration camps if he gets his way.'

'I agree,' Michael said simply. 'That's why we should have term limits here – we disqualify the old brigade from standing again. And the Bill of Rights would be there to protect the minority, any minority.'

'And if my community doesn't agree with this?' Spock asked.

'Like I said – Sarajevo. Worse, though, because both sides will have arms. It won't just be like the UN who let the Serbs move in and kill everyone they please without so much as putting thumb-tacks under their tyres. If the international community can let it happen in Bosnia, it'll let it happen here. So, do you Republican gentlemen have any interest in a deal? Or have you got any more realistic proposals?'

At about half-past six, the terrorists were distracted from their discussions by chanting and shouting from outside the theatre. 'I'll go and find out what that is,' Charlotte offered, and hared off to investigate.

From a first-floor window she craned her neck and saw along the side street up to the front of the Grand Opera House. Great Victoria Street was filled with banners and Union Jacks. Thousands of people were surrounding the building, and someone was yelling hysterical slogans through a loudhailer. It was a voice that Charlotte would have recognised anywhere: God Bob had arrived with his followers.

She rushed down to the stage door and made sure it was securely locked. Then she called Tim at the BBC Ulster newsroom. 'How could Reverend Scott have found out about this?'

'Grace must have tipped him off. We're just getting reports in that say Scott is denouncing the Government and the Minister and everybody else for breaking bread with the men of blood.'

'Damn.'

'How's it going?' Tim asked.

'No one's dead yet,' she replied in an absent-minded frenzy. 'Look, we have to move this onto a different footing. I think it's time for the CNN option. Maybe you can liaise with Johnny Burleigh and the Army boys. See if they agree.'

'Shame it had to happen so early.'

'Any chance you could get the Irish Prime Minister into a studio in Dublin for a live link into our little tea party?' she asked, but was distracted by the volume of the chanting coming from the crowd outside.

'Your wish is my command. I'll see you soon. 'Bye.'

When Charlotte returned to the talks she explained that they had visitors, and watched Michael's guests stiffen visibly. 'Not that fucking tool,' grunted the man from the UDA. 'That's typical. Reverend Fucking Scott, come to spoil our games as usual.' Then he noticed the terror on the faces of their opposite numbers in the IRA. 'It's OK, Spocky mate. They'll tear us apart long before they get to you.'

'They're not going to tear anyone apart,' Charlotte announced authoritatively, while metaphorically crossing her fingers. 'I have a plan, but I need your permission to open this discussion up a bit.'

'Oh God,' Michael muttered, and rubbed his eyes. 'What now?'

'Oh ye of little faith,' she responded with a hurt frown. Then she explained herself as quickly as possible, and the Minister was outvoted by ten to one.

The terrorists thought Charlotte had a good idea.

Chapter Twenty-Nine

At exactly seven o'clock, normal programming on BBC 1 was interrupted by a special announcement from the Ulster studio. The woman who usually read the bulletins had been hurried in front of the camera, and she looked slightly startled as she glanced down at the paper in her hand, and up again at the lens.

'We apologise for this interruption, but this is a flash from the Belfast newsroom. The Army has made an emergency request for the friends and relatives of victims of the Troubles to immediately go to the Grand Opera House in Great Victoria Street in Belfast. They are asked to attend a special evening session of the peace talks to put their views forward direct to the paramilitaries from both sides of the sectarian divide.' The newsreader coughed and reread the next sentence as if she couldn't quite believe it. 'This is a meeting for members of the public and paramilitaries only. No politicians will be admitted. There is already a demonstration of supporters of the Reverend Robert Scott outside the Grand Opera House. But the Army is now securing a corridor into the building, and they have guaranteed safe passage for those who wish to attend.'

Then it was back to a sports quiz. Charlotte switched off the set, and rubbed her hands together. She was so nervous that her whole body was quivering with cold and sweating at the same time.

'So,' she announced to the assembled terrorists, 'that went OK. Now we try to get the link to the Irish Prime Minister.'

'What makes you think he'll want to talk to our illustrious company gathered here?' Michael asked with a gallant gesture at the leading paramilitaries. 'Won't he consult Downing Street to find out how they feel about him chatting to Neil here? These friends of ours haven't renounced violence, after all.'

Charlotte tried to avoid his glare. The turn of events had obviously left him a few mental blocks behind her, and besides, it was clear that he was struggling not to strangle her.

'Well, Eddie and Johnny are talking to Dublin right now.' She watched Michael roll his eyes heavenward.

'I don't believe this. None of it.'

'It's OK.' She sounded like the leader of an expedition into uncharted territory who knows she must keep team spirits up. 'Let's have some sandwiches. Neil – what can I get you? Prawn and mayonnaise?'

'Yes, please.' Neil appeared to be enjoying his evening out.

'How did you get the BBC to cooperate with this . . . crazy idea?' Michael asked.

'It's Tim, my friend in the BBC Ulster newsroom. He told his bosses that CNN was about to get the broadcasting scoop of the century. You see, they're already here in the Opera House. Sorry, Michael, I forgot to tell you, but CNN set up a whole outside broadcast unit earlier today, so they're ready to go on air when the audience arrives. And so Tim explained to the BBC that the only way the Corporation can get access to the Opera House is to carry this announcement. Then I gave them permission to set up here too.'

'But you work for the BBC,' said the increasingly confused Michael.

Charlotte shook her head and took a bite of the smoked ham sandwich. 'Not any more.'

'So who do you work for?' Neil asked. 'CNN?'

'Nope,' she said between slurps of mineral water. 'I'm currently looking for a job. The BBC sacked me earlier today. A little misunderstanding back at Westminster.'

'You're mad,' Michael commented from the other side of the table.

'That's a bit rich, coming from a politician,' the nun-killer laughed. 'Listen, we've had enough of these fucking dildo Loyal Unionist Party tosspots; them with their prissy bloody shite. They dump on my boys every time they do a job, but it's my boys kept them from getting fried when the RUC and the Army had fucking well disappeared off the streets. But do we get any credit for it?'

'Have you noticed that all the women in God Bob's church have got mouths like puckered arseholes?' remarked the third Loyalist prince. 'Prim fucking snooty bitches. Never come down here to help our working-class women who have to cope with fuck-all money, and a husband inside for possession or whatever.' Whatever presumably included slitting nuns' throats, Charlotte reflected as she went through her wine-waiter routine with the mineral water.

'What makes you think anyone will show up? Why would they want to be in an auditorium with terrorists?' Michael asked the hostess.

'Hey,' objected one of the IRA heavies, 'the people in our communities are with us, and don't forget it. It's the RUC and the Army and God Bob that give them the shits. Same for their people too, I bet.' He gestured vaguely at Neil's side. The Loyalists nodded and kept eating.

'Can we do a sound test, sir?' the technician asked Spock, and clipped the microphone onto his Aran jumper. 'Just a few words, if you don't mind.'

'I'll have some of that make-up,' the UDA brigadier affirmed. 'The wife says my nose gets red when I'm angry.'

'Which camera are we starting with?' Charlotte asked Tim, who was seated beside the director in the control booth in the gods of the theatre. She had a microphone clipped to her silk blouse, which carried her words to their electronic nest high above her, and she could hear their responses through her earpiece. The former BBC reporter, who was about to become a presenter, stood centre-stage before the closed curtain. She was feeling as wired as a cocaine addict as she nervously rehearsed the running order of the programme with the director. There had been no opportunity to install an autocue, so Charlotte would be winging it. Under the circumstances, a script would soon have been redundant anyway.

From the other side of the curtain, the terrorist high command could hear the audience assembling. It was only forty minutes since the appeal on TV, and the theatre was already full. Crowds had gathered outside in the street where there was an almighty shouting match between the general public and God Bob's pilgrims. The Army had the unenviable task of keeping the two contingents separate; and in a rare and touching gesture of reconciliation between two lifelong enemies, the BBC and CNN were working together to set up a big screen against a wall in Great Victoria Street, opposite the Opera House.

As news of the event spread, more people arrived. Smelly

hot-dog stands materialised out of nowhere, and a man warned anyone who would listen about the dangers of eating meat. Tim was on the mobile phone, placing camera crews in amongst the crowd on the street so he could feed their comments into the programme. When he was happy with the situation outside the Opera House, he leaned forward and spoke into the director's microphone that fed into Charlotte's ear.

'Good luck, superstar. We're a minute till air. And just so you know, Trevor Grace has been touring the early evening news programmes telling everyone this isn't his idea, and saying how irresponsible Fitzgerald is. And we're still negotiating with Dublin to get their Prime Minister live. But not surprisingly, he's somewhat preoccupied by today's bombs. Twenty-two dead so far.'

The director interrupted. 'OK, Charlotte. Thirty seconds. Stand by.' The reporter shushed the terrorists who were now arranged in a more audience-friendly semicircle behind her. Michael was in the middle between the warring factions, and for a split second their eyes met. He smiled at her with the kind of smile he used to give her, when they were friends. She pulled a face that conveyed her panic, which was one hundred per cent.

'Twenty seconds, Charlotte.' It was the invisible director with the comforting Belfast voice in her earpiece. 'Tim says ABC has just bought into our feed. We're going across the States, live. Good luck everyone. Two. One. On air.'

When the curtain opened the terrorists blinked in the glare of the lights, and surveyed the Opera House, ornate and golden and twinkling like a jewel box. Then as their eyes adjusted they noticed the people, who were sitting in the aisles, and at the front, and standing at the back. Charlotte was about to begin her spiel, when she noticed a woman in the first row holding up a photograph. The man beside her also had a snapshot and he raised it above his head. And the family behind them did the same.

'Turn the cameras around on the audience,' Charlotte whispered into her mike, hoping that the director had noticed the forest of arms, and wasn't broadcasting her voice. Her hunch was right, and for the first minute the cameras tracked row upon row of the audience, who sat in dignified silence, holding up photographs, large and small, battered, and more recent elaborate coloured portraits. It had been spontaneous: every person had arrived with pictures of the victims of violence who had been near to them.

After a minute of eerie and poignant silence Charlotte stepped forward to the edge of the stage, looked straight into the camera, and wondered if she was about to faint. 'Good evening, ladies and gentlemen, good evening Northern Ireland, and hello to the viewers of CNN, the BBC and ABC.

'Tonight the people of this Province are going to have their say about the Troubles, and the so-called peace process, and the paramilitaries and the politicians who claim to represent them. No one has ever asked the people of Northern Ireland what they think, other than giving them a choice of "yes" or "no" in a referendum. Or asking them to choose between politicians on a ballot paper.

'Tonight we'll hear words for a change; not guns, or the results of votes, or stitched-up deals. Tonight the people of Northern Ireland are here to give their views. We have victims of the violence in the audience, their friends and relatives, and members of the paramilitaries. We are going to listen to what they have to tell us about the past, the present and the future.

'Later, I'm going to ask Michael Fitzgerald, the Northern

Ireland Minister, to put forward some new ideas on how we could bring a lasting peace to the Province. But now we are going to listen to the people who have not spoken with words until now.'

With that, the CNN technicians raced around the auditorium to bring microphones to contributors who had raised their hands. And the testimonies began: from young and old, Protestant and Catholic, terrorists and victims, inside the theatre and out on the street. There were harrowing tales of bombs and assassinations and mistakes that had claimed the lives of innocent bystanders; there were expressions of sorrow, anger, defiance and futility. The unedited outpouring of grief was enough to silence even the God Bob mob outside who were glued to the giant screen.

Occasionally Charlotte called on a paramilitary to add his ten cents' worth, but generally they were glad to stay quietly in their places on the stage as the audience vented its collective spleen against the politicians, the system, the terrorists and the media. Neil turned a queer shade of red when one young mother brought down the house by attacking 'him and his thieving, money-grubbing, drug-pushing mafia'. It was hardly a comfort to Neil that Spock was later savaged just as comprehensively by Catholic shopkeepers and taxi drivers who recited precisely how much protection money they handed over every week to keep the boss man in sheepskin coats.

While this was going on, Charlotte listened to her earpiece and followed developments in the director's booth where Tim was pulling together the broadcast. Whenever there was a pause between very angry people bearing witness, the reporter turned to the camera and welcomed the viewers of the Canadian Broad-casting Corporation, or Australian television, who had just joined in the live feed. Or they watched the big TV monitors that had been put on the stage so the audience could view the videos of grainy newsreel footage from the worst period of the Troubles. Then it was back to high octane testimony.

Charlotte stood quietly to one side of the stage, feet aching, and hands trembling. How on earth was she managing to compère the strangest discussion programme in history? Best not to think about it, she concluded, and steered the show outside for another selection of wrathful comments from the people waiting patiently in the street.

It was compulsive viewing, to be sure, but for Sir Trevor Grace, skulking in his office at Stormont, sucking on his third gin and tonic of the evening, Charlotte Carter's terrorist telethon was torture. He had already done his circuit of the news shows, but the channels soon bored of his disapproval, and returned to the live feed. As Grace watched it now, it seemed impossible that the pleasing course of recent events had been so disrupted by Michael Fitzgerald's little friend. The referendum was on course; Dublin was clearing up after the bombs – London wouldn't be hearing much more about a united Ireland out of them, he hoped – and God Bob's demonstration and the wave of ethnic cleansing had scared the shit out of the PM during his satisfyingly dire visit to Belfast earlier on. In fact, dozens of Tory MPs would be questioning their leader's judgement in even going to the Province today. Better and better.

But since then things had fallen apart. Now the PM was back in London, watching TV, like everyone else. Until an hour ago Downing Street had been pestering the Secretary of State to find out what was happening. But then Johnny Burleigh had intervened, and now the little fuck-head at Number 10 believed something was being achieved by this televised love-in. Downing Street had told Grace that the US President was laying down the line with Dublin, and the Irish leader was consulting his Cabinet colleagues.

But uppermost in his mind was one simple question: was Charlotte Carter going to broadcast the video of the Northern Ireland Committee? Would the little bitch keep her word? Grace had fulfilled his side of the deal: NIPD had stayed away, and the terrorists were in place, making fools of themselves with choked-up speeches from the heart, and declarations of regret. 'Pass the sick bag,' he had muttered to his PPS, as the hard men described their remorse, and then laid the blame at the feet of the politicians who had left them no other option but violence. The gunmen were metamorphosing into party candidates before his eyes.

Grace pillaged the office minibar for another drink and tried to calm his nerves: he still had the photos of Fitzgerald and the useful, but now absent, Mandy tart. And this Ulster rubbish could be deflected into a broader debate about Euro-interference in the British way of government. The telethon was meaningless and ephemeral. That was what Trevor Grace told himself as he swigged his gin and tonic. But then again, Trevor Grace didn't understand the power of television.

'I think it's horrible,' a gaunt young man in grunge denims commented, 'all this talk about sacrifice and heroes and martyrs and people spilling their blood and starving themselves to death. It's medieval, and I wish we could forget that stuff and concentrate on the future.'

He sat down to polite applause. Then a middle-aged woman in a smart skirt-suit had the microphone. 'Speaking as a member of the Catholic community, I think we can't have real peace until we feel at ease with each other. When the Protestants ran

Northern Ireland they behaved like bad parents who hurt and neglected and abused their children. They had power over the Catholic minority, and they misused it.' She was interrupted by applause at this point, and she glanced around the theatre in stark terror, as if she had only just noticed the other people.

'I know that the Protestants who suffered in the Troubles weren't the same ones who ran this Province, but they've got to recognise that what was done to the Catholic community was wrong. It's just like a little girl who has been abused by her father. We need the father to accept that what he did was wrong, and to apologise. That's all we're asking.'

This contribution encouraged another Catholic, a bald man with a beer belly straining at a plaid shirt, to get to his feet. 'It's no good the Protestant working classes blaming us because there aren't any job these days. Everyone's got to skill themselves. Computers and all that stuff. We can't be like them on the Faroe Islands who think there's nothing wrong with killing whales, and they expect to be subsidised to keep on killing whales because generations of them have always done it. Now they have to learn other skills, like coal miners have to retrain.'

The beer belly waited until the applause had died down and he cleared his throat self-consciously. 'There was something else I wanted to say. It's about what the lady talked about. When I was a lad I was in the IRA, and I did some wee jobs, and although I told myself I was doing it for Ireland at the time, now I see I was also doing it for a lark. And I'm sorry about the consequences of that, because I'm not sure we really achieved much in all those years.'

Michael, who was listening keenly from his place on the stage, tried to imagine the Joe Couch Potato in the plaid shirt as a lean young Republican, hiding his sniper's rifle in attics, and running through back alleys to avoid Army patrols. It was like James Bond with a Zimmer frame.

The next speaker was also inspired by the Catholic woman's talk of forgiveness and denial. He was outside, standing in the crowds watching the big screen, and his face looked pinched with the cold. The minute Michael heard the Old Etonian drawl he knew to whom it belonged.

'I'm a Protestant, and my family has been here since 1603, and I consider myself to be an Irishman,' boomed Sir Edward Montgomery. 'Of course the Stormont regime was rotten, and it deserved to go, and we should say so and apologise while we're at it. But some Unionists were trying to reform it before the Troubles began. The real blame lies with the Loyal Unionist Party, who've given Protestants such a bad name in this Province. They're the ones who always tried to stop reform. Whenever a moderate Official Unionist has made a gesture of conciliation, he's been hounded by that Scott man, and his religious fanatics. That's what's gone wrong here!' he shouted above the jeers from the Loyal Unionist brigade who were still being held at bay by the Army.

'And incidentally,' Sir Edward continued after he had waved two fingers at God Bob's followers, 'we've heard enough about what the Army did. We have to put it behind us, and remember they were human too. You imagine what it must have been like to be an eighteen-year-old, wet behind the ears, and you're sent to a place that looks like England, except that the people are trying to kill each other. But you can't tell who's a Catholic and who's a Protestant, because they look and talk the same. And suddenly you're surrounded by a crowd of hysterical screaming harpies banging dustbin lids; foul-mouthed bags who'll tear the skin off your face, given half the chance.'

Sir Edward Montgomery's second point was largely lost on the audience because his first remarks had incited the Loyal Unionist Party into a noisy frenzy. Through her earpiece Charlotte listened in on the director's booth high above her. As producer of this event, Tim had decided to take a contribution from the Reverend Scott, if only to stop his supporters drowning out everything that happened outside the theatre. Tim took a crew and headed into the crush. But before they could hear from God Bob, a quietly attractive woman in her early forties got uncertainly to her feet, and introduced herself as Jane from Belfast. She read from the piece of paper in her hands.

'The only way we can stop the hatred is to remove the ignorance in both communities,' she began in a quavering soprano. Neil's head shot up, and he searched the audience to see the source of this most unwelcome intervention. 'We must have integrated schools, all across the Province, and they must teach a common history course,' his wife continued timidly. 'Only then will we learn to live with each other as human beings, and not as two separate communities that can be conveniently pigeon-holed by politicians or terrorists.' When she sat down she got one of the warmest roars of approval of the evening. Neil hung his head again, too embarrassed to meet the eyes of his fellow Loyalists.

There followed several women who harangued the audience and terrorists for excluding women from the political process, thereby removing the people most able to heal and nurture society.

Nurturing had never been one of the Reverend Scott's objectives, but he wasn't listening to anyone else because he was about to hold forth into Tim's microphone. 'I demand the right to be heard,' he began with a forthright but high-pitched bark when the camera was on him. 'I am a representative of my people and I have been excluded from this meeting. It is a disgrace.'

'Hang on,' Tim interjected loudly. 'Earlier on you were criticising everyone in the Opera House for breaking bread with the terrorists. Now you want to be in on it. What's changed?'

'I am the elected representative of my people,' he bellowed above the reporter's voice. 'I demand to be heard! There is blaspheming going on here, and I will not be slandered by murderers and criminals,' he frothed.

'But you've been telling the world what you think for years, and it hasn't done anyone any good,' the dogged Tim insisted. Then he suddenly turned his massive back on God Bob, thereby obliterating him, and spoke directly to the camera. 'Charlotte, perhaps we should let the people in the theatre tell us if they want to hear what the Reverend Scott has to say.' Behind him God Bob was swallowing air like a stunned goldfish.

Charlotte had barely registered Tim's question when the UDA throat-slitter leapt to his feet. 'Where were you when the Unionist people needed you?' he screamed at the TV monitor on the stage. 'Have you ever made the sacrifices you demand of everyone else? You're just a bag of wind, you are, and your Church is full of hypocrites. And we've had enough of you in this Province, because all you care about is yourself. We can see through you and your bloody great ego, and it's time the working-class people started electing their own who might do a better job for them.'

'Tell them about 1974,' Neil yelled from behind him.

'Yeah,' the throat-slitter said, catching his breath. 'When we were organising the Ulster Workers' Strike in 1974 you didn't want anything to do with us, but when you saw we were bringing Ulster to a standstill you tried to take the credit for organising it.'

'Tell them about the secret negotiations,' Neil bawled.

'Right,' the throat-slitter said with a jerk of his head towards his prompter. 'A few years ago we were meeting with his lot,' he jabbed a finger in Spock's direction, 'and we managed to agree on having an independent Ulster with a Bill of Rights and a power-sharing Government. But little God Bob there got wind of it, and he didn't like the sound of this because he'd be out of a job if the working classes got their act together and stopped fighting each other. So guess what? He had one of the IRA's commanders bumped off. Yes he did!' the UDA man insisted as the audience erupted. Michael tried not to cheer as he heard his own words to Neil repeated with such authority by another more persuasive speaker.

The director cut to the outside camera where Tim was asking Reverend Scott for his reaction. The man of God was choking with fury, saying curses would be on all of them for their lies, and that this was the devil's work, but he was drowned out by booing and yelling. Inside the theatre the audience was booing too, and Charlotte struggled to get order. The throat-slitter was still on his feet, hurling abuse at God Bob's image on the monitor, but when he saw that Michael wanted to speak he shushed the audience with violent waves of his arms. 'Quiet, you lot!' he howled.

'I want to ask Reverend Scott something about his referendum,' Michael said, once he could make himself heard. 'Is it true that the only reason you've called these by-elections and the referendum is to frighten off the Irish Government? Have you any intention of really demanding a repartition of Northern Ireland? Or is this part of a game you're playing, a game that is causing panic across the Province, and making people leave their homes, and leading to brutal ethnic cleansing?'

There was more shouting in the wake of Michael's question, then people outside began to chant, 'Answer!' at God Bob. The Reverend was purple-faced by now.

'I will answer no questions put to me by a so-called Minister of the Crown who is acting directly on behalf of the evil, conniving government in Dublin,' he spluttered.

'Does Reverend Scott deny that he and a member of the British Government plotted to invent the flag competition to incite hatred and unrest in the Province, and that it was nothing whatsoever to do with a European directive?'

Everyone's attention was rooted on God Bob's dark, flashing eyes. He gaped stupidly at the camera for a moment, as if the Minister had been speaking to him in an incomprehensible tongue. Then a chorus of, 'Answer! Answer!' started to build. God Bob's supporters were no longer vocal or visible, and the Reverend Robert Scott found himself isolated, in front of the camera, with Tim ramming the microphone down his throat, and asking him to respond. He blinked as if his brain was working double time to calculate the lie of the land. Then he took a deep breath, as if he was the Michelin man puffing himself up.

'I will bear witness,' he wailed, 'and I shall demand the resignation of the Secretary of State, Sir Trevor Grace, who single-handedly instigated the competition for a new Ulster flag, and who wanted to destroy the Assembly with a referendum. I can reveal that he foisted this upon the Assembly. He is a disgrace to the Crown, and he must go,' God Bob concluded with a shake of his ginger head.

'Will you revoke your resignation from the Assembly, and withdraw your demand for a referendum?' Tim asked, before Michael could get the question in. 'Are you on the side of keeping Ulster's borders as they are?'

From the way Reverend Scott's eyes swivelled around at the crowd before he answered, it was obvious that some rapid mental calculations were taking place. Once a shrewd and populist politician, always one. The leader of the Loyal Unionist Party nodded his assent to Tim's questions. 'I am always on the side of Ulster,' he shouted with a new-found clarity of voice. 'And Sir Trevor Grace must go.'

By half-past eight the telethon had moved on to Michael's talks with the terrorists. By this time, several dozen Assembly members from Sinn Fein, the Official Unionists and the SDLP had turned up outside the Grand Opera House. But the audience inside voted not to listen to them until they had all heard about the deal that the men of violence had cooked up. Then the show was in Michael's hands, and he outlined his idea for fifty-fifty power-sharing, removing the British Army from the Province, a Bill of Rights, and an international agreement to keep Ulster's borders for the next twenty-five years.

The audience seemed content to let the men of violence play a central role in deal-making, which was more than could be said for the cold and irrelevant politicians skulking in the crowd.

From her position on the stage, Charlotte sensed that there was universal agreement that the politicians had achieved nothing, and represented nobody but themselves. Hence they were superfluous to negotiations to stop violence, and the audience was much keener to know if Spock from the IRA would be satisfied if the British Army packed up and went home; or how Neil's brigadiers would treat the prospect of an independent Ulster.

They moved to the specifics of power-sharing and what the Irish Government would do. Meanwhile Charlotte could hear an interesting discussion up in the director's booth through her earpiece. Apparently, all the women manning British Telecom's directory enquiries service had voted to offer their services to take down the results of a telephone poll of Ulster citizens. They would even bring colleagues in from home to man the phones until midnight if CNN and the BBC asked their viewers to call in.

The politicians shuffling about outside were less than happy when Charlotte announced that there would be a telephone poll. Who cared what the Assemblymen thought of Michael's ideas if the people could ring directory enquiries, or the BBC, or the VISA credit card centre, or any of the other organisations who were offering their services to man the telephones?

By 9 p.m., 30,000 votes had been logged, each with the name of the caller, in an attempt to reduce the incidence of over-zealous multiple callers. Then the Irish Prime Minister joined the telethon in a live broadcast from his office at Government Buildings in Dublin. Like a true professional, he did not even need a question or an introduction from Michael, who was standing by to interview him. The Taoiseach looked intently at the camera, and read a prepared statement from his teleprompter with a dignity and calm that commanded even Neil's attention, if not his respect.

'It's a privilege to have this chance to address the people of Northern Ireland this evening,' he began. 'Thank you for allowing me to contribute to this important discussion. Let me say that my Government, and I believe the Irish people, will abide by the will of the people of Northern Ireland. We do not seek to prolong the conflict by holding out false promises to those who demand a united Ireland today or tomorrow. You won't get it from this Government, because the will of the majority in Northern Ireland is paramount. In the interests of peace and security and economic stability, I would like to commit my Government to signing the International Declaration suggested by Mr Fitzgerald. And you have my word that we will work to promote greater understanding and cooperation on this island, but never at the expense of alarming the Unionist tradition in the North. I sincerely hope that this initiative will lead to constructive talks, and genuine power-sharing, and I wish you all the luck in the world.'

If Spock and the IRA commanders had been worried about the affront to their manhood earlier in the evening, they were now turning white from the well-aimed kick in their balls from the Irish Prime Minister. The moment the Taoiseach was off air, CNN went to a commercial break, the BBC showed a short video recapping the evening's highlights, and Neil and his brigadiers began shaking each other's hands and slapping each other on the back. Michael thought it was a bit early for such self-congratulation, but he fought the urge to grin widely.

A moment later Charlotte was shushing them as they resumed the television broadcast. 'We're now going live to Number Ten Downing Street where the British Prime Minister joins us.'

'I wish to commit my Government to work with the Irish Government to frame a document that will guarantee the current shape of Ulster for the next twenty-five years,' he announced. This had Neil punching the air with his fist. 'We will immediately begin discussions with all parties to the Northern Ireland conflict, provided they cease their violence, to find a power-sharing arrangement that gives both communities an equal say.' This also pleased the terrorists – they instantly joined the ranks of world statesmen and Nobel Peace Prize winners. 'And we shall recognise that just as the Unionist population has every right to want to remain British, so the Nationalist community has an equal and proper right to wish to be Irish. In twenty-five years' time they will have a democratic opportunity for a refer- endum on the status of the Province. In the meantime, all British troops will be removed within the next six months.'

Those final promises meant that Spock and his colleagues could start breathing again.

Charlotte's attention snapped back to the TV monitor as the PM announced that he had accepted Sir Trevor Grace's resigna- tion, but that he believed the negotiations, and the Province, would be in excellent hands with Grace's successor. 'The new Secretary of State will be Michael Fitzgerald, and I am confident that he will do an excellent job. Welcome to the Cabinet, Michael.'

Like everyone else in the theatre, Charlotte turned to look at the new Secretary of State, whose mouth was hanging open in awe. He glanced at Neil, who had started to applaud, and at Spock, who was also clapping. Then his eyes settled on Charlotte, and he mouthed a stunned, 'Thank you,' and tried not to appear too overwhelmed by this sudden promotion.

At a quarter to ten Charlotte told the audience that calls in favour of Michael's compromise were running at seventy-eight per cent; then, because there was nothing left to say that hadn't already been said, she wrapped up the broadcast. CNN went straight to an orgy of advertising, and self-praise that would numb the viewers, if they weren't already numb. The BBC went to a weather forecast.

Half an hour later, as Charlotte was leaving the director's booth, someone handed her a mobile phone. 'It's a man. Won't say who he is.'

'When do I get my video?' the caller asked. 'I've kept my part of the bargain, and allowed you to get away with this appalling display.'

Charlotte listened to the man who had just been sacked on air, and whose political career lay in ruins. 'So when will you bring it here?' he asked.

'I have no intention of letting you have this.'

'I thought we had a gentleman's agreement,' he blustered, the panic palpable in his voice.

Charlotte hesitated as her fingertips prodded tentatively at a pimple that was developing on her forehead as a result of too many chocolate bars. By tomorrow it would have ripened into a satisfactory Vesuvius, she thought with a shiver of disgust and fascination. 'But Sir Trevor, that agreement worked on the assumption that you are a gentleman, which you manifestly are not. And that I am a lady. And I can assure you that I'm no lady,' she added, and clicked off the phone.

On her way out of the director's booth, the chief CNN personage collared her. 'First of all, that was amazing, and you were brilliant. Did you realise that we sold that feed to twenty-two different broadcasting companies around the world? We had advertisers begging us to take their money, and bidding against each other to get the slot just before the Irish Prime Minister spoke. Nothing like it since O.J. Simpson. Would you like a job?' he asked matter-of-factly.

Charlotte resisted the urge to jump into the man's arms, and instead she inclined her head to one side as if she was mildly interested as the personage continued. 'Tim tells me you have plans for a whole series of cathartic discussions where you bring the decision-makers into direct confrontation with the victims of their decisions. Nice idea. Let's talk about it.'

'Yes, let's talk about it.' After I've spent two weeks in bed recovering from this, she thought. In bed with Alfred the Rabbit, most likely.

'And the video of Trevor Grace – when do we use it?' the CNN man continued.

Charlotte winced and bit her lower lip. 'Ah, confession time. The quality's not awfully good, and if I'm absolutely honest you can't make out everything Grace is saying. In fact, it wouldn't stand up in a court of law.'

'*What?* Then how did you get Grace to agree to all this?' The CNN producer indicated the emptying theatre below them. 'And how did you get CNN in London to put on this show?' he asked more in wonder than anger.

'I sort of guessed what Grace was saying. You know, I filled in the gaps. It's the kind of thing he would have said.' She smiled unconvincingly. 'It would have been in character. And I suppose he really was saying it, because the moment I mentioned it, he agreed to what I wanted.'

She braced herself for the CNN man to withdraw the job offer, but he laughed, and handed her the video. 'Awesome. I like it,' he remarked and wiped the tears from the corners of his eyes.

Michael was finishing the last in a series of TV and radio interviews up on the stage when Charlotte reappeared and retrieved her mobile phone. He kept half his attention on the interview while straining to listen in on Charlotte's conversation. She was telling someone called Tim, who had gone back to BBC Broadcasting House, that she would spend the night at the Europa Hotel next door.

'That's very sweet of you, my giant angel, but I'm not going to trouble you to do the hostess routine . . . No, really, I'll be fine at the hotel . . . I'll let you get on . . . You're in the middle of the broadcasting coup of your career, and you are incredibly good at what you do . . . and I want to thank you again for having enough faith in the idea to make it work. I'll see you soon . . . 'Bye.'

Out of the corner of his eye Michael saw her collect her coat and handbag, and head for the stage door without even looking back over her shoulder. He terminated his interview with a cheery, 'Now it's up to the people of Northern Ireland. Thank you!' and scuttled after her.

'Are you hungry?' he asked when he caught up with her on the iron staircase. 'Would you like to go out for something to eat?'

From her withering expression he guessed that relying on her ever-present appetite might not work this time. 'Charlotte, I have so many apologies to make to you.'

'No, you don't. I should apologise for endangering your daughter. I'm so glad she and Delva are safe.' She smiled sadly and turned to go.

In a flash Michael had overtaken her, and blocked her way on the steps down to the car park. 'Please let me explain. At least give me a hearing. Over dinner. There's a good Chinese I can recommend – the Dragon City Restaurant, on Botanic Avenue. Peking duck,' he continued with a bit more optimism when a grin twitched around one side of her mouth.

'Charlotte, today has been a bit odd, what with one thing and another, and I'm sorry I was so sour to you. I was preoccupied with the kidnapping, and Elvis's little murder plot and—'

'I understand.' She tried to get past him, but he held his ground and clung onto the banisters on either side to prevent her passing.

'Not good enough. You have to let me grovel, and ask your forgiveness for the way I treated you.' He gabbled at high speed, as if he knew he had a limited time in which to make his pitch. 'Of course, now I see how right you were to bring about this paramilitary telethon. But this afternoon, I was going out of my mind because of Laura. And as to our earlier misunderstanding, I honestly believed your brother was your boyfriend.'

'Oh, let's not go into that again, Michael!'

'But Eddie warned me you were seeing someone. And when I saw the picture of Jeremy in your kitchen—'

'Eddie? He told you I was . . .' she fumed. 'He is a lowlife piece of scum, isn't he?'

'The worst. Now look, I would have been much keener to – you know – if I hadn't believe you were already tied up with someone else. So what I wonder is if you could forgive me for my stupidity, and whether we might try to be friends again.' She looked unconvinced so he plunged on recklessly. 'I think we get on well, and I love talking to you and listening to you. And I find I can tell you about things no one else understands.' He paused when he saw her defrost a degree or two. 'And I think about you all the time.'

She smiled at his earnest expression, and his chaotic mane.

'Perhaps in time we could pick up where we left off?' he ventured hopefully.

'Remind me where we left off.'

'You might not want to recall it, but we were kissing on your doorstep.'

'And now you want to take me to a Chinese restaurant,' she commented, as if he had suggested sodomising her with a milk bottle.

'Charlotte – don't be cruel.'

'And where, pray, is this Chinese restaurant with its famed Peking duck?'

He looked bashfully down at his shoes. 'Around the corner from my house. I was hoping, well, I was going to suggest that you stay the night.'

'Mmm. Must be a big house: a room for Laura, a room for Delva, and one for you. And of course a spare bedroom.' She feigned amazement.

'There isn't a spare bedroom,' he admitted hopelessly, and gripped the banisters so hard that his knuckles turned white. 'I know it sounds presumptuous, but I wasn't implying—'

'What *were* you implying?'

He sighed. 'It's been a long day. We're both exhausted. I'm not going to force myself on you. I wouldn't dream of suggesting anything. I just thought it might be . . .'

'Let me get this straight. I spend eighteen months lusting after you from the Press Gallery, and when I finally get you into bed all that's on offer is a hug?'

He looked up in surprise, and she leaned forward and kissed him on the lips. Then she slipped her arms around his neck and pulled him closer. They stood like that, kissing, for some time, arms locked around each other on the draughty back stairs of the theatre, until they surfaced for air.

'Come home with me, Charlotte. I'm not going to expect anything. I don't want to blow my chance with you now.'

She pushed past him and started down the stairs. 'How disappointing,' she called over her shoulder.

'Hang on – stop! Don't go.' He caught up with her in the car park. 'Let's really make this work together. You know, see how you can bear bloody Bosnian Laura, and whether you like being with a boring, forty-one-year-old Minister.'

'Correction: boring, forty-one-year-old Cabinet Minister.'

'Then we can be on Lobby terms permanently,' he suggested.

'For someone who's only got as far as swapping a bit of spit with a girl you certainly lay all your cards on the table, don't you?'

'Sorry.'

She shrugged enigmatically, and strolled down the street.

'Charlotte,' he asked as they drew parallel to the Europa entrance, 'have I blown it?'

'No,' she said, and reached for his hand. 'Let's start with the Chinese restaurant.'

Epilogue

The Arrivals Hall of Lester Pearson International Airport was in its usual state of chaos: it was packed with Italian Canadians hugging their relatives who had just disembarked in the Land of Plenty. Bill Anderson found their loud displays of joy both vulgar and disturbing, but when he caught sight of Mandy emerging from Customs, he too was choked with emotion. She looked like a bedraggled waif, and when she ran into his arms she felt as fragile as a half-starved bird.

'Thank the good Lord you made it,' he whispered through his daughter's big blonde hair. Then he examined her pale, fraught countenance. 'You were very brave, and your mother and I are proud of you. So's the Reverend Patterson, and—'

'Daddy, what happened? Tell me,' she pleaded impatiently. 'I've been on the plane all this time and—'

'I'm afraid it didn't work. The British Government is breaking bread with the terrorists once more, and courting those vipers in Dublin. It's been on television all afternoon. The whole disgusting performance is a humiliation for Ulster—'

'—but did they get Fitzgerald?' she interrupted, too much the committed terrorist to indulge in her father's sentimentality.

When Bill shook his head sadly, Mandy's face contorted into

the hard scowl of an old fishwife. The papist bastard had escaped.

'The battle's only just begun, dear,' her father added as he reached down for her case. 'And thank heavens you're back safely.' But Mandy would not be comforted. She had failed in her assignment, and she had let down the cause that was most important to her.

They walked in solemn silence through the kissing, weeping arrivals from Sicily, and headed for the elevator up to the parking lot.

'Ms Amanda Anderson?'

Mandy swung around and found herself face to face with the identification badge of a member of the Royal Canadian Mounted Police. She looked back at her father, but he was being guided away by another plain-clothes officer who had him firmly by the elbow.

'It'd be a good idea if you and Mr Anderson came with us.'

A selection of bestsellers from Headline

BODY OF A CRIME	Michael C. Eberhardt	£5.99 ☐
TESTIMONY	Craig A. Lewis	£5.99 ☐
LIFE PENALTY	Joy Fielding	£5.99 ☐
SLAYGROUND	Philip Caveney	£5.99 ☐
BURN OUT	Alan Scholefield	£4.99 ☐
SPECIAL VICTIMS	Nick Gaitano	£4.99 ☐
DESPERATE MEASURES	David Morrell	£5.99 ☐
JUDGMENT HOUR	Stephen Smoke	£5.99 ☐
DEEP PURSUIT	Geoffrey Norman	£4.99 ☐
THE CHIMNEY SWEEPER	John Peyton Cooke	£4.99 ☐
TRAP DOOR	Deanie Francis Mills	£5.99 ☐
VANISHING ACT	Thomas Perry	£4.99 ☐

All Headline books are available at your local bookshop or newsagent, or can be ordered direct from the publisher. Just tick the titles you want and fill in the form below. Prices and availability subject to change without notice.

Headline Book Publishing, Cash Sales Department, Bookpoint, 39 Milton Park, Abingdon, OXON, OX14 4TD, UK. If you have a credit card you may order by telephone – 01235 400400.

Please enclose a cheque or postal order made payable to Bookpoint Ltd to the value of the cover price and allow the following for postage and packing:

UK & BFPO: £1.00 for the first book, 50p for the second book and 30p for each additional book ordered up to a maximum charge of £3.00.

OVERSEAS & EIRE: £2.00 for the first book, £1.00 for the second book and 50p for each additional book.

Name ....

Address ....

....

....

If you would prefer to pay by credit card, please complete:
Please debit my Visa/Access/Diner's Card/American Express (delete as applicable) card no:

Signature .... Expiry Date.............